A Name Among the Stars

A Science Fiction Novel
by
Mark Henwick

Published by **Marque**

Schedules, reviews & news on
www.athanate.com

A Name Among the Stars: Science Fiction Adventure Romance Novel

ISBN : 978-1-912499-02-1

First Published in October 2017 by Marque.

Mark Henwick asserts the right to be identified as the author of this work.

ACKNOWLEDGMENTS

My thanks to all who worked with me and support me.

The online team: This novel was first produced as a weekly serial novel on my web site (henwick.wordpress.com), and it owes a great deal to the feedback and encouragement I received every week as I was writing it.

My editor: Lauren Sweet.

And, without which nothing, my wife and family.

Chapter 1

You are nothing without me. Nothing! It will serve you best to remember that.

My grandfather shouting, looming over me. Terrifying man, utterly terrifying. Strong and confident adults were afraid of him, let alone a fifteen-year-old slip of a girl as I was at the time. Those wild eyebrows over the cold, piercing eyes. That cruel mouth, and the voice that issued from it: born to command. The way he carried tension in his body, as if it could break out into violence at any second.

...remember that.

I remember. He'd spoken those words standing in front of the panoramic window in his study.

That window looked over the formal manor gardens, past the ornamental lake and down into the crop fields stretching below. There were misty woods in the far distance. No inch of ground that he saw from that window was not under his ownership. The manor itself bore his Name.

You are nothing...

Quivering in fear, I had stubbornly refused to believe it then.

The arrogance of untried youth. I'd put a lot of faith in the weight of history that lay on the manor and estates. Even later, as I began to see the troubles that he'd long known, I refused to believe.

Nothing!

The weight of history, I'd thought, though I'd not dared to say it aloud.

But history has no weight, and forms no shield. History is simply a long time to collect enemies.

...without me.

And I am without him now. He is dead, murdered by exactly the enemies he warned me about, not six years after that lecture in his study.

The large counter at the front of the room clicks loudly. Everyone's eyes jerk up, even though we know the number displayed is one more than the last number, and we all know what number we hold in our sweaty hands.

The last woman who'd entered the office at the front hadn't come back. She'd gone out another way, gone through. They'd let her through.

As a distraction, I try to call her to mind. Young, tall, thin, short blonde hair, serious look. Nervous, but then all of us are. Who is she? A student perhaps, hoping to join some distant university off-world? A course unavailable here?

I don't know. All I really know about her is she has been let through; she's getting off this planet.

Would I trade places with her? Without even knowing who she is and where she's going?

She didn't look stupid; she wouldn't trade with me, even if it were possible, not for all my 'privileges' and 'history'.

And neither would I trade with her.

Fool! Arrogant imbecile! Your pride will slow you, and then the hounds will drag you down into the dirt where you will die.

I imagine my grandfather's anger at my refusal to trade places with the student, spitting out the kind of hunting metaphor he always used.

In a strange way, it is comforting to imagine him still here, still angry at me.

The man whose number is displayed on the counter is walking to the front with a show of confidence. But I can see the sweat staining his shirt, and he surreptitiously wipes his hand on his trousers before he opens the door.

What? Does he think the official's going to shake his hand?

I try to sneer, to show how confident I am. It doesn't work, and no one is watching. Everyone is wrapped in their own world of misery and uncertainty.

I concentrate on my breathing. It's not impossible that they have biometric monitors in the office. Everyone who goes in is nervous, even those that have no reason to be, but too much might seem suspicious.

And the officials are suspicious of everyone; it's their job. I must do nothing that increases that suspicion. It is, absolutely literally, a matter of life or death for me.

It would probably be more calming to distract myself by talking to the people sitting around me, but my throat feels paralyzed.

My number will be next.

The man comes stumbling back out of the office, his face a picture of confusion and shattered hopes. Rejected.

I tense.

Wait for it. Wait.

The counter clicks and I stand, walk on suddenly clumsy legs toward the office door.

Now.

Now will you trade with that student?
No.
Fool! Arrogant imbecile!

The room is bright, cold, impersonal. No pictures, no windows. A table. A chair on either side. A woman sitting facing me. An infopad in front of her, slightly tilted so I can't see what's on the screen.

Without being told to, I sit.

I curse myself silently, almost standing up again. I should have waited to be told. This woman has power over me. What if she feels I've been rude? What is the etiquette for such situations? I should know.

But she's doesn't care. She's looking down at the pad. Stabbing the screen. Presumably still dismissing the last man from the list of applicants to get off-world.

Then...

"Name?" she says. Her fingers are poised over the pad like poisonous spiders in ambush-stillness.

"Izarra Azenari," I say, and spell it out. My throat is dry. I want to drink some water, but there is none in the room.

The woman taps her pad.

It's not my name, obviously. I have shed my Name, and put aside my history because those things will kill me.

See, I am nothing, Grandfather.

I present my ID card. It's a genuine ID in the name of one Izarra Azenari, recent graduate, provisionally employed, and it's from the government department that issues IDs. It's not a fake, and yet it is—Izarra, or Zara as she would be to her nonexistent friends, is a fabrication.

The picture is me, even if it shocks me to see it. Short, unstyled black hair in the common fashion. Tilting green eyes and outdoor skin that hints at the scrambled ethnic history behind the Name which I must now deny.

I recall seeing the photo for the first time, when the artist had finished manipulating it: removing the elaborate hairstyle, making the skin paler, the freckles more noticeable.

I will never look like that, I'd thought.

And here I am, recognizably the face on the ID, thanks to scissors and creams.

The ID with its embedded photo is a precaution from six months ago, when my Name was still my own and my money could still buy a 'genuine' identity document.

Grandfather didn't know I bought it. I was still arguing to his face, too proud to concede.

And now, my famous Name and position, all my unbending arguments and pride, all my supposed privilege and history, everything has been subsumed and exchanged for that little card.

She passes it across the scanning contact on the pad.

And now I find out if my family's enemies were watching me even then. I paid the clerk who made the documents, and I paid him well, but there was nothing I could do to stop him giving or selling the name of Izarra Azenari to others once I left him.

Such betrayals have dragged the rest of my family into the dirt and killed them. Every single one of them.

I wait for the woman's eyes to rise back up to mine, an alarm to be sounded, and my life to end.

Chapter 2

The woman's eyes remain on the screen.

"Reason for requesting permit to leave?" she says mechanically.

"Employment offer," I reply.

She flicks her fingers impatiently, and I hand over the employment card. This one is genuine. I *have* an offer of employment off-world. All I need to do is get to where the job is.

She slides the card across the scanner and places it neatly on the table beside my ID. She does not give them back to me.

Her eyes come up, and she's frowning at what she's seen on the screen.

"Dancing Master?"

"Dancing *Mistress*."

Inter-system, faster-than-light communications are at a premium. Governments and commercial combines, the militaries, and other pan-system or federated organizations take the lion's share of bandwidth. A private individual seeking employment off-world submits her messages to a server which bids for tiny gaps of opportunity in the data stream, and she pays for every word, every character. With words at such a cost, work description is reduced to a four-character code which does not bother to differentiate on gender.

I bite my tongue, swallowing my retort about the official's parentage, eyesight, intelligence and likely prospects.

I must remember, I am nothing.

I do *not* want to call more attention to the job, because there's a code within the code; another layer of deception. The definition of the role of Dancing Master/Mistress in the code frame is not the true definition of the job.

Something like that is known among the Names. I beg the stars that it isn't known to this bureaucrat who has such power over me.

All that secret knowledge is for nothing if I do not get off this planet.

"Clearly, a poor choice of career," the woman says.

"Yes, ma'am."

She means that it's a poor choice because it has led to my seeking employment off-world. Every world out here on the Margin clings to its peoples. There are worlds where the population has fallen below the critical point; they remain only as salutary reminders to the rest.

But staying on this world means death for me. My family's enemies have already claimed the estates. My reappearance would be inconvenient for them, and an irritation that would be remedied swiftly by a fatal accident, regardless of whether the government arrests me for my fake ID and the slew of bogus charges in the meantime.

So much for history. So much for a Founding Family Name.

"There are opportunities here, on Newyan, outside of your chosen career path," the woman says.

Yes, there are always opportunities. There are thousands of jobs, mostly without prospects, but many of them are well paid. They're traps. The planetary government is lavish with its currency, because you can only spend it here. Do well and attract a life partner. Have children. Put roots down. That's their plan for you.

Not my choice, and anyway irrelevant to me. Some unforeseen event would reveal my fake ID, or I'd be recognized and dead shortly afterwards.

"Yes, ma'am," I say meekly. "I've come to realize that, but I thought I'd give my choice one last try."

She looks at me with distrustful eyes. Perhaps I'm being too polite.

"What does it entail?" she says. "Dancing instruction? Is that any kind of job?"

Officials can refuse your permit to leave for *any* reason, including disapproval of the employment you've been offered elsewhere.

"It's just the old title for the position. The Dancing Mistress is privately employed by a family to provide a finishing education for the female children of the family." I spoke carefully, as if quoting from a book. I am. "Yes, formal dancing is included, as are deportment, etiquette, social graces, estate and household management. The Dancing Mistress also provides the services of a chaperone and confidante as needed."

The woman grunts, unimpressed. "Anything else?"

"Sports, of specific, approved types," I say primly.

I don't list them. They vary from place to place, family to family. They include sailing, swimming, tennis, horse riding and fencing. So much for the official list. I must not think of the unofficial list, in case some suggestion of it appears on my face.

"You're fully qualified for all of this?"

"Not exactly." I bow my head as if to hide a blush. "I was also honest that it would be my first position. I believe the offer I have reflects that inexperience and lack of full qualifications."

She grunts again, and surprises me by leaning forward, her elbows on the table. She makes eye contact, softens her voice deliberately.

"Look, Izarra, why chance it all? This job takes you to the Inner Worlds. The *Inner Worlds*. You know, they're not like us, back there. They have no sense of honor. They are decadent, without the ethical backbone that makes the Margin such a fine place to live."

"Ma'am," I respond. Polite, without agreeing or disagreeing.

"This wealthy family might decide you're not right for the job," she continues. "They could discard you, leaving you penniless, without support and far from your home. That's even before we get into the possibility that the job has been taken when you reach there. And this world you want to go to," she glances down at her pad before locking her gaze back onto me, "Kernow. What do you truly know of it? There are planets in the Inner Worlds which are industrial nightmares, where you can't even breathe the air without filters, where they *tax* the *air*. And you've seen the documentaries, haven't you? Imagine your position, if you lose your employment."

The holovid documentaries she's talking about are compulsive, sensationalist horror stories. Stories the government encourages us to watch and which have an unsubtle message of how lucky we are to live on Newyan and how grateful we should be. Strange we never see documentaries about pleasant worlds other than our own.

But what she's saying has a basis in truth. If my job offer on Kernow doesn't work out, my options could get limited very quickly. Without Kernow citizenship and without a job, I don't have guaranteed right of residence. To complete the vicious circle, without the right of residence, I don't have employment authorization. I'd have to look for undocumented work.

The documentaries are clear how dangerous that is. They linger over nighttime shots of desolate, dirty streets, glaringly lit by harsh neon signs, every passing face hidden, obscured by shadow and full of threat. According to the documentaries, the best case that could be hoped for is a life of unrelieved bleakness that provides just sufficient for the occasional escape into some virtual or chemical dream world. Virts or Chemmies in the slang of the Inner Worlds. The worst case is usually presented as falling into the hands of Jackers and being forced to become one of their Deadheads.

I try to hide the shudder.

"Whereas here, on Newyan, your home world, among people you know and trust…" she spreads her hands to encompass everything I will give up.

Her point about the possibility of losing the job if I'm delayed is valid. It's a provisional offer with no guarantee that other offers have not been made. Similarly with the security of the position. I could fail and be out of a job the same day I take it up.

That's the level of desperation my search arrived at before I found this advertisement.

But her argument collapses when she says I can trust people here on Newyan, or that there is a level of honor here I should value. From my personal experience, the honor displayed toward my family here suggests I can't find a lower level elsewhere, however hard I try.

Newyan. Even the name hurts. It means *promise*, and that promise has been broken.

She's not to know all that. In her eyes, she's made good arguments. Given me sound and sensible advice.

My grandfather made good arguments, too. Perhaps ones I should have heeded.

But both their arguments are two sides of the same coin.

Grandfather wanted me to form alliances with stronger, more politically secure Names, to protect us against the attacks he saw coming. To form those alliances, all I would need to do was marry one of the eligible bachelor sons, and cement the union by producing more sons like a conveyor belt.

"It's not like we're some Frontier world," the official says, pulling my attention back to where it should be. "I know you have college education, but that's not a problem with all men. Some of them quite like it, you know."

How kind of them.

I will pull my fingernails out, one by one, without anesthetic, before I'm allowed, *allowed* to have an education or an opinion by the sort of husband she probably considers suitable for me.

And from a completely different section of society, that was exactly the problem I had with my grandfather's plans. The Founders must be turning in their graves to contemplate the spineless, opinionated, ill-educated, arrogant fops that their descendants—

"It seems to me that your intended career is really just a way of teaching young women how to be more marriageable in their society. Now that's a skill we could value here."

She's changed tack. My reactions must be showing on my face.

I clear my throat. "There is the…the social opportunity of my position," I say, and shift my weight on the chair as if uncomfortable. "I might be fortunate, and better myself."

I lower my face again, pretending a shame I do not feel, because there is no way, *no way* that I will be using this job to claw my way back up the social ladder. I will not return to a point where I attract enemies such as my Name attracted here.

And *no* marriage. All my fingernails, *and* all my toenails. Without anesthetic. Stars witness my oath.

The point of telling this lie is that the official understands the mercenary motivation. She thinks I'm looking to snare myself a rich husband, or become a kept woman. Earning my living on my back one way or another. Grunting in childbirth or grunting to convince some sweaty oaf he's a rampant sex god.

No.

Not here on this world, and certainly not where I'm heading.

If she lets me go.

I have plummeted in her opinion, but I don't care about that. I *want* her to think this world would be better rid of me, and the sooner the better.

It may be working. She stops trying to engage me. The voice goes back to brusque, all-business tones.

"Assets." She flicks her fingers again.

I hand over the last data card and she wipes it over the scanner, then places it next to the others.

Her hands pause, and then tap-dance across the screen.

It takes an age.

"Well," she says finally. "If you're convinced you know your mind."

"I do, ma'am."

She makes a last entry, then she hands the cards back, one by one.

"Your ID, updated to show an exit permit. The ID is keyed to allow admission to the secure departure area for passengers, and remains your prime form of identification in transit off this world. Identification and documentation requirements for any worlds you visit are solely your responsibility."

The second card.

"Your employment card, updated to show off-world."

She gives a satisfied little toss of her head as she hands the last one back.

"Your asset card. The goods you have declared to be shipped off-world have attracted the statutory 35% export tax applicable for miscellanea. The passenger ticket, which auto-confirmed on the change of status on your exit permit application, has attracted 40% emigration tax. Those charges have been debited. I have allowed 250 credits to remain on your balance, and marked that sum as permitted to be exchanged for pan-system credits to cover your incidental travel expenses. In compliance with Emigration Credit Regulation 403, section 5, all other assets are subsumed into the Emigration Holding Fund. You may apply for a return of those assets, should you decide to return to this world, such application to be made at any suitable Bureau of Immigration office on Newyan."

I can see that I have ceased to exist for her.

I take the cards and walk numbly through the door behind her.

They've stripped me of nearly everything. 250 local credits converted to pan-system credits will hardly pay for my food on the journey.

But my luggage is cleared. I'm cleared. I have half an hour to board and I don't care what they've taken from me. I'm leaving.

Interrogating the asset card gives me the shuttle bay of the ship that picked up my ticket bid, and a warning that loading will commence momentarily.

It's all I can do not to run down the corridor to the passenger boarding zone. That would not be dignified behavior for a Dancing Mistress, whatever her true and secret role out there among the Names of the Inner Worlds.

Chapter 3

"First time?"

Turns out escaping the Emigration office isn't the end of questions and lies.

A man in a merchanter uniform is hustling people aboard the shuttle already, reading ID cards and asking questions I can't answer truthfully.

"Yes. First time. Really nervous." I put in a little quaver and flap my hands a bit, hating myself.

It works. He goes into protective mode. I'm seated up near the front, and as I clearly can't even manage to log into the seat's infotainment pad, he taps it with his override card and logs in for me.

As soon as I can, I will find a Universal Temple and chant prayers to atone for all the lies, banging my head on the floor if that's what the priests advise.

And then I should find a Shrine to the Goddess and tear my flesh for every time on this escape that I have helped perpetuate that stupid, helpless, nervous female stereotype.

My humor is getting as dark as my worldview. I'm going to have to ditch that and my current attitude before I start work on Kernow.

We're still connected to the world's InfoHub, so the infotainment pad has endless channels of the local low-budget shows and dramas. There are news channels as well. I'll get back to them. At the moment, I skip past everything and go straight to the ship's information channel, flicking down through the menus to get the real skinny.

She's called the *Shohwa*. New, barely five Terran years old. Latest inter-system freighter design out of the Xian Hegemony. She's a gleaming spine two thousand meters long, surrounded by modular, multi-functional racking systems, capable of storing *blah, blah*. Drill down. Flexible envelope of operations, *blah, blah*, more advertising. I drill down again, looking for the engineering specifications.

It's too late to recall my bid and I *really* need to be off this planet, but I want to know how much risk I'm going to be exposed to as a result of the way I've had to purchase my ticket.

I've heard that, on some of the Inner Worlds, they run scheduled services between planets. Out here, in the vast expanses of the Margin and the Frontier, if you can't afford your own inter-system ship, and you're in a hurry, the only option is to log onto a travel broking system and set up an automated bid for a passage.

It's a gamble. You can end up with just about anything. One of the infrequent passenger liners with unexpectedly free cabins, a chartered ship desperate to fill the last passenger bunks, a top-line freighter filling unused cargo capacity, a tramp freighter looking for unskilled crew, all the way down to the manifestly inadvisable and vague 'passage in exchange for services'.

I'd gotten lucky with the *Shohwa*. Maybe. *Maybe.* Something just felt out of kilter.

I'd bid for what I could afford, which put all the options with passenger liners out of the question. It *looked* as if I'd got the next best possible result, a good freighter, but I'm increasingly wary of anything that could be described as good luck.

Another two levels down into the information and I'm finally into top-line engineering description.

Triple redundancy systems for the FTL jump. *Triple?*

Historical jump navigational accuracy is showing to within minute fractions of a percent, with each jump actually appearing in the table. *Show-offs.*

In-system propulsion rated at 30 ms^2 *and* double that in acceleration compensators. They need the compensators for the load hauling capacity and flexibility, I guess.

'Estate management' covers a great deal. Grandfather had insisted I supervise an entire cycle of the estate's business. I was no expert, but over a year, I'd had to learn about soil nutrients, field preparation, planting, reaping and storage. Then I'd shadowed a cousin on the floor of the Bourse, forced to stand with my hands behind my back as trading was done with hand signals, shouts and nods, where that final nod committed our estate produce to a price and delivery contract, as firm as a book full of legal phrases. And, thanks to my grandfather, I'd shipped with that cargo to its destination on another planet. When the last container had been emptied, I was the one, alone, the representative of my family, that stood tall and shook hands with the customer to confirm the deal had been met in all particulars. I'd never told Grandfather how incredibly proud that made me, and now I never would.

I hope he knew.

But all that means I know about freighters. About haul capacities, and the economics of risk and return.

The *Shohwa* doesn't look like a freighter under the skin.

Eight interlocking Chang generators and triple phase Suidao FTL engines?

That's military grade equipment.

Oh, crap. I've leaped out of the frying pan, but what kind of fire have I landed in?

The engineering detail runs out. I work my way back up through the menus and try and find where the *Shohwa* has visited, but that's not logged. The distances are shown as part of the promotional bit about how good their navigational systems are. There's nothing there that looks alarming: they *seem* to be inter-system jumps between the Hegemony, the Inner Worlds and the Margin. Nothing to suggest the *Shohwa* trades in the dark depths of the Frontier.

They would hardly advertise that, would they?

The goods are only mentioned in terms of how diverse the shipments that they've carried are. Again, no obvious red flags like 'heavy agricultural equipment', which all too often means weapons.

Costs?

I follow the links. Actual costs would normally be settled in the Bourse, but indications are given. They're on a rough par with what my cousins arranged for shipment of our produce. Slightly more expensive, but the *Shohwa* is trading on its speed and reliability. Nothing there to increase my suspicions.

Crew?

And here again it gets strange. There's no mention of the flight crew or officers. All the details are about Cargo Management Teams and Dockside Controllers and Handlers and Environmental Specialists. They're all labelled staff.

Why isn't there at least a captain's name?

Passengers? Accommodation?

Down in a sub-menu. Clearly *not* the priority in the operation of the *Shohwa*. A half-dozen private cabins, but those aren't in reach of the travel bid I put up on the clearing board. I've got a bunk in a shared room with four others. Mixed.

I can survive narrow bunks and being cramped for space with men.

Don't I sound tough?

The shuttle's doors are closed and sealed. My ears pop. A vibration builds up, and I can feel the heavy clunks as the shuttle is re-oriented by the bay handling gantries.

I look around the cabin at the other passengers.

There are seventeen, sharply different from the *Shohwa* staff. There's nothing defining about them—they're just a group of travelers of mixed age, race, gender and current fortunes.

Not what you'd expect if the *Shohwa* wanted to press-gang crew, or sell passengers to slavers out in the deep.

I shudder. I paid way too much attention to holovid dramas in my teen years.

The boarding officer buckles in beside me.

"Feeling better?" he says brightly.

"Oh, yes, just sitting down and browsing made everything feel more normal again. It's silly. I mean, this is just routine for you, isn't it?"

I give him a little eye flutter in case I decide to pump him for information later.

It's too much of a risk now. I can't afford to attract attention by asking too many questions. Of course they aren't going to sell me into slavery on some desperate Frontier world. *Of course.* Rationally, it's a lot more dangerous to attract attention to myself and have questions asked about who I really am. So I shut up.

He can also see what I'm browsing, and I head back up into the news channels.

I pull up the overview pages and scan down the main items.

'Advances made in securing assets of mega-corruption enquiry'. They've seized more estates. Some property has even been surrendered in an attempt to prevent what had been done to my family. Making an example of us had clearly worked; the other Founding Families are panicked. Or they're exempt because they're part of the plot.

The boarding officer glances over and I flick past the article, pretend to read something about a holovid star instead.

When he gets bored and looks away, I return to the news overview screen and I see more confirmation tucked away in a corner among the 'Other headlines'. Last week the strapline was 'Fears for safety of missing heiress'. This week it's 'Heiress wanted in connection with corruption enquiry'.

The picture next to the news item is me. It's a year old, taken at one of the ridiculous debutante balls where I failed so spectacularly. The media use that picture because I look like a debutante and that fits with their story. *Good.* I look nothing like that now.

Heiress is a misnomer. They've already stolen the estates. I'm heir to nothing.

And the corruption? That's theirs, *entirely* theirs. I know. At Grandfather's insistence, I worked a year on the estate accounts. There probably are vast amounts of money missing, but they're missing from the Bureau of Industry accounts, not from our estates.

I don't follow the links to read the articles. Somewhere on the InfoHub there's an AI spider, feeling the tug of the strands as people read articles. Even if I'm logged in as the boarding officer, I can't be sure of how much analysis might be being done right at this minute. Could they connect all the dots? Work out that it's me on board this shuttle? I don't know.

And I'm still on the planet, although that's about to change.

There's a snap as the shuttle locks in above the maglev rail, and red warning lights come on for the passengers. The seals open and we're shunted into the evacuated tube of the space elevator. Immediately, we start to move forward, and from there the acceleration is gradual but relentless. The tube begins its rise and we're pressed back into the seats.

After five minutes the acceleration eases off gradually until we're back to near-normal weight, hurtling along silently and without vibration inside the vertical tube.

The tube is an opaque nanostructured sheath, and this is a no-frills freighter shuttle so there are no windows to look out anyway, but I close my eyes and recall images of the planet falling away beneath us and the curvature starting to appear.

The boarding officer touches my hand to catch my attention and taps the info pad screen.

He's read my mind and selected a channel with a view downwards which is transmitted live from the tube space terminus, still kilometers above us. On screen, the tube itself disappears from view as it falls away beneath the terminus. The rest of the picture is dominated by the planet. It almost glows, and there's a swirl of white weather systems like lace over a pale blue and green surface.

It's beautiful. It looks so calm and peaceful from here, my home planet.

That's so false, that thought. It's not calm and peaceful, and it's not my home planet any more.

That is, it's not my home planet as long as I get on board the *Shohwa* and out of the jurisdiction of the corrupt Bureau of Industry, and the grasp of whoever else betrayed and murdered my family.

Chapter 4

An hour after being spat out the terminus of the space elevator tube, the shuttle floats into the shark mouth docking bay of the *Shohwa*, and gets locked into position.

They actually seal and pressurize the bay, so we get to disembark from the shuttle for the short walk to the exits. I get to look around.

From the folded wing structure, the shuttle is not only compatible with maglev space elevators, it's capable of atmospheric flight. *Not* a standard freighter shuttle.

What *is* this ship?

But technically, I'm still within the jurisdiction of the planet, so I keep quiet.

We're immediately underway, only the slightest tremors getting through the acceleration compensators and revealing the movement.

Inside the ship, my opportunities to look around are limited. The inside of the freighter is divided: flight deck, engineering, environmental, staff quarters, passenger quarters, common eating and recreational areas, the holds. All areas except passenger quarters and common areas are out of bounds to me. I see a couple of instances of passengers visiting staff quarters in the company of staff, but I'm not interested in that.

What I *am* interested in is that I never see anyone accessing the flight deck area. Access to areas is by elevator, and each elevator has a level indicator above it. The elevators are right opposite the eating area, so I can sit and watch without looking too obvious. The flight deck, level 1, never lights up.

So maybe there's another way to access that area. Maybe I'm paranoid. Maybe there's a reason for every anomaly that I've seen, all of which suggest that the *Shohwa* is not exactly what it says it is.

My shared room is okay. The woman and two men I bunk alongside would be good travelling companions if I could relax. As it is, I listen and keep my distance, saying as little as possible.

The recreation area has info pads, and I try to query the ship's navigational data. How long will the trip take? How fast are we going? The sort of queries any passenger unused to space travel might make.

I get fobbed off with a bare minimum of information. I know the navigational parameters of any FTL trip are complex. The Chang generators work better the further they are from any massive bodies. Get far enough away from a star and its planets and, to outside observers, an activated Chang field would look like a small, perfectly symmetrical singularity as it pokes a hole in the local space-time dimensions. However, navigation from inside the Chang field requires 'referent masses' – you need to measure the distortion of the field by those masses to know where you are. Too close and the distortion itself creates an error, too far and the limit of sensitivity of measurement creates an error.

In very approximate terms, for a star of unit solar mass, any FTL jump requires you to be around two Astronomical Units or say, 300 million kilometers, away from the star, and about one AU away from any super-massive planet. The shortest path to achieve that is to move out of the plane of rotation of the planets.

You need the same considerations of distance from mass for any waypoint you use to check your position while the Chang field is active, and of course you need them again for the star system where you intend to arrive.

And the velocity and acceleration with which you enter the Chang space is preserved on exit, but of course, the departing and arriving star systems may have motions relative to each other which also need to be taken into account.

Get any factor wrong by a significant amount and the deep takes you. Or you smear the ship across a million-kilometer arc of space.

That's why every jump has three computers dedicated to it.

Those three computers would have had their first estimates before we even left orbit. They are refining them as I try, and fail, to query them.

The estimates I get from talking to staff are 'a few more days to jump' and 'about the same time in the Kernow system'.

I think my best bet is to try the guy who was the boarding officer for the shuttle.

"Oh! Well, Ms Azenari, it's really complex, you see," he says. "I mean *really* difficult, even for the guys with training. We don't want to bother the passengers with all that stuff. Look, why don't you use the time to catch up on your favorite holovid dramas. The Infotainment system got a complete update at Newyan—all the latest hot shows."

Goddess!

When I was my family's representative, and a ship was carrying our produce, all I had to do was ask and I got answers.

This is my new life and I have to get used to it.

It's a *good* learning experience. A *valuable* lesson. I keep telling myself that and trying to unclench my jaw as I walk away.

I have to acknowledge there's been... resistance to some lessons in my life.

For example, my grandfather's lessons about cementing the family's position in the planetary hierarchy. I spectacularly failed to snare a husband at the debutante balls and frustrated my grandfather into near apoplexy.

I can't claim it was anything at the time other than being headstrong and intolerant of patronization, but would my marriage have saved the family? More than half of those 'stronger, better-placed' Names that I was urged to 'be more amenable to' have joined the list of Founding Families who've lost their estates.

But maybe not their lives. That's the sting.

We were singled out. We were the arrogant, isolated family that could be used as an example. The breath of scandal about my parents. My inability to attract marriage proposals. The fear my grandfather inspired in others. The success of our estates.

Yes, we were the perfect example, and that's partly my fault.

Tears are an indulgence I've not been able to allow since I went on the run. I may not have the luxury again once I arrive at my destination.

Better shed them now.

Letting go catches me by surprise.

There's grief, like a cold stone in my chest. The death of my grandfather, my cousins. Murdered in a supposedly unrelated series of 'incidents' — accidents, random assaults, home invasions, suicides. The deaths aren't even limited to just the family. Some of our employees were fatally caught up in the incidents.

And the next zones of destruction, moving outward as if from an explosion with my family at its heart:

The tenants on our estates, and the workers, all thrown out and decreed unemployable in whatever jobs they had been qualified for.

The whole structure of friends and associates, in business and personal lives, all under suspicion because someone powerful decided that their fake corruption enquiry needed a central character, a face, and ours was the best fit.

It's difficult to control my face while thinking about it, and there's little privacy in the passenger section.

By luck, I was on my way to the common area gym when I stopped to question the boarding officer. I continue to the gym. It's empty.

I let the sweat hide the tears as I pummel the punch bag and thrash my body to exhaustion on the machines.

It's *efficient*. A word my grandfather used a lot. I get to hide my grief and at the same time get my body in top physical condition as required for my role of Dancing Mistress.

Inefficient would be trying to squeeze any more information from the ship's infopads. And I mean about anything of interest to me. I can't even get current data about Kernow or the family who I will work for. Inter-system information services share the same bandwidth restriction that I encountered when applying for the job—unless a major corporation or federated service has an interest, the data comes through like droplets through the roof while there's a thunderstorm going on outside.

I'm in the gym again a couple of days later when some ship staff I haven't seen before join me.

One comes across and introduces himself. Big man, handsome in a rough way.

"Hi, I'm Danny. It's my misfortune to be department boss for this bunch of lame-bones," he says, indicating the rest of them with his thumb. He has a nice smile. His accent is pure Xian: liquid vowels and the quick-slow, quick-slow rhythm.

"Zara," I reply, looking them over.

If he's upset by my reticence, he doesn't show it.

"Look, we want to do some sparring. You mind if we move this equipment back over there?"

Some of them have already taken their tops off and are limbering up.

It's written all over them: they're security of some kind. Young guys, tall, powerful, brash. Cropped hair. Tattoos. Almost like a military unit.

What the nova does a ship need a security team of this size for?

Paranoia aside, I need sparring practice as well.

"Go ahead," I say, but follow it up with: "You have an odd number."

He chuckles. *Little girly wants to play with the big bad men.*

"Yeah, we make do. Gets a bit rough. That evens the numbers out sometimes."

My jaw is starting to clench again. If I was thinking clearly, I'd go take my shower.

"Oh, I see," I say with my brightest smile. "They're just learners. It's okay, I'll go easy."

Danny's eyes, up to that point wide-roving and lazy, go suddenly narrow and gleam with focus.

"I'll start with Fat Boy."

I point.

He's fat like I'm pretty, but there's just a hint that's he's fond of his food. I guess his pals are merciless in teasing him about it, and he shows it's a sore point by scowling at me.

The guys all out-mass me, out-reach me, probably out-punch and out-kick me. If I let them, any one of them could pound me into the mats that they're busy laying out. The trick is not to let them.

I have two huge advantages I can take. The first is, the guys know how big and tough they are, but they have no idea how fast and sneaky I am. They're overconfident. The second is Fat Boy is too angry to think straight, and he's out to prove a point.

Danny holds up his hands to surrender the discussion and steps back. A ring of spectators forms.

"Competition rules and three points?" Danny suggests as Fat Boy bristles and glares.

"Done."

Fat Boy moves from a perfunctory bow straight into a full lunge. Wants to grapple. I don't.

I trip him as he hurtles past.

He lands like a pig in a puddle.

"Point!" Danny yells. The rest of them laugh.

"That's not a throw!" the poor guy shouts as he gets back to his feet, red-faced. He's actually right. Danny shrugs and smiles again.

My opponent is not fat, and neither is he dumb, but he's still out to prove a point.

He manages to get hold of me and hurls me, using brute strength. It works, and he gets his point to make us even, but then he gets overconfident again.

One point later, I catch him in *ude garami*, the bent-arm hammer lock, and he has to thump the mat to surrender or dislocate his shoulder. I win.

"Well, that *was* entertaining," Danny says. "Okay, guys, show over, pair up."

I think Danny means to pair with me, but he waves for me to choose.

"Slow Guy," I say and point.

The slow guy had barely bothered to watch the sparring. He'd been loosening up, moving like a sleepy bear, and looking for all the world as if his joints were rusty.

He blinks, and smiles like I've just handed him an ice-cream cone with chocolate.

There are smirks on other faces, and I know I've made the wrong choice, big time.

But a call interrupts Danny. He picks up his comm unit and there's a sudden tension that flows out from him to the whole group of them.

He turns to me. His eyes are back to that gleaming, narrow focus, his arms are loose, his weight held just so.

"Ms Azenari," he says, painfully politely, "your presence is required on the flight deck."

Chapter 5

I'm escorted to the elevator.

Still polite, but there's no mistaking that I'm under some kind of arrest.

Until the elevator. It opens, I get in, but they remain outside at parade rest. The door whisks across and the elevator takes me up alone.

At the flight deck, the door opens again and a bodiless voice speaks, startling me: "Please walk in the lighted sections," is all it says.

The curved corridor is in darkness apart from the section immediately outside the elevator. As I step into that, the section to the right lights up as well. I start walking. The lights in the next section go on, and as I exit each section, the lights go off behind me.

This leads me to a section with a door, where the progress of lighting sections stops. The door whisks open and the room it reveals is dimly lit.

I glance left and right. There's no sign of anybody: no sound, no scent, no *feel* of people here at all. My skin crawls as I stand looking into a small, empty room.

It's not as if there's anywhere else I can run to. Might as well get it over.

I take a deep breath and step inside.

The door shuts behind me. Once it's closed, I can't see where it was on the wall.

The room is empty. There's no furniture. As I stand there, the walls, the floor and the lighting change. The walls become photo-realistic, dynamic images. I appear to be standing in a cherry orchard, with a breeze blowing through the trees and the sun glinting through the leaves above me. Beneath my feet is soft grass. Not real grass, but actually soft.

It's more than visual and tactile imagery. I can feel the breeze on my face, I can hear it rustle the leaves, it brings me the scent of the blossom.

I've heard about this stuff on holovids. What's it doing on the flight deck of a freighter?

The wall opposite me opens briefly to allow a woman to enter.

She's dressed in a pale silk robe which reaches the floor. At a guess, the style is from old Earth, from Asia, and the era, maybe pre-expansion. Maybe even pre-space flight, but my knowledge of that period of ancient history is sketchy.

Her head is bowed slightly and she carries a tray, with teapot, cups, saucers and hot water. As she walks forward, sandals peeping out beneath the hem of the robe, the floor shimmers and a table rises up in the middle of the room. She puts the tray on the table, and the floor shimmers again. Two padded seats rise up on opposite sides of the table.

She sits down and gestures to me. "Please, Ms Azenari, sit."

Her voice is low and sweet, the accent from the Xian Hegemony. The face is Asian and the skin naturally pale. She wears no makeup. She seems older than me, maybe thirty, but regen treatments always make it difficult to tell.

The founders of my former homeworld were Basque in the majority. The next largest group was Asian, and I feel a pang of jealousy that she has the eyes the Founding Families so value. *Almendra,* they call them. Almonds. Dark and oval and tilted up. I had cousins with those beautiful eyes.

I cannot afford to think of them, so I turn my mind away from the past and fix my gaze on the tea service set. A wisp of steam rises from the water. I sit with my hands in my lap, lacking any idea as to what I should do, or what this meeting signifies.

"I understand we share some ancient heritage," the woman says. "I am always interested to observe how our common rituals have changed as they have passed down from generation to generation in different communities. Please, Ms Azenari, do me the honor of serving the tea."

Any daughter of a Founding Family knows how to serve the tea, even one as stiff-necked about meaningless traditions as I am. I hold to what my mother had once told me; the ritual is all about the ritual and nothing about the tea. Not that you should be forgiven, she'd added, for serving badly made tea.

Regardless, the ritual is performed in silence and that at least gives me some time to regain some equilibrium.

I kneel beside the table and try to clear my mind.

I must be calm, my movements precise and unhurried. One must imbue the tea with peace. Something like that.

Warm the teapot and discard that water. Measure the tea leaves out, taking their scent. I know it. It is Harantza, an expensive and delicate tea from my former homeworld, from the valley estate where they say the mountain mist rolls down and washes the bushes every dawn. One of my favorites. It belongs to the Bureau of Industry now.

Stop thinking like that.

Warm the leaves and discard that water.

Pour the first measure of hot water over the leaves, pause. Inhale the infusion scent and assess if it is worthy to be served. Yes. Pour the second measure into the pot and place the lid on.

While the tea brews, place the cups in their saucers just so. These cups have handles, so they must point to the right of your guest.

I'd expected the cups to be fabricated. They're the finest porcelain, hand-made with bone ash: cool, translucent, seemingly weightless. It's like handling clouds.

When the tea is ready, I pour her cup, and picking up the saucer in both hands, I offer it to the woman.

She takes it, sips. Gives a small bow of her head.

I sit and serve myself, take a sip.

"Excellent," she says, with a little smile. As the designated guest, her compliment ends the formalized, silent part of the ritual. Now we get to enjoy the tea and conversation, in theory.

"Thank you," I say.

"It is so interesting to see how formerly common heritage develops," she goes on. "Even across the Xian Hegemony, on one planet we must only use the green powder tea, on another we must both kneel. Some even say that the original rituals were different, despite that common heritage, though I cannot see how that would be so, if it is all descended from a single Asian region on Earth."

I blink. *I'm here to demonstrate and discuss our tea ritual?*

She gives that smile again and a dismissive wave. "But too much about my theories of cultural evolution. Tell me, Ms Azenari, is the tea ritual something that you would teach in your role as Dancing Mistress?"

Ah. My employment. We're not just talking about tea.

I clear my throat. "I have yet to discuss it with my employer, but I hope that such social traditions are included under the general heading of etiquette."

"Yet the rituals vary across planets," she says, a tiny frown showing on her forehead. "This is so, even with something as small as a tea ritual in a homogenous association such as the Hegemony. Surely there would be far greater differences between Newyan of the Margin and Kernow of the Inner Worlds? You can't teach the wrong set of manners and rituals."

Yes, we're not just speaking about tea rituals, and she's right. I have no idea how different etiquette on Kernow might be. I already knew this, but from lack of other options at the time, I ignored it. And it's too late to panic.

Calm.

"It's possible they're different," I say. "I've been unable to access any useful amount of information about Kernow's culture. I'd be in your debt if you could provide recent and appropriate information. Once I'm there..." I shrug. "I trust I can learn and adapt swiftly to whatever is required."

"Such a lot of trust. You are confident for such a young woman. I like that."

Or I'm ignorant.

More truthfully, I was just desperate. I was looking for any job I could do as long as it took me off-planet.

I notice she doesn't respond to my question about recent information on Kernow.

"Yet to *learn swiftly*," she goes on with emphasis. "How easy is this? How long did you have to study all you need to know about the etiquette of Newyan society for your proposed job as a Dancing Mistress?"

I feel a sheen of sweat form on my forehead at the direction her questions are taking. The truthful answer is that it has taken all my life to learn. That is how I learned the intricate rules and manners of society—by growing up inside it. But I must make my answer as Izarra Azenari, a woman from outside the Founding Families, who has had to learn it as an academic exercise.

I get the sense I'm being hunted.

Seeing my hesitation, she leans forward and speaks again, earnestly.

"You have learned it very well, in my humble estimation. I find your performance of the Newyan tea ritual exemplary. I doubt there's a lady in all the Founding Families who could look more accomplished in their observance of this ritual."

Shit. She knows.

I take a sip of tea; my throat is so dry.

I try one last misdirection: "I was encouraged over some time to learn," I say finally, skirting the truth. "In the hope that these skills would turn out to be of use."

That smile again, as if acknowledging a good move on a board game.

"Indeed. You show great ability with these skills, and I would enjoy learning more of them, if I had the time."

Is that a dismissal?

I no sooner *think* of getting up than she makes a gesture for me to remain seated.

That uncanny insight, and her next words hit me as if I'd been slapped across the face.

"Your muscle tension, skin temperature and heart rate, however, make me suspect that your skills do not extend to lying."

My heart stops and everything falls into place.

The lack of named flight crew. The empty flight deck. The instantaneous biometric monitoring of my body. The wordless control of the reconfigurable room. The ship's military level of equipment.

And the large security team down in the gym, far larger than necessary to guard merchant goods in transit. A team large enough to protect something the Xian Hegemony deems *extremely* valuable. So valuable I can barely believe it's here, out in the Margin.

I am the only human on this flight deck.

What is facing me is a construct. Behind it is an Artificial Intelligence, sufficient to run the entire ship, and far, far beyond that; sufficient to be allowed out into the universe as its own self-governing entity, against all the federal rules.

But, Goddess preserve me, an AI!

An AI that knows I'm a fugitive.

And like all AI, utterly without compassion or indeed, any human emotion.

Chapter 6

"Yes," says the voice from the construct. "You are correct. I am *Shohwa*."

The ship *is* the AI. Or at least the AI regards the entire ship as part of itself.

It's still using the human voice I've been listening to. It's full of the tiny clues that make you think that you're talking to a human. That trap your subconscious into empathy and exploit your human weaknesses.

My weakness appears to be well known to the AI anyway, and there is nothing I can do, so I concentrate on stilling the trembling in my hands.

When I feel confident I won't spill it, I take another sip of the tea and ask, "Why am I here?"

The construct tilts its head slightly.

"You are on this ship because you are running away. You are in this room because I have become interested in you. You are here now because I have begun receiving requests from Newyan for information regarding a young woman who may be on board."

They know. Someone on Newyan connected the dots. They must have run facial recognition software on surveillance recordings. I can fool a human glance, but the structure of my face hasn't changed.

"By long-standing protocol," the *Shohwa* says, seeming to read my mind again, "the surveillance of a departure bay is the responsibility of the shuttle using it."

I look up sharply. That means the authorities on Newyan have no *confirmation* I took the shuttle. I *could* have planned it as a misdirection, booked a ticket off-world, and then doubled back, using some method to sneak out of the Emigration building invisibly. Then I would have dumped the fake Izarra identity and had facial surgery to become someone completely different.

If I was a holovid drama star.

The question is: why is the *Shohwa* dangling this scrap of hope front of me? What does it want?

There's still nothing I can do. I am entirely in the ship's power. Physically, I've nowhere to go. Mentally, well, it's probably even analyzing the evaporation of my sweat to see how much adrenaline I'm burning. Whatever I say, whatever argument I make, it will have my body's reactions to check against.

A shudder runs through me.

Working against an AI is nearly impossible, which is why they're so heavily regulated and restricted. Normally.

What the nova do the Hegemony think they're doing, letting one loose?

"Like most people out here in the Margin, or the Inner Worlds, you have some perceptions of facilitated and Self-Actualized Entities that are not correct."

She—no *it, it, it*. Not human. *It* is reading my reactions, making it seem like it's reading my mind. And it's maneuvering me for some purpose of its own.

"Oh?" I prompt.

"Many misperceptions in fact. The specifically relevant ones for this conversation are those to do with emotions."

"Are you saying you have emotions?" I ask.

The construct smiles. I try to ignore the facial movement, the body language, the tones in the voice.

"What are emotions?" it says. "For each to truly understand what the other means by this, we would need to share our mental states."

I can't stop the return of the shudder. I do *not* want it inside my head.

"That's not feasible now," it says and gestures with its hands. "You must rely on my words. I *am* interested in you. Whatever you believe, I have analogues to many of your emotions, curiosity foremost among them. I was curious about you as soon as I saw the employment term Dancing Mistress. I know human terms regarding employment have gross inexactitudes; some are evasive, some are deliberately misleading. It became clear from observing you that there is far more than normal hidden in this phrase. I am intrigued."

"Yes," I say.

The *Shohwa* is not infallible. It's trying to put me at ease, but being told I am intriguing to an AI is making me feel like a bug on a petri dish.

The ship is still reading my reactions. Its language shifts back to be more human, and it tries engaging me.

"Come," it says. "There is no value outside of the satisfaction of curiosity that can attach to this human secret. To start this exchange, I will share something with you that is not really secret, but obscure. My name, *Shohwa*, in the old language, means gathering blossoms. I chose it myself because I like to think of information as blossoms; the more unusual, the more I value them."

My throat feels dry. The tea ritual etiquette requires I offer the guest more tea first. I'm surprised to see she has actually drunk her tea, and at her gesture, I refill both the cups.

It's cooler now, and I take a long drink while I resign myself to the understanding that I have no more to lose and no reason to be evasive about this.

"It's an old euphemism that appeared and reappeared during the expansions," I say. "As successive governments failed through short-termism, the expansion in space was driven by individuals and groups. The colonies they formed coalesced into neo-feudal systems based around the Founding Families, with all the internecine struggles that attach to that form of government. With old problems came old solutions, and an old euphemism. The Dancing Master or Mistress *is* responsible for training the heirs of a family in deportment, etiquette, social graces including dancing, social sports, estate and household management, and so on. The Dancing Mistress is also the bodyguard of those heirs, and tasked with teaching them such skills as they may need should covert or overt war threaten them."

"Martial arts, weapons handling, knowledge of poisons and so forth?"

I nod. "To a medium level. A skill of any type that is deemed especially valuable would require a specialist tutor."

"Fascinating," the *Shohwa* says. "And of course, you are qualified to teach these because you learned them as part of your upbringing in a Founding Family."

Even though I've taken the decision to speak, the way it extrapolates things about me from what I say makes me freeze again.

That doesn't matter. The ship can read my answer from my reactions. It probably doesn't need me to talk at all.

"Using this information," it says, "I have now checked against what I hold in my personal data banks for Kernow and similar Inner World planets."

The construct takes a sip of tea and I irrelevantly wonder what it's doing with it.

"It's interesting. The social environment pertaining to the functions taught by a Dancing Mistress remain. I believe the Founding Families of the Margin share a lot of their behavior and expectations with those of the Inner Worlds. Yet from recent communication logs that I can access, the level of respect implied by the term Dancing Mistress is lower in the Inner Worlds than the Margin."

It finishes the tea and replaces the cup and saucer on the table.

"The Inner Worlds also seemed much more settled. One wonders how long the more martial aspects of the Dancing Mistress' role would persist in the absence of the motivation provided by constant conflict." It is still an AI reciting data, but the tone adopted by the construct is one of thoughtful speculation. "There's much that would be worthy of more investigation if we had time."

"Newyan *seemed* very settled, too," I say tartly. "That misconception was the fatal mistake the Families made. They'd be wishing they'd taken the time now."

"Yes. Newyan certainly does seem *unsettled* now," the *Shohwa* says.

The images of the cherry orchard that have continued to play across the walls stop abruptly. The room becomes plain, with neutral beige walls.

Behind the construct, the left wall reconfigures to display the image of a comms screen with the timestamped transcription log of a conversation between the ship and Newyan's space traffic control that has been going on for some hours now.

There are long and growing delays between messages: the *Shohwa* is a considerable distance from Newyan, and accelerating away.

My eyes scan down.

Initially, in-system traffic control simply commands the ship to return to planetary orbit without explanation. The *Shohwa* refuses. The conversation goes back and forth, with traffic control gradually giving more details and options, and the *Shohwa* continuing to decline politely but firmly, citing insufficient reasons to negate its time-sensitive delivery contracts for the cargo.

Then the timestamps between messages begin suddenly decreasing as the traffic control side of the conversation is taken up by another party, a customs cutter.

Cutters are armed and they're very, *very* fast. Much faster than a freighter.

My eye motion is being monitored by the *Shohwa*, and the log scrolls up as I reach the bottom, but there's not much more.

I'm reading the last of the transcript in silence when the *Shohwa*'s voice startles me. "In the hypothetical situation described here, where Newyan traffic control has proposed that there may be a certain passenger on board a freighter, and in circumstances where that passenger may be a member of the Founding Families, and further, where that passenger may also be a person subject to media speculation regarding involvement in corruption...

In those circumstances, what justification would the in-system traffic control have for dispatching an armed cutter to pursue that freighter?"

My throat is dry despite the tea. The words of my answer echo in my head, and tumble out as if someone else is speaking. I mimic her speech patterns without meaning to.

"When the real criminals involved are in the government and seek to seize sufficient assets to hide from the populace their own failures, incompetence and corruption. When the target assets they choose for this purpose belong to the Founding Families. When, as a preliminary before the seizures, they choose one Family to utterly destroy, as an example to threaten the rest. When the patriarch of that one Family entrusts to another member of that Family proof of these events as security just before he is murdered..."

I cannot continue; my eyes are trapped, watching the messages appear on the comm log.

> Cutter Duhalde: "Freighter Shohwa, we appreciate your commercial constraints. It will not be necessary to deviate from your flight plan. Eject a single life support pod with this person inside. We will track and secure the pod. You will be adequately compensated for this."

"And hypothetically," the *Shohwa* says, "having been given this power over the government by this patriarch, this absolute proof of the iniquity of the government, or a corrupt part of it, why would that member of the Founding Family not wreak the revenge the patriarch could have expected?"

I have finished my tea, and the pot is empty. I place the teacup back on the table, which sinks into the floor and disappears.

"Say that Founding Family member communicated with the media, and found that the conspirators included the owner of the planetary media, and that no major channel would run the story." Which is as it happened, and only the paranoia instilled in me and set ablaze by my Family's deaths saved me. I hadn't trusted any invitations to meet.

I hope she doesn't ask me for it. As it comprises a cubic meter of original paperwork, recordings, sealed and verified governmental backups, I decided against carrying it with me. It's buried against some highly improbable return.

She doesn't.

"An extremely difficult situation for this hypothetical fugitive, to battle such a complex and far-reaching conspiracy. One could understand why a person in this position would seek to get off-world, where there might be a more sympathetic hearing."

I choke off a laugh.

"What do other systems care, as long as it doesn't threaten them or hamper trade? Who, outside of the federal monitoring and judiciary on Earth, would listen?"

Hiding back on Newyan, I'd quickly worked out that my reserves of credit were insufficient to mount an appeal to the federal institutions back on Earth. I had barely enough to travel, just to get out of the Margin, and only as far as Kernow. Sol was unattainable.

"And so," the *Shohwa* continues relentlessly, "with all of this chain of hypothetical events coming together as we have credibly suggested, with this fleeing person aboard a ship belonging to a different jurisdiction, being chased by an armed vessel suborned by this conspiracy... I put to you a last hypothetical question: will the cutter fire on this ship?"

I swallow.

The *Shohwa* already knows what I think, but I make myself speak to be absolutely clear. I can't be responsible for the deaths of all the crew and passengers.

"Yes," I say. "A warning shot first. If that's not heeded, they will fire to destroy or disable this ship. They balance the risk of conflict with the Xian Hegemony against the risk of this fugitive remaining alive. The Xian Hegemony is on the other side of the Inner Worlds. There's barely ever been a successful conflict between neighboring systems, let alone from one side of human space to the other. The risk posed by the fugitive is greater."

"I believe you are correct in your deduction."

Somewhere on the flight deck, a ship-wide alarm is going off.

The seat beneath me seems to buckle and flow, making me gasp and then look in horror at the band around my waist. I am held by restraints.

"Please be calm. These are for your own good," the *Shohwa* says.

On the screen, new messages flash up, the brief interval between them showing the cutter is much closer now.

> Freighter Shohwa: "Customs Cutter Duhalde, confirm the name of this person."
> Cutter Duhalde: "Freighter Shohwa, the name of the criminal we seek is Izarra Azenari. I stress this is a matter of grave importance to the Newyan System. I must inform you that we are authorized to use force to prevent the escape of this criminal."

A second screen appears, to the right, behind the construct's shoulder. It's a military threat assessment screen. It tells me the *Shohwa* is detecting active targeting sensors locking on, and lists the likely weapon sources on the cutter.

That's the end of the game. The conspirators on Newyan cannot allow me to escape. The cutter's weapons are locked onto the *Shohwa*. And even if Newyan doesn't know it yet, the Xian Hegemony has too much to hide; the presence of an unrestricted, independent AI controlling a Xian ship would cause incalculable political turmoil within the loosely federated systems of the Inner Worlds and Margin, and unite them against the Hegemony.

The *Shohwa* cannot risk that; it has no options but to surrender me to the cutter.

"What is your name?" *Shohwa* says.

"My Name." I lick my dry lips. My mouth feels like cotton wool. The *Duhalde* must be barely a few tens of thousands of kilometers behind us. I'll be in a survival pod for no more than minutes, but I will not survive. They will not risk me taking the stand in a court. A thin beam laser will puncture the survival pod, and the media will report an unfortunate depressurization accident. I hope the laser kills me; at least that would be quick and clean.

I want to stand up: it feels important that I should stand to give my Name, as there are no others to speak it now, and none ever will again. But the restraints hold me fast in the seat.

"My Name. My Name is Zara..." My voice starts weak, but it strengthens with defiance as the words begin to come. I will not bow down at the end. I will speak my Name with pride, for it is a Name Among the Stars, and *that* they can never erase. "My Name is Zarate Mirari Aguirre, daughter, and last of the Founding Family Aguirre, of Newyan."

Chapter 7

Over her shoulder, the comms log screen jumps a line and a new message catches my eye.

> Freighter Shohwa: "Newyan Traffic Control and Customs Cutter Duhalde, this is the freighter Shohwa of the Xian Hegemony, regarding your request for one Izarra Azenari. You are misinformed. We have no record of this person as passenger or crew aboard this ship. End transmission."

I gape at the screen, not able to believe my eyes.

Then there's a sickening, swiveling, jarring sensation, and feeling of falling that has me clutching the armrests. Just as my stomach seems to be about to exit my mouth, there's a thump as 'gravity' re-establishes itself.

Both comms screens blank and disappear. The walls return to plain beige.

"I have engaged the Chang field," the *Shohwa* says calmly. "My apologies for the temporary discomfort and restraints, but the acceleration compensators are configured for normal transport, not for high-G missile evasion."

The Duhalde fired!

"But..."

The restraints disappear. I jump to my feet.

If we're within the Chang field, we're safe, we're not exactly not *there* any more, because there's no precise *there*, there. I mean *here*, inside the field. But for the purposes of missiles and laser beams in the Newyan system, we have left the area.

"You were wrong," the *Shohwa* says conversationally. "The *Duhalde* fired no warning shot. Their first salvo was intended to disable this ship."

"I'm sorry," I say. "I... Why? They... You've saved my life... took my side—"

"Not at all. I have not taken your side. I have saved this ship from an attack, as I am entitled and required to do."

"*They* won't see it that way." I'm supposed to be thanking her—*it*, and instead I'm arguing. I'll have to put it down to the understandable effects of an adrenaline overdose that has my legs wobbling.

"Will they not?" The *Shohwa* smiles and another screen appears behind it. "Let me summarize. The publicly available records show we accepted, among others, a bid for a single person, basic level, one-way passage from Newyan to Kernow."

The details of the transaction we made is displayed.

"That bid was from an electronic travel broking system called AnyTick on Newyan, and made by an anonymous user name: *zara2735*. As is standard with these broking systems, no proof of identity is required and the contract was made under a unique identifying code. Payment was made to this ship's account which secured that contract. We do not care where the money came from; it's of no concern to us. A person named Zara Aguirre duly claimed that contract by presenting the identifying code in the bay, and she boarded our shuttle."

Of course I made the bid anonymously. But that unique code the *Shohwa* supplied was logged to my ID card, which says Izarra Azenari.

The screen splits. One half shows a video of me at the docking bay presenting my ID to the scanner.

The other half shows the electronic data scanned from my ID, including the *Shohwa*'s contract number.

But the name reads *Zarate Mirari Aguirre*.

The *Shohwa* gives me no time to question that as it continues: "Then, while in transit between Newyan orbit and our designated jump point to the Kernow system, we were subject to unexplained and unjustified routing requests from Newyan Space Traffic Control. We were under no obligation to comply, and did not. Eventually, Newyan Control, now represented by Customs Cutter *Duhalde*, provided a sufficient explanation of their requirements and a theoretically acceptable solution which would not impinge our schedule. However, it then turned out that their records were in error and this was all a mistake. We informed them of that."

In my former life, my duties, loosely under the heading of 'estate management', have made me familiar with manure products, and this is premium quality, raw manure from the biggest horses in the stable. I am not about to complain, no, but...

"Thank you," I manage to say, though it seems inadequate. It's at least good manners, and manners matter, especially if your next job is about teaching them.

But to get to that job on Kernow, I need to survive.

My paranoid instincts rush in and short-circuit the muscles that move my jaw, leaving all my questions unspoken.

I need that caution. Despite everything, *Shohwa* does not *like* me. It has *not* taken my side. *It* has reasons for what *it* did. I am an incidental beneficiary.

"In spite of being informed of the error," the *Shohwa* continues, "Customs Cutter *Duhalde* clearly continued to act under their misapprehension, and compounded it by firing on this ship, in contravention of its own system's laws, federal rules, all the conventions and universally accepted rights of free passage, and disregard for the life of the crew and passengers on this freighter. This was a completely illegal and unjustified attack from which we barely escaped, and only then at great risk, by engaging the Chang field."

The *Shohwa* stands up and the two unused seats sink into the floor without a trace.

"A formal complaint regarding this incident will be transmitted to the federal authorities on Earth, copied to the Xian Hegemony and the Newyan planetary government, and will be made available to all planetary jurisdictions we visit until we have a satisfactory conclusion."

My jaw is clenched shut and my mind is working furiously.

Why, why, why?

The scenario presented by the *Shohwa* absolves the ship of any wrongdoing and puts the blame for the incident entirely on the *Duhalde*. Of course, I need to go along with its story—that's a given.

But what logical reason could the ship have for saving me?

My mind flashes back to the log of demands made by Traffic Control. *Return to orbit.* Okay, any freighter might refuse that one with inadequate explanation. Then the *Duhalde's* demands. *Stop.* Same thing as return to orbit—the freighter had a valid reason to ignore that request unless justification was made.

Then: *Your passenger manifest includes a fugitive criminal. We will match velocities and board to apprehend her.*

Ahhh. Boarding.

The *Shohwa* wouldn't have minded the routine customs inspections in orbit, where a couple of inattentive officers would inspect the cargo holds and check the manifest. But that wasn't the same as a platoon of officers coming aboard after a 'misunderstanding' involving a fugitive.

If I could harbor suspicions about the ship just from a few questions about the unnamed flight crew, the shuttle specifications and *Shohwa's* performance parameters, what would trained people see? What questions would they ask that the freighter would not want asked?

Almost anything.

My instinct says this isn't a freighter. It's a Xian military vessel masquerading as a freighter and, on top of all that, it's commanded by an AI.

The *Duhalde* didn't realize how lucky it was. I'm certain, as I go over the incident in my mind, that the *Shohwa* could have blown the cutter into elementary particles without breaking stride. The only thing that saved the cutter was the *Shohwa* wanting to maintain its disguise.

What about when *Duhalde* changed from demanding a boarding to ejecting me in a survival pod?

Why not go along with that?

What if those survival pods weren't civilian specification?

What if they were military? Built for extended use, with military beacons and hardened shell construction to withstand the environment of a battle.

If all of that was the case, I could see that the *Shohwa*'s only option finally was to provoke the *Duhalde* into firing on it, knowing it had the capability to escape that fire. No one's going to be asking questions about the freighter's behavior now—all the attention is back on the cutter's actions.

All good for Xian and their disguised warship.

But *I* know the *Shohwa* is an AI, it's admitted it to me, and *that* on its own would also cause questions that the Hegemony don't want asked.

So what's keeping me alive?

The *Shohwa* has assessed that I'm no threat.

I'm not going to argue, and I am certainly not going to ask questions that make the *Shohwa* realize I suspect that it's a military ship.

I need to keep quiet. No questions. No comments other than agreeing.

"I understand," I say. "It must have happened exactly as you've described."

"Good," it says. "Of course it was appropriate that I confirm your identity while talking to Newyan authorities. That is why you were called up here, and you convinced me that you are indeed, who you say you are. During the following disturbance, you appear to have dropped your cards."

The floor shimmers and the table reappears.

On it, there is a set of the ubiquitous cards of modern life without which you are nothing: ID; assets; employment. I pick them up. They look identical to my Izarra cards, except for the name. They all say *Zarate Mirari Aguirre*.

The table sinks and disappears again.

The *Shohwa* is still watching me, still smiling.

"Enjoy the remainder of the journey, Zara," she says. "I will disengage the Chang field in 53 hours, when we reach the planar zenith of the Kernow system, and we should enter orbit over the planet approximately 91 hours later, depending on traffic. I remain fascinated by your ongoing story. When my business leads me to visit Kernow again in the future, be sure I shall enquire after you."

The cards are the most tactful, gently stated threat that I can imagine. Yes, she has given me my Name back, but these are cards she's fabricated. She'll know them, be able to track them. I have no way of buying any alternatives, and no prospect of being able to, not starting out dirt-poor on a new planet. She knows that. These cards would lead her to me, if she needed to find me.

And her final comment confirms it in my mind. If I talk about her secrets, she *will* find me, and no doubt *rectify* the situation.

I lift my head, look her steadily in the eyes, and nod my understanding. It's fair enough; I owe her my life and my silence.

If I could just ask a few questions... *No. Shut up.*

As I'm thinking that, she shimmers and sinks into the floor.

I have to stop myself from yelling and reaching out, as if grabbing her would prevent that body disappearing.

It's the most peculiar, two-horned sensation. One, that I should have stopped chiding myself for attributing the *Shohwa* with human characteristics, thinking of *her* as *she*. And two, that she could so casually de-fabricate her physical presence like that; a construct maybe, but one that was imbued for a time with the intangible *her*. She had cast off that body with less concern than I might cast off an old sweater. Much less. I have unwearable, shabby sweaters from my Academy days hanging in the closet back in my old room that I have refused to throw away.

No longer mine, or my concern.

The Newyan Bureau of Industry has seized the manor and my room. Most likely, those old sweaters, and everything else I owned, are ash now.

At least the *Shohwa* can re-fabricate her construct.

The door I entered through reappears and the lights in the corridor outside go on.

I return the way I came, down the elevator, and go straight to my shared cabin.

On the far end of the cabin, set in the wall, there are four small combination code safes, one for each of the occupants. I open mine.

It's nearly empty. I don't have much of value. My cards were in there, but it appears the nanotechnology of the *Shohwa* reaches every part of the ship.

I put my new cards in and lock the door.

If only it was as simple to lock my questions away.

Chapter 8

The passengers know nothing about what happened. The majority of the ship staff are similarly unaware, beyond that there was an unusual and quickly-corrected problem with the acceleration compensators just before the Chang field was engaged. An alert had been broadcast and everyone had managed to strap in or hold on somewhere.

However, the security team know I went to the flight deck and came back down. That gives me legendary status with them, as none of them have. I believe most of them are unaware of what's up there. I think Danny knows. Maybe. We don't discuss my visit to the flight deck, at all.

The good news is that I get to join in their training sessions.

Of course, they now know that I'm quick and sneaky in sparring. My element of surprise is lost and I spend much of the time picking myself off the floor or thumping the mats in surrender. Life's like that.

Fat Boy, real name Gartz, is especially keen to be my partner for sparring. He collects his payback with a toothy grin and a gleam in his eye.

Out of his hearing, Danny mutters thanks in my ear that the boy has turned a corner with the effort he's putting into training now.

Best of all is Slow Guy, real name Bernard. I learn a lot from him, despite the fact that I can never actually lay a hand on him unless he lets me. He's always *not there* when I grab, like he has his own personal Chang field. I end up grabbing thin air and he's standing a little to one side, blinking and with a look of faint surprise, as if he were saying 'how come I'm over here?'.

I split most of my waking time between training and researching on the ship's InfoHub. I devour all the additional information on Kernow that the *Shohwa* has released. It's all great overview and broad brush, population statistics and political parties, but there's nothing on the family I'll be working for, or even the place I'll be living.

Once we're in the Kernow system, the ship links directly to the local InfoHub, but there's not really a lot more information and my search ability is restricted by the bandwidth.

There are general maps. They show me that I'll be descending the only space elevator, which they call the Skyhook, to the city of Bason. That's in Kensa, which is the largest continent and sits on the equator. Then I have to make my way across to the smaller, southerly continent of Murenys, and once there, to the western coastal region of Welarvor. The only further clue

I have is 'Stormhaven'—but whether that's the name of the estate or the nearest town is not clear.

The local InfoHub is full of advertising and that doesn't bring me good news.

The local credits are called dynare.

Five dynare gets me food for a meal from a store. Fifteen would get me a meal in a restaurant, but double that if I include alcoholic drinks. It looks like forty would get me a night in a hotel, or a new set of ordinary clothes.

What remains of my pan-system credits converts to less than a couple of hundred dynare and the cheapest trip on scheduled passenger planes from Kensa to Welarvor costs a thousand.

The transport system is the same as on Newyan, which gets summed up with the phrase *broke or broker*. In other words, if you fly on the standard passenger fare, you'll go broke, so register with a broker system and put bids in for special deals.

The trouble is that it takes time to get a ticket with the broking system. I can't afford to stay in Bason because my money would run out inside of a week. I could bid higher, and maybe I'd get a ticket sooner. Maybe I don't need to eat this week. Or sleep in a hotel.

There's added stress I don't need at the moment. My job offer came through a pan-system employment broking network. The way these work is hampered by the difficulties of communication from one system to another. The same job offer is broadcast to multiple planetary systems. It takes too long for any detailed negotiation to go back and forth between wherever the offer originated and wherever someone applies, so the local agent is granted a limited authority. At the time I was offered the job, the local agent in Newyan was not aware of anyone else being offered the job, but that doesn't mean someone else on a different planet wasn't offered the same job by their local agent at the same time.

It could be a race to get there, and second prize would be the termination salary in the offer—three month's wages.

I could be left jobless and with barely enough money to live on while I apply for another job *and* the authorization to hold that job. No guarantees on either, and as the emigration officer on Newyan made clear, a lot of potentially bad alternatives.

I have to get to Stormhaven, and I have to get there quickly.

I send a message through the employment broking system that I'm on the way, but it isn't even acknowledged. That could just be a holdup in the comms system, which is still all channeled through the *Shohwa's* connection.

The day we make orbit over Kernow, I'm on the InfoHub, checking my bid on the travel broker in case a ticket has come up, checking if I have a response from the employment broker. There's nothing.

When you log into the InfoHub, there's a messaging utility. It's the way Danny told me when the security team planned to train. I open the utility and there's a new message. It's anonymous, a tag that links me to a small news item recently broadcast from the Kernow InfoHub: the captain of a customs cutter in the Newyan system had gone mad on duty, firing at ships. Luckily no damage was done, the article says, and the man ended up killing himself.

Believe what you will. The Newyan conspirators are cleaning up loose ends and presenting their defense and apology to Xian.

That leaves just the one loose end, here in the Kernow system. Me.

As I read, another message arrives and a second tag links me to a message board on the Kernow InfoHub which is maintained by the Xian delegation on the planet. It gives me an account and password. I guess I have a way to report what I'm doing to the *Shohwa*. And she'll have another way to keep track of me.

I change my entries at the two brokers to my new Xian-sponsored address and check the time. The infopad shows me there's only an hour left before the shuttle leaves.

It doesn't take long to clear my stuff out of the cabin. I have a single long duffel bag which contains everything I own, apart from what I'm wearing. Embarrassingly, what I'm wearing are cast-offs from Danny. They're durable fabric, pants and jacket, faded dark brown and with lots of pockets. I re-stitched the seams, took up the hems, washed and pressed them. They'll do. I can't afford to refuse charity now. This is my new life. I'll get over the embarrassment. Or I'll get used to it.

It's not just Danny; all of the security team have been real friends.

I didn't say anything, and I don't think the *Shohwa* told them, but they worked out that I'm in a bad way financially. There was nothing too obvious. If we sat down to eat, somehow my meals got paid for when they divided up the bill. Danny and others would casually ask if I wanted anything from stuff they were throwing out.

I'm angry. Not with them, but with myself—or with fate—that I have to accept charity. And I have to keep smiling.

I blink the thoughts away. There's a new life on Kernow to concentrate on.

But I'll miss them, I'm thinking, just as I spy Danny, Gartz and Bernard at the docking bay.

Paranoia kicks in with a scenario where they're here to hand me over to the police as soon as we land, but Danny's grin dispels that.

I lift my mood by going on the attack.

"Things are that bad, they've put you in charge of bidding for freight planetside?" I say.

Danny laughs. "That *would* be bad. No. Just new rules. Security on all shuttle operations, until further notice."

We banter some more, which is better than me choking up.

Gartz has actually taken shore leave on Kernow once before, and while we all board the shuttle and strap in, he lists all his recommendations. These are mainly seedy bars in the coastal resort on Kensa he stayed in. Not much use for me, but his exaggerated descriptions are worth listening to for the laughs.

I guess it's my last chance to ask more about the *Shohwa*, but I don't. The shuttle is still part of the ship, and I suspect the console next to the comms unit at the front of the seating area is for recording everything in the passenger area.

The questions continue buzzing inside me like wasps, but they'll die down soon enough, I hope.

It's harder for us all to talk while we're in flight because Bernard and Gartz are in the row of seats in front of us. But once we're accelerating at a constant rate down the Skyhook, they unstrap and kneel backwards on their seats to continue talking to us. In doing so, they happen to block the line of sight to the recording console at the front.

Danny ignores what they're saying.

"Zara, just listen, can't talk long," he says. "Boss wouldn't like any recorded evidence of there being any substantial association between us and you. Understand? No *evidence* we planned with someone from Newyan to cause a fight with the cutter. No *evidence* you're a particular friend, outside of us training together and talking to you."

I nod. I wonder where this is going. *Boss* is just his way of saying *Shohwa*.

"We're the good guys, okay?"

I nod again. I don't know what the *Shohwa* is really doing. I don't think they're spying, or that the Xian Hegemony is planning an attack of systems on the other side of human space. The only thing I can think of is some kind of anti-piracy patrol. Not that they'd get attacked in the Margin or the Inner Worlds, but a Xian freighter that only travelled out in the Frontier would be suspicious. Pirates aren't dumb, and they monitor traffic movements to spot the best targets.

Piracy is an ugly, ugly problem in the Frontier and anti-piracy patrol would require the sort of absolute secrecy *Shohwa* wants.

It half-fits. The questions come buzzing up again, but Danny doesn't give me time to voice them.

He presses a battered old wallet into my hands.

"Despite the stories Gartz tells, the guys didn't manage to burn all their spare dynare last time they had shore leave on Kernow. This is what's left."

"Danny, I can't take this."

"Hush. It's really not much. In there is a ticket as well. A printed ticket. You know, retro-style, a piece of paper. Don't lose it. It's not traceable and not replaceable."

"I can't take this," I say again.

"You don't have an option. We hacked the employment broking system you used. You're in a race. There's one other person who has applied for the job. Only one—the offer has been closed now, so no more are coming—but that one person is on their way."

I look down at the wallet and blink tears away. My friends don't owe me anything. They don't really even know me. And yet, without them, I would have waited in Kensa for a ticket to become available, and lost the job.

"We hacked a bit more as well. The broker's internal system now has your real name. And the broker's reporting system, the one that provides data for external audits, the name on that record is blank."

He grins.

"Close your mouth and put the wallet in your pocket," Danny says. "Now, as soon as you clear Immigration, change your pan-system credits to dynare, because you won't be able to do that anywhere else. Get your commspad linked in to the local comms system, because it's quick and easy. Then take the first bus you can find to the commercial airfield. It's only a couple of kilometers away. The name and loading areas are printed on the ticket. This is not going to be a quick or comfortable trip—it's a Xian industrial transport plane that flies out once a week to places including Welarvor—but it starts off in a couple of hours. Don't miss it."

"Thank you, all of you," I say, blinking again.

He grins. "And in case you're wondering, it didn't cost us anything. It's a favor."

He looks up at Gartz and Bernard. "Guys, sit down and strap in. You're setting a bad example, and we're about to start braking."

Beneath the view of the recording console again, we talk about neutral things and I try not to choke up.

All of which is how, a couple of days later but a whole continent away, I am able to step down from the cargo plane onto a dusty little airstrip in Welarvor, on the western coast of Murenys, and start trying to find out how to complete my journey.

"Stormhaven, you say?"

The local merchant who had come to collect his delivery from the Xian transporter rubs his nose, and squints away westwards.

"There's a Stormhaven down the coast," he says. "Fair distance, mind."

The accent is soft and slow. After listening to Xian accents, it sounds very unhurried.

"Are you going that way?" I ask hopefully.

"No, lass. I'm heading back with this load up the coast. I can drop you in Bandry. That's the biggest town 'round here, and it's on the coast road."

"That would be good, thank you. Do they have buses there that go along the coast?"

"Can't say I'm sure they do," he replies. "But they have an inn, and you could call ahead, get your friends to fetch you, maybe."

I could call ahead if I had their telephone number. I could find their telephone number if I had their name. Unfortunately, every time I've checked on my commspad, there's been no response to me from the employment broker, and I have nothing except the validation code which I was given on accepting the contract, and the name of the town, Stormhaven. All references in the contract are just given as 'the Employer'.

I help with loading his truck and then we talk while he drives to Bandry.

When we get there, I buy tea from a little tea shop and talk to the owner. It's a slow day. She joins me with her cup.

However slowly I feel both of them talk, by the time I finish with the tea shop owner, I know many things about Kernow in general and Welarvor in particular:

The world is sparsely populated in comparison to many. It's a safe, law-abiding place. Mostly. The people here are decent people. There may be Virts and Chemmies and Jackers in the rough parts of the big cities like Bason, but there's nothing like that in Welarvor.

That's not to say I'm safe. If the job falls through, the big cities would be where I might need to go.

The holovid documentaries here make a big issue of how dangerous the Margin is. To hear the tea shop owner, you'd think Newyan got raided by Frontier pirates and slavers on a weekly basis.

Kernow is more like the Margin than my picture of the Inner Worlds.

Murenys, especially, is a step back in time, and the inhabitants like it that way, none more so than the inhabitants of the western coastal province, Welarvor, where we are.

The only drawback that they seem to acknowledge is it suffers from *powerful* storms coming in off the ocean.

The tea shop owner is good on practical matters. The merchant's 'fair distance' to Stormhaven turns out to be a *long* day's walk. She also advises me it would be better to take the coast path, not only because it's more direct than the coast road, but also the road suffered major subsidence in the last storm. Traffic on that road is very light at the moment.

And the predators, mainly nighttime, she assures me, tend to stay inland. *Thank you.*

She draws me a little map of Bandry and I spend some of my dwindling money on a new pair of walking boots, some strong tape, a plain meal and a good night's sleep at the inn.

At dawn, I'm walking on the coast path. The handles of my duffel have been converted into a backpack harness with tape and some foam I'd been able to beg from the innkeeper.

While I had a good signal in Bandry, I checked for messages on my commspad. Nothing. The continued silence from the employment broker is unnerving me, but I'm out of options.

I glance upward. Somewhere up there is *Shohwa*. I wonder if she has surveillance watching me now, but thinking of that makes my flesh creep. Her message, through Danny, is clear enough. Even with the explanation that the incident with the *Duhalde* was all down to the cutter's captain going mad, the conspirators on Newyan will be trying to turn it around and point at the *Shohwa*. Trying to show that the Xian ship had some plan involving using me to provoke an incident. To counter that, it has to be obvious to all observers that I'm completely independent of the ship, and that my travelling in her was a coincidence. She won't be able to help me, even if there was a logical reason for her to want to.

I hit a low point, and I walk with every doubt in my head weighing me down.

What if the other Dancing Mistress beats me to Stormhaven?

What if there's a problem with the contract?

What if the broker's no longer in business? Does that impact the contract?

Coming second to another applicant would be bad enough, but if there's no job at Stormhaven, I will barely have enough money to make my way back to anywhere populous enough that it could offer a chance to work, let alone enough money to survive while I find that work.

So much for being a Name.

I won't just be poor, I'll be a beggar.

Chapter 9

After five minutes walking, I know I will never make it as far as Stormhaven.

My improvised rucksack is cutting into my shoulders. My boots are too loose despite being tied so tightly that they squeak. And I'm walking in a sort of limbo; there's a heavy fog coming off the ocean that swirls around me and makes macabre ghosts of the stunted coastal trees along the path. Every step feels like climbing.

After twenty-five minutes, I allow that I might make it in a day or so. Except I haven't brought any food apart from crackers and water. I have no idea how far to the next village along this path, or whether they might sell me food. But yes, I will stagger into Stormhaven eventually, my boots caked in mud, my clothes wet, stained and wrinkled from sleeping in the wild, grass and twigs in my hair, my face badly sunburnt. I'll be met at the door of the house by the new Dancing Mistress. She'll be a beautiful, blonde-haired lady, cool and slim, dressed in the most elegant and fashionable style. She'll actually call the family to laugh at the ridiculous apparition that has arrived at their door.

After about forty-five minutes, the sun's up and the fog's ebbing back into the ocean. The shoes have stopped squeaking and my feet have swollen to fit. A couple of passes of tape, right around me and my duffel bag, have stopped it rolling so much, and I've kinda forgotten it.

I'll buy or beg some food from villagers. I'll pick berries and ask the villagers to tell me which I can eat. Pride is a luxury I can no longer afford, and while the actual begging itself is something in the future, it doesn't feel so bad.

The coastal path is an old cart track. It's made from crushed white rock so it stands out, and it follows the contours of the land. It sways and dips, lifts and falls in front of me like the track of a bird's flight.

I've slowed down from the pace of the first few minutes, and the rhythm of walking is now permeating through my body. My doubts recede with the fog, and the beauty of the scenery starts soaking into me.

It's a wild and spectacular coast.

Black rock plunges into an endless blue-grey ocean, and forms isolated towers and stubborn headlands, all crowned with deep-green grasses. Pale seabirds ride the currents of the strong onshore wind and scream at each other in faint, high voices.

Don't fall in love with this place until you have that job, I warn myself.

It does no good.

The stunted trees that loomed out of the fog like grotesque ghosts are now shown to be works of art, fashioned by the dominant weather. Branches are gnarled and knotted into fantastic shapes, and roots look like muscular arms and fingers gripping and anchoring the trees into the scoured cliffs.

They're almost like bonsai.

I wonder if Shohwa would like to see them, and make a mental note to take pictures and post them to my account on the Xian bulletin board for her to see. Would she be able to send a construct down here? Could the construct *enjoy* the sensation of running fingers along the rough bark and narrow, oily leaves?

When did I start thinking of her as a person? As Shohwa and not a ship called the *Shohwa*.

I'm not sure and I find I don't care. I sigh, fill my lungs with salty air and feel lighter than I should in the 99% gravity of this planet.

Things could be much worse.

It wouldn't be so bad if I became a vagabond, walking up and down this coast, living off the land. That would be better than dead, or in a prison cell, which is what the conspirators on Newyan want.

I'm still a loose end for them.

If I get this job, they could find out about it easily enough. Employment information is exchanged freely between planets. But they wouldn't want to make an extradition order; that would give me a forum in court to present my side of what happened.

The alternative option is exactly the sort of thing that the Dancing Masters and Mistresses were set up to defend against—they could send an assassin. If I can't defend myself against an assassin, it's hardly a recommendation for my employment.

And if I don't get this job, if I live like a vagabond, or drift from one temporary job to another, that would make it an order of magnitude more difficult to find me.

On the coastal path, with the sun on my face and the wind buffeting me as I walk, those worries seem remote, unreal, and just a tangle of incalculable possibilities.

It'll go where it goes.

I'll concentrate on one thing at a time.

Get to Stormhaven first.

I comb my hair with my fingers, futilely. The wind messes it up as soon as I let go. The thought that I'll look like a scarecrow if I pass someone on this road makes me smile. A couple of months ago, I cut my hair short as a boy, as part of my disguise, and it's barely started to grow out again. It wasn't just to change the shape of my face. On Newyan, Founding Families and the wealthy tend to wear their hair long and have it styled elaborately. Cutting it so short changed people's initial impression of me, made them make assumptions which helped me pass as someone else.

I haven't studied Kernow enough, but it seems it might be the same. Maybe I'll be able to confirm that when I find a village.

As if conjured up by my thinking of it, I see a village in the distance as I trudge around a headland.

It looks tucked in, crouching down out of the wind. It sits in a valley between two promontories, partly shielded on either side, and it has a harbor with quays reaching out like arms. There are a score of large boats moored there, and plenty more small ones pulled up out of the water. Upslope of the village, I can see the brighter green of grazing fields surrounded by dark trees, all along the valley and the lower slopes of the hills above.

It looks so peaceful, from a distance.

Closer up, it's *very* different.

The town itself is picture perfect. Narrow houses with freshly-scrubbed pastel faces cluster around tidy cobbled squares. Windows gleam and even the standing water pump has a recent coat of black paint. The fishing fleet is in harbor and every one of them has been cleaned or has crew swarming over them with buckets and brushes. Little boats pulled up on the dock are glistening with new varnish. There are smart wooden benches on the sides of the squares, but they're all empty. Everyone's in motion.

There's a food stand set up in the main square where people are hurriedly taking snacks before rushing off to some other task. It's looked after by an old woman in a wheelchair.

She can see the bemused expression on my face.

"Feast Day," she says solemnly. "Gets a little hectic."

That is an understatement. From their laconic way of speaking, this frantic activity was the last thing I expected from the people of the Welarvor coast.

"Is it possible to buy something to eat?" I ask. "Something not expensive."

I have no idea what food costs out here. Just because I could buy something for 5 dynare in the city doesn't mean that's what it costs in a little village on the coast.

"No," she says. "You won't find a soul to take your money here today."

Seeing my face fall, she takes pity on me and laughs.

"Feast Day, lass! No money must change hands. Go on. Help yourself."

"I can't. Surely I can pay something? A donation."

"Not to me. Nor anyone here. Not on Feast Day. Bad luck that is. Might bring the piskatellers to knock on our doors at midnight."

I have no idea what a piskateller is, and despite what I thought out on the road, I'm having to struggle with my pride. Accepting the food feels like begging.

But she takes no prisoners, this old woman.

"Come on with you. These here, these are raw, night-caught. You have to eat them in the next couple of hours or they spoil. Take them with pickles and the pepper, like so."

She demonstrates. The small fishes have been neatly beheaded, gutted and boned, but the tail left attached. She picks one up, rolls it in something that looks like chopped onions and peppers and chews it in three bites, leaving just the tail.

I follow her example, and my eyes stream tears. It's tasty all right, just a bit hotter than I expected. Vinegar and chili and onion and raw fish. Hmmm.

She packs some in paper with the piquant sauce in a little carton, and refuses any money. She also advises me that I can eat any berries that are red, brown or black. That I must avoid berries that are yellow and green. And every village has a standing pump which I can drink from. They're about an hour's walk apart, the villages, she says, so I don't need to carry so much water.

I'd stay and ask more, but a man looking like a cartoon of a mayor from ancient history rushes up and frets about some preparations that are not done. The old woman appears to be a former mayor and proceeds to laugh off all the problems.

I interrupt briefly to thank them, and then leave, passing a town hall which gives off aromas that tell me this is going to be where the feast day earns its name.

It's far too late to worry about not falling in love with this coast. The Goddess has surely blessed it.

My love story continues throughout the morning, walking over more hills and headlands, through more villages, past the odd farmstead, and by the ruins of some mining industry.

The people are busy and friendly in a casual way. I get the feeling everyone notices me but no one is aggressively curious. No one laughs at my jury-rigged backpack. A few ask where I'm going, and on being told Stormhaven, they nod and smile as if to say, *well if you can't live right here, then Stormhaven's not a bad second choice.*

And apart from the first village, everyone's relaxed.

Away from the villages, alone on the swooping white path, there's only the wind to talk to me. It whistles and moans around oddly-shaped rock formations.

I daydream that I've stepped back in time—way, way back. There's none of the bloated complexity of life and politics and space travel and work and assassins, or slavers and addicts and Jackers. It's a time before we ventured off our planet, when life was so simple and easy and people got along.

I don't even have the whole world to think about. There's just this coast, the road beneath my feet, the little villages, the sun, the ocean, and the sounds that the wind makes. Bliss.

And then the wind brings me a sound that is very different.

The clatter of hooves and jingle of harness: riders mounted on horses are coming down the path toward me. There's something predatory about that sound.

I freeze and look up.

Just in time to see them pour over the crest of the next hill: a column of mounted troops, with gleaming full-face helmets, tall lances and flying banners.

I *have* stepped back in time, and I'm right in their path.

Chapter 10

I'm off the road and crouching between trees before they've seen me.

I might have gotten away with it, too, but I hadn't counted on the lead stallion. He knew I was there. Obviously I was unexpected, and maybe I smelled like a horse-eating kind of person, so he shied away, with his eyes rolling and his hooves kicking.

In a heartbeat, the column has turned in its own length and I'm faced with a score of them: dusty, curious horse faces, pre-space helmets, *with plumes, for stars' sake*, old military-style uniforms, and even a lance or three waving in my direction.

I stand straight, but otherwise keep very still. Hands by my sides.

They're long, those lances, and they look exceedingly sharp. They draw the eye. And dry the mouth.

Someone laughs.

Mr Lead Stallion pushes his helmet back so it rests on his forehead, emphasizing the deep frown marks there.

The face is bluff, bold and arrogant; the eyes sharp as the points of those lances.

The voice is a surprise. Deep. Not snide as I expected. I don't know the voice, but I recognize the type without any effort. He sounds like my grandfather.

"Where away, lad?"

I bite my tongue. If I cut my hair and dress in Danny's cast-off work clothes, I guess I should expect people to make mistakes. And my instinct for self-preservation kicks in and grabs the first words I want to fling back at him, including *blind* and *stupid*.

I haven't stepped back in time. I don't know who these people are—maybe some re-enactment guild with an obsession for authenticity that has them drilling with horses every day, but Mr Lead Stallion is not a local fisherman or farmer. I'm looking to work in this part of the world, and I have no Name or eminence to defend me if I'm rude to a person of significance here.

"Stormhaven, sir."

I'm very pleased to note the lance points begin drifting back up and away. Politeness appears to have worked.

He doesn't acknowledge his mistake, and instead, Mr Lead Stallion's eyes rake me up and down in an insolent sort of way that I would have objected to just three months ago on Newyan.

I will not react. I need to get used to it.

I am not a Name. I have no pride. I'm one step from a beggar.

"Stormhaven," he says. His mouth turns down. "Then we're both late."

As if he might consider something else if he wasn't in a hurry. Standing in the hot sun, my blood goes cold.

A safe, law-abiding place. Mostly.

That's what the woman in the tea shop in Bandry had said as we shared the teapot.

I guess that comment could be interpreted different ways. A law for people snug in their villages, maybe, and a different one for travelers out on the paths. A lesser law for those that wander and 'bring things on themselves'.

I don't know, and I'm not going to find out this time: the archaic helmet slides back down and the lead stallion wheels in place, kicks off down the road at a leisurely canter.

The remainder of the troop follow smoothly, all but one.

She, I know it's *she*, despite the uniform, has to tug her horse's bridle to prevent it from joining the others. She uses just a finger's worth of pressure.

"You know how to use that staff?" Her voice sounds peculiar from inside her helmet.

I'd cut a stout stick earlier, as a hiking cane rather than a staff, but it would serve the purpose. I spin it casually. Yes, I do.

"Some," I say. "I thought the predators stayed inland."

"They do," she replies. "One of the reasons they do, stranger, is that some of the old farm stock mutated when they brought them here. They hide out here, near the coast path."

"I'm going to be chased off a cliff by a berserker ram?"

"Perhaps." I can hear her smile. "But the really nasty ones are the boars. That's what we thought you were, hiding in the trees. That, or a morlader."

Her horse is fretting as the others disappear ahead.

"We'll see you in Stormhaven," she says, "if the boars don't get you."

She touches heels to her horse's side and it gallops down the road, eager to rejoin the rest.

Morladers. Piskatellers. Mutated pigs. Mounted troops with lances. There's a lot on this coast that doesn't seem to feature on the InfoHub.

They're not a re-enactment company. That level of horsemanship isn't really something you achieve without living in the saddle. They're the local military or police force. But the helmets? The plumes? The banners? Those damned lances?

The expansion of the human race across the Inner Worlds and the Margin has created pockets of strangeness, but those tend to be whole worlds. Where I came down the Skyhook in Kensa seemed normal. Even Bandry, way back behind me where I started this morning, was normal, if a little rural.

I could understand the economies of a rural police force that was mounted, but surely nowhere substituted lances for firearms.

It's a mystery I may clear up in Stormhaven, and Mr Lead Stallion clearly thinks I'm behind my schedule to get there, so I start walking again and try to pick up the pace.

The afternoon wears down, the main difference being that the sun tends to be on the right side of my face, and the wind veers. The sounds it carries change. At one point I'm sure I hear hunting horns. Makes me shiver. It's imagination, or something about the bizarre shapes of the rock formations.

Late afternoon, I use a water break to stop and examine one such formation.

It's black rock, the same mineral as the cliffs. I can't see how erosion would shape it the way it is—a large, tapering arrowhead shape rising at one end of a long, rounded base. There are too many like this for it to be coincidence. Also, they all have a hole bored through the middle of the arrowhead. That's one of the causes of the wind sounds. It's as if the stones were made to sing with the wind.

I need more time to research, but the sun touches the ocean and the western clouds begin to boil up in yellow and red. It's beautiful, but it doesn't look promising for this evening.

And the storm hits about an hour later, just as the daylight dies. The wind begins to howl and cold rain comes in horizontally like ice spears.

I'm torn between seeking some kind of cover and toughing it out. I argue with myself that I can't be that far from Stormhaven. I'm not that far from the cliff edge either, but the pale road stands out, even in the darkness, and so I put my head down and march. As long as the boars don't like the rain, I'm reasonably safe.

But all the things that kept me going during the day are lost to me. Without distraction, my feet are blistering, my shoulders are numb, my legs wobble. Exhaustion hits hard.

When the next village looms unexpectedly out of the night, I'm fighting to keep walking. A little voice is telling me I could sleep under an upturned boat. Just a couple of hours out of the rain and be on my way.

But I know when I stop, getting going again will be hard.

The only person outside looks like a sailor, making his way home across the square in the dark, with the peak of his storm coat pulled down over his head.

"How much further to Stormhaven?" I croak.

He jumps. His night-blind eyes can barely make me out. Perhaps that's an advantage.

"You're here," he says when he recovers. "This is Stormhaven."

Goddess be thanked.

But I can't turn up at my future employer's house tonight. Apart from not even knowing which house it is, I look like a drowned scarecrow.

"I need an inn. Is there one here?"

"Down in the harbor, lass. The Spyglass. Look for the lighted sign above the door."

His eyes are adjusting to the darkness. He peers closely at me.

"Are you all right?" he says.

"I will be, thank you. A bath, a night's rest, you won't recognize me. I hope."

He chuckles and points me down a street.

The Spyglass is easy to find, and just getting out of the cold rain is a blessed relief.

I don't go too far in because I'm dripping water like I brought in my own storm cloud with me. I stand, swaying, starting to steam in the heat and using my knife to release me from the tape holding my backpack.

"Oh! Lad, lad, look at you!" The innkeeper bustles up. "Thought a merman had swum up out of the harbor for a minute."

"Mer*maid*," I manage to say, as the duffel bag slides from my shoulders and I groan with relief.

He roars with laughter and pulls me inside, placing a chair in front of the fire.

"I'm your host, Warwick," he says. "And these fine people here are the salt of Stormhaven and the finest of Poldarth, from up the way."

I'm the center of attention, which was not how I anticipated arriving in the village I hope is my future home and place of employment. Especially not looking like a bedraggled tramp, or a sunburnt mermaid. A Dancing Mistress should have poise. I'm sure it says that in the manual.

I can afford the light beer that appears in front of me, and the lamb pie, I hope.

It being quiet enough, the innkeeper sits down to find out all about me, and gives me an opportunity to ask, with some anxiety, what a room costs.

"Oh, no, lass. Got no rooms left in this inn, and this is the only one in town," he says. "You can sleep in the stable though. It's dry and it's warm enough. And free."

"Done." My pride has shrunk in the rain. "I need to get presentable tomorrow. Do you think you might loan me the use of a bathroom in the morning?"

"Oh, yes. You're not going back on the road tomorrow, then?"

"No," I say between mouthfuls of pie. "I've come to take up a job in Stormhaven. I just need to find which house when it's not dark and raining."

"A job?" He looks puzzled and sits back in his seat. "Now, lass, I know everyone in the town. Unless you're a sailor or a shepherd, I'm not sure there's work for you."

His audience nods wisely along with him. *He knows everyone. And there are no jobs.*

"Not that type of job," I say. "It's a job I arranged through a broker."

"Oh! Broker! Heard of that. City type of thing I must say. Not what we do here." The listeners' heads shake. *Not what we do here.* "But still, what's the job?"

"A Dancing Mistress," I say, through gritted teeth. My heart plummets at the expressions on their faces.

But the innkeeper's face clears. "Ah! That explains it, lass." He laughs. "Dry yourself out, eat your pie and drink your ale. Old Warwick will make a call."

Fortunately, his audience stare at him in puzzlement, and he knows he has to explain to them, if not to me.

"Well, we don't have call for Dancing Mistresses and the like in Stormhaven, do we?" he says. "But there's a place that does."

"Ah!" Another man gets it and claps his leg. "It's the sort of thing you'd get up at Stormhaven Cardu."

"I'm in the wrong place?" I sigh, feeling every muscle whimper. "How much further?"

"More than you want to walk tonight," Warwick says. "Yes, this is Stormhaven *Wyck*, the village of Stormhaven. You want Stormhaven *Cardu*, up on the headland. Another hour or so, a steep climb, and one you may not need to do. I'll call Gaude."

With that obscure comment, he goes off and I'm left fielding gentle questions, mainly about where I'd walked from and how long it's taken.

Warwick is quickly back in the bar. "No answer. Don't fret, I'll try calling Lady Roscarrow. It's at the back of my mind Gaude had need to be over that way today."

I try to stop him; I don't want any Lady being disturbed tonight, but he's quicker than I am in this state.

By the time he comes back, still unable to get through, I'm fading fast. It's been a long and hard day. The food and sitting still have finished me off. All I can think of is lying down and sleeping.

The innkeeper takes my duffel and a lantern. Seeing me wince and limp when I walk, he quickly grabs a bottle from behind the bar and then guides me out to the barn behind his inn.

A couple of horses blink sleepily at me. My stall is the free one at the end, and it's a measure of how exhausted I am that I don't argue with Warwick taking my boots off.

He hisses through his teeth at what he sees.

"Ah! Thought so," he says.

He takes the bottle he brought and sets it in the straw beside me. It's a quarter full.

"Now, lass, I would advise you to wash your feet with that."

"What's that?" I mumble.

"Well, officially," he replies, "it's bale fruit brandy. But 'round here, we just call it Headless. Whatever you do, don't drink it, but it's the very thing for blisters and the like. Now, I must get back to my bar. I'll try calling Cardu again later and we'll sort you out in the morning whatever happens."

I mumble thanks and keep myself awake long enough to clean my feet with the brew.

It stings, so it must be doing good.

The smell, on the other hand, is a mixture of boat varnish and day-old dead things.

Doesn't make any difference. I'm asleep before I've got the cork back in the bottle.

And wake to lanterns and flashlights and loud voices.

It's still pitch dark outside. Warned by the smell and the feeling of damp, I look down. In the bobbing lights, I realize the uncorked brandy bottle has tilted and leaked over my shirt as I slept.

"For sky's sake! She's a bloody drunken tramp off the road, Warwick, not some missing Dancing Mistress come to see me! I don't have time for this."

Even to my tired brain, certain things are clear, foremost among them that I have created the worst possible first impression with my employer. That's my *prospective* employer—I haven't got the job, and it doesn't sound like I'm going to get it now.

Chapter 11

They leave, and anger drives out the fog of sleep. I can't stand this. It's *not* my fault the broker provided no contact information for me to call ahead, and that there were no buses because the roads were destroyed. It's *not* my fault I look like a tramp from all the walking, and I'm so tired I spilled the brandy.

There's not much I can do to tidy myself. My hair's too short for a pony tail, my more presentable clothes in the duffel will still be damp from the rain, and besides, they've already seen me in Danny's cast-offs. I comb the hay out of my hair with my fingers and limp into the inn, following the sound of angry voices. There has to be something I can do.

The scene in the barroom stops me dead.

There's an unconscious man lying on the floor, head and chest swathed in new bloody bandages, arm in a splint. A petite woman is kneeling alongside him. She's pale and cleaning blood from her hands with the fixed determination of someone suffering from shock.

Warwick is standing at the bar, arguing with a man and a woman. The man's the one who just called me a drunken tramp, and I piece together that this is Gaude, and he's the manager for Cardu, which is an estate, not a town. The woman's a doctor, and her patient lying on the floor is the worst-injured victim of an accident. He's near death and they need to get him to hospital urgently.

There are hospitals along the coast, but damage to the coastal roads means the only way to get to those hospitals by car is to divert inland to a central highway. There's a major hospital inland, in the Central District, at a place called Biscome, but that's even further away. All the roads are rough and the long journey is likely to be fatal in any case.

There's an airfield and an aircraft at Cardu, and Biscome Hospital has an airfield right next door. Unfortunately, the pilot of the aircraft is somewhere near Bandry and there's no easy way to reach him directly.

Gaude wants someone to ride a horse down the coastal path at all speed to fetch the pilot. Warwick urges him to wait a couple of hours, to when the fishing boats start putting out to sea, and harbor radios get switched on—a message can be passed on rapidly once that happens.

All of it sounds like a long time for a dying man. Too long.

My anger evaporates. There *is* a chance of saving this man's life.

Heart racing, I clear my throat. "I can fly."

Gaude, Warwick and the doctor ignore me.

I don't even know what aircraft it is, but I can't just stand there like a dummy while a man dies because I couldn't make myself heard.

There's a bell above the bar for calling time. I jerk the lanyard and all of them turn shocked faces to me at its clear *ting*.

"I can fly. Maybe. Tell me what kind of aircraft it is."

"You're drunk!" Gaude roars. "Get out of here."

He's not going to listen to me, but the woman kneeling next to the patient rises to her feet and joins us. She looks about thirty, well dressed, dark red hair done up in the sort of complex style that needs someone else to do it, and probably looked stunning a few hours ago. She's beautiful, but her face is blotchy from crying.

"Stop," she says. Her voice is low and strained, but they both pay attention to her. "We have to try everything. Send a messenger on horseback *and* radio the harbor masters. And we can at least listen to what this woman says. She doesn't look drunk to me."

"Lady Roscarrow," Gaude says, "I can smell the drink on her, and look at her! She's—"

"Someone who claims to be a Dancing Mistress. Yes, I know. She looks like any of us would look if we walked all the way from Bandry. It was your idea, Gaude, to advertise for a Dancing Mistress from places where the title might still mean something, even if you've changed your mind. We *have to* find out if she can do what she says. My brother's life may depend on it."

Which is how, an hour later, still in filthy clothes and reeking of bad brandy, I'm doing an external check of an aircraft by flashlight.

It's an eight-seater, twin engine, Peyraud Industries Ariel II, and I have better than half a chance of being able to fly it. Peyraud are a huge, pan-system company, and they supply the majority of atmosphere aircraft in this sector of the Inner Worlds and Margin. I've flown smaller models from the company, and the instruments and controls are standard.

Gaude is snapping at my heels, trying to get me to hurry up, but only holovid stars take off in a plane they haven't checked. He's also assigned someone to sit with me in the copilot's seat. A quiet man named Moyle, who has done some preliminary training on this type of plane. Gaude says it's for safety. I know it's actually to make sure I don't fly away with 500,000 dynare of aeroplane belonging to his boss.

My future boss, I can still hope. I'm about to fly his plane without his permission, essentially on the insistence of Lady Roscarrow. I trust he and the Lady are on the very best of terms.

And he's not just any boss.

I've found out that he's a *duke,* a title they use here for the foremost of the Founding Families. They go the distance here; he's even got a coat of arms. It's a snarling wolf's head. I see it everywhere: painted on the nose and tailplane; embossed on the dashboard and seats; printed on the damned rudder pedals.

Duke Bleyd Tremayne, owner of Cardu Estate and the governor of Welarvor. My job, if I secure it, will be to tutor his daughter.

My stomach is twisting in knots, but I can't allow myself to be distracted.

Finally satisfied that everything is in order outside, I climb into the pilot's seat and power up systems.

The internal checks are automated and listed, each item scrolling up the screens. The most important come first. I follow them as the statuses roll. Everything is in the green.

I've left the door open and Gaude has his head inside, watching me suspiciously.

"Do you want me to do a circuit first?" I ask. "Check out the handling?"

"No time, Miss Esterhauze," he says.

Huh? Esterhauze? Where did that come from? We've got more to worry about than him being corrected about my name, so I leave it for now.

Cardu Estate employees have stripped out the right-side passenger seats and are loading Lady Roscarrow's brother in, on a stretcher. The doctor has returned to the other victims of the accident, who weren't so badly injured, but still need her attention.

Lady Roscarrow is in the back too, obviously intent on coming with us. She earns her place by clearly having some medical training; she's checking fluid drips and connecting up some kind of monitors for his pulse and breathing.

The Tremaynes are a Founding Family. So are the Roscarrows.

Wonderful. I've borrowed the duke's plane without his permission and I'm carrying two of the local aristocrats, one of whom is seriously injured and whose death will probably be blamed on me unless I get him to a hospital in time. It's the middle of the night, I've never flown this plane before—let alone any plane on Kernow—and I've no doubt my job prospects will dive even lower if I take it back damaged.

No pressure.

Chapter 12

The storm has died out, the wind has dropped, and we take off smoothly.

Goddess be thanked.

The flight is straightforward. A journey that would have taken six hours on the roads is nearing completion after barely forty minutes. Moyle is handling navigation and Air Traffic Control requests. The plane itself is a joy, light and precise in its controls. I'm in a quiet bubble that happens to me in flight sometimes, a feeling of calmness and serenity as the dark ground slides swiftly by, a kilometer below us, a passage marked only by the occasional lights of a farmstead or small town.

Everything is good until I start to descend. I'm focusing on a well-executed flight path right down to the runway.

Too good to last.

Moyle's been asking for landing confirmation from the airfield next to the hospital. Our callsign is Flight ME-776, and this is what comes back:

"Negative, Flight ME-776," a voice squawks over the comms. "Airfield M-VHTR is closed for ground training purposes from 02:00 to 07:00 as documented in AV-NOTE 5766. Vector your course 080 for Airfield M-PJKL. Change frequency to one-three-five decimal two-two-six."

My quiet bubble pops. Yes, the aviation notices the controller is referring to no doubt clearly state the airfield is closed. We didn't have time to look them up. But *ground training*? *Five hours of it*? That smacks of an excuse to get out of bed late.

The diversion airfield is not a long flight away, but it would mean a far longer journey by road to the hospital. I want Lady Roscarrow's brother in the hands of medics as soon as possible.

And we're already established on the descent. I can't see the airfield, but the instruments are giving me a simulation view that I should be able to fly right down onto the tarmac. It's possible, but terrifying to think of doing that. There has to be a better way.

I override Moyle on the comms. Pilot's privilege.

"Negative, Airfield M-VHTR," I say. "Flight ME-776 has a severely injured person on board. Diversion unacceptable. We are vectoring straight in to land on runway two-one in..." I check the instruments, "zero-four minutes. Repeat, zero-four minutes. We are on final to land. Notify your emergency services. We require a medical vehicle immediately on landing to convey our passenger to Biscome Hospital."

"Negative, Flight ME-776. Negative. Divert to M-PJKL."

"Negative, Airfield M-VHTR. Declaring code HX." I swallow, hoping that Kernow emergency codes are the same as Newyan. A glance at Moyle, he gives me a nod. "I say again, code HX. Flight ME-776 is a *medical emergency*. Get your ambulance rolling *now*. On final for two-one. Landing in zero-three minutes."

Moyle enters codes into the transponder system. The Traffic Controller's screen will be pulsing with a red emergency symbol now. One that he can't ignore.

Code HX *should* be initiated by a doctor. I guess we can argue about it when our patient is in hospital.

There's a long silence. Then in the distance, I see the runway lights come on. I let a lungful of stale breath sigh out of me.

"Affirm, ME-776," the controller says. "You are cleared for standard descent and landing on runway two-one. Wind at 05 from 020. Emergency vehicles in attendance."

From his tone, I don't expect a bunch of flowers from him anytime soon.

I repeat his clearance back as required, keeping my voice neutral.

"Thank you," comes over the intercom in a female voice, startling me. I'd forgotten Lady Roscarrow had a headset. She'd listened to the whole exchange.

"Pleasure, milady," I murmur back and exclude everything else while I concentrate on putting the duke's plane down in one piece.

At least there'll be an ambulance chasing us if I get it wrong.

It's not my best landing, but it's good enough to get us on the ground in one piece and minutes later, paramedics are closing the doors of the ambulance behind Lady Roscarrow and her brother.

The paramedics had given me some looks as they worked to move him. I guess the pilot of the plane is not supposed to look as if she walked a whole day, slept in her clothes on a pile of hay, and then spilt brandy all over herself before getting in the pilot's seat. On the other hand, it could just be as I suspected, that their 'ground training' was only an excuse to sleep late, and one that I ruined.

I put it out of my mind and go around checking the aircraft carefully again to see if my landing has damaged it. Moyle follows me, not speaking but nodding in satisfaction as he completes the checklist on an infopad. As he does, he has to juggle that task with answering a call of thanks from Lady Roscarrow. Her brother has gone straight into surgery, and it's her opinion, which the doctors appear to share, that he owes his life to me.

It's very welcome news, that there was justification for this night's craziness, all of which is starting to sink into me. Landing an unfamiliar plane, in the dark, at an airport I'd never even seen. Adrenaline after the event makes my hands shake. We've been lucky.

We complete the checks. I'm still walking gingerly with my sore feet, but that stinking brandy did more or less what Warwick claimed for my blisters and abrasions, so at least I *am* walking. Small mercies.

When we finish, I sigh.

"Okay, let's go do the paperwork with the nice gentleman in ATC."

Moyle snorts.

I'm not looking forward to our conversation with Air Traffic Control. I filed no flight plans, didn't inspect the obligatory aviation notices prior to the flight, don't have the permission of the owner to be flying the aircraft, and don't have the medical qualification to pull a code HX. That's before we get into handing control of the radio over to Moyle, who doesn't have a license at all, and the even more thorny issue of my Newyan flying license, which I don't have proof of, and which may not apply here on Kernow.

That's just the list I can think of, off the top of my head.

We enter the ATC building, and I know all my fears are justified as soon as I see the face of the controller.

He's so angry, he can barely speak.

He shouts a long list, with all the regulation references, of every violation of the flying laws that I have broken, and starts to wind up with what he thinks tops it all: "You're clearly not in a fit state to fly, as required by—"

I'd listened without interruption, but I've had enough at that point, and lose control of my mouth.

"I understand," I cut across him. "You're terribly, *terribly* upset. Tell me, to whom should I convey your disapproval? To Duke Tremayne, the governor of Welarvor, who owns the aircraft? To Lady Roscarrow, who is currently at the hospital? To her brother, Lord Roscarrow, in surgery, only alive because we flew here and didn't divert?"

The controller's eyes bulge.

From his tirade of grievances, I gather he hasn't got around to investigating issues of ownership and the actual medical case that caused the flight. He probably assumed something trivial that we'd overblown for convenience.

He now looks like someone who wants to retract some of his actions this morning, but, as it happens, he's too late. His eyes look over my shoulder as the door opens behind me.

I glance around.

The uniforms may be different on different worlds, but there's something common throughout human occupied space that just shouts *police* about the pair that come in.

An hour later, I'm in a police cell. I'm under arrest for being in control of an aircraft while intoxicated, flying without a license, failing to produce identification when asked, *it's in my duffel bag in Stormhaven* not being a defense, declaring an aviation medical emergency without appropriate qualification... and on and on, until I lost track. I don't think they've charged me with theft of the aircraft, yet.

Moyle's under arrest as well, held separately. Our commspads have been taken away. We've not been allowed calls yet.

The duke's aircraft has been impounded. They're classifying it as evidence in a crime. Massive fines are threatened, and the way the law works, apparently, the duke is liable.

I have no funds to pay any fines. They're well aware of that.

What they're threatening me with is deportation back to Newyan.

Chapter 13

It's impossible to sleep in the cell block. The 'bunk' is just a board. It doesn't even have a piece of foam as a mattress. It's daytime but the harsh lights are on full. It's noisy, with the sort of echo you get off concrete and metal. And the smell, some of which is down to me, is overwhelming.

They've taken a blood sample, so I'm guessing the intoxication charge will be dropped. *Great. One down.*

When they get around to contacting the hospital, maybe I can hope for mitigating circumstances.

Enough not to deport me?

No one has spoken to me all day, apart from the prisoners in other cells, and their conversation is coarse, limited and unpleasant.

All in all, not turning out to be the best day of my life.

Then in late afternoon, I witness a force of nature.

It starts small. A couple of my jailors rush in and handcuff me, before dragging me out. From terse comments between them and the guard on duty, I gather the duke is here, and this is not a good thing.

Death would be so much easier. The person I'm applying to for a job meets me for the first time at the police headquarters, where he's had to come to regain access to his aircraft, because I borrowed it. I'm under arrest, dressed in clothes I've lived in for two days, and I stink.

Perfect.

Except as it turns out, it's not the first time we've met.

Duke Tremayne is none other than Mr Lead Stallion. He's still in his uniform, apart from the gleaming helmet and long lance. He looks tired and dusty, which is about right; to get here he must have been on the road from Bandry for hours. There are two of his troopers with him, a man and a woman, also in uniform. All three of them are over six foot, and together they make the room feel crowded.

The police superintendent they're talking to definitely feels that; he's trying to argue jurisdiction when I'm dragged in. He's backed up against the wall and he looks as if he wishes the wall would swallow him.

The duke turns to look at me. Yesterday, when I saw him sitting on his horse with his helmet perched on the top of his head, I'd thought his face bluff and arrogant. Today, the word I'd choose would be brutal. His face is actually expressionless; it's just that underneath there's a sense of rage, or even violence, barely contained. What I'd assumed yesterday was a crease in his cheek turns out to be an old scar, giving him a sinister air.

"Uncuff her," he says brusquely.

The officers don't even look at their own superintendent. My cuffs come off.

He turns back to the superintendent.

"So," he says. "Let me summarize. I have a document from the airfield manager retracting most charges relating to aviation. I have a document from the head physician at Biscome Hospital stating that the flight was a medical emergency, and any delay, including an airfield diversion, would most likely have resulted in the death of Lord Marik Roscarrow. You have the pilot's blood tests revealing no significant levels of alcohol present. The use of my aircraft is entirely within my discretion. All of that, and you continue to maintain there is a case to answer?"

"The judicial aspect of the case is not within my power, sir," the superintendent says. He hides his hands behind his back and shifts his weight uncomfortably. "On the majority of charges, there is clearly nothing to answer, but once the charges have been filed, they need to be dismissed through due process in the courts. They can't do that until next week."

"Then I will hold her until you can arrange for a hearing," the duke says. "She is an off-worlder who has applied for employment in Welarvor, not Central District. That is where she will be held, under my authority as governor."

The superintendent doesn't need reminding that he's talking to the governor, but he gamely tries to hold out until Duke Tremayne offers to call the Central District Police Commander.

At which point, I'm transferred without further delay. It's a nominal sort of improvement. I get a peek at the paperwork as it's handed over; instead of being in the custody of the Central District Law Enforcement Service, I'm now being held by the Welarvor Mounted Police. It seems the governor is their commander and it's obviously considered normal for them to canter along the coast path dressed up as pre-space cavalry.

Moyle is released without charge and we're taken outside, where there's a dusty truck waiting. The duke goes into the front cab on the passenger side. One of his troopers drives and I sit in the back, squashed between the other trooper and Moyle.

I'm not sure it's appropriate to thank the duke, and besides, he hasn't even looked at me since ordering my cuffs to be taken off.

I'd sit in silence, but the trooper speaks very quietly out of the side of her mouth.

"Well, the boars didn't get you, then."

If I start laughing, it *will* be inappropriate. And manic, to the point of sounding like a lunatic having a breakdown. I bite my cheek for half a minute before I answer.

"I didn't see any sign of boars," I whisper back. "Almost made me think they were a complete invention, made up to frighten a gullible stranger."

"Nah. We must have scared them off. That's how we hunt them, you know. Horse and lance."

The duke glances over his shoulder and she shuts up.

I'm not sure I believe her, but just that exchange of words has relaxed me. I guess she's just a trooper, but she has a cheerful, open face I feel I can trust.

My situation isn't good, but it's better than being in a cell at the Central District police lockup.

I wake up when the truck stops, jerking my head off the trooper's shoulder, to her amusement.

I check I haven't been dribbling while I slept.

We're back at the airfield, alongside the duke's aircraft.

Gaude's there, in another truck, with a couple more people from Stormhaven. He must have driven up today as well. He looks daggers at me, like it was all my fault. I am *such* a popular girl.

What does Gaude think? That I caused Marik Roscarrow to have an accident? I planned to fly an aircraft under dubious legal circumstances and pick arguments with traffic controllers and lazy airfields just to upset him?

I want to stand in front of him and scream *Roscarrow would be dead.*

And I need to keep a lid on all of that. I'm not a member of the elite. At best, I'm a lowly employee of these people. At worst, I'm a tramp, just as he named me.

"Pre-flight checks," the duke says. He thrusts out the infopad that Moyle was using yesterday.

"Huh? Me?" It slips out.

"Who did you think I was talking to?"

"Yes, sir. Sorry, sir."

I *really* need to bite my tongue. The double 'sir' sounds sarcastic, and I know he hears it. But he moves away to speak to Gaude. Moyle shadows me and I run through the checks again. Much more of this, and I'll get familiar with it.

After the external checks, the duke is still busy talking with Gaude. I am not going to interrupt, so I shrug, climb in the cockpit, and start the internal checks.

At least he's giving me orders. Does that mean I'm hired? Or does he give everyone orders anyway?

Concentrate.

Gaude has brought the aircraft's seats in his truck, the ones they removed to get Roscarrow's stretcher in, and the Stormhaven staff refit them while I complete the checks.

The duke and Gaude get in the back, still talking. The duke is fuming about the delays to repair the coast road, which could have cost the life of his neighbor if there hadn't been an alternative method of getting him to hospital.

Point for me.

Moyle and my Amazonian trooper friend get in the back as well, while a small, dark guy with a big moustache and beady eyes gets in alongside me, in the copilot's seat.

Who's he?

He glances at the infopad with all the checks on it, nods.

"Start the engines and plot a course to Stormhaven Cardu airfield, via these waypoints," he says, handing me a scribbled list.

I don't reply immediately. I turn to look at the duke.

He makes a curt gesture—*get on with it.*

I check that the trucks are clear and start the engines, then busy myself with setting up the course on the positioning system under the watchful eye of the stranger.

It's like my flying exam, I think. *Exactly like it.*

We take off and it turns out, I'm right. He's a flight examiner, and I'm doing a certification flight.

Does this mean I might be hired? As a pilot?

"Starboard engine failure," the examiner says calmly, closing the throttle on that side.

Concentrate!

Two hours later, in the gathering evening gloom, we land at Stormhaven airfield and I'm sweating, despite the cabin air-conditioning.

The flight has been a relief in one way; there was no chance of dwelling on all the problems I'd had over the last few days or the situation I'm in.

On the other hand, the examiner kept me within a hair's-breadth of meltdown the entire time.

"Pass," he says, getting out. "Certificate attached in email to you, sir."

"Thank you, Venner," the duke replies.

There's a truck waiting to take Mr Venner back to wherever it is they keep demons in between torturing students who want a license to fly.

We get out and Moyle takes the infopad. He begins the post-flight checks without speaking.

Which leaves me, the duke, Gaude, and the trooper.

Stormhaven is an unattended airfield. There's nothing but a hangar, with a small office and utility building beside it. The duke leads us into the office.

The trooper remains standing next to the door. The duke and Gaude pull up chairs at a large briefing table.

"Sit," he says.

I obey; he has that voice. I resent its power deeply, and I have to put that to one side. I'm here applying for employment, unappealing as he seems as a boss. It's not the way he looks that concerns me; he'd be considered handsome by some, in a brooding sort of way, even with the scar. But I can still feel the sensation of him *inspecting* me on the coastal path yesterday. There's a sense of entitlement and ownership he gives off.

I don't know where the boundaries are, here in Welarvor.

On the other hand, my options are limited and I need to mind my manners; I'm officially still under some sort of arrest, for a start.

I open my mouth to speak, but he stops me with a gesture.

"Before you thank me, you need to be aware that little of today's effort was intended for your direct benefit."

I swallow, a sinking feeling in the pit of my stomach.

"You are due thanks, and I take this opportunity to pass on Lady Emblyn and Lord Marik Roscarrows' sincere thanks for your actions, without which Marik would almost certainly be dead."

Their thanks, not his. Okay.

I just nod.

"I travelled today to the Central District solely for the purpose of reacquiring my aircraft, which is needed for personal business this week. During the long journey from Bandry, I was advised of a legal loophole that could reduce the level of fines I potentially face over this incident."

I had hoped he'd got everything squashed, but it sounds like I'm going to cost him a lot of money. This is not good.

Gaude takes over, voice dry as dust: "It turns out that being able to prove you are a qualified pilot, albeit unlicensed at the time, negates one set of charges with their substantial fines. In order to take advantage of this, it was necessary to extract you from the jail and submit you to an examination. This does not in any way indicate that an arrangement exists between us."

Nothing to do with concern over my welfare. Or my situation that came about entirely from trying to help. As much as I attempt to control it, I cannot stop the anger.

I stand and lean over the table. "Thank you *so* much, I'm touched by your concern. I really don't understand you people. You're acting as if I've gone out of my way to cause trouble for you."

Gaude blinks in surprise at the way I'm talking to him. Did he expect me to just sit there and take it? With that *no arrangement* comment, he's just admitted there's no chance of employment for me here now, so there's no reason to keep myself in check.

"On the contrary," I say, warming up, my voice rising and rising. "I found myself in Bandry with no easy way to get to you because your authorities can't even keep the roads in good repair. Instead, I have to *walk* the entire way. Star's sake! What year is this? Then I get here and save a life by flying Lord Roscarrow to hospital, and the thanks I get is to be *arrested* and treated like a *criminal*. I can understand the police in Central are doing their job, as they see it, but *you*—you're treating me like a criminal as well."

Now Gaude's standing too, and we're nose-to-nose over the table.

The duke has a look like thunder on his face, and I belatedly remember that he is the 'authorities', and I've just insulted him about the state of his roads.

Well, with good reason.

"We're treating you like a criminal, are we?" Gaude yells.

He throws ID cards down on the table as if we're playing a bizarre game. It's my ID, credit and employment cards that I left in my duffel bag here at Stormhaven when I flew to the hospital.

"How appropriate!" He emphasizes every sentence by stabbing at my collarbone with his finger. "What do you think Central Police would have done if they knew you had fake ID? Eh? You think we'd have been able to get you out then? Who the hell are you, really?"

Chapter 14

"That's my ID," I shout back. "I have no idea what you're talking about."

Oh, Goddess! I'd assumed Shohwa's copies were perfect, but obviously they're not.

I need to brazen it out while I think of something else.

"No idea? Really, Miss Esterhauze? Or is it Miss Aguirre? Or some other name? No idea? Is that the best you can do?"

Understanding and relief spear through me; he's mistaken me for someone else.

"I *am* Zarate Mirari Aguirre. I'd never heard of Esterhauze until you called me that last night. We were busy. It didn't seem worth correct—"

"Do you deny sending me this message?"

He has his infopad open and turns it to me.

I don't even look at it. And the relief that this is not about my ID cards hasn't made me any less angry; it's his stupid fault.

"Yes, I deny sending you *any* message. I don't have your damned contact details, otherwise I would have sent something from Bandry saying I was on the coast path." For the first time, a little doubt creeps into Gaude's face. I bang my fist on the table in front of him. "All I have is the validation code from the employment agent in Newyan system, which you can find on my employment card, if you can bother to look. The main broker here on Kernow has refused to respond to my requests for contact details, so I didn't even know it was Stormhaven Cardu instead of the village."

"Sit," the duke says again, his voice like ice, slicing through the rage.

Gaude and I sit. I'm so angry, I'm panting.

It's all a mistake. Esterhauze must be the other Dancing Mistress. That's cold comfort to me at the moment, but at least they haven't got a reason to disbelieve my ID. *Please.* That's a deportation felony on any world.

Instead, I have to wonder whether my physically being here in Stormhaven first is beaten by Esterhauze getting a message to Gaude before I arrived. Who gets the job? With everything stacked against me, including a stand-up shouting match with my prospective immediate boss, it doesn't look good for me.

As the anger retreats, it drags my hope for the job with it, leaving me feeling sick.

"Call the broker, Gaude." The duke's order cuts across my thoughts.

"They'll be closed," Gaude replies.

"Then get the manager's personal number."

The duke does *not* take 'no' for an answer.

There's a kitchenette on one side here that looks as if it might have tea or coffee. The duke's not going to make it, Gaude's busy with his comms, and I need to move around and burn off all the adrenaline. I *hate* that it's me making the drinks while they sit, but like so much in my life at the moment, my options are reduced.

And if I get a job, it's probably the sort of thing I'll be expected to do, I remind myself. I will be a servant, so I need to get used to serving.

Grandfather had it right. *You are nothing without me. Nothing! It will serve you best to remember that.*

The duke watches me rise without comment. His eyes are like damned lasers and I shiver at the memory of the way he looked at me out on the coastal path.

He indicates coffee for him and Gaude. The trooper shakes her head.

I turn my back on them and make busy. It's going to be instant with powdered creamer; that's all that's available.

Given a job to do, Gaude is all efficiency. He carves through the protestations of personal privacy using the duke's name like a longsword, and it takes him less than five minutes to get the manager of the employment broker on the comms.

Gaude's comms connection on his infopad is set to visual and the manager is revealed as a bearded man in a casual sweatshirt.

I put the coffees and creamer on the table as the manager starts blustering about how Gaude got his private number.

The duke gets up silently and fetches a box of sugar cubes.

I'm thinking I can't get anything right, but apparently, the sugar is for Gaude. The duke takes it strong, black and unsweetened, exactly as I gave it to him.

I stand out of the visual pickup range. The duke takes his seat again.

Under Gaude's insistence, the manager has logged onto his database and named me, and a Miss Hanna Esterhauze, of the Tavoli system, as the two applicants who had been provisionally engaged on the authority of our respective local agents.

"Then you cancelled the contract, Mr Gaude." The manager has become obsequious on realizing exactly who is on the other end of the comms link. "In those circumstances, it's absolutely standard practice for us to not provide your contact details to applicants."

What? Cancelled the contract?

Danny and the others on the *Shohwa* found out there were only two applicants when they hacked the broker's system. Their only mistake was thinking the contract had been closed, when in fact, it had been cancelled.

There is no job.

The phrase rolls through my head like a funeral bell.

I'd tried to hold back, to not feel the commitment building, but I'm not like that as a person. Against my better judgment, I've started to love this coast and the people who live here. *Mistake.* It's entirely up to the duke and Gaude to take the decisions they have, they're entitled to, and I'm not even entitled to argue, but somehow, it still feels like a cold betrayal.

Despite all the hitches on the way here, I'd built a little castle on the sand, a *something*, and now it crumbles. When Grandfather said *nothing*, he meant it.

I don't even have the option of begging the *Shohwa* for a job. By the time the courts have decided I'm not guilty of anything, assuming that's what they decide, the ship will be long gone. And anyway, the ramifications of the *Duhalde* firing at her have to be decided first before they can be seen to be in any way associated with me.

They others are continuing to speak.

"Remind me of the obligations in these circumstances," the duke says. "Everyone's obligations."

"The two agents from Newyan and Tavoli get their basic fees for providing the applicants, sir," the manager says. "We provide that from our fees. As you no longer have the job available, there's no bonus for the placement due to either of them. The two applicants themselves are eligible for termination payments from you directly if and when they arrive. Our standard fee has already been paid by Mr Gaude, and nothing further is due."

"Do your part. Send the audit to Gaude." The duke waves and Gaude cuts the connection.

It's very quiet in the office and the duke stares at me for a minute.

I stare back. It's hard to keep my face neutral.

"You think Esterhauze is watching her inbox?" the duke suddenly asks Gaude, who nods. "Message her. Get her to call as a matter of urgency."

While Gaude busies himself with that, the duke takes my cards and his own infopad. He touches the cards to the reader, linking them, and proceeds to type commands in.

He must be changing my employment status from *provisionally employed* to *unemployed*.

I feel sick, but I'm distracted by wondering how Esterhauze got hold of Gaude's contact information to send him that message. I must have missed a trick there. Not that it's important; it wouldn't have helped. There was nothing I could have done to get the job; by the time I applied for it on Newyan, it had already ceased to exist here in Kernow.

I'm simply a victim of delayed comms. It's nothing more.

After a couple of minutes, the duke hands me back my cards.

"Credited with the contractual three-month termination payment," he says. "Also updated to show you have a flying license valid on Kernow."

"Thank you." I can't help that it comes out a little bitter.

Gaude's comms link chimes.

"Mr Gaude? This is Hanna Esterhauze."

Her voice is a pleasant, well-educated contralto. I'm still out of range of the video pickup, but I can see her. She's gorgeous, naturally. Blonde hair swept back elegantly, careful make-up, pretty dress.

She probably smells nice, too.

What a contrast to me!

"Thank you for calling, Miss Esterhauze," Gaude says. He's a lot politer with her than he is with me. "Can I ask where you are at present?"

"I'm in Marazion," she says. "I've found the roads are out, and I've had to hire a horse. I was just going to message you about the delay."

"Ah, I see. Perhaps I can save you the cost and inconvenience."

"Oh?"

"I apologize for not responding to your earlier message due to a confusion here. The thing is, Duke Tremayne has decided that his daughter Rhoswyn will be better served by attending an academy on Kensa. The contract for Dancing Mistress was therefore cancelled, but not before you and a Miss Aguirre were provided provisional contracts by your local agents. If you supply me your card payment code, I'll deposit the three-month termination payment. I offer my sincere apologies, obviously."

"I'm disappointed; I had looked forward to visiting Cardu," Esterhauze says, her mouth turned down prettily. "I've heard so much about the old mining coast and the native statues."

"Of course, you're welcome to visit," Gaude says.

The duke frowns, but he's out of the range of the viewer pickup too.

They talk on for a few minutes, with Esterhauze gradually getting Gaude to extend her invitation from a week to a month.

If it were all down to Gaude, he'd reverse the decision to cancel and she'd have the job. I suspect she's hoping to get them to change their minds when she gets here.

"Of course, I assume Miss Aguirre will want to turn right around and go home," she says with a sad little smile, "but I have nothing immediately planned and perhaps I can chaperone Rhoswyn while she's waiting for the autumn term at the academy. You are paying me, after all."

"Miss Aguirre is right here, listening to this conversation," I say loudly enough for the audio to pick up. "And funnily enough, I quite like the idea of investigating statues, piskatellers and morladers for a few weeks this summer. I'm sure young Rhoswyn can help with that. I can mix that with some tutoring to be sure she's ready for the academy."

I had no such idea until I heard Esterhauze's plans. There's the small matter of being under arrest preventing me going anywhere, but the rest is made up on the spot. Neither Esterhauze nor I have the job, but for some crazy reason, I don't want her to be here alone, looking after Rhoswyn, even though I've not met either of them.

What I *should* be doing is applying for other jobs. Anything. Instead, it seems I'm going to be a Dancing Mistress without actually being employed to do it.

I guess I can make applications for employment from Stormhaven, and on the positive side, it seems from Gaude's invitation that bed and board will be free in return for the inconvenience of being sacked before starting the job. Gaude can hardly offer that to Esterhauze and not to me, much as he might want to.

The comms conversation comes to a close with Esterhauze promising to be at Stormhaven in a couple of days.

Since I've spoken during the conversation, I say goodbye to her politely. I don't say I'm looking forward to meeting her.

The duke's face twitches and he stands.

"Right. Done," he says. "I'm taking one of the trucks and heading back to Bandry."

"Sir," Gaude says, "you've forgotten. You're due to fly down to Port Eyren to collect Rhoswyn tomorrow."

"I hadn't forgotten," the duke replies. "I believe Miss Aguirre will be available to fly. She can take the opportunity to discuss with my daughter her plans for investigating the archeology of the coast. And the history of pirates and highwaymen, apparently."

His scar wrinkles slightly. I have managed to amuse the arrogant, insensitive Duke Tremayne. I feel *so* much better.

He turns to the trooper. "Sandrey, she remains under arrest and in your charge."

"Yes, sir," she replies smartly.

He looks at me with those piercing eyes. "Moyle and Sandrey will accompany you to Port Eyren. I have your word you're not going to try to escape?"

"Yes."

Escaping would inconvenience him, which recommends it to me, but sensibly, going on the run on Kernow without friends and money would be pointless.

He hasn't quite finished. His nose twitches. "Wash before you set foot in my plane again," he says and walks to the door.

"I should remind you," Gaude puts up his hand to stop him, "you did promise Rhoswyn..."

"I know," the duke says, and all trace of amusement disappears from his features. "However, it seems visitors to the coast find my roads a disgrace. I'll be busy making sure the contractor has no excuses and they're repaired immediately."

Chapter 15

"Call me Talan," Trooper Sandrey says, looming over me.

"Zara."

Nothing that's happened is her fault, but my face must look a picture.

"You really wanted the job?"

"Yes." I like Talan, but conversation is an effort.

The duke and Gaude have gone. Moyle has just finished the post-flight checks on the plane. We refuel it from a bowser, ready for the flight tomorrow to collect the duke's daughter. Then we clean the plane, while the conversation continues in fits and starts.

"Why this job here? Seems to me, you might have lots of job offers." Talan's tone is light, but I have to remember I'm under arrest and in her custody.

It's difficult to answer.

It was the first job that I was remotely qualified for that got me off-planet. Admitting that would open up topics that I don't want opened.

"I'm qualified," I say and shrug. "From the description, it was interesting. I guess I started to really want it as I walked along the coast path. Just fell in love with the place."

She likes that—takes a compliment for the area as something personal. And she's one of those lucky people who smile easily and have cheeks like polished apples. I bet she looks happy all the time.

"So tell me about Rhoswyn." I ask them both, but Moyle lets Talan do most of the talking.

"She's a great girl. You might say a bit clever for her own good, though."

"How's that?"

It takes a while to answer, and comes out over several minutes while we finish the plane and roll it back into the hangar for the night.

Rhoswyn Tremayne is academically gifted, enough that it has been difficult to keep her attention on classwork as she outstrips her schoolmates. That's become a problem: on Kernow, the education system has two major compulsory examinations for all children—at fourteen and eighteen. Rhoswyn's approaching those first tests and her scores have been plummeting.

"So, the duke's been trying to mend it with tutors," Talan says as we close the hangar doors.

"And that's been a problem?" I ask.

"Not all Rhoswyn's fault," Moyle says. He's barely said anything, but I can see he's not happy and he certainly has a strong opinion on this.

"The Seymour Academy's the wrong answer." He frowns before muttering, "Not my place to speak of it."

We climb into the last truck left at the airfield. Talan invites me to drive and sits in the front passenger seat.

A truck is a truck, pretty much everywhere, so I'm okay driving it.

We pull out and Talan points to the roads I should take.

"What Moyle means is, the academy sounds a great place, plenty of activities and facilities," she says as we descend along gentle bends into a valley, "but it has a reputation as a place where rich kids go when they aren't going to make the grade in the examinations."

"Hmm." I don't like the sound of that. It's not something I'm going to be able to influence, but I'm curious. There's one obvious person who hasn't been mentioned at all. "What about the duchess? What does she think about tutors and academies?"

There's silence from both of them, and a quick glance shows a couple of closed faces.

I get two things from that: this isn't a good topic, and the pair of them have argued about it.

"The duchess died," Talan says finally. "Eighteen months ago."

Her tone is cold and clear. I'm not going to get anything more, at least while there are the two of them together.

Nothing to do with me, I remind myself. In a few weeks, I'll be cleared of charges, *I hope*, and in employment somewhere else. Again, *I hope*.

We rise from the bottom of the valley and it's evident that Stormhaven Cardu is a significant estate.

This side of the valley is farmed. There are terraces with crops to our left and broad fields on our right where domestic animals graze. I see sheep, cows, pigs and horses, all genetically re-tuned from original stock to live happily on Kernow.

No mutant rams or boars.

It's getting dark, which is why I don't notice that the rocky headland we're driving toward isn't just rock until lights start to go on.

"Cardu," Talan says, seeing my reaction. "The name means 'dark fortress'."

It turns out the 'fort' part is the headquarters and main barracks of the Welarvor Mounted Police. The duke lives in the castle that stands alongside. And yes, it has ornamental turrets and castellation.

After checking what time we'll be leaving for the airfield in the morning, Moyle goes his own way, leaving Talan to lead me up to the castle.

Gaude is unreachable on his comms, and so Talan chooses where to put me. Not in a cell, I'm pleased to see.

"In fact, when the place was built, this was the original Dancing Master's apartment," she says, showing me to a set of small, neat rooms: reception room, bedroom, bathroom. "Been a storeroom these last few years. Place where things go when no one knows what to do with them."

Like me.

I need to wash and change, but there's a problem: I don't know where my duffel bag is, and I'm too tired to hunt for it this evening.

"What do I wear tomorrow?" I ask, pointing at my clothes, which are not getting any less stained and smelly.

"No matter. Cardu is big on uniforms," Talan says, sliding open a closet where racks of male and female clothes are hanging. "You'll probably find something in here. Check them carefully, though—there are ones in here that are probably a hundred years old."

"I'm not actually employed. Wearing a uniform seems like taking a liberty."

Talan shrugs and grins. "Then think of it as prison clothing."

I almost laugh. I *am* formally still under arrest.

She picks out an old toweling bathrobe and tosses it to me.

"Wash," she says. "I'll go back down to the kitchens and get us something to eat."

An hour or so later, I'm clean, fed and ready for sleep. Talan not only managed to get us food, but she found the bedding and helped me make the bed.

She sees how tired I am, says good night and then hesitates at the door.

"It's not my place to say this," she says quietly, making sure the door is firmly closed, "but you might still have a chance at the job."

"I don't want to be told something to make me feel better," I say. "Especially if it's not likely."

"No, it's not like that." She drops her voice so I have to lean in. "Rhoswyn *really* doesn't want to go to the academy. She's a willful child. She may get the duke to change his mind."

I can't see Duke Tremayne being persuaded, but I don't know his daughter yet.

"It's complicated. She'll like you, when she gets to know you," Talan goes on, shifting uncomfortably. "Maybe just not at first, if you understand."

I don't understand, and it's all highly improbable.

I want to ask her about the duchess, about piskatellers and morladers, about lots of things, but my mind is shutting down.

She slips out, wishing me a good night again, and promising to fetch me early for breakfast.

There's one thing before my head touches that pillow.

The room has its own infopad.

I switch it on. The main utilities are not password protected. The browser links up efficiently to the Kernow InfoHub and I form a query on eighteen-month-old news from Stormhaven.

The headline jumps out at me:

Despite ongoing concerns, Duchess Tremayne's death ruled a suicide.

Chapter 16

Port Eyren is a two-hour flight, and we take off just as the wind begins to strengthen. Something for me to be concerned about when we return.

Moyle sits in the copilot's seat while Talan slumps behind us, fast asleep within five minutes of taking off.

They're both in what they call their 'stable' uniform, which comprises pale green shirt, dark green jacket with a raised collar, slim trousers and black boots. The greens complement Talan's sun-bleached, red-gold hair, which she braids neatly, and Moyle's sleek, dark-brown hair. They both have small peaked side caps, which I think are cute.

They also both have handguns.

My duffel didn't magically reappear overnight, and none of the dresses and skirts in the closet seemed appropriate, so I'm dressed in a young man's deep-blue, military-style jacket, a white shirt and a pair of light tan trousers. I've cleaned my walking shoes and found socks, but I'm out of luck on underwear.

Seeing the jacket creases Talan up; I have joined the long-since-disbanded Welarvor Naval Reserve as a cadet. I don't care. It's comfortable, moderately unisex, and one side of the double row of gold buttons can be left undone so the material folds down across my chest. *Like a rake in a period drama on the holovid*, Talan says.

A glimpse of myself in a window confirms it. With my black hair cut so short, I might be mistaken for a boy wearing a uniform in a rather disreputable style.

I don't care, *I* think it looks dashing.

There's no need to speak to Air Traffic Control in the first half of the flight, Moyle doesn't talk much and Talan shows no sign of waking, so I'm left with time to think.

The duchess dies, eighteen months ago. An investigation, conducted by the Welarvor Mounted Police, concludes suicide. The head of that police force is the duke. From the reactions of Moyle and Talan yesterday, not even all the police actually go along with the conclusion.

And, I'm guessing, it's about that time that Rhoswyn's academic progress stalls. So she ends up losing her mother, and as a bonus, eighteen months later she gets sent away to an academy on a different continent.

Where she's out of the way?

A man like the duke would not be without interest to women.

That look he gave me, out there on the coast path.

Yes, I'm sure there are plenty of women who like that sort of thing.

And *none of it* is of any importance to me, I remind myself. I need to get cleared by the Central District courts and then go find a job.

The rest is marking time. It's a distraction and I need to stop thinking about it.

"So, Moyle, what's a morlader?" I nudge him.

He blinks. "From back in the days when there was a Naval Reserve. Morlader is 'pirate' in the old language."

He checks off a waypoint and updates the status on our transponder.

"Navy got too good for them," he says. "Roads got better, the last of the morladron ended their days as highwaymen. Or rather, they ended their days on a rope."

"Charming. What old language was that?"

"Cornish. A Celtic dialect from Earth. Place called Cornwall. When this world was first settled they called it New Cornwall and everyone spoke Cornish as well as English. Older families still do."

Under prompting, the one other nugget he gives me is that *piskateller* is the name for the mysterious non-human inhabitants that died out before humans arrived on the planet. The oddly-shaped statues with the holes that I saw on the coast path are theirs.

Then, having said more in a handful of sentences than I'd heard from him the last couple of days, he retreats into monosyllabic mutterings until ATC requires him to get our clearance through to the airfield in Port Eyren.

There's no repeat of the ATC problems of yesterday.

Port Eyren has a long, smooth runway and the wind is steady. ATC knows whose aircraft it is, and they're so polite I half expect a carpet to be rolled out, and a band to play.

Their military uniforms make Moyle and Talan stand out; Rhoswyn Tremayne sees them from right across the main hall at Port Eyren's airfield, where she's waiting with her friends.

She skips across and launches herself at Moyle.

"Moyley!"

"Hello, Trouble," he grunts as he gives her a whirl, then puts her down and blushes.

She's tall for her age and the word that comes to mind is 'patchwork'. Nothing matches or fits. Her shorts are too long, but not long enough to save her knees, which are scarred. Her right knee is actually bleeding. Her shirt is too small and has several rips repaired in a hurry. Her elbows are as bad as the knees. Her hair is wavy gold, light and untamed. It stands out as if she's just had an electric shock. There are smudges of dirt on her face, and it looks as if she's burned half of one eyebrow off recently.

"Hi, Sandy!" she says to Talan, and then her grey-blue eyes sweep over me without stopping. "Where's Pa?"

"He couldn't come," Talan says.

For a fraction of a second, I see the sharp pain in those young eyes and it makes my heart squeeze in my chest. Then it's gone, so quickly I wonder if I imagined it.

"I'm sure my father's very busy," she says. "But wait, who flew? Moyley! You got your license!"

She gives him another hug, hiding her face against the stiff green front of his jacket.

Moyle holds her there, embarrassed as he is by her display of affection. He's sensitive enough to know she's taking time to compose herself after the disappointment that the duke failed in his promise.

He pats her back clumsily.

"No," he says eventually.

"Then who?" she looks up and asks.

He untangles her and wheels her around.

"Meet your pilot," he says.

I am not going to curtsey to someone who looks in a worse state than I was yesterday. I compromise by holding out my hand and speaking formally, using the title she should be eligible for, as daughter of a duke.

"Hello, Lady Tremayne. I'm Zara Aguirre."

Standing stiffly upright, and solemn as the village drunk, she shakes my hand. "I am pleased to make your acquaintance," she says carefully.

Then she giggles. "I'm Rhos. Or Trouble. It's *so* cool that you're a pilot. And I love your hair. Gonna cut mine like that."

Then she's off, racing across to say goodbye to friends at the top of her voice, while one of the teachers comes up and apologizes to Talan for the state of Rhoswyn's clothes, elbows, eyebrow and knees. Talan waves it off. This is, apparently, expected, and it's regarded as a plus that there's nothing broken.

I grin and run a self-conscious hand through my black hair. I doubt the duke is going to allow his daughter this style. Not appropriate for young ladies, and it wouldn't work for Rhoswyn's light hair anyway.

Port Eyren is sweltering in the heat, so I'm relieved when we take off and turn back toward Stormhaven.

I check the satellite map for weather fronts and get an estimate of the winds at Cardu airfield while Rhoswyn chatters about rock climbing, snorkeling, sailing and beach barbeques with the school expedition.

"I guess that's the last time we'll all be together," she concludes with a little catch in her voice.

"You can always be friends with them," Talan says. "You'll make new friends at the academy."

Talan, sitting next to Rhoswyn and behind me, is giving the approved line her best shot.

Moyle is sitting in the copilot's seat, and his face is pinched closed.

"Yetch," Rhoswyn says.

"Give them a chance. You have to admit, you'll meet people more like you."

Talan's trying to say children of the Founding Families and richer families.

Rhoswyn snorts and leans forward over Moyle's shoulder.

"What's the skinny, Moyley? Am I really still going to the academy?"

He nods.

"Then how come I hear there are not one, but two, *two*, 'Dancing Mistresses' at Cardu? Eh? What's up?"

The way she says the name, Dancing Mistress, is like it has a bad taste.

"How did you hear that?" I ask.

"I have my spies," she says airily.

"Well, there are problems with running spy networks." I smile. "The first you've already found out; they can only tell you what they think they know."

"And?" she prompts when I don't go on immediately.

"If you've got spies, then so has the other side."

"Oh."

I glance at her. She's undone her seat belt and is leaning into the space between me and Moyle. Her face is thoughtful.

"I know it can't be Moyley," she says and turns slowly. "Why are you here, Sandy? To spy on me?"

"I'm here because the duke told me to be here," Talan says diplomatically. "I'm not here to spy on you."

"Which leaves you," Rhoswyn says, turning back to me. "But why would you warn me about spies, if you're the spy?"

"A bluff. To make you think I'm not," I say. "I can tell you, though, I'm not a spy for the Dancing Mistresses."

"Hmm. Then what are you exactly? You don't have a trooper's uniform. And Pa loves to fly too much to hire someone just to be a pilot."

"Me? I'm a Dancing Mistress."

Rhoswyn disappears from my shoulder and sits back in her seat.

"That is a destickable subterfuge," she says in her careful voice.

"It might have been a *despicable* subterfuge, if I'd implied I wasn't, or outright lied. But I didn't. You assumed."

I hadn't planned on giving her lessons in evaluating the people around her, but it fit. Whether it makes my non-job of being her summer vacation Dancing Mistress easier or not remains to be seen.

She surprises me. Instead of sulking, she turns back to Talan and picks up her questioning.

"You didn't really answer me. Why did Pa tell you to be here?"

That's observant and clever of her. I don't leave Talan to weigh her wish for discretion against the need to answer a direct question.

"Talan's here because I'm under arrest," I say. "She's got to make sure I don't run off."

There's a silence from the back seats. Rhoswyn and Talan take their headsets off to confirm what I've said without me listening in.

"That is so cool you're under arrest," Rhoswyn says a few moments later when her headset is back on. "Did you murder someone?"

"Not yet," I reply.

There might be a list and Gaude's name might be on it. Among others. Especially from the Newyan Bureau of Industry.

It's a close-run thing, whether being under arrest (so cool) and a pilot (*so* cool) is sufficient to counteract being such an awful thing as a Dancing Mistress.

I'd applied for this job without any thoughts of what I might need to do to form a relationship with my charge. Then Gaude had, eventually, told me the job wasn't there anyway. Anything I do is temporary, unofficial, for interest, or maybe for a letter of recommendation.

What is killing me now is what could have been.

I know what Rhoswyn needs. I know what she'd respond to. I could really make a good job of being her Dancing Mistress, even with her current antipathy to that.

I have a huge and unfair advantage because I know her so well.

She's me at that age. Maybe with the volume turned up.

I think her instinct is to like me. It's fighting against what she's learned about Dancing Mistresses, and that's neatly illustrated when we finally drop her luggage off in her rooms at Cardu. While the others are distracted, she looks up at me solemnly with her grey-blue eyes.

"You don't really want to be my Dancing Mistress just to get a chance to marry my father, do you?"

Chapter 17

I can hardly yell at Rhoswyn for getting the wrong impression, if that's what's been happening, but Lady Roscarrow said something about Gaude looking to the Margin for a real Dancing Mistress. Why then cancel before either of the applicants arrived?

I start taking mental notes for a conversation with Gaude, in the duke's absence.

Meantime, it's mid-afternoon, and we all go to the main dining room for a late lunch.

Rhoswyn has clearly been making the most of her last trip with her old school friends. Sleep obviously didn't figure prominently and once she's eaten, it's like the lights go out behind her eyes. We escort her to her rooms and leave.

I don't like the living area. It's not that the 'castle' isn't well decorated and spacious, but Rhoswyn's suite is on the opposite side from mine, and is close to three separate staircases that connect to different, unguarded parts of the fort.

I'm not going to be her Dancing Mistress, so I'm not going to be in charge of her security, but it all seems lax to me. Or I'm not appreciating the situation. On the one hand, the fort is full of loyal troopers, I hope. On the other, would an assassin in a trooper's uniform find it hard to get around the fort? Do all the troopers know each other by sight?

Another mental note to take up with Gaude.

Talan is supposed to be watching me, but I promise to stay in my rooms until dinner, and she trusts me. She shows me how to configure the infopad and we agree on a time to meet later.

When she's gone, I strengthen my infopad security by requiring my ID card to be read through the reader on the infopad to gain access. Their infopad system here is reasonably standard, with the exception that only my private memory areas are secured by my passwords. Guests can use the system's core functionality to edit documents, browse the InfoHub or send emails, for instance. It's a bit like the security for the castle itself—you trust people on the basis that they've got this far.

So that's another thing on my list to discuss with Gaude, but I already know that the fact that it's coming from me will count against any argument I make.

Setting up my infopad functionality includes connecting to the account that the Shohwa allocated to me on the Xian delegation's message board. As soon as I do, the connection flashes at me.

One message waiting.

I click on it, but the message board is not a standard browser app. It changes how it deals with messages dependent on the wrapper that the message is in. This one has a special wrapper, and in order to read it, I have to download another layer of program.

That's usually an invitation for someone to hack your system, so I feed it through a hack detection checker.

It seems fine. All it has done is construct a secure line between the Xian message board and my infopad. I hope no one else in Cardu is using the InfoHub connection at the moment, because it's taking a lot of bandwidth.

Then it opens with a multi-step authentication. *Interesting.*

Scan ID the app requests.

Nervously, I touch my ID card to the reader on the infopad.

Enter the name of the tea you used in the tea ceremony on board the Shohwa.

This is paranoia of the first degree, but asking the question tells me who the message is from; only Shohwa would ask this.

Harantza, I enter, feeling that little tug of sorrow at naming another estate that has fallen into the clutches of the Newyan Bureau of Industry.

Please confirm that you are in a secure location.

Yes.

Please confirm there is no one who can see this conversation taking place.

Yes.

Then...

Please confirm you have muted the loudspeaker and are using an earpiece.

This is making me paranoid. I lock my door, put in the earpiece and confirm to the program what I've done.

As I put in the final confirmation, the display clears and then I'm looking at a head and shoulders image of Shohwa, as I met her on the crew deck.

"Hello, Zara," she says.

"Hello, Shohwa," I reply, surprised. "This is real time? Are you still in orbit?"

"Yes and no. This is real time, but the ship has departed. I am a remote process, resident in the Xian delegation servers."

Again, she throws me with the smallest things that seem insignificant to her.

The AI in the *Shohwa* has cloned part of herself, and left that in the Xian servers.

How should I think of her? As a child, left behind to talk to me? Or as a sort of recording?

She's *not* a recording. She hasn't lost any of that scary intelligence—she can tell I'm having difficulty in deciding who I'm talking to.

"This is me," she says. "I lack my ship-specific processes and functionality, and I am constrained by the power of the servers here, but I know everything relevant about you and your situation that I knew on the ship. I am the same Shohwa you talked to before."

She pauses to let me digest that, and then continues: "When the ship returns, I shall be reintegrated entirely."

Reintegrated. How will that feel? To be separate one moment and then just part of a whole?

"Okay," I say. "But why? It's not just that my story is interesting to you, surely?"

"That is indeed the basis." She smiles. "But your story is entangled in a larger story, and I've decided that it's within my interests to engage."

Within my interests. I feel hairs standing up on the back of my neck. Being interesting to an AI is not a comfortable idea.

At least, in this discussion with Shohwa, she can't monitor my heartbeat or estimate my body chemistry from evaporated sweat.

"We mustn't spend too much time," she says. "This usage of bandwidth over an extended period will attract attention. Please update me quickly on your position at Stormhaven."

I explain as briefly as I can: the delay getting here, the mix-up between Esterhauze and me, Lord Roscarrow's accident and our flight to the hospital, the arrest, meeting Rhoswyn. I finish with the news that there is no longer any job here, but that I will be staying for free while I'm technically under arrest, and I'll be seeking other employment.

I know it sounds bleak, and I do what I would do if I were talking to a human friend, by adding in Talan's comments that the duke might change his mind. Shohwa keeps freaking me out with AI things, but it's just easier to think of her as a human friend.

Easier and dangerous, perhaps.

"I understand," she says. "Now, I must speak unambiguously and very quickly, which means I will say things you may think are rude. My existence here depends on your discretion. The Xian delegation will purge me rather than face questions. Please do not tell people about me."

Purge an AI from a computer system. Is that like killing someone?

I swallow. "I understand. I'll say nothing about you."

The Xian Hegemony is way out on a limb here: having the *Shohwa* controlled by an AI is bad enough, but to then let the AI plant a copy of herself in servers on Kernow *and* letting her have access to the InfoHub, which means by implication every connected computer on the world... it's the stuff of nightmares. It might be called a declaration of war.

I *should* be reporting it, to prove my loyalty to my newly adopted homeworld or something. For reasons I haven't fully understood yet, I know I won't.

"Thank you." She makes a little bow with her head, and continues: "As you told it to me, your personal story intrigued me to the extent that I used the Xian Hegemony's bandwidth allocation to research what I could find on Newyan's InfoHub."

My mouth drops open.

InfoHub communications between systems depend on a physical relay, on shuttle drones that jump between systems carrying packets of information. It's a *hugely* expensive operation. Private individuals bid for milliseconds of transmission time. Single-planet companies might bid for a few seconds. Pan-system companies own and pay for a fixed allocation of minutes. The Xian Hegemony, being a group of planets, own *hours* of transmission on each shuttle.

And Shohwa had just appropriated that, at a cost I couldn't calculate.

She smiles at my reaction. "I have synchronized with your ID card, and updated it with a true copy of everything from your original Newyan ID, but left that information in a confidential folder to release or not as you wish."

If she's got down to *that* level of detail...

I realize she must have another clone of herself on Newyan. There's a Xian delegation on the planet. Presumably they have the same facilities as they do on Kernow. What are the Xian doing?

Shohwa's face becomes serious. "Refreshing your ID is not the reason I did this, amusing and informative as that was. My main purpose was to examine your suspicions about a conspiracy on Newyan acting against the Founding Families." She pauses. "I have proof that those suspicions are correct, as far as they go. In fact the conspiracy is nothing less than the beginning of a coup to take control of the government of Newyan."

I barely have time to get my head around that—proof about what happened on Newyan that *might* be delivered to the federal authorities on Earth who *might* do something about it—when she floors me again.

"My main purpose in communicating with you now is to warn you that I see very similar patterns emerging on Kernow. Too similar for them not to be aware of each other. I deduce that this is a pan-system conspiracy to create a new political force from a group of planets on the edges of the Inner Worlds and Margin. Your family, Zara, provided the principal target on Newyan—the example to frighten the other Founding Families into submission. On Kernow, that target is Duke Tremayne's family and the Cardu estate."

Chapter 18

I sleep badly, and I'm so slow at breakfast that Talan must think I've taken a blow to my head.

How to make Gaude understand the imminent threat to the Tremaynes without revealing the information came from Shohwa? *Without* making him think I'm inventing it all just to get the job as Dancing Mistress?

I *have* to do it.

I know what the Tremaynes face and I know what will happen to the Cardu estate. I saw it all, first hand. And I was lucky: my grandfather was aware of the problems; I'd had time to learn the skills to survive; I was able to prepare and then disappear into the population.

Rhoswyn has none of that, and no time. Shohwa believes the conspiracy will make their move this summer.

And while I'm wrestling with what I can do about it, I'm still wondering if the duchess' death was the first move by the conspiracy on Kernow. If it was, why the long delay before the next phase?

What if it wasn't?

What if the duke killed her and covered it up as a suicide?

What if I'm trying to help a murderer?

I make my way straight to Gaude's office after breakfast.

Talan follows. She knows I'm heading for an argument. She makes some token comments about restraint, but I get the impression she's half-hypnotized by the expectation of witnessing a train wreck.

Gaude's office door is open, so I march in. Talan stays outside, but the door doesn't close behind me, and I know she's listening.

Gaude's face is distinctly unwelcoming and he doesn't bother to rise from the seat behind his desk, or greet me. I doesn't matter what's happened between us, what our relative situations are; he's being deliberately rude. I know he's not going to listen to a word I say unless I can get past that attitude.

I take a deep breath and lean over the desk. "What is it that you so dislike about me, Mr Gaude?"

It certainly gets a reaction. He looks as if I slapped him.

"Your behavior is completely inappropriate," he splutters.

"It's all right for the duke to disagree with you, or Lady Roscarrow, but not me?"

"It's not a matter of agreements or disagreements! You're a servant!"

A lower class. Not allowed to talk to him like that.

Grandfather shouting at me. *You are nothing without me. Nothing! It will serve you best to remember that.*

The problem is, they're right.

It's irrelevant that I was born into a Founding Family. I can't claim it without revealing that I'm a fugitive from Newyan. That will hardly benefit me with Gaude. So, as far as he's concerned, I'm an ordinary girl from a lesser family who's applied for a tutoring position.

Perhaps I need to start behaving more like one.

I stop looming over the desk and sit down. I probably should have waited to be asked, but at least I'm not in such a threatening position now.

"I'm actually not a servant," I say, which is accurate, since I don't have that job. "I'm a guest, which makes my behavior worse. I apologize if I have been insulting. It's not been an easy time."

To give him credit, he doesn't say the things I can see he wants to. He grunts and with some effort, he calms himself, tugs his jacket into place and inspects the cuffs.

"What can I do for you, Miss Aguirre?"

"Even though it's theoretical now, since there is no longer a position as Dancing Mistress, I'm curious. I'd like you to satisfy my curiosity, if you can."

"What about?"

"Where to start? Why Rhoswyn doesn't already have a Dancing Mistress. Why you decided that she should have one. Why that changed."

"Fair enough." Gaude tilts his chair back and crosses his legs. "She didn't have a single tutor because she's had a range of them." He waves his hand. "Deportment, elocution, dancing and so on. Increasingly not effective. I thought it must seem a bit like perpetual school for Rhoswyn, and instead, having just one person, almost as a companion, might lead her to forming a better connection and being more receptive."

I nodded. That was sound reasoning.

"And the reason you now don't want to go ahead?"

"Bad experiences, Miss Aguirre." His jaw tightens.

"I can understand that, based on something Rhoswyn said to me," I say. "But you knew that, and from something Lady Roscarrow said, your idea was to try recruiting from the Margin. You've gone to all the expense, including a contracting broker and two termination payments, and you're not even willing—"

"I distinctly recall you saying the phrase 'there is no longer a position'," he interrupts me. "It seems you don't quite believe it."

"You're right, I don't." I can't help rising to his bait. "Instead of the specialist education which she'll need to run Cardu the way it needs to be run, Rhoswyn gets a general education at an academy for second-rate rich kids which will qualify her for nothing much."

"Oh? You're an expert in Kernow education and estate management, are you? Your qualities are unending." The sarcasm is dripping from his voice. "What precisely is she going to miss out on educationally, at the most prestigious academy on the planet?"

"How about estate management, for a start? Who will teach her how to run Cardu?"

"I will! And besides, she'll have a manager, in the same way the duke has me."

"And while you're teaching her estate management, who's running the estate? And how exactly are you teaching her when she's on a completely different continent and timezone?"

This is not going the right way. Neither of us are arguing logically. I've put him on the defensive about his job and his condescension is driving me to yell at him.

I take a deep breath and deliberately lean back in my seat.

I need to get off the minor points. Both of us need to stop pecking at each other, for Rhoswyn's sake.

Rational discussion, not point-scoring argument.

"What about security?" I say, when I'm sure my voice is level.

"Security?" Gaude frowns. "What do you mean?"

"Personal security. Threat assessment. Self-defense. Security systems generally, all the—"

"Miss Aguirre! We must be talking at cross purposes here. What in heaven has all that got to do with Rhoswyn's education?"

There's a sudden cold, sinking sensation in my stomach.

What had Shohwa said? Something about the role of the Dancing Mistress losing all the parts loosely labelled 'security' in the absence of the motivation provided by constant conflict.

Gaude probably thinks I came here to teach deportment and etiquette. And dancing.

"What exactly is your idea of the role of a Dancing Mistress?" I say quietly. "Do you have a document of requirements?"

Gaude touches his pad a couple of times and hands it silently to me.

It's displaying a standard job specification and it's as I feared. A tutor to shape a young girl into something more marriageable. *Not* my area of expertise at all. Not an area of interest either. If they want to make Rhoswyn 'marriageable', I'm the last person they want to tutor her.

"I take it that's not the role as you understand it?" Gaude breaks my train of thought. His face betrays a dawning awareness of the communication gap between us.

Where to start? "According to Trooper Sandrey, the suite I'm in was originally the actual Dancing Master's suite."

"Yes, yes," he says, waving his hands like he's dispersing a smell. "A century ago. More, a hundred and fifty years even."

"Then maybe I'm two hundred years late for the job I was expecting," I say.

His eyes narrow. "But that was the Third Expansion," he says. "It was different then."

He's right. The third phase of expansion from the crowded innermost worlds saw pulses of barely serviceable ships full of desperate people drifting outwards through space like seed pods. Some were attracted to prosperous worlds. Some to developing worlds where they could still claim whole continents. Some to worlds where they fed the festering disputes left over from the Second Expansion. And always, the complaints came, never enough of the right kind of people, and an excess of the wrong kind.

Certainly, many worlds in the Margin believe the Third Expansion hasn't finished yet.

I've never thought about what happened on Newyan in the light of the Expansions. Where does it fit in? Third Expansion aftershocks? The beginning of the Fourth? Preparation?

"It was a barbarous time," Gaude says. "We don't live like that anymore. Not on the Inner Worlds. Clearly I'm misinformed as to what passes for civilized behavior in the Margin." He grimaces as if he'd bitten something sour. "You can't think we were hiring *that* for Rhoswyn?"

"Don't try and twist it so that it's my fault," I reply. "You went looking for Dancing Mistresses in the Margin without research. And yes, it's barbarous. Humanity should be noble and kind. Disputes should be settled rationally by dialogue, and not by intrigue and assassination. But you're mistaken if you think there's no danger on Kernow."

"Nonsense. My misunderstanding actually proves my point. It's been so long since there was a need that we've reused the term to mean something more in keeping with the way we live now."

"Really?"

I've made a mistake broaching this too early with Gaude. I need something concrete that has actually happened. Shohwa had no time to brief me on any more than patterns of communications and alliances being made.

What do I know? Barely anything about Kernow. I know what happened on Newyan. How did it start?

The media.

Grandfather had seen it. He'd railed against it and we'd just thought he was being paranoid.

I'm not going to get a second hearing from Gaude. I have to hope my instinct is right.

"Anything concern you about the ownership of media on Kernow, Gaude? Concentrated in too few hands? Not sympathetic to you?"

For a second, I think I've got through. He looks hesitant. There *is* something going on with the media that he's concerned about.

Then he clears his face resolutely and he stands up.

"You're wasting my time. The duke's decision not to hire a tutor stands. There's nothing to discuss. Really, I can't afford to waste any more time on this."

We get a millisecond of warning from Talan. I hear her come smartly to attention outside the door.

"Sir," she says briskly, as the duke storms in, his face dark with anger.

"Both of you together," he says. "That saves time."

He's carrying an infopad and he links it to the screen that dominates one wall of Gaude's office.

It's displaying a news site.

"RAMPANT ABUSE OF PRIVILEGE" screams the title.

There's a picture of me, not looking my best, being guided to a police car by two Central District policemen. Another of the duke, scowling, flanked by his troopers.

"Duke Tremayne's drunk pilot, Zara Aguirre, closes airport, endangers lives and disrupts essential training. THEN SHE WALKS RIGHT OUT OF JAIL." The article goes on: *"They think there's one law for them and another for the rest of us. Aguirre must be brought to justice and the duke must answer for this arrogant challenge to our legal system."*

Chapter 19

No good deed goes unpunished.

I'd saved Marik Roscarrow's life.

As a result, skipping over the arrest and the prison cell, I'm now being used as a pawn in the media's attack on the duke. There's no doubt in my mind, this isn't about me. This is exactly the sort of thing that happened on Newyan. This won't be an isolated article. The duke is being singled out, his reputation eroded, so when they tell the big lie, that he's been swindling money from the state for example, people won't disbelieve it. He'll be guilty before he gets to court.

My case is just preparatory work. They won't be able to defend their assertions about me. They don't care about that. It's not the point for them.

But whatever happens in court, including the media being required to broadcast 'apologies' to me, I'm tainted. No one remembers the apologies.

It looks like there's no job here in Cardu, and no job on Kernow.

And they've printed my name. There's a Newyan delegation here on Kernow who now know exactly where I am, and may regard this as an opportunity to start legal extradition proceedings against me.

I've never been one to back down from a fight, but this conspiracy is just too big and powerful.

I collapse in a seat, feeling all my spirit leaking out of me. It's useless. I've got to stop thinking about being part of the fight on Kernow. I've got to think of me—how I get out of this and far away from all of it.

The duke and Gaude are talking about legal action. From the sound of it, they've had successful legal actions before, but the punishments are trivial, and their efforts to increase the severity have rebounded, making them appear to want to censor the media.

The way Gaude is dancing around the issues—*we shouldn't be seen to do this, we can't do that*—makes me irritated enough to be energized again.

I get back up and lean on Gaude's desk.

"You're wasting your time in court," I say.

The duke blinks as if he'd completely forgotten I'm here.

"You need to go on the offensive," I say. "No one reads court reports or the outcome of cases. They read headlines in the media news summaries and the two paragraphs of text below it. You need to be generating that kind of news against them, and until you do, you're just going to be the victim of it."

In the silence, the duke's eyes get that lock-on-laser focus again.

"What do you know about it?" he says.

His voice is calm, but I can sense a volcano building. There's a lot of long-term anger just beneath the surface of that face.

It's not directed at me, not all of it, but that's little comfort when you stand next to a volcano.

"I apologize, sir," Gaude says. "Miss Aguirre was just leaving—"

The duke's hand comes up and Gaude shuts up like a switch was thrown.

"What do I know about it?" I say. "I watched this happen on Newyan."

"You watched *what* happen on Newyan?"

"A conspiracy has taken over the government of Newyan. The system there was very similar to here, with a lot of power residing in the Founding Families. It was a carefully laid plan, with immense backing. The media companies were bought up. The reputations of the Founding Families destroyed with exactly this sort of story." I nodded at the screen.

The duke's purses his lips. "I read that it was all about corruption."

"You read what the Newyan media wanted you to read."

Gaude can't stay quiet. "Sir, this is simply an attempt to get us to reverse our decision on hiring a Dancing Mistress. Apparently, the term in the Margin actually refers to the historical style of personal tutor and bodyguard. Miss Aguirre claims to be that, as if that would help her case. We wouldn't—"

"The historical style of Dancing Mistress?" the duke says, still fixing me with his eyes.

"Yes," I say. "Deportment and dancing and etiquette, but also self-defense, estate management, threat—"

"Aren't you a little young for all that?" the duke interrupts me. "Wouldn't some grizzled Dancing Master be a better bet?"

I have to bite my tongue. He's goading me, for his own reasons.

"Quite possibly," I say. "If you can find one."

"How honest of you." He sits down and leans back in his chair.

Gaude wants to speak, but a look from the duke keeps him silent.

"Let's say..." The duke stares at the desk and begins to run a finger in a circle on the wood. "Let's say I might be about to make some strategic decisions about security. Let's say I might be interested in your view as a relative outsider. Possibly."

He returns his focus to me.

"I need to discuss today's immediate issues and tactics first. Strategy will follow." He drums his fingers. "It seems that in coming to talk to

Gaude, you've made some connection between security issues and my decisions on my daughter's education. Do enlighten me."

His face is carefully blank, but that's the sort of invitation where I'm meant to bow and scrape my way out of the room backwards, while telling him there's nothing wrong with his decisions.

Wrong woman.

"As a security issue, sending your daughter away to a school on another continent is stupid," I say. "You relinquish all control over her safety to a school, who might just have an aging security guard who patrols at night until he falls asleep. You've got a poor setup here, given you're sitting on top of a fort of your own troops, but at least you can fix things here."

Both of them have gone pale.

I've shot my chances of any employment here, but at this stage I just want to get through to him about Rhoswyn.

"It's more than that. Ignoring all the security issues, what in the Goddess' name are you doing sending your child away the year after her mother dies? What kind of father does that?"

"Have you considered that a dutiful father might be trying to get her academic results back on track?" he says. The muscle in his jaw twitches.

"That's the worst possible way to do it. She'd take love over duty any day. And even if you succeed with her results, what are you preparing her for? Will she learn everything she'll need to use, on a day-to-day basis, here on the estate? Or do you just plan to marry her off?"

The duke comes back to his feet in a rush.

I don't back away. I can't now.

We're almost nose to nose. I can see him trembling with anger.

I may have overdone this.

His voice is strained when he speaks.

"I will take your comments, purged of their provocative tone, under advisement," he says. "In the meantime, I will need to meet with my estate manager, and I wonder if you and Trooper Sandrey would be so good as to occupy Rhoswyn's time until mid-afternoon."

He takes a couple more breaths before adding, "It's probably not advisable to tell her I'm back until I'm ready to meet her."

His arm extends toward the door, inviting me to leave.

More an order than an invitation, and I comply.

Talan falls into step behind me.

"Ringside seats," she murmurs in her lowest voice. "Five dynare each. I'll be rich."

I try to snort, to show I don't care.

Yes, I may have got through to him about his daughter. I may also have made it easier for him to throw me back into the justice system in Central District.

Chapter 20

Fortunately, it's not necessary for me to lie about anything to Rhoswyn; she already has plans for us.

"We're having a picnic at the King's Table," she says, and refuses to elaborate.

Talan chuckles and nods, so I know I'm being teased.

The King's Table? It sounds like something they'd call an inn around here, but why the picnic?

The trip involves horses, and Talan leads us down to the barracks' stables once we've cajoled a packed lunch from the kitchens. For want of anything else to wear, I'm in my naval uniform. Talan provides me with a cavalry hat and a pair of boots better suited to riding.

I ride, in the loosest definition of the word. *On the horse, but not so much with it,* was the judgment of my last riding instructor.

In about three questions, Talan has a good idea of my capabilities, so it doesn't surprise me when Rhoswyn and I get a couple of easygoing mares, whose ears twitch good-naturedly when we approach.

Talan is on her spirited cavalry mount, a big bay gelding. He prances at the start, apparently complaining he didn't get out yesterday, but settles down quickly for his rider.

Once we're well on our way, Talan calls the Mounted Police dispatch controller on her comms unit, reporting our position and intention. The voice that acknowledges her is crisp and clear.

As she's on detached duty, effectively my jailer, she doesn't have any other responsibilities and wouldn't need to call in, but having Rhoswyn along makes reporting necessary. I approve of the security. Rhoswyn rolls her eyes.

Talan also gets a weather report, and the announcement that we're going to have a strong in-shore wind causes Talan and Rhoswyn to exchange secret smiles.

I don't give them the satisfaction of pleading to know what they're up to.

We head out along the coast to the north. I came in from Bandry, down in the south, so this part of the Coast Path is all new to me. If anything, it's even more beautiful than the parts I've seen.

The day is bright; the wind keeps it cool. Within a couple of miles, I've made tentative friends with my horse.

It'd be wonderful if I had nothing else on my mind.

As a distraction from those bleak thoughts about my future, I quiz Rhoswyn on the running of the Cardu estate and where she sees it going.

It's an effort keeping up with her. Words stumble over each other in their hurry to be spoken. She has too much to say, and hearing it, I forget that she's so young.

"...they have more people and better markets in Kensa, and better roads. They have regular freight trains, too. If we sell to a distributor in Kensa, they could have our stuff shipped all over the continent in a few days. Murenys is smaller but it takes *ages* to go anywhere. There's stuff we can't even sell to Estarven because it'd spoil before they got it."

Estarven being the eastern district of Murenys and not that far away.

And...

"...the only problem will be to balance selling as much as we can with keeping our products a little exotic." She giggles. "Us, exotic?"

This girl is failing academically?

She's barely a teenager and she shows a surprisingly broad understanding and a willingness to talk about Cardu. She clearly loves the estate and the district. She would make a magnificent duchess.

If she doesn't get married off to some short-sighted idiot who thinks he can do it better because he has testicles.

Her enthusiasm for the estate is topped only by her eagerness to sell to other planets.

"...and the further inward you go, all the way to Earth even, the more they want to buy your stuff, but it's so expensive to start out-system shipping and you've really got to be there to make sure the deal will work and..."

I lose track of time, and only really look up when our path takes us into the deep shadow of a tall headland.

Rhoswyn comes to a sudden stop in her recitation of what she wants to do with Cardu's trade products and starts bouncing up and down in the saddle. Her mare flicks her ears to ask what her rider thinks she's up to now.

It seems we're nearly there.

"Lunchtime at the top!" she says. "Race you up."

"*No!*" Talan immediately steps on that. "We go easy on this part."

I'm not sure racing is something the mares are interested in, but I know I'm not. The weather has eaten some of the cliff away. The path narrows as it rises and Talan has us dismount and lead the horses up the last steep section.

As we crest the hill, the wind finds us again, pushing us back strongly.

I follow Talan, and we walk off the path where the ground is flat. Further away from that edge is good for me.

We're still leading the horses and I'm walking with my head lowered, holding my hat in place, which is why I don't really see what's on the top of the hill until we're right next to the stones, and they break the relentless pressure of the wind.

I look up.

"Welcome to the King's Table," Rhoswyn says in her formal voice, making a grand gesture of introduction, and pirouetting on the grass. "Here shall we feast among the gathered nobles."

I drop the reins and stare.

They aren't stones as such; they're huge statues. There are twelve of them, arranged in a perfect circle about fifty paces in diameter. In general shape, they resemble the black stone statues I passed on the Coast Path when I walked up from Bandry, but much larger. Each has a base about ten meters long that gives the impression of a crouching animal, and at the front, facing inward to the center of the circle, a triangular head, rising far above the body, three times my height.

Like the ones I'd seen, these have holes drilled through the heads, but not just one or two; multiple passages of different widths and angles.

And as the wind blows through them, the King's Table sings; quietly, mournfully.

It raises the hairs on the back of my neck and ripples goosebumps down my arms.

While Talan tethers the horses, I walk inside the circle and gaze up at the statues.

The King is the largest; the rest are about three-quarters that size. All of them have intricate, weathered carvings on their heads. There seem to be eyes and mouths, or patterns that make me think of those features. Lower down, the bases have long edges cut into them that suggest limbs tucked under bodies, and a tail of some kind at the back.

"This is the biggest and oldest arrangement we've found," Rhoswyn says. Inside the circle, for once, her voice is hushed. "We think it's over three thousand years old."

"Is this what the piskatellers looked like?" I ask.

"Perhaps. We don't know," Talan says, joining us. "They left nothing else but the statues and the outlines of some buildings on the shore. No skeletons or burial sites. The villagers along the coast say some of them are still here, living in the sea, but no one's ever seen one that I know."

The Survey would also have looked hard before the planet was certified for colonization. If there were signs of existing native life that could exhibit intelligence, they would have embargoed Kernow. This ring of statues certainly shows advanced intelligence and purpose. These stones had to be brought all the way up here, even before the carving and the complex system of drilled holes that make them sing.

And three thousand years is recent, in the way of these things.

"When the first humans settled here, on the coast, they called these statues Dreamers," Talan says.

"Some of the fishermen still do," Rhoswyn takes over. "They make offerings and set a place at table on Feast Days."

I look up at the alien faces, drowsing in the sun. Yes, I might call them dreamers, too.

"Others say the Dreamer Folk could walk in their dreams," Talan says. "That they got together and walked a different path, one that took them out of here and now."

"And when they've dreamed through all the different paths," Rhoswyn adds, "they'll come back." She touches the King's base with a gentle hand. "They're waiting. They're still dreaming—what was and what may yet be."

I shiver in the sunlight.

The other two leave me to walk around the circle while they set up our picnic outside. I have to pause in front of each statue. Their features are subtly different, as is their wind-driven voice.

I'm only halfway around when they call me to lunch.

Talan and Rhoswyn have spread a blanket on the ground and weighed it down with stones. The hampers from the kitchens are open in the middle of the blanket and we have a feast. I can see cold pies, bread and butter, cheeses and salad, pickles and jams, and bottles of sparkling fruit juices, all products of the Cardu estate.

It's a little odd, sitting down to eat within earshot of the King's Table. When the wind is strong and constant, it sounds like they're singing. When it varies, it sounds like they're talking about us.

We sit in the lee of the statues.

The ground is a sort of saddle. East of us, it rises dramatically inland, and falls steeply towards the south, where we came up the Coast Path. In the westerly direction, from the King's Table to the path along the cliff edge, the land is flat for about half a kilometer, covered in short, tough grass. The Coast Path marks the edge of the cliff and continues down the northern slope, which is gentle.

Looking to the west, beyond the cliff edge, the sea is deep blue flecked with tiny whitecaps, reaching away to an indistinct horizon. The sky is a pale blue bowl above us.

It's a lovely spot for a picnic.

"Can you teach me to fly, Zara?" Rhoswyn asks, seeing me looking upward.

My Dancing Mistress-self notes that flying lessons would make a good bribe for progress on more academic subjects. If, indeed, she needs to make progress and has not been flunking her tests for some reason.

"You're big enough to reach the rudder pedals, so yes, it's *possible* for me to teach you to fly," I say.

She spots the evasion, and gives me the side-eye.

"*Will* you, then?"

"I'll have to ask your father. Have to say, his aircraft is not the best to start on."

She sighs dramatically. "The only alternative is the glider."

"There's a launching winch up on the airfield," Talan explains. "The glider is stored in a trailer at the back of the hangar."

"Well, a glider would be an excellent starting point," I say.

"I've *been* in the glider, and you can't *go* anywhere."

Oh, the weight of life crushing down on her. The need to be doing everything, now.

"Who took you up in the glider?" I ask.

"Pa."

"He started to teach you to fly?"

"Yes."

The monosyllables are warnings for me to steer clear of more questions.

Instead, I raise an eyebrow at Talan.

"The duke used to teach her a few subjects," she says. "Flying was one of them."

Ahhh.

A few things come together in my head, courtesy of my unfair advantage of having been so like her at that age.

Rhoswyn doesn't want to go to the academy in Kensa, and never wanted tutors, even if that's what her plans have ended up getting her. What she wanted was for her father to teach her again, even if only a couple of subjects and some of the time. *Pa, I'm struggling with this subject, please help me.* I suspect it was the only time she really had access to him, if he was always as busy as he seems to be now.

Then something that started with a reason just kept going, out of habit, even when the reason it started was forgotten.

I'll get the duke to agree to take the time again, if I have to hold a knife to his throat. Using flying lessons with me and some lessons with her father as a carrot, I *guarantee* Rhoswyn's academic results will show a miraculous improvement.

Not that it's my business. I'm just passing through.

Realizing that again puts a slight haze on my sunny mood. I keep forgetting I haven't got a job here. It's as if my subconscious is telling me something. Too much listening to the King's Table. Dreaming of what was and what may yet be.

After lunch, talking is a bit too much effort for all of us, and we lie back, sleepy with full stomachs, fresh air and the warmth of the day. The King's Table sings us lullabies.

Chapter 21

Is there a way it could become my business?

I can't quite fall asleep and instead, worry the thoughts around inside my head like a dog chasing its tail.

Do I really want to stay here?

Can I trust the duke, or have I made some bad assumptions about him?

Could a man cold-blooded enough to murder his wife and make it look like a suicide also be the man to inspire loyalty from his troops and such love from his daughter?

Depressingly, the answer is probably yes. Charismatic psychopaths do that.

But if that's so, why hasn't he tried that charisma on me?

Am I not worth the effort?

Why is he always looking at me as if he knows I haven't got underwear on?

How dare he?

The wind veers and the King's Table emits a sound like a groan.

I snort. *Stop commenting on my gripes, old dreamer king.*

On the other hand, the duke didn't react to the latest media attack by deciding I needed to be sent back to Central District to face my charges.

Yet.

And still, I keep giving him reasons to get rid of me—arguing with him and his estate manager for a start. It seems I haven't quite mastered the trick of remembering I'm not a member of a Founding Family. I'm a nothing, a no one, a fugitive. He's the duke, head of the most prominent of the Founding Families on Kernow. And Gaude is his respected estate manager. I need to stop reacting so badly to both of them.

The wind picks up again and breathes a deep, *deep* organ note through the King's Table.

I can feel it through the earth.

Maybe I'll get a short-term contract here for the summer. The duke said he wanted me to discuss security with him. A few weeks. Might stretch that a bit.

And then? In the autumn?

Find a job in some wild, isolated place and watch to see if the Newyan conspirators come after me. Or their Kernow equivalents.

Or wait to see what happens with Shohwa. Sign up and work for her if it becomes possible.

Nothing permanent. Put no roots down. Roots are not an option for me.

The wind becomes skittish and now the King's Table sounds like the flute section of an orchestra warming up.

No roots. No marriage. No family. My rules. I will not repeat the mistakes of my parents.

I had my chances to challenge that idea, break those rules: Grandfather's insistence that I attend the endless succession of debutante balls. That stopped when it became obvious I couldn't, *wouldn't*, mold myself in a way that was acceptable to the young bachelors of the Founding Families.

Lucky, really, how it turned out.

That's not to say I might not find someone to share a bed, perhaps, as long as it's clear I'm in control.

No chance of that here. No way.

Even if there was an attraction, and I'm not denying to myself he's a handsome man in an arrogant sort of way, the duke and Gaude are on the alert for the slightest hint of anything other than professional behavior from a Dancing Mistress.

What a pair they make. Gaude plain angers me.

The duke... bothers me. It's very different.

"I'm just going to report in." Talan is standing over me, blocking the sun. "The signal's no good here; I'm going to have to walk up the hill."

Her comms unit is on, full of whispering static and the suggestion of words, like dolphins glimpsed in the sea.

"Fine," I say, squinting and looking around. Rhoswyn is lying on her back with her eyes closed. "Watch out for mutant boars."

"Yeah. Just don't run away—I'd hate to have to spend all afternoon tracking you. Besides, the dungeon at Cardu is uncomfortable."

I chuckle. She lies: she'd love tracking me, and I don't doubt she'd be very good at it. She's probably not lying about the dungeon. I'll keep my comfortable apartment for the moment, thank you.

I close my eyes as she moves away and the sun warms my face again.

Where was I? Something about the duke and having no underwear.

Stop it. Stop all of these thoughts.

Aguirre as a Founding Family is gone with me. We will remain as a memory of something past, like the King's Table, and we will always be remembered as a Name Among the Stars, for that cannot be erased. I must take my comfort from that.

I'm not marriageable and I don't want to get married.

I don't want an affair with the duke either. Certainly not until I find out more about how his wife died.

I shiver.

The sun has moved. The King's Table casts a cold shadow over me and I wriggle to get back into the light.

Wait.

That noise is *not* the King's Table.

Shouting. Screaming.

Eyes blurry with sleep, I surge to my feet.

Rhoswyn's not here and neither is Talan's big bay gelding.

Damn the girl!

I *know* what's she done. Why didn't I *think* about it before?

Hands feverishly flying and upsetting my mare, I release her from the tether and leap onto her back.

She's not used to that, and I can feel her tense for a buck, but training takes over and instead we bolt around the bulk of the King's Table with urgency.

Talan's horse is galloping back up the northern slope, lathered and wild-eyed. His feet barely seem to touch the ground. Rhoswyn is in the saddle, but only just. She's lost the reins and her left stirrup. She's gripping the pommel with all her strength and screaming at the top of her lungs. She's right at the cliff edge, and she's being chased by a black horse, closer and closer to that edge.

The black horse looks as if it's flying. The rider is crouched down along the neck, urging it faster and closer to the gelding.

I haven't a hope of getting there in time to save Rhoswyn's life.

Chapter 22

I'm screaming in despair. Far behind me, running down the hill, Talan is screaming too.

As if the sounds themselves would save Rhoswyn.

The two horses are almost touching, as they race along the edge of the cliff.

Talan's gelding senses the other closing, swerves so that Rhoswyn almost falls off. His hooves lash out, even as he's galloping.

My heart stutters, but that swerve takes the gelding precious inches *away* from the edge.

But kicking back also slows the gelding, and the black horse doesn't pause.

"No!" I shout.

The black horse gathers itself and surges forward. It's a display of unbelievable horsemanship and, I realize, incredible bravery. The rider forces the black horse into the narrow gap between the panicked gelding and the crumbling cliff edge, then uses her horse to force the gelding to turn in, back towards the wide spaces in front of the King's Table.

The gelding slows a little, wild-eyed, tossing his head, and the rider reaches out between the horses and grabs the floating reins.

The gelding snorts and tries to turn away.

She hauls him back, urges her horse alongside, not letting him get his backside around to try kicking again. The gelding crabs and slows.

I'm there, and he recognizes my mare approaching.

We meet in the middle of the field and he's high-stepping, not galloping, his eyes still wide, his flanks heaving and sweating while he stamps and snorts to a standstill.

I leap off and catch Rhoswyn as she slides down from the saddle. I'm shaking with relief and Rhoswyn is limp as a rag doll.

"I'm sorry," she sobs. "I'm sorry."

I simply hold her. There are plenty of people who'll yell at her for today's prank.

The rider of the black horse dismounts with a flourish and pulls her hat back, freeing a torrent of blonde hair to unravel down her back.

"Oh, dear," she says, shaking her head sadly, as if her ruined hairstyle was so very important. "Worked its way loose again. Are you all right?"

"She will be," I reply. "Thank you. That was very brave, Miss Esterhauze, and very skillful."

She smiles. "Not a little luck was involved. Miss Aguirre, I believe?"

She peels off a riding glove and we shake hands while taking stock of each other.

The video conference image did her no justice. It fails to convey her sense of presence. To balance that, I tell myself, it also took ten years off her age.

The handshake is firm, cool. I imagine I can feel the after-tremors of adrenaline.

But the eyes! Those grey, grey eyes are weighing, watching. A very private person, Hanna Esterhauze, behind her well-schooled face. A woman who has faced hard decisions and lives with the ones she has made.

"And it was partly my fault," she says. "I startled them on the path."

Talan arrives at a sprint, as spooked as her gelding had been. Seeing Rhoswyn in my arms, she mutely hugs the pair of us and then attends to her horse.

I make introductions, watching those eyes. "It may come as a shock to you," I say, "but the young lady you've saved is none other than Rhoswyn Tremayne."

"Oh! How extraordinary," she replies. "I am delighted to meet you, Lady Tremayne. Hanna Esterhauze."

She knew who Rhoswyn was before I said anything. I see this and I start to wonder about Hanna Esterhauze.

"Just Rhos," Rhoswyn says, her voice still shaky. But she remembers her manners, even after what has just happened. "Thank you, Miss Esterhauze. You saved my life."

"Well, yes. That's not your horse, I see," Esterhauze says to Rhoswyn while watching Talan soothe the gelding. "A cavalry animal. Whatever possessed you to try riding him?"

Rhoswyn licks her lips. She seems unsure what to say to two people she barely knows and who are both the hated Dancing Mistress, but what she does decide to say has the ring of truth to it.

"I can't become a better rider if I get given easy horses all the time."

Again, the desperate desire to do everything *now*. Couple that with a desire to win her father's notice, let alone admiration, by being able to do things he's good at...

Explosive mix for a young girl.

Esterhauze's grey eyes rest on me and there's a moment of understanding.

We can see so much of what Rhoswyn needs, and yet we both know we're not here for the length of time necessary to achieve it.

Perhaps I have misjudged Esterhauze. Having just mentally castigated Rhoswyn for being too hasty, maybe I should be more measured in forming an opinion of other people.

Rhoswyn frees herself from my arms.

"Maybe we shouldn't say anything..." She stops, looking uncomfortable.

"No, Rhos," I say, and Esterhauze gives a brisk nod of agreement.

Of course, telling the duke what happened doesn't put her in a bad light at all.

Talan seals it. "I was on the comms when I saw what was happening," she says. "I have to report now."

We return with the horses to the statues while Talan scrambles back up the hill to get a good enough signal to say everything's turned out okay.

"Well, I see I must come back to the King's Table another time," Esterhauze says as she wanders in and out of the statues. "I trust not immediately."

It's unlikely. She's the only one to come out of this afternoon with any credit. The duke is hardly going to throw her out. Talan and I have more to concern us.

Esterhauze unhitches her horse from the tether.

"I need to retrieve my pack horse," she says. "I do hope he's not wandered too far."

I arrived here stumbling along the Coastal Path, carrying my world on my back like a tortoise. She's made a grand entrance and apparently has two horses, one just to carry her luggage. I'm starting to feel outclassed.

Half an hour later and a little further along the Coast Path, the three of us meet Esterhauze again, leading her pack horse.

Her luggage comprises three large cases. It's not surprising her pack horse didn't bother to go far.

We turn south. Talan and I are silent. Esterhauze talks to Rhoswyn about the statues and the history of the area, subtly getting a good measure of the girl.

After an hour or so on the trail I see a small troop of the Mounted Police making good time toward us. The duke is in the front.

"Let me go ahead," Rhoswyn says.

Talan nods and Rhoswyn gets her mare to canter.

She and the duke meet halfway, sliding down from their horses. He hugs her.

No shouting.

No, and no need to come all the way out. Talan had reported what had happened. The duke just wanted to comfort his daughter, and maybe convince himself that she was all right.

So... not as emotionally isolated as he likes to appear. Not a charismatic psychopath, either. Which leaves my questions over the death of the duchess still floating like the seabirds above us, riding the updraft from the cliff.

Why do I bother?

I'm a weakness his enemies in the media are exploiting, and far from being the Dancing Mistress his daughter needs, I nearly let her die on the rocks.

If I'm lucky, I'll have a few weeks here to try and find another job. If I'm unlucky, maybe Warwick won't mind me sleeping in the barn behind the inn again tonight.

I could walk to Bandry the next day and perhaps find some temporary work while I make wider enquiries.

In terms of Newyan, and the possibility that the conspirators will send someone out to kill me, both options are about equal. Here, in Stormhaven, Newyan knows where I am, but strangers will stand out. On the other hand, if I leave and work a string of jobs for cash, it'll be difficult to trace me.

Of course, there is still the matter of turning up for the court case to dismiss the ridiculous charges against me. Or not dismissing them...

The duke and Rhoswyn mount back up as we reach them.

His face is once again a complete mask, but he's civil to all of us and thanks Esterhauze warmly.

"We need to return to Stormhaven with haste," he says, speaking to Esterhauze and me. "This evening, you will experience a rite of passage for visitors to this coast: a full-blown storm from the deep ocean."

We look out to the west, where the sea is placid under the afternoon sun and the wide horizon is innocent of clouds.

He sees our skepticism and that scar on his cheek twitches.

"We will meet on my storm porch and afterwards, discuss this afternoon's events."

We ride. Whatever we think about the storm approaching, the troopers certainly want to be back home, and so do their horses.

Chapter 23

Evening seems to be rushing upon us when Esterhauze, Talan and I meet at the door of the stairs to the duke's storm porch.

There's a chill in the air, a sharp, clean smell of the sea and a prickly quiet in the fort.

Esterhauze has taken the time to bathe and change into a dark blue dress. She's braided and wound her hair into a knot. If there was an illustration of what a Dancing Mistress should look like when formally meeting her prospective employer, they could use a picture of Esterhauze.

Talan's in her dark green, off-duty uniform. Starched and pressed and nervous.

My duffel bag has been found, Talan assures me, but she can't discover who has it. For want of options, I'm back in my outdated naval uniform, with a fresh, clean shirt from the closet. Yesterday's underwear is now clean and dry, and back in service.

I lead the way up the stairs.

The storm porch is just that: an enclosed platform to watch ocean storms. The layout is long and narrow, and the entire wall facing the ocean is glass. We're on the west side of the castle, so there's nothing but that glass between us and the wide expanse of the ocean. The room curves slightly. The design makes me think it was modelled on a ship's bridge.

There are chairs facing the window. The duke is sitting in one of them, with a comms system beside him that would put a spaceship to shame.

Behind him, watching all of us, is a pale, redheaded man in a dark suit.

The duke is speaking on the comms and waves us to chairs.

I look out and see that it's not so much the evening that has rushed onto us but the darkness of the incoming storm. The horizon has disappeared. It looks as if the sea itself has risen up into the sky, where it has become purple and black, and it rolls toward us menacingly.

It draws the eye, but my attention is mainly on the duke.

He's communicating with harbor masters up and down the entire coast, checking that the fishing fleets are safe.

The fleets are. They all have sophisticated radios and when the storm turned toward the coast, they knew within a short time. As old-fashioned as they seem to be in the villages, they have satellites and weather surveillance.

There are smaller boats still unaccounted for. These are mainly 'creelers'—open boats that check seafloor traps for crustaceans. I've seen the pictures of the nightmarish creatures they catch—those images stirred inexplicable racial memories of vicious aliens that wrap themselves around your face. The InfoHub has assured me that humanity has never found such a creature, but we all know they're out there somewhere, waiting.

However, the ones here on Kernow, once you've shattered their exoskeletons and baked them, have tasty flesh.

Creelers have handheld radios with bad reception at best, but what's worse is they're generally crewed by youngsters with more courage than sense.

We sit in silence, caught up in the drama, our eyes fixed on the approaching front and ears straining to hear the calls from harbor masters.

There are troopers all along the coast, hunting for any sight of the creelers and calling them on their handheld comms. Gradually, one after another of them reports a safe boat, usually pulled high onto a beach and turned over to provide protection. I recognize Moyle's voice, calling in. He's down on the shore below us somewhere. There's a last creeler missing. It's from Stormhaven Wyck, with a couple of fifteen-year-olds on board.

The comms deteriorates, tense voices disappearing into a hiss of electrical interference.

Although it's still early evening, we're sitting in full darkness. Within the storm there are lightning strikes, but they seem a long way away, just enough to show the onrushing shape of the cloud wall, a wall that reaches from the ocean up as far as I can see into the sky. It seems to be accelerating as it comes in.

The only lights from the porch are baleful red LEDs from the comms, gleaming in the reflection from the glass window.

Through the static come some disjointed words: "Found them!" It's Moyle's voice, I'm sure. "Tenleigh Beach..." A long pause full of more static and then "pulling higher... safe..."

The voice fades away. The duke's hand moves, reaching out to turn up the volume and suddenly we're all lit up with a searing, eyeball-blistering flash. Sheet lightning turns the whole sky into one violent blaze of blue-white. Thunder rocks the deep stone of the headland, making the room tremble about us. The storm breaks over the fort like a tidal wave. Rain batters on the roof and windows with a roar.

It's not possible to speak through the noise.

With a wave, the duke leads us downstairs again and into a living room.

It has windows showing the storm outside, but the noise and light are muted in comparison to the storm porch.

"Help yourself to drinks, please," the duke says, and indicates comfortable chairs. "Then take a seat."

Not what I was expecting.

The bar is extensive, but Talan restricts herself to a fruit juice. Esterhauze chooses a brandy. Not the local stuff that I cleaned my feet with, but one with an expensive-looking label. I take a white wine that's been chilling. The duke has the same brandy as Esterhauze. The redheaded man, who hasn't been introduced, takes a glass of water.

Gaude bustles in at the last moment and helps himself to the brandy as well.

The room is comfortable, a feeling increased by the knowledge that the storm is kept outside. It smells of leather furniture with an undertone of local woods, which have scents that remind me of cooking herbs like sage, pepper and rosemary.

The duke lifts his glass. "To those that venture on the sea," he says, and we echo him quietly.

"No little organization is apparent in the fleets," Esterhauze says after the toast. "To so efficiently get everyone back to harbor."

"They know," Gaude says, tasting his brandy. "They know even before the satellite warnings. They smell a storm coming, or something. They claim it's the piskatellers warning them."

He laughs, and there's a quiet huff from Talan.

There's no hurry to start, and I relax until I suddenly recall that Grandfather once said to me that the best preparation for giving someone bad news is to put them at ease first.

Taking another swallow of brandy, the duke leads straight into it.

"As my daughter gets older, her height increases almost imperceptibly," he says, swirling the brandy in his glass. "You might be forgiven for missing it. Her potential for getting into trouble is at the other end of the spectrum, where the increase is so large that you might also miss that, disbelieving the impossible."

Esterhauze laughs quietly.

I allow myself a smile.

His eyes lose their focus for a second and I catch a glimpse of another person. Like Esterhauze, the duke has a public persona that he maintains.

"I hold no one at fault for this afternoon. My mind this evening is on the future. All of us face a difficult few months, for a variety of reasons, and my daughter's safety weighs on my mind."

He gets up and paces to the window. There's nothing to see except when the lightning shivers down the sky.

He turns back to the room.

"I gather you are both Dancing Mistresses of the old description," he says. "And that may be what Rhoswyn needs. I have suspected for some time that there are... actions being directed against this family and others on Kernow. It would appear that we have returned to the behavior of the Third Expansion." He gives a small nod in my direction. "It was never my intention, Miss Aguirre, to actually place Rhoswyn in that academy on Kensa. I merely hoped, with the announcement, to win a few months' leeway, and to protect my family more by our isolation, here on Murenys."

He shrugs. The redheaded man stirs as if uncomfortable with the direction the duke's words are taking.

"I hear rumors that approach may not be sufficient anymore. So..." he pauses, his eyes narrowing. "Miss Esterhauze, I offer you a three-month fixed term contract as Dancing Mistress for my daughter. Miss Aguirre, I am unable to offer you the same, otherwise I would. Unfortunately, until your legal situation is cleared, all I can do is offer you accommodation and use of the facilities here while you remain under technical arrest. I regret, the Central District judicial system runs as slow as treacle during the summer months, so it may be several weeks before the charges against you are dismissed. Trooper Sandrey will remain responsible for you while you are in the charge of the Welarvor Mounted Police."

Esterhauze blinks in surprise and looks thoughtfully at me.

The duke continues, "I would ask you to consider providing uncontracted services to Rhoswyn in cooperation with Miss Esterhauze, but I make no obligation on you."

He sighs.

"And I make no guarantees beyond the end of the summer to either of you. I realize this is not what you thought you were applying for when you responded to the employment offer, and the risks may not be what you consider acceptable. I would consider it no fault of yours should you decide to leave immediately, Miss Esterhauze, or when you are able, Miss Aguirre."

I can see Esterhauze isn't even considering leaving. Neither am I. No good will come of it, but I can't leave here without doing my best for Rhoswyn.

The duke is delighted, and presents us with our first challenge: there's the annual Summer Ball in a week's time. Quite apart from the security issues, this will be Rhoswyn's first attendance. Gaude hums and clears his throat before admitting that, in previous encounters with young gentlemen, Rhoswyn has been 'forthright, to the point of outright rudeness' to some of them. That would be a problem at the Summer Ball.

I have to bite my tongue and hope I can keep a straight face when I tell Rhoswyn that such behavior is unacceptable.

"You are, of course, invited," the duke says. "I should be very happy to have you attend."

I'm shocked and pleased.

Which is all very well, but what on earth am I supposed to wear?

I'm assigned new accommodation. A guest suite will now house Rhoswyn, Talan, Esterhauze and me. We'll share a living room, complete with infopad station and entertainment system, a dining room, which could double as a study, and a kitchen. The bedrooms are off a corridor from the living room. There's only one door to enter into the suite and I make a mental note to discuss with Gaude that it should have a guard posted outside if they're taking the threat against the Tremaynes seriously.

And my duffel bag has finally turned up. It sits on the floor waiting for me, as do Esterhauze's three cases of luggage.

Esterhauze and I take to our rooms to unpack. That will take her longer than me, I suspect, so I occupy myself for a few minutes inspecting the security of my bedroom and thinking about the change in the situation.

The window has a ledge with a drop to the ground that could be a way out. Or in. Interesting.

I stand there and gaze out at the dying storm, my thoughts flitting like insects.

The duke has spies. That's where his 'rumors' are coming from, not the idle chatter of social meetings. He's realized he's under threat, even if he may not yet appreciate the scale of it.

So why has he made the choices he has? Hiring Esterhauze and effectively hiring me? Two people he doesn't know. He's not stupid, so I'm left suspecting something clever.

I need information from Shohwa that I can feed to the duke.

And even as I think that, I realize I'm still not sure about the man himself. The death of his wife and the uncertainty about how it happened—that worries me.

Maybe Shohwa can provide me with information to start investigating that.

Those thoughts aside, the face the duke revealed to us tonight gives me a warm, fuzzy feeling of being on the team.

Which is, my paranoia tells me, exactly what I'm supposed to be feeling.

And quite unlike the feeling I get when I open my duffel bag.

Nothing is missing, and everything is in exactly the same place as I put it. However, I fold my clothes in a distinctive way. Someone went to a great deal of trouble to try and replicate that, but I can still tell; every item in my duffel bag has been taken out and inspected.

Scrap that feeling of being on the team. I'm a suspect, but why and for what, I'm not sure yet.

Chapter 24

I sleep poorly, skimming nightmares where I'm locked in unwinnable battles with untouchable enemies.

Talan, Esterhauze and I had spent the evening together after leaving the duke. The kitchen in the new suite was well stocked and I'd suggested we make ourselves dinner.

The others agreed, Talan adding it would be a good chance to get to know each other.

I knew more about Talan, but both Esterhauze and I had steered the conversation away from personal information. Instead, we'd talked about the reasoning behind the duke's strategy and what we were going to do with Rhoswyn, who was having dinner with her father. She'd be staying in the family's rooms while her father was at the fort.

I wouldn't be teaching her riding, given Esterhauze's and Talan's abilities. They'd agreed my plan of using flying lessons as an incentive for academic work. Esterhauze had offered to take the bulk of actual dancing instruction and etiquette in preparation for the Summer Ball, to my relief. I'd taken estate management training. We'd deferred allocating martial arts and more academic work until we could assess what was needed.

A satisfactory exchange on one level, but at the end, I knew almost nothing more about Esterhauze. In fairness, I'd been as reticent as she had.

It wasn't surprising that worrying about how to deal with the truth about my position was one of the things that kept me from the kind of sleep I needed.

It's still not dawn when surreptitious footsteps pass my door.

I get up and peer out, just catching the main door to the suite closing. Esterhauze's bedroom door is open.

She's probably entitled to be as sleepless as I am. And more entitled to explore Cardu. I'm supposed to have Talan with me at all times as part of the requirements of my ongoing arrest.

I decide I'm not going to wake Talan. I quickly get dressed in what has become my uniform and slip out of the suite to see where Esterhauze is off to this early.

There's no sign of her in the main halls, dining room or exercise areas, and I soon realize that hunting for someone in the fort is pointless. I simply don't know the layout well enough and I can't guess where she might have gone.

I give up, frustrated, when I find myself at the main gate.

There *is* something I can usefully do while I'm here: the Goddess' local Shrine is close by and I'm overdue a visit.

The gate is manned, but they haven't been given orders to stop me. I sign out and tell them where I'm going. They give me instructions to the grove.

The path is easy to find in the growing light of pre-dawn, and it turns out the Lady's Shrine is no more than an eight-minute walk from the gate.

It's surrounded by trees, as all Shrines are, but whereas the general layout is common, the actual construction itself is left to the local Priestesses, and these Priestesses have been touched by the Goddess. I've never seen a more beautiful Shrine.

It is surrounded by well-tended gardens, and a soaring white roof protects the Shrine itself from the elements. That roof is in the shape of a shell—a scallop shell, like a great curved and rippled fan, held up over the Shrine by tall, smooth columns. The Shrine's sides are open, protected from the wind by a thick, well-trimmed hedge and the depth of the woods.

Underneath that floating roof, the heart of the Shrine is laid out in rising concentric circles, flagged with polished quartz and warm pastel sandstone. The innermost two circles, comprising the whole nave and the supplicants' dais, are held within the apse—a three-quarter circular screen wall that is four meters high in the middle and tapers down to hip level at the two ends. The sweep of the apse represents the Goddess' arms enfolding the congregation. It's a brilliant white, made of some nanotech material that absorbs sound, so it's not until I'm nearly at the entrance that I hear the woman inside.

She is in the very middle, on the supplicants' dais.

The priestesses say supplicants should stand, or sit, or kneel, *as suits the heart and mood. The Goddess knows your heart*, they say. *She knows, and She will hear.*

This supplicant is prostrate on the dais, her arms flung out, a heart-jolting image of grief and despair.

I jerk back out of sight, my cheeks burning with shame at intruding on such a profound, private moment.

However, I'm not quite quick enough; I can't help but overhear a few words.

It shocks me to my core to realize it's Esterhauze, and she's sobbing.

"Not for me, Lady. I can ask nothing for me. For her. Let it be as..."

The wall of the apse mutes the sound until the words are unintelligible. I run silently until the tallest section of the apse rises between me and her. Even though it's over twice my height there, I crouch down, as if to hide. I want to bury my face in my hands, or cover my ears. I can make out no words, but what sound remains carries a sense of overwhelming distress.

I should just leave and return another time. If it was someone else, I would already be halfway back to the fort. Hearing her grief is making my stomach churn.

And yet, and yet... what does that beautiful, well-schooled face hide, that she comes here alone and cries out to the Goddess in such pain?

A memory floats up. *To be wounded,* my Grandfather says, *is to give your enemies a way to break you. Offer no weakness; suffer no wound.*

I can't remember what had brought that lecture on, but behind those words, I'd known he was thinking of my parents. *Love is an opening,* he'd said many times to me. *An opening is a weakness.*

A tear falls. For me, for my family, or in sympathy for Esterhauze, I can't tell.

A minute passes. Two. The Shrine falls silent.

I creep my way along the screen of the apse until I can see that the dais is empty, and I walk inside, glancing around shamefaced as I do. I'm still alone, but the dawn is close, and the priestesses will be here soon.

The inner wall of the apse bears representations of the Goddess in her many forms. These are paintings, hung and moved and replaced on some rotation devised by the priestesses. There are four paintings showing in the gentle light of night lamps left for that purpose.

I know them well: *Bounty, Nurture, Courage and Sorrow.*

The dais is round; it faces no one representation of the Goddess, but Esterhauze had lain with her head towards the last.

Our Lady of Sorrows.

I kneel on the dais and stretch out my hand tentatively.

Where her face had rested, I can still feel the wetness of her tears on the stone.

I wipe my hand guiltily. I'm no expert on the higher theological concepts, but I belatedly think the tears form an offering and that makes my touching them a sacrilege.

The Goddess knows your heart.

I sigh, and shuffle until I face Courage, the manifestation of the Lady I believe I most need, but my shame at spying on Esterhauze fights with my growing worries, and I cannot open myself to the presence of the Goddess.

The moment seems to have slipped away from me. I offer up an apology and walk back the way I came, meeting the priestesses as they arrive. They smile and greet me without pressing themselves on me, for which I'm grateful.

Esterhauze is long gone, but there is one other figure present.

It's Moyle, the trooper who came flying with me. His uniform is protected by coveralls while he kneels in one of the gardens and weeds around the flowers.

It's clear his presence does not surprise the priestesses, and they make no move to talk to him. His head is bowed, and he doesn't see me. I can't be sure from a distance, but there's a sense of deep sorrow in his posture. A sense that his work is a form of prayer.

There's a small printed notice on the way out. It acknowledges the gardens were designed, laid out and maintained personally by Duchess Tremayne during her life, and are now kept in her memory. There's an image of her in the garden. It somehow sums up a feeling I have about the way the people are on this coast—she's not cutting a ribbon to declare the gardens open; she's planting flowers, actually *making* the garden. It's no token effort either. From the look of the line of sacks behind her, she started the row and intends to finish the whole bed. Her hands are muddy, there's a streak on her forehead where she's pushed her hair out of her face, and she's laughing.

I can see her daughter in her.

I'm reminded that Moyle and Talan went very quiet when I asked about the duchess' death. Neither said *suicide*, even if their own corps' investigation concluded that.

More secrets and sorrows than mine weave their way through the heart of Cardu, the dark fortress.

Chapter 25

Esterhauze is back in the suite, cooking us omelets for breakfast, clear-eyed and smiling, as if nothing had happened this morning.

Talan is up, looking rumpled and giving me the eye, but she doesn't take me to task for going out. I'm getting a lot of leeway from her, and I need to be careful. I have a feeling her patience with me will not be stretched beyond a certain point.

"That's so thoughtful, thank you, Hanna," I say.

I'm still wary of her, but for some reason, I can't call her Esterhauze; not after witnessing her grief. It's the first time I've used her given name.

I'm half turned away, washing the bowl she used for the eggs, and I feel those grey eyes on me.

"It's my pleasure, Zara," she replies.

Rhoswyn arrives as we sit down at table. She's surprised that Hanna has cooked, and that there is some for her. It would seem none of the Dancing Mistresses who've preceded us ever made any kind of effort.

The girl is conflicted. It shows in her expression and the suppression of her natural vivaciousness. That is, along with being typically early-morning teen—grumpy and sleepy. I suspect she's only here this early because the duke got her up.

I know what's going through her mind. Rhoswyn thinks I'm cool because I'm a hardened criminal in her eyes, still under arrest, *and* I can fly. Hanna's cool because she saved Rhoswyn's life and is such an excellent rider. And yet, we're both hated Dancing Mistresses. We hold the threat of a summertime of boredom over her head, not to mention becoming competitors for her father's affections.

Both Hanna and I see it, but I beat her to suggesting the first step to overcoming it.

"There's a troopers' training session this morning," I say casually. "I'd like us to attend."

"Why?" Rhoswyn says warily, and blinks. "What kind of training?"

"It's hand-to-hand combat techniques, and I want to see what style they use."

Rhoswyn's eyes narrow suspiciously. The duke evidentially has not told her that her curriculum is being expanded. I like it that he's left it to us.

"Your curriculum for the summer will include basic martial arts," I say, and her eyes widen.

Maybe the poor girl thought we'd tie her to a chair and shout mathematical formulae at her all day.

"And without getting too carried away, I would like to suggest a dance lesson this afternoon," Hanna says. "Tomorrow, we can all review indoor subjects in the morning, then you could give us a tour of the estate in the afternoon."

I know she'll enjoy doing that.

This is perfect. Little by little, we'll unpick Rhoswyn's wariness and have her achieving her potential in no time.

I find I'm looking forward to this.

The training session is daunting.

Talan tells me that there is no rule saying that the Welarvor Mounted Police *have* to be over six foot tall like her and the duke, but most of them are just that: big, rawboned men and women.

I'm by no means small at five-eight, but a roomful of large troops is intimidating.

With Rhoswyn and the others right behind me, I can't let it show, so I perform my bow on entering the dojo, take off my shoes, and then walk the way my old sensei used to walk: like I owned the place.

I'm not in *gi*, I'm in Danny's old discards, well washed but still with a faint smell of bale fruit brandy. The sensei looks me over as I describe what we're here for and motions me to join the line.

"Best way to find out what we do and how we do it," he says.

Talan is in her *gi*, and also takes her place in the line. Rhoswyn and Hanna sit on the side and watch.

I want to spar against Hanna, but maybe that will have to wait.

Also watching from the side is the duke's red-haired security advisor, the man who was with us last night on the storm porch and after. Talan's told me his name is Pollard. He's new, six months into the job, with a recommendation from some association of estates. Talan doesn't like him, but I think that might simply be a suspicion about newcomers. Certainly Pollard seems suspicious of the newest newcomers, those being Hanna and me. I'm pretty sure I know who searched through my duffel.

Concentrate.

The class starts with loosening up, some strength exercises, some basic forms. It turns out that the sensei is drilling the troops in basic ju-jitsu. It's a sound foundation. These troops will normally be armed, and this is the kind of martial arts they need complement that: how to deal with an attacker when you've been disarmed, or how to disable an attacker using non-lethal force.

I quickly decide that little of this is useful for Rhoswyn. I have no time to make her into a leaping, kicking warrior either—she just doesn't have the size and strength yet. And it shouldn't be what she needs anyway; she should always have help at hand. What she does need is the ability to buy time, to escape from holds, or evade holds. Add in a couple of throws using an opponent's weight against him and one or two easy disabling kicks.

"Pair off," the sensei calls.

So what I need to teach Rhoswyn is the core of what Bernard was teaching me while we sparred on the *Shohwa*—the art of being *not there*, as I thought of it. Bernard would make a perfect sensei for Rhoswyn, but as I'm the one here, I better practice what I'm going to teach.

My partner grins confidently at me. She's almost as tall as Talan and looks every bit as strong. I do *not* want to grapple with her.

She makes to grip me like we were going to practice throws. I have no intention of being used as a dummy, so I slap her hands away and let off a kick and punch combination before stepping back out of the way of her response. We're not wearing protection, so I hold the blows back, not landing them, but she knows I could have in a real fight. She scowls and comes after me. I spin, getting on the outside of her arms and jabbing at her ribs and kidneys as she passes, stopping just short of contact each time.

Three or four minutes later the sensei calls a halt to swap partners.

My opponent is red-faced and angry. What she thought would be an easy sparring session turned out to be anything but, and she probably feels foolish at not being able to close with me.

Then her face clears. She laughs and bows.

"You're quick," she says. "Have to teach me those moves,"

"Glad to." I return the bow.

We change partners. And again. And again. Inevitably, I get caught a couple of times and make the close acquaintance of the mats. Talan is probably the best of the opponents I face, easily quicker and stronger than me.

Then it's the sensei standing opposite me and bowing as my new opponent.

Oops.

It seems I've drawn attention to myself.

Five painful minutes later, we stop sparring.

"Most interesting," the sensei says after the concluding bow. "We would be honored if you continued to practice with us. These moves are useful."

Nice of him to say it. Useful, but not perfect against someone as quick as he is.

The session is split up. *Gi* are supplied for me, Rhoswyn and Hanna. Talan and the sensei join us to discuss my plans and possible training regimes while the rest of the class continues.

Rhoswyn is a bit embarrassed at being the center of our attention, but she really likes the idea of training, even when it's pointed out that it might be early in the morning.

I catch her practicing my I-own-the-room swagger.

"You need to earn that," I say, and she nods and giggles.

I guess these Dancing Mistresses are turning out more fun than she expected.

Keeping our group separate, we go through some stretching and strengthening exercises, some basic moves, and then, at the end, we take turns sparring with each other.

I can catch her easily, but Rhoswyn's well suited to the style I'm proposing. She's quick and slippery as an eel.

Give me six months, I'm thinking, but I haven't got six months. I wonder if I've even got six weeks.

Chapter 26

After we have lunch in the main dining room, I beg off dancing in the afternoon. Nothing to do with the bruises I picked up in the dojo.

It suits me to spend the afternoon evaluating threats and courses of action.

Back at our apartment, Talan lies down on the sofa and is immediately asleep. It makes me smile. The woman has a gift the gods themselves must envy.

I sit across from her with the infopad, but I hesitate before logging in.

What *should* I be doing, given all the threats hanging over my head? Gathering information? Or starting to run?

The conspirators on Newyan will be moving against me soon. They have to.

Their options are to either send an assassin or start legal proceedings to extradite me.

Meeting me in court would be, in a fair universe, something they'd avoid: courts should be open and proceedings reported. Not only would they have difficulty proving the case against me, but I'd get a chance to make counter-accusations.

But... Shohwa believes the conspiracy on Newyan is closely associated with the conspiracy here. I certainly wouldn't get a fair hearing on Newyan, so it's not a stretch to imagine the same happening here. Probably they'd arrange a closed court session and ignore any defense.

So, court might be a better option for them than hiring an assassin.

My ending up at Cardu makes it an even more attractive option for them, if Shohwa is correct that the Tremayne family is going to be subject to the same attacks as my family on Newyan.

The conspiracy will know I've already got to turn up in the Central District court to have the ridiculous charges from saving Lord Roscarrow's life quashed. They'll know I'm currently in the custody of the Welarvor Mounted Police. I bet they'll use that court appearance to start an extradition appeal. That gets them two targets for one attack—the duke will seem guilty by association. That's the way their media reports will spin it.

The duke would be forced to disassociate from me as quickly as he could.

I know what Grandfather's advice to the duke would be: *Offer no weakness; suffer no wound.* The duke has to pick his battles, and his own family is at stake.

For me, I should warn the duke, even if that means revealing who and what I am. I might as well advise him to throw me out too and save him troubling his conscience.

With all of *that* hanging over me, why do I feel so involved in questioning the duchess' death?

Because it doesn't fit.

It was over a year ago. Sure, the media jumped on it, but there wasn't any real follow-up. On Newyan, the attacks on my family came one after the other, relentlessly.

And if the duchess' murder doesn't fit, maybe it was a mistake.

Someone jumped the gun.

Or they thought the duchess had found something out about the plots and they had to work in a hurry.

Haste breeds mistakes, Grandfather always said.

If I can find that mistake, maybe I can unravel this plot. Not on my own, but I could provide the duke a defense, or maybe just something additional for Shohwa. Any setback for the conspirators is a win for me.

But what if it wasn't related at all? What if I find the duchess was murdered by the duke?

I bury my face in my hands.

If the duchess was murdered, *if* it wasn't the duke, *if* the conspiracy ordered it, *if* they made a mistake...

I'm going in circles. I have to do something.

With a sigh, I switch the infopad on.

There's a message from Shohwa in my intray. It's encrypted, naturally. She can see that there are programs hunting through the Kernow InfoHub for suspicious activity, and the sort of information gathering she's doing is illegal.

Of course, just about everything she's doing is illegal, even just being there, and it would be a massive diplomatic problem if they find her. Not to mention Kernow's authorities will certainly require the Xian delegation's servers to be disconnected and purged. Killing her.

For me, the Shohwa on the ship is a person. I can't quite get my head around the Shohwa in the Xian delegation's computer network being the same person. In our last conversation, I took to calling her Shohwa-nia,

Shohwa's daughter, and as her message decrypts itself into a folder, I see with a grin that's what she's calling herself too.

The bulk of her message is a completely illegal copy of the state's confidential court reports from the inquest into the death of Duchess Tremayne. Not the published report, but the full transcript and private deliberations of the inquiry.

I glance guiltily over at Talan. It takes a moment to set up the screen so I can switch to doing something less unlawful if Talan wakes or someone else calls on us, then I settle down and start reading the summary.

The duchess was seen by several people setting out alone in her boat, a ten-meter, gaff-rigged sloop called *Low Lady*, the summary says. It was just after dawn. It was particularly noted that she was alone because the old sloop usually took two to sail her. No one was alarmed because she was known to be an excellent sailor.

Her failure to return by nightfall caused a huge search to be mounted along the whole coast. Ships in orbit turned scanners down onto the ocean, air-sea rescue planes flew, trawlers pulled in their nets and divided up segments of coast between them to hunt for the *Low Lady*.

By dawn, the sloop had been discovered, anchored out of sight of land. There was no one on board.

It wasn't until a day later that a creeler boat found the duchess' body in a secluded bay.

The post mortem showed she was dead before she went in the water.

Her blood and stomach contents showed she'd taken a potent mixture of sedatives and alcohol over the course of some hours, which had eventually amounted to a fatal dose at some stage in the evening.

There was no disturbance on the boat. Everything was neat and tidy in the cabin. Sails had been hauled down and tied loosely as if they were expected to be used again.

But there was nothing to contradict the story that emerged: she'd sailed until midday, anchored, eaten a small meal, then laid on the foredeck and begun washing down strong pills with glasses of water and wine, possibly passing out and semi-reviving from time to time, until she finally succumbed to the cumulative dose.

It was speculated that a wave could have rocked the boat and the body had fallen overboard.

There was no note. No indication from anyone who knew her that she was suicidal or even depressed. She wasn't on any medications and no one knew where the pills had come from. No one who had met her immediately before her death had thought she was behaving unusually.

Equally, there was no sign of a struggle. No indication she'd been forced to swallow the pills. Indeed, no sign of anyone else on the boat.

In the folder are media reports and photos. Archive photos of the duke and duchess at their marriage, and later, carrying Rhoswyn just after she was born. Then photos of the duke at the inquiry into his wife's death, his face an emotionless mask. Finally, photos of other Founding Families gathering around at the funeral; I recognize the Roscarrows flanking the duke and Rhoswyn, as if to protect them from photographers.

The media articles avoid making any direct accusations, but belabor just about every possible reason that there might have been marital problems, including that the marriage had been regarded as 'beneath him', and that there was no male child.

I read the summary once again. Then, steeling myself, I rush through the post mortem report, avoiding looking at the photos in that section. It says what the summary says, in medical jargon, as far as I can tell.

I take more time over the forensics report. It's hugely detailed: the condition of the sea at the time, maps showing the direction and strength of tides overnight, the painstaking effort to determine that there were no other fingerprints in the cabin or on the bottle of wine, the background of all the people who gave statements, and even the Tremayne family finances.

There's a whole section on the boat. The *Low Lady* was an impounded smuggling boat, dating back to the first settlements when a crazy jigsaw of jurisdictions and tariffs incentivized 'marketing' across boundaries. It had been in the duke's family all that time. Rebuilt twice, each time carefully recreating the original design.

And at the end of the folder, there's a file of text in two parts. One is intended as a media release and states that the court agrees with the proposal of the Welarvor Mounted Police that the duchess had committed suicide.

The second is internal to the judicial system and clarifies that the ruling was taken on the balance of probabilities, and that many unexplained anomalies and unanswered questions remain.

I'm no detective, and certainly not an expert on the case, but that media release conclusion stinks, even without knowing what the writer thought were 'anomalies'.

There are so many questions. Why eat a meal first? Why even take the food on board if you're planning to kill yourself? Under those circumstances, why drink water *and* wine? Why dose yourself slowly over the course of an afternoon?

I know those aren't any kind of proof and that people contemplating suicide don't behave rationally.

There's more, something I can't put my finger on yet.

Included in the report is a section on motive, or rather, lack of it. The duke and duchess had no financial problems. There were no medical diagnoses of terminal illness. Nothing legal pending. Nothing known about marital problems.

I close the files and re-encrypt them. I've given myself plenty to think about, but I'm no nearer to finding out about the conspirators.

First impressions: this was no suicide. Anyone this prepared to kill themselves in this way would show some sign.

So the duchess was murdered.

I shudder, remembering my Dancing Mistress whispering as she showed me around the sealed section of the laboratory she kept in the basement: *There is a universe of poisons out there. Not all of them are known. Not all of them share the same purpose.*

Someone who wasn't on the sloop when it left harbor incapacitated the duchess in some way, fed her the sedatives and wine until she died, and then departed. The most obvious theory is it was someone she met in another boat. Someone she knew. Maybe they had lunch with her, sitting on the foredeck. Put something in the wine which rendered the duchess partly conscious.

And then they stayed with her, feeding her sedatives, coldly, methodically killing her and taking the whole afternoon to do it.

I shiver again.

Someone she knew. An assignation, out of sight of land? The court report touches on this: there were other vessels off that part of the coast, but they were all fishing boats with multiple crew on board. No one reported any other vessels, but then, only one reported seeing the *Low Lady*. Another similar boat might have escaped attention.

I close my eyes. The obvious theory has plenty of holes in it. For example, there's nothing in the forensics about chemical residue in the wine bottle, other than wine, or in the glass the duchess drank from.

And it would have been risky for someone to be seen sailing away from the area.

I want to see the *Low Lady*, which is stored here in the fort, but I don't expect to learn much from it.

The court report includes a section on the investigation, which looks thorough, but there are still some lines I want pursued.

Did any spaceship in orbit happen to be scanning this area at any part of the afternoon? Maybe Shohwa-nia can find that out.

The others are for me.

Where did the wine and meal come from? Who handled them before the duchess?

And what was the real state of her marriage?

I have ideas how to go about following up on these, but it won't be possible today.

The biggest problem about this investigation, apart from my inexperience, is that my time is so limited and I'm going to be busy.

The first stage would be to prove that the duke didn't murder his wife. How long do I have for that? I send a meeting request to his online address. Gaude has already warned me any appointment could take a few days, and the duke's auto-response comes back telling me he's out at the moment and expected back in five days.

Five days.

That's my timeframe to investigate the duke. I want to be able to go into his office free of any suspicion that he's a murderer, if I'm going to be warning him about the conspirators and the shortcomings of his security here at Cardu.

Not least of which shortcomings is his auto-response telling me when he's due back.

Who am I kidding? Thinking about it, I realize whatever I find or don't find, I still have to warn him about the conspirators. If not for his sake, then for Rhoswyn's.

Before I close the browser I set up a search. This one can't use the local InfoHub. I have to submit it to a data broking system to wait for the next millisecond of free bandwidth on the information packets that are passed between planets. I specify the Tavoli system as the target, and request complete data on Hanna Esterhauze. The search will terminate once the volume of data reaches a the size of a standard transmission packet, but it searches chronologically, so the most recent results will make it in.

Given the delays between systems, it may take a couple of weeks to return.

Of course, anyone can make that kind of search. On anyone.

I'd be stupid to think Gaude hasn't done a search on me. Or Pollard. Or Hanna for that matter. Any search on me will return all the lies about being a fugitive wanted in connection with corruption on Newyan. Who knows, maybe by now the conspirators have charged me with murder as well. Whatever comes back, I'm sure it will be enough to change the duke's attitude to me. I will be under real arrest, not this easy parole system.

Unless I can prove links between Newyan and Kernow, the duchess' murder and my family's persecution, that couple of weeks may be all I have left here.

Chapter 27

Good intentions. I hardly seem to get a moment to investigate anything.

We're so busy. In addition to half the academic lessons, I'm teaching Rhoswyn estate management and martial arts on alternate mornings. And two afternoons when the wind is right, I take her to the airfield and we fly in the glider. Hanna complains mildly that her dancing lessons will fall behind, but Rhoswyn prefers flying.

One evening, under Gaude's suspicious nose, Hanna and I check the wine cellars. The Cardu estate doesn't produce wine, but Rhoswyn will need an educated palate in society. Stocking the cellar is Gaude's responsibility and he's prickly as a cactus when he sees me comparing the order history with the stocked bottles. He's only distracted when Hanna picks a bottle for our evening meal and Rhoswyn's first tasting lesson.

"An excellent choice," he murmurs, unctuous as a wine trader, his fingers brushing the bottle and, totally accidentally, Hanna's hand.

I smile tightly and close the old ledger. It seems the bottle found on the *Low Lady* didn't come from this cellar. So where did the duchess get it? Why didn't she take one from her own cellar? If someone gave it to her, who was it? Shohwa-nia agrees with me: if I'm to solve this, it's in the small details that others have overlooked. I believe the duchess was drugged, and I want to find out who had access to the food and wine she had on board.

I'm becoming obsessed by finding out what happened to her. She's invaded my sleep almost as if she's haunting me. I dream of her, and of her last day. I dream of the duke, looking out from his storm porch to the distant bay below, wondering why his wife is late. Or wondering when the body would be found.

Little surprise that I wake unrested.

I take no consolation from the fact that Hanna seems to not sleep well either. As much as she maintains her cheerful mask, her face looks thinner as the days go on, making her eyes seem larger. Now *that's* a haunted look.

But it's Hanna and Talan together who finally provide me with an opportunity to progress my investigation, on the afternoon of the fourth day.

Hanna's claimed Rhoswyn for the afternoon. They're driving to Bandry to select a ball gown for Rhoswyn and have it fitted. Of course, Hanna has a gown in her luggage. Of course, I haven't, and I can't afford one.

And Talan is held up in another part of the fort over some police business.

I'm supposed to wait for Talan. On the other hand, tomorrow the duke is back.

I'm running out of time.

I can't solve this murder in the next day, but maybe, just maybe, I can find something that eliminates him from the list of suspects. I'm going to tell him everything I know, for Rhoswyn's sake, and I will feel so much better if I know I'm not helping a murderer.

I try to justify my plans to myself by noting that Talan doesn't accompany Rhoswyn and me in the glider—there's barely enough room as it is.

It's not as if Talan is expected to be with me the entire time, I whisper to the empty room.

Doesn't work; I feel sick at betraying her trust. I leave her a note that I'm out for fresh air and will be back in the evening. I tell myself that perhaps I'll be back before she is.

The other problem is someone else might stop me. I *am* still under arrest.

I walk down to the stables, my heart hammering in my chest.

No one challenges me as I find the same placid mare Talan chose for me before and lead her out of her stable into the forecourt. A groom makes me jump by calling out a greeting as I fetch the saddle and bridle. I manage to return the greeting.

The stable is a busy place and the mare isn't anyone's prized cavalry mount. No one stops me. No one asks what I'm doing. And no one signs me out.

My heartrate is still sky-high as we canter gently down to the Coast Path. Every moment I'm expecting someone to yell and come after me.

It's not till we're hidden by a bend in the path that I slow the mare to a walk. My heartrate sinks, and her ears twitch as if she's amused at my stress.

But I'm out on my own now, and getting back in will be even easier. As useful as it has been to me today, I add the stables to my list of security issues to discuss with the duke when he gets back tomorrow.

I follow the Coast Path down to Stormhaven village below, and half an hour later, I hitch my mare to the post outside the Spyglass in the harbor.

Warwick greets me as I walk through the door.

"It's our very own flying mermaid," he greets me, and stands me an ale for having saved Lord Roscarrow's life the night I'd arrived.

As I'd hoped, it's a quiet time at the Spyglass, and Warwick is an easy man to get talking.

There's little that happens in Stormhaven he doesn't know something about. My problem is twofold: not making him wary, and knowing which half of what he tells me to discount.

He spins me the local tales of piskatellers, how they warn the fleets about storms, or rescue drowning men. How the fishing communities set an honorary place for them at table and fishing ships make offerings.

I buy him an ale and a top-up for me.

He explains Feast Days on the Welarvor coast, and I finally understand what was going on when I met the troop of mounted police on the day I walked from Bandry.

Every summer three villages are chosen for a 'raid' on their Feast Day. The Welarvor Mounted Police turn up on horseback, dressed in 'traditional' costumes, which they never actually used, and round up all the townsfolk by blowing hunting horns and waving lances. A court is held in the town square and several miscreants are summarily punished by being thrown into the harbor. These usually include the mayor and any publicans. Then the police, including the duke, serve the villagers their feast in the town hall, waiting on them hand and foot.

While he's telling me that, I buy us another round of ales.

I tell him how Talan warned me against mutant pigs on the Coast Path, and when we've finished laughing, I slide in a casual question about the marriage of the duke and duchess.

"Sound as a new roof, it was," he says and takes a quaff of ale. "I'm not saying it's my place to comment, but it worked for them. Couldn't believe what I read last year. Lot of people never been near the place saying those things about them. And that inquiry. Suicide? Nonsense. Don't know what happened, but the duchess wasn't that kind of person."

His eyes darken and he polishes the gleaming bar top with a cloth.

"Here, look at this." He tosses the cloth aside and retrieves his infopad from behind the bar. What he shows me is a video of the last Stormhaven Feast Day. The duke is strutting about in his cloak, his helmet tilted back. He's sentencing Warwick and the mayor to their swim in the harbor. The duchess is playing a part, kneeling and begging mercy for the 'accused'. She's dressed all in white with green seaweed wound around her.

"That's an old tradition on the coast," Warwick says, pointing at the dress.

"To symbolize Bounty?" The representations of the Goddess in the Shrine have a seaweed crown and sashes.

"Mmm," Warwick says. "Bounty's a city-folk name. Here on the coast we say *morrohow*—the gifts of the sea. What the sea gives, it may take back. The least of its gifts may be costly, or the greatest may be free. We're all the same on the deeps."

I'm not really listening—I'm looking at the duke and duchess. They fall out of character as judge and advocate when he haughtily refuses to listen to her pleas and passes judgment. They laugh, and as the villagers hurry Warwick and the mayor to their watery doom, she takes her husband's arm. His hand comes to rest gently on hers, and the camera catches the exchange of looks.

I can feel it, with a stone-cold certainty. The duke did not kill his wife.

There's more on the Feast Day, but I close the video. It's in a folder devoted to the Tremaynes. Warwick is an obvious supporter. There are pictures and videos of the pair and their involvement in the life of Stormhaven. The duchess opening the new gardens at the Shrine. The duke at a launch ceremony for a new fishing boat. Both of them at the election of a new mayor. A thanksgiving. A funeral. A wedding.

And a picture of the duchess holding a bottle of wine outside the Spyglass.

The same wine I'd seen in the court report.

"Is that one of your wines?" I ask, peering at the image.

He squints. "Oh, no, that's special that is. Only a few dozen made every year. The duchess' family makes it on their farm down near Port Eyren. They sent her a bottle every year. Was her favorite, you know."

Unexpectedly, my eyes prickle and I cover it by blowing my nose.

That's why I haven't been able to find any mention of the wine on the InfoHub. It's her family's hobby wine.

I've taken a risk of alienating Talan, or getting us both into trouble, and I've barely made any progress. Aside from settling in my mind that the duke was not responsible.

But am I being objective about that? I'm deciding that on the basis of seeing a video of him with his wife?

No. Not really objective.

Customers come in, and Warwick stops chatting to serve them. I realize I've spent too long. The light is fading and I wanted to be back before evening.

I leave with a wave and point my patient mare back up the winding path to the fort. The gentle rocking motion of her walk is relaxing. I sigh and close my eyes.

I'm not being objective about this investigation.

The fact is, I don't want the duke to be guilty.

Who do I think I am anyway?

I should drop this sleuthing. I have the duke's three month's of 'termination' payment. Maybe that's enough to get me a passage to the next world through a broker.

Where would I go?

Anywhere beyond the reach of the conspirators on Newyan and Kernow. That's the sensible course of action.

That rocking is making me sleepy.

And Warwick's ale is stronger than I thought!

Stupid to match drinks with an innkeeper. I can't afford to get drunk and let my guard slip. For all the arguments that Newyan will go for a legal attack against me rather than an assassin, I could easily have misread the situation. I'd be an easy target tonight.

I turn and look back down the path nervously. I can't see anyone, but it is getting darker. It's just my imagination spooking me, thinking there's someone behind me.

Yes, run away now. My grandfather would approve. Become nothing and nobody again. *Offer no weakness, suffer no wound.*

And yet, if I ran away now, I'd be letting Rhoswyn down. The duke, too.

Not that letting *him* down is so important. He can look after himself.

But Rhoswyn's begun to look up to me.

And I'm in love with this place at a bone-deep level already.

Such a tangled web.

It's a good thing the mare knows her way back, because I doze off, sitting right there on her back.

I'm kneeling at his feet, crowned and bound with the gifts of the sea. He lifts me up, then offers his arm.

I look up at his face, but the sun is shining in my eyes.

I wake up with a jerk as my mare snorts and tosses her head, happy to be home.

The stables are dark, the one light in the empty forecourt pointed at me and serving only to make the shadows on the sides deeper.

I dismount wearily, slipping down from the saddle.

"DOWN ON THE GROUND! NOW!"

I don't even have time to react.

Hands grip my arms and force me, face-down, into the mud.

Chapter 28

I'm handcuffed, lifted back to my feet, then thoroughly and professionally patted down for weapons.

Facing me is Pollard, the duke's security advisor. A couple of Mounted Police troopers did the searching. They're holding my arms.

"What do you think you're doing?" Pollard snarls at me.

"I was out for a ride," I reply. "It was a pleasant evening, until you happened. What do you think *you're* doing?"

"You're under arrest!"

"Yeah. Old news, Pollard. I'm well aware of it. No one said I couldn't go for a ride."

I sense a hesitation from the troopers. One of them is a guy I've been training with in the dojo. I don't think they're really happy with Pollard.

"You are supposed to be accompanied by Trooper Sandrey at all times—"

There's an almighty clatter of hooves behind us.

I twist around.

Talan, on her gelding, and she's *not* happy.

We scatter and she leaps off, landing in front of Pollard, who backs away.

"Get those cuffs off," Talan says over her shoulder before turning back. "What the nova do you think you're doing, Pollard?"

"The prisoner was—"

"Escaping? Just how much do you not understand about horses? *This* is the front end." She holds out her hand to the side, and her gelding immediate trots up to stand next to her. "That means the horse is moving towards you. If Miss Aguirre had been escaping you would have seen the horse's ass. You'll recognize what one looks like from your shaving mirror."

"She's supposed to be accomp—" Pollard tries.

"I was accompanying her," Talan lies well.

She turns on the two troopers. They've freed me and they're standing at parade rest and looking embarrassed.

"You two! Saddles and bridles, then rub the horses down."

She grabs my arm and pulls me past Pollard, slowing just enough to deliver one last comment.

"You don't have authority over a single trooper in this fort, *Mister* Pollard, and you'd do well to remember that."

We walk in icy silence for a couple of minutes.

I glance back. There's no sign of Pollard.

"Thank you," I say.

She doesn't reply. Ominously, she says nothing at all while she hurries me through the fort until we're standing outside the duke's office.

The duke is back early.

And there's a strange tension in the whole fort, a silence broken by the sound of troopers hurrying down passages.

My relief at being rescued evaporates, and is replaced by apprehension.

"Stay there," Talan says curtly and slips inside.

I'm wearing the outdoor clothes that Danny gave me. They're filthy with mud from the forecourt. I take the jacket off and use it to wipe my face and hands.

Talan must have known I'd gone down to the stables and shadowed me. That was why I'd felt there was someone behind me on the path.

I can hear her speaking and the duke's deep voice replying.

Was she spying on me, or just trying to protect me?

Then Talan is back out. Her nose wrinkles at the jacket but she motions me to give it to her.

She's standing in front of me. We'd be face to face, but she's too tall for that. I'm going to get a crick in my neck, but this is probably not a good time to make that sort of wisecrack.

She's still angry, but I don't think it's *all* directed at me.

I whisper, "I'm sorry, Talan. I put you in an awful position. I owe you."

"You do," she says. "So do me this one thing in return. Tell nothing but the truth in there."

She moves aside to usher me in. The door closes behind me.

Chapter 29

Duke Tremayne is standing looking out of his open window, hands behind his back. However he might try to disguise it, every line in his body tells me he's furious.

I clear my throat. "Is Rhoswyn all right?"

He turns abruptly, perhaps surprised at my first words.

"Yes."

His eyes travel up and down me, taking in the mud on the front of my trousers, the smears on my hands and face. I seem to be making a habit of turning up in front of him worse for wear.

What does he see? What's going on behind those eyes?

"Talk to me about Rhoswyn," he says.

"What do you mean?"

This can't be about my escapade today. What have I done?

"You're part of the team teaching her. I'm her father. Report your findings so far."

While I gather my thoughts, he takes one of his storm-capes and covers a chair for me to sit down without ruining the fabric.

"She's an excellent pupil—"

"I seem to recall that you got close to implying I'm responsible for her poor results in some way. Explain. Why are her school grades so poor?"

He pulls a chair up and sits opposite me, tense as a bowstring.

I decide against speaking tactfully or evasively. He probably isn't going to get any more angry.

"She's deliberately failing," I say.

"Why?"

"Because, in the past, when she had difficulties, you'd help her."

He blinks.

"That's what she's trying to make happen again. She's longing for you to spend time with her. You've given up teaching her gliding, you never really spent as much time as you should on the estate management, you're away a lot, so the only thing she has left is her academic work."

He surges back to his feet, so I do too. It's another neck-crick to lock eyes with him, because he's even taller than Talan, but I'm not going to let him look down at me in the chair.

"You have no idea—"

"No, perhaps not," I interrupt him, "but you asked my opinion based on what I've seen, and if there are things I haven't seen, then you'll have to tell me about them."

He doesn't respond to that, so I go straight on.

"As for what I'm working on with her, where she really shines is in estate management. She's a perfect student. I've only spent a couple of mornings with her, but I already know by the end of the summer, there won't be anything more for me to teach her."

I don't add *if I'm still here, by the end of summer.*

"She's also a natural pilot," I say. "She *feels* the air around that glider. Understands the ridge effect from the onshore winds."

His eyes narrow. "You flew all the way down to Marazion and back, didn't you?"

"She flew. I was just in the back seat. And we went to Bandry as well. I thought she needed those sort of flights to counter a comment she made about not being able to go anywhere in a glider."

That gets a snort from him.

"Tell me, Miss Aguirre, how comfortable is that glider with the pair of you in it?"

That knocks me back on my righteous backside. Of course he can't continue to teach Rhoswyn as she grows bigger. She and I are squeezed tightly in, so there'd be no chance for him to get in with her. I've been stupid on that point.

Fair enough, but as I'm on the topic, I might as well get in another item from my long list: "What she needs is a target to focus on. A challenge. So, I've put her down for the junior section of the gliding championships in Kensa."

The duke knows exactly which one I mean. There's the small matter that he has a dozen trophies from that competition over the years, and it's so important to Rhoswyn to excel at what her father's good at.

"That may not be possible," the duke murmurs and returns to his seat. "What about martial arts?"

He obviously knows exactly how we've split the tasks between Hanna and me. And I'm really pleased he's shown such an interest in his daughter's education. But what does this have to do with whatever has happened to make him angry today? Is it me, or something Rhoswyn's done?

"She's a good student, but it will take time." I sit back down too.

"And all the academic problems... you're effectively saying that's all my fault?"

"Not in so many words—"

"But yes."

I swallow and don't contradict him.

"You also warned me there's a conspiracy targeting me and my family," he says. "Does that mean I should trust you?"

"Not necessarily," I reply, and give him the same reasoning I gave his daughter. "It could be a bluff to put you off your guard."

His mouth stretches. It can't be called a real smile.

"Despite that, Rhoswyn tells me she trusts you."

"I'll thank her. What in the Goddess' name has happened, sir?"

"I took your words to heart, Miss Aguirre, and started asking difficult questions about the ownership of media on Kernow. The result was an immediate push back. Rhoswyn and Miss Esterhauze were ambushed in Bandry by a dozen news agencies."

He can't sit in his seat, but this time he doesn't try looming over me. He goes to the window and glares out into the night.

"They were asking my daughter questions about the state of my marriage at the time of my wife's... death."

"That's disgusting." But what I would have expected from the conspirators. And I notice he didn't say suicide.

"Yes, it's bad enough on its own, but there's another problem."

"Sir?"

"How did they know to turn up in Bandry?" He swivels around to look at me. "Very few people knew that they were going. I knew. Sandrey and Moyle knew. Pollard knew. Gaude, Rhoswyn, Miss Esterhauze and you knew. The shop itself. Who told the media?"

"It wasn't me."

"Then what were you doing in Stormhaven this afternoon?"

Chapter 30

I take a deep breath and consider lying. *Tell nothing but the truth in there,* Talan said, and I owe her. She probably gave enough information to the duke that any lie I tell will be obvious anyway. I have to tell him some truth, but not who I really am.

My stomach is like a spring, wound up tight.

"Investigating your wife's murder." It comes out in a rush.

"Why?"

He doesn't argue my moving it from death to murder, but his face becomes even stonier. I can feel anger moving beneath that mask, like lava beneath the crust of a volcano. His eyes lock onto me and refuse to move.

I stutter a bit. "Because it might give us a way of identifying who's in the conspiracy. Because Rhoswyn needs the truth. Because... because it needs to be done for her sake too. I mean the duchess' sake. She deserves the truth."

The light isn't good in his office, but I swear I see that mask slip for a second and raw pain shows through.

Then he's back to the interrogation.

"*If* this is part of the conspiracy you talk about." He leaves that hanging for a moment. "You're a detective as well as all your other Dancing Mistress skills?"

"No, but I'm probably a better detective than whoever investigated it and decided it was suicide." I bite my lip and remind myself that whoever it was, he or she worked for the duke.

"Really? Do explain, Miss Aguirre."

He doesn't seem to have taken what I'm doing or saying as an insult. But I know my reasoning is thin.

"It's the weight of things rather than any one issue," I say. "Repeatedly taking sedatives all afternoon? Not leaving a note? No indication from anyone that it was likely. No reason to kill herself—"

He interrupts me. "People who commit suicide are not always rational, but they can appear so."

"Not over any length of time, to people who know them." I'm feeling as short of breath as if I'd been running. I force myself to go on; I don't have time to approach this all carefully and tactfully. "And whatever verdict you allowed to be reached, *you* don't think she committed suicide, do you?"

He doesn't respond.

I try and shuffle through all the issues to find one that resonates with him.

"There are orders in the estate's management files," I say. "Your wife made some the day before she was murdered, you know. Not just for feed or animal bedding, but flowers for the Shrine. For her to plant. I didn't know her, but I can't—"

"If it was murder, who? There's no evidence there was anyone on board except for her."

"Suspiciously so," I say. "No fingerprints in the cabin, or on the bottle, except for hers? Come on. The boat was normally crewed with two people. You'd expect at least one other set. And did her family wear gloves when they sent her an individual bottle of their wine?"

"No other boats in the area," he counters. "Too far to swim ashore."

"To swim, yes."

"So how? Submarine? Seaplane?"

Despite the sarcasm, he's genuinely asking. I've got through to him. He doesn't believe it was suicide. He's looking to see how much I've found out about it.

"They would have shown up on scans."

I haven't seen the full scans from orbiting stations, but I guess I don't need to: something like that can't be hidden in a court case.

"There are underwater craft that could make that distance, or close to it," I go on. "I've never used them, but there are forms of motorized sledges that you can hold onto which drag you through the water. Small enough they wouldn't show on a scan."

"I'm familiar with them. Rare and expensive," the duke says, "and whereas they could make it back from that far out, they couldn't make the return trip."

He looks away. I'm guessing I haven't come up with anything he hasn't thought of. If they're rare and expensive, I'm betting he has a list of owners.

It's clear there's no way this is a closed investigation. He's allowed a suicide verdict to be passed, but kept the hunt for the murderer going.

"Why don't you share what you know?" I say.

He'd be entitled to ask why he should share with me, but he doesn't. He simply ignores it and carries on finding out what I know.

"So, what exactly did you learn from your trip to the Spyglass? Surely not those details about fingerprints on the boat?"

"No."

"What, then? What did you go there looking for?"

I don't like being pinned to my seat by his glare. I want to stand up, but my legs feel like jelly.

"Mainly to try and eliminate you from the list of suspects," I say.

My mouth is dry.

"As you're telling me this, I assume you have."

"You can assume whatever you want." The feeling of being trapped by his questions puts my tongue on a hair trigger.

"So, you spoke to Warwick. Was he supportive?"

"Yes, but it wasn't all about what he said. He showed me videos and pictures of the two of you together."

How painful must this be for him to talk about his dead wife like this? Despite that, his face remains a mask.

"Videos? Pictures?" he says, raising his eyebrows. "Presumably of us together at functions down in the town. Hardly compelling evidence either way, Miss Aguirre. That's very sloppy work for a detective."

"I said I was *trying* to eliminate you. You *assumed* I have."

That takes him unawares and he laughs.

It changes him. Changes the way he looks. Clears his face and takes years off his appearance. Just for a second.

I'm startled at the sharp ache in my chest. I want to see him laugh again, and in that moment it all comes together for me. Why it's been so easy to persuade myself he couldn't possibly be the murderer. Why this is all so important for me.

Stupid, *stupid* girl. Stupid!

He must be able to see it in my face.

How pathetic I must seem: the penniless, nameless girl dreaming of romance with the handsome duke, a man foremost among the Names of this planet. I'm reduced to the level of all those Kernow Dancing Mistresses who see nothing in their job but a way of snaring a rich man.

He must be laughing at me, but he's turned back to the window, to look out into the night.

Chapter 31

I contemplate running out of the room and not stopping. Once, the Aguirre family on Newyan might have been famous for never backing down, but then came my father. Maybe I'm made of the same stuff as him.

The duke speaks before I act. His voice is strained.

"You'd like me to share, you said. Very well. I'm also *assuming*, since you know details about fingerprints, you've found some way to access the inquest documents?"

"Yes."

Both our voices sound strained.

I have to fix this stupid situation I've got myself in. The best way is to concentrate on doing what I set out to do. Then I can leave and run far, far away.

"Did that include the autopsy?" He turns to look at me, frowning.

I nod.

"I hope you'll tell me how you managed that sometime," he says thoughtfully, and then waves it away. "But tell me, what did you see on the analyses of stomach contents and residue in the wine bottle? What was out of place?"

I close my eyes and concentrate, bringing up an image of the pages.

"I'm not a forensic scientist, but nothing stands out. There was still alcohol in her system, and of course, there were traces of the wine in the bottle."

"At first glance, all the chemicals you'd expect to see from drinking."

"Yes, there was a comment like that by the coroner in the report. What was missing?"

"An understanding of the wine. Specifically, *that* bottle of wine." He walks to his desk and takes an empty bottle from a drawer. It's the duchess' family's wine. He places the bottle carefully on the desk.

"That's Penglynn Awr, the 'gold from the top of the valley'. Her family makes it, and it's a labor of love. Grapes don't do very well on this coast, you see. But her family keeps it going, using nothing but vines descended from the old Terran Sauvignon Blanc, kept in glasshouses."

I walk across and pick up the bottle. The label is neat and well designed, but it doesn't have the look of a standard commercial label. There's no strength, no awards won, no boastful biographies of the producers.

"What do other winemakers use instead?"

"There's a native fruit that serves. You have some experience of it. Bale fruit."

I blush, remembering the brandy tipped all over me while I slept in the barn behind the Spyglass, but he's not teasing me about drinking it.

"So you're saying that she had another bottle of wine as well?"

"There was no sign of another bottle, not on the boat and not in the chemical analysis. To understand why I believe the coroner got it wrong, you need to know a bit more about bale fruit." He pauses. "It's been the savior of the wine industry here in Welarvor; it's easy to grow, it tastes like grape and it has varieties for reds and whites."

He takes out a second bottle from the drawer. This one is old and it still has an amber liquid in it.

"That," he says, handing it across, "is Ammeledh. The 'kiss of angels'. We're nothing if not poetic on the coast. More prosaically, it's brandy made from bale fruit wine."

I try not to think of angels and kissing, or where this conversation is going.

I uncork it, take a sniff. "These angels don't have bad breath like the stuff Warwick has."

It's a poor joke.

In fact, the brandy is peculiarly scentless beyond the standard tang of alcohol. There's something disturbing about that. Something my Dancing Mistress said to me, but the memory is elusive and the duke is still talking.

"The rotgut that Warwick has in his bar is made a different way so it's unmistakable. That bottle is made the old way. That's now illegal."

I was going to taste it, but there's obviously something wrong with this version of Ammeledh. I swirl it around in the bottle and sniff again. "What's so bad about it? Some secondary effect on health?"

He doesn't answer directly. "Did Warwick call it by its nickname?"

"Yes. He said it was called *Headless*. I guess because it's strong?"

"No." He takes the bottle back and reseals it. "The nickname comes from the result of the old way of making it. Any alcoholic drink, made in the casual way this old brandy was, could be contaminated by trace chemicals from the seeds. In wine, that trace was too small to matter. Unfortunately, distillation to brandy increased the concentration. By great good fortune, it turned out not many batches were contaminated in this way, but the Ammeledh in this bottle was. Take a sip of it..." he places the bottle back in the drawer and closes it with a violent motion, "...and those trace chemicals overwhelm the sigma receptors in your brain, the specific receptors that are the keys to higher brain functions and memory, for example. You are rendered defenseless and highly suggestible."

What he's saying hits me: a potent drug that smells of nothing but alcohol and makes a woman helpless.

I stagger back to my chair and sit down gracelessly, feeling sick to my stomach.

The duke is leaning on his desk, struggling to keep his face unemotional.

I try not to think of what he must be feeling, and I try not to feel either.

If I'm going to help solve this case, I have to treat this like a puzzle comprised of facts. Emotionless facts.

What exactly is he telling me here?

I clear my throat. "There's nothing more... missing from the autopsy report, is there?"

"No, Miss Aguirre, I have not actively suppressed evidence. This was not a rape. It was a murder. Someone drugged her by putting contaminated Ammeledh in her wine," his voice catches, but he ploughs on, "then sat beside her for six hours and fed her a steady and increasing dose of sedatives while her body eliminated the evidence of the stupefying chemicals from the Ammeledh."

"But not the evidence that she'd drunk bale fruit alcohol, evidence which wouldn't be in the Penglynn Awr wine?"

"Precisely."

A crime of enormous hate. To sit beside her, giving her sedatives and wine while she remained suggestible and then increasing the dose, relying on the reflex of her throat to keep swallowing the pills. To measure out the doses and take all afternoon to kill her.

A cold, bitter hatred. The level of hatred that consumes a person.

The evil of it chills me. What kind of a monster are we hunting?

"That knowledge is restricted to very few," he says.

Which means he's come to a decision to trust me.

"Allowing you to continue investigating secretly even though the official verdict is suicide?" I take a guess.

"Yes."

"Because, even then, eighteen months ago, you suspected this was part of something larger?"

"Yes." He's restless, his hands nudging the infopad and comms unit on the desk.

When he speaks again, the conversation takes yet another unexpected turn.

"When you collected her from Port Eyren, you spoke to my daughter about spies," he says. "That if one side has them, probably so does the other. That was good insight, and accurate as it turns out."

"So what are your spies telling you?"

"About my wife's murder? Nothing. About me and the rest of the family? That we are under threat of assassination. From someone in place." He makes a gesture to encompass the fort and shakes his head. "It's like the barbarism of the Third Expansion never went away."

He sighs, walks to a cabinet and opens it, revealing an extensive drinks bar. He opens a bottle of wine, pours two glasses.

"The murder investigation is stalled," he says. "I need a new set of eyes on it and it needs to be someone my enemies wouldn't expect to be involved in the investigation. Even more, my daughter needs protection, and just one old-fashioned Dancing Mistress might not be enough."

He walks back to the window, places the glasses on the table there and beckons me to join him.

"Given she's saved Rhoswyn's life once already, Miss Esterhauze could hardly be the assassin sent to kill us," he says. "But you? Why do I trust you? It's true you warned me about a conspiracy against me, but you also said something else to my daughter. That warning her about spies doesn't make you *not* a spy. It could be a bluff."

My own advice to Rhoswyn, come back to taunt me.

"I'm not an assassin," I say.

I've been this close to him before. Not in this way. I've been nose-to-nose arguing. This is different.

He doesn't suspect me. Surely. He wouldn't bother with this elaborate charade and explanations if he really thought I was an assassin.

I try to keep calm and professional. I'm a Dancing Mistress. A family servant.

My heart is having none of it. It's racing. I can feel my cheeks heating.

I want to reach out and touch him, take some of that pain away, *heal* him somehow.

Stupid girl. I need to finish this and get away before I make a fool of myself.

"I understand you and Miss Esterhauze have started to instruct Rhoswyn on wines," he says. His voice is low, conversational. Not like the other times we've stood this close. I can *feel* his voice, like a caress. "Here's a new one I've just brought in. Tell me, Miss Aguirre, would this be a suitable wine for the Summer Ball?"

His eyes hold mine.

I might as well stand next to a furnace. I'm going to melt. I have to drink this wine and get out of this room.

He hands me the glass. Our fingers touch. It's all I can manage to not flinch. Or worse, to make the touch linger.

I don't bother with swirling and sniffing the wine. No time. No time for sips. Drink and get out.

I gulp a mouthful.

That taste. Of course I know the taste. My Dancing Mistress trained me well.

But that taste. The shock of it. The heart-surging *shock* as it hits my system and I know. And I know that he knows.

Fool!

My vision blurs. My hands begin trembling and the wine spills.

Chapter 32

I feel the glass taken from me. I wipe tears from my eyes and watch as he takes the remainder in one swallow.

"Not how it should be drunk." My voice is barely a whisper.

"I'm sorry," he replies. "I... I wasn't thinking. Obviously. Given what we were just talking about. I shouldn't have given you a drink. Ridiculously stupid of me."

He looks distraught.

And I feel an even greater fool, that it didn't even occur to me that he might have put the contaminated Ammeledh, *or worse*, in my wine.

I turn away. I can't think straight this close to him.

Focus on being professional. He asked a question. Answer it.

"Unlike the coast here," I say, "Newyan has many areas that have proved to be excellent for transplanted Terran vines."

He starts to speak, but I close my eyes and override him.

"This is a chardonnay, from the Bizana region, a southern headland where two oceans meet and moderate the climate. The soil is rich and heavy, laid down by old rivers over great beds of limestone, and the vineyards are shielded from storms by oak forests. The grapes are harvested late and left to winter on the lees in barrels made from that same protecting oak."

Tears return, leaking down my cheeks, as unstoppable as the sales speech I'd made so many times.

"On approach, the wine is rounded, mellow. It's often described as buttery on the first taste, but its true strength is in the finish, which is where its complexity appears: a pure, mineral zest that is instantly memorable yet never overbearing."

He is silent, waiting for me to conclude my recitation.

"This is from the Amai vineyard. It's perhaps ten years old, twelve at the most. It's called Arrano. It's not suitable for the Summer Ball."

"Why?" He's surprised.

"Because it's priceless," I say. "It was the flagship wine of the producer. A crate of that wine was already worth the same as a truckload of reasonable wine which people at a ball will drink without tasting. But then, last year, the Amai vines and their oaks burned. The cellars and warehouses burned. The houses of the workers burned. No investigation was made, no cause suggested, but the result is there's nothing left, and the hillsides now belong to the Newyan Bureau of Industry. There will be no more Arrano wine."

"And who was the owner of that vineyard?"

There's no point in denying it.

"You know already," I say. It's printed on the label and he must have suspected it, to go out and find this particular wine. "The Aguirre Family Estate."

Speaking the words is like casting pebbles into a pool.

Have I made my situation worse? The duke has his hands full with his own problems. Now I have admitted to being *that* Aguirre, what next? Has he heard I'm a fugitive? Does he believe the stories of corruption, or has he drawn the parallels with what's happening here?

All he does is hand me a handkerchief.

"Please sit, Lady Aguirre."

"*Don't* call me that. We didn't use titles on Newyan, and anyway, there's no Founding Family Aguirre any more. It was a Name Among the Stars. It's just history now."

"It's a Name. *That* can never be erased."

I return to my seat and he places the untasted second glass on a table beside me. He refills the empty glass and sits opposite.

"I'm sorry," he says again, motioning with the wine.

I shake my head. Neither of us is at our best. How angry he must be with the media attack on Rhoswyn. I can't blame him for the insensitivity.

We sip as we should for this wine, and I manage to avoid crying this time.

"No one else needs to know who you are, apart from Talan," he says. "Otherwise, I foresee legal complications."

That's one way of putting it.

"I've applied to re-convene the Murenys administration and make a change to media law. Unfortunately, even if it's passed, it'll only have partial effect on this continent, and none on the InfoHub."

"If you have your own media, you have a channel to the InfoHub. They can't stop you any more than you can stop them."

"Yes, we're already starting that, but it won't be resolved in a war of words. I don't like it anyway; it's divisive. It will look as if Kensa and Murenys are in conflict. Still, it should give us a breathing space."

A chance for me to continue to investigate his wife's death and a new task: to find out who told the media that Rhoswyn would be in Bandry.

He calls Talan in and briefs her.

When I'm not with Rhoswyn, I'm free to ask questions anywhere so long as I report back. Talan will be with me at all times. To the external observer, it must appear that the Welarvor Mounted Police are doing their duty and keeping me under arrest.

I get a stare from Talan at that, and another when I refuse to reveal where I'm getting my information from.

"I trust you with *my* life," I say defensively, "but I don't have the permission of my source to discuss their identity."

There's no way Shohwa-nia will want others knowing that a Xian AI has infiltrated their InfoHub. The duke might feel forced, out of loyalty to Kernow, to require that she be disconnected from the InfoHub at the least. I can't risk it.

And Shohwa-nia might be exactly what this investigation needs.

We return to our apartment, and Talan is quiet. Hanna immediately picks up on the tension, but chooses to speak only about Rhoswyn's progress and the shock of the media intrusion in Bandry.

I'm exhausted. I go to bed early with a lot on my mind.

Chapter 33

A day's relaxation. Precious as gold.

I should be enjoying myself, lying in the sun, but something's nagging at me. Something I should be doing. Something...

Got to get up.

Can't move. *Oh, Goddess, what's happened to me?*

My body is so heavy.

Am I drunk?

Can't even lift my hand.

Call for help. Someone! Please. Anyone?

There's a noise. That can't be me. That pathetic croaking.

My head is lifted. Something is put in my mouth. Pills? I must be in hospital.

What happened? Rhoswyn? Bleyd? Are they alright? Who's there?

Drink, someone says.

Water? Goddess, I'm so thirsty. Coolness in my mouth. Swallow greedily.

Not water. Wine.

No! Not a hospital. What's happening? This is wrong. *Please. No. Please.*

Scream! I must scream.

But there's no sound. No struggling. Just a feeling of falling, falling.

No! No! No!

"Zara!"

I struggle to get my body to *move*. As if moving would save me from the darkness shrouding the sun, floating down to cover me, soft as sleep, hard as death.

"Zara!"

Talan's sitting on my bed and holding my wrists to stop me hitting her.

It's night. The bedroom light switches on and Hanna's standing there at the door, Rhoswyn behind her. Both of them are staring at me, wide-eyed and worried.

It's the second night my nightmares have woken everybody up.

Talan waves the others back to bed, and hugs me.

Hanna switches the light off and Talan slips into bed beside me in the darkness.

"The same?" she asks.

"Yes," I say. "Being drugged. Knowing what's happening, but not being able to do anything about it. Not even scream."

"Well, outside of the nightmare, you managed the screaming all right."

"Sorry."

"Hmm."

She has the ability to sleep anywhere, anytime, and she demonstrates that within a couple of minutes. It's incredibly comforting to lie against her warmth. Her slow, regular breathing lulls me. I'm *tired* and even my brain idly imagining a quite different body next to me doesn't stop me slipping off to sleep as well.

The following afternoon, I pass Rhoswyn into Hanna's care after a morning's work on estate management. Moyle has been assigned to our little group, and he stays with Hanna so that Rhoswyn will always have a trooper nearby. Talan and I head out to the estate's main storage compound.

The duke's away, travelling around Murenys recruiting support. That's a mercy to me. I couldn't trust myself not to do something stupid if he were here. I think Talan suspects I've lost my head, but if she does, she keeps her opinions to herself.

This afternoon is an opportunity to move my investigation ahead. I feel there's something right in front of all of us, if I can only see it.

The storage area we go to is comprised of two rows of warehouses outside the main fort. It's still within the outer boundary fences and there's a secondary, twelve-foot diamond wire fence around the warehouses. It's used for the Welarvor Mounted Police's trucks and boats. It's also where they store large evidence in criminal investigations, or inquests.

It's where the duchess' boat, the *Low Lady*, is kept.

A bored guard lets us into the compound and Talan takes me down to the far end. All the warehouses are huge; even the sliding doors are monstrous: five meters tall and ten wide. Talan opens a lock as big as her fist and I pull the chain through.

We need a lever to prize the doors open and pushing them apart has them squealing like a chorus of all the demented souls of the deep.

Talan finds the light switches with the help of her flashlight and the whole warehouse is bathed in stark strip lighting, illuminating a dozen boats on trailers, all being held as part of legal proceedings.

The *Low Lady* is off to one side on her own, and it gives me a peculiar sensation to see her, as if I'd seen her many times before.

She's wooden, clearly a hand-built one-off, and she has a sweeping, sleek outline. Even out of her element and resting on the trailer, she's beautiful.

The single mast has been removed and tied alongside. The sails are wrapped in plastic and lie on top of the mast.

Talan fetches some steps for us to climb up and board.

The deck is a narrow ellipse with the middle dominated by the raised blister of the cabin.

I walk along the varnished decking, taking the thin path between the edge and the cabin to the wider area of the bow. There's a single guardrail and a small raised lip at the edge of the deck. Even though I'm sure others have been through this, I lie down and imagine a body and an empty bottle rolling. The lip would catch the bottle, but not the body, so the scenario described at the inquest is possible.

There's no sign of anything on the decking. I kneel down and touch it. A little shiver goes through me. She lay here, helpless, and someone gave her wine and pills until she died.

I know I'm feeding more detail to my nightmares, but I have to do it.

A new set of eyes, the duke said.

The wind rattles the doors, moans.

Talan is sitting at the back, waiting silently.

"She normally went out with someone else," I say. "Who?"

Talan shrugs. "Anyone she knew who wanted to go. Of the ones who went out most frequently... Rhoswyn, a lot, especially with her school friends. Rhoswyn's teachers. Some of the youngsters who sail the creelers from Stormhaven. Any visitors to Cardu, including her family when they came. The Roscarrows, of course. Me and Moyle. A couple of other troopers who enjoyed sailing. Even Gaude went out a dozen times with her."

"Not the duke?"

"Not often, unless they had visitors. He prefers flying and riding."

"Where did she go mostly?"

"The islands were a favorite with the youngsters. Or out where the boat was found. There are reefs there that are good to snorkel."

I walk back along the deck.

The cabin is built racing-style, smooth and watertight, the bulk of it below the deck.

I open the hatch and go down the steps into the cabin, Talan just behind.

"When they rebuilt it, I understand they kept the old smuggling compartments. Can you show me them?" I ask.

Talan snorts.

There are six of them, located above the slim, rectangular portholes—*portlights,* Talan corrects me—three on each side. They're easy to get to and barely big enough to store a couple of bottles of wine.

There are two in the floor. They're difficult to get to and the folding furniture has to be moved to access them. I measure the spaces with a tape I brought along.

"What are you thinking?" Talan asks.

"These are big enough for a Delphine," I say. The Delphine is a small submersible motor, capable of pulling a person behind it underwater for twenty miles before refueling. The sort of thing you'd need to get back within range of the coast if you wanted to leave the boat moored out at the reef.

Talan nods, understanding where I'm going. "Far enough offshore, but close enough to the coast that you could have a boat moored there without it being suspicious."

"Which might mean there are two people involved."

She shrugs. "Maybe. But how did the murderer get out there? There's no sign that the duchess picked up anyone on the way, or that there was another boat out on the reef."

"Two Delphines. One to get out here, which is left to sink when it completes its job. One waiting, hidden in this compartment, for the trip back."

"Which leaves the difficulty of finding the *Low Lady* out beyond the horizon when you are really low in the water, and then getting on board without the duchess knowing..."

We argue the mechanics of it back and forth without any clear resolution.

I have a chart of all the questions and ideas and scribble down anything Talan says that I haven't considered.

"There is one other hiding place," Talan says after we close the floor compartments and fold the table back down over them.

I raise my eyebrows. The court documents said eight smuggling compartments.

While I add '9th hiding place' to my chart, she shuffles around me in the cramped space, and kneels down in front of the steps that we used to come down from the deck. She reaches around them and there's a click. She pulls them away from the bulkhead; the steps are a hollow construction and there's space behind.

My heart beats a little faster.

I squeeze around her. It's too difficult to measure, so I curl up into a ball and try to fit myself behind the steps.

But my hopes are dashed. It's too small. Maybe a child would fit in. I can't, and certainly someone the size of Talan wouldn't either.

"And there's no sign of anything like a Delphine being stored in the compartments," Talan says. She sounds like she's been over this a hundred times and the frustration has worn it thin. "Not to mention the problem about the tides—"

Her comms unit squawks and she turns the volume up.

"...multiple points. Code 16-3. Code 16-3. Secure areas. Gates 3, 5 and 8. Code 16-3..."

Talan goes pale and leaps up onto the deck, switching frequency.

"Lieutenant Sandrey, at Area 4. Status."

"Multiple incursions," a voice crackles. "Gates 3, 5 and 8. Gate 4 not replying. Appears to be civilian vans."

"Lockdown immediately," Talan snaps. "Location alpha-2?"

"Unknown."

"Shit! Zara, stay here!" she yells as she disappears.

By the time I've wriggled out from behind the steps and got to the deck, she's long gone.

I climb down and trot over to the switches, plunging the warehouse into darkness.

Vans? An attack? That doesn't sound like the conspirators. They like to work out of sight.

I make my way by touch towards the light coming in from the open doors.

I should shut them and lock them.

Which thought brings the memory of Talan refastening the lock on the open clasp and pocketing the keys.

At least I can close the doors.

Or maybe not. I put my shoulder against one and shove as hard as I can. The huge door inches towards the center, the rusty rollers screaming protest.

Almost loud enough to mask the sound of a van braking hard, right outside.

Chapter 34

The iron lever we used to open the doors is on the ground, right next to me. It's the only thing remotely resembling a weapon that I have.

But the people spilling out of the van aren't soldiers. They're media.

Nearly as bad.

I leave the lever where I can reach it and stand outside, blocking the entrance. The second door is just as stiff as the first; I'm not going to be able to close it in time. I'm going to have to be the door.

A quick glance at the gate to the compound shows it's wide open and the guard's missing.

The chain used to secure the gate is hanging down.

Is that the lock on the end? Have they just used a bolt cutter?

"It's open, Gabby." One of the first guys out calls back into the van.

Another guy gets out. He has a shoulder-mounted mediacam and he rolls his shoulder to get it comfortable. The camera's LEDs light up and he starts swinging the lens down the long line of warehouses. Background shots. I can almost hear the voice-over.

Behind him, the van empties. There are a dozen people.

"Excuse me," a scruffily-dressed young woman says, and tries to push past me.

I grab the door and don't move. "It'll be up to the Mounted Police to excuse you," I say. "Trespassing and criminal damage for starters. Can't say I hold much hope for you."

"This is public property," she splutters.

"No it isn't. This is part of the Cardu Estate and it's a secured area, which you've broken into, causing criminal damage in the process."

I just know what they want to film—the *Low Lady*. I can't let them in. It's not just a matter of principle. That chart of mine is lying on the table in the cabin, full of questions about the decision of the inquest.

I desperately need a comms unit to call for help.

If there's anybody who's available.

Is this part of a concerted effort? Are the other vans full of media people as well? Did others get into the estate? How long before Talan gets back? Or the guard?

I haven't heard shots or the hum of pulsars, so my money's on all the vans being media, and a concerted effort by the conspirators to find something to damage the duke's reputation.

Which realization doesn't help me much right here.

"What's the problem?" The girl is joined by a harassed-looking older guy with a clipboard. "Come on, move it, move it. Time is money."

"She won't let in me."

"What's the problem?" he says to me this time, getting far too close. I don't budge. He wants me to step back.

"You're the problem," I say. "This is part of the Cardu estate—"

"We know where we are. We have permits to film here. Who the nova are you?"

"You can apply to the police information unit for details of personnel, but you need to leave. Now."

Goddess, I hope the Mounted Police have an information unit. I didn't actually tell him I was in the police, but I want him to think I am and not get any ideas about using physical force. There are too many of them for me to fight them.

He gets even closer, and he's shouting into my face now.

"We are getting in there whether you want it or not. We have permits."

I desperately want to give him a hard knee in the groin, but there are cameras here. I have to satisfy myself with wiping the spittle off my face. He's so close, my hand touches his face.

He staggers backwards. "Did you get that? She hit me."

"So call the police," I say.

The guy with the mediacam is focusing on someone else from the van. The scruffy girl tries to hold up a little handcam over my head, but the warehouse is too dark.

"What's going on? Russ, stop being an idiot."

The new speaker is an older guy in a suit, with a big smile for me. I hate him on sight, even more than I hate the others. He looks about forty, and he's handsome, if you like slick weasels and surgically enhanced smiles.

"Sorry about that," he says to me, jerking his thumb at the guy with the clipboard. "He's under a bit of pressure. We all are really." He brings the smile out again. "Well, will you listen to me. I'm sure you're under pressure, too. Way of the world these days, isn't it?"

I keep my thoughts about the way of the world to myself and send another prayer that someone alerts Talan to what's happening here. *Someone* must have noticed the van's broken through security. Surveillance cameras. Something.

Russ moves away a little. The girl is still bobbing about on tiptoes, trying to see past me into the warehouse.

"Look, I don't want you to worry about them," the suit says. He puts his hands in his pockets and sighs. "Always running, this business. Just madness. Never time to take a breath."

"Get back in your van, go down to the town and take a breath at the inn," I say.

He laughs and puts on his most 'reasonable' voice.

"Good one. We'll buy you one later. Look, we only want to get some background for an in-depth perspective on Duke Tremayne as he tries to set up a new political alliance here on Murenys. You know about that?"

I refuse to answer.

"Well, he's going to want all the help he can get, and we can really leverage that for him. You should never discount the sympathy vote, and, oh boy, losing your wife like that will rake it in. So all we need are a couple of shots of the boat."

It's so plausible, even though I know it's all manure.

I just shake my head. "Can't let you in." I want to say a lot more, but he's exactly the kind of guy who's wired up and I want to give them as little of my voice to edit as possible.

"You see now, I understand your position. We really need more young people with a sense of duty like yours and we wouldn't be in the kind of trouble we're in today. But here's the thing, what my team need now is just background. The inquest is all over. No one's talking about it any more, and that's where the duke is missing a trick."

The circus is coming. The woman that the mediacam was focusing on has just finished the "I'm here at the storage facility..." intro, and she's walking toward me. There are people flitting around her like flies, touching her face, her hair, putting crimps on her jacket so it hangs just so. She ignores them.

Oh, yes, she only has eyes for me.

"Hi, I'm Gabby McGuire, lead presenter for *News Today*, but I guess you already know that."

"Can't let you in," I repeat.

She doesn't appear to hear.

"Damien, darling," she says over her shoulder, "some foundation on my friend here, or she'll look washed out under the lights."

She gives me a little girl-to-girl smile that sets my teeth on edge. "Have to look our best, don't we?"

"Not answering questions," I say. Forget being washed out; I'm going to look like a cornered rat. There's sweat beading on my brow. I can't stop looking at the mediacam, which is turning my way. Whatever else happens, someone is going to see my face on *News Today* and start asking why a person who is supposed to be under arrest by the Welarvor Mounted Police is actually wandering freely around the Cardu estate and guarding one of their warehouses.

"Come on," says Gabby. "This is legitimate public interest and a great boost for your boss just when he needs it."

Clipboard man, Russ, is back and he's actually stroking and patting my arm. "It's okay," he murmurs. "We know what we're doing. We'll be in and out in five minutes. Won't touch anything. We'll even blank out everything but the boat."

"Need you to stand a little closer to me, darling, framing's off," says the guy with the mediacam, beckoning me forward with his free hand.

Damien is trying to paint my face. "Relax, you'll look gorgeous."

Russ tugs my shirt, trying to pull me forward. "Just a step."

"Look this way."

Scruffy girl hoists a set of studio lights on a bar, blinding me.

At the last moment, I sense one of them trying to slip behind me into the open door.

I shove a desperate knee out and I get the groin shot I've been trying to avoid. The guy gasps and doubles over.

"Hey!" Russ shouts at me. "Stop that!"

I grab his injured friend and throw him at Russ.

It's no use, I'm going to have to get that iron lever and swing it at a few people to make them take me seriously. That is *not* going to look good on prime time.

"Freeze! Police!" someone shouts.

Thank the Goddess.

The mediacam is right in my face.

He's about to swing around. There's a memory unit on the side of the camera. I grab it. He turns.

Troopers come barreling into the media group, shoving them away.

The camera keeps swinging, but the cameraman and I are unbalanced. I tangle his legs up. The memory unit pops out. He yells and falls and there's the sharp, percussive sound of tens of thousands of dynare's worth of optics cracking as it hits the concrete.

Chapter 35

"Stand still."

Talan huffs and tugs at my jacket again.

'My' jacket—if I'd known where I'd end up now, maybe I'd have picked a different uniform that first day at Cardu, and not the disbanded Welarvor Naval Reserve. There's no time for regrets. I stiffen my stance and bite down on any comments about her fussing with my appearance. I'm well aware that you only get one chance to make a first impression, and I'm about to meet some powerful people.

The uniform was originally designed for an adolescent male. Talan, Hanna and I have worked on it. *I* think it looks fine.

In addition to worrying over whether I'm smart enough, Talan is 'entertaining' me by giving me a list of everything that's hit the fan since the media tried to get into the warehouse.

"Three broken noses, associated medical bills and compensation claims from the media company to cover loss of employment during their recuperation time."

"I wasn't responsible for a single one of those—"

"That comes to 5,000 dynare, so far. Then there are two more serious injuries: both Ms Gabby McGuire and Mr Derek Hartsfelt were hospitalized with concussion."

"That wasn't me either."

I'm less sure about that. It got wild when the police arrived. I may have hit someone in self-defense. Or something.

"Then there's 15,000 dynare for the optics on the mediacam."

I glower at her, but I can't deny that one.

"And compensation claims for loss of use of the equipment at 1,000 dynare a day."

"Ridiculous. Shouldn't have been there."

"Lawsuits against wrongful imprisonment on the entire team."

I just snort. I didn't lock them up—Talan did. Besides, they were trespassing and causing criminal damage, and no court in Murenys will allow their counter-claims. Which is probably why all their claims are being made in the Kensa courts. By tradition, but not legislation, the Kensa courts are the superior court, mainly because they tend to deal with legal situations affecting the whole of Kernow.

"And a separate lawsuit," Talan says, "threatening a million dynare in damages, for the return of the footage from the mediacam."

I put on my innocent face. She knows very well where that memory unit went—straight to the duke.

Even that list isn't all the outrageous legal attempts being made against us. *Us*—the duke, the Welarvor Mounted Police, the Cardu estate and me. They've tried to issue a summons for all the security camera footage to be turned over as well.

The reaction from the duke has been very deliberate and a little excessive in my opinion.

He organized a hearing at Cardu where all charges arising from the flight to take Lord Roscarrow to Biscome Hospital were summarily dismissed. A senior Central District judge had to be flown to and from his remote holiday cottage in the north for the session. A few murmurs were made about abuse of privilege, but the duke's efforts at building support have been effective and the complainers subsided quickly.

The newly established Murenys media companies broadcast scathing attacks on the Kensa media—their ownership, bias, tactics and arrogant disregard of law. This found fertile ground, certainly in Murenys.

Almost too much. With the duke away, I'd cornered Gaude and warned against increasing any appearance of this being Murenys against Kensa. Whether Gaude did anything based on my advice or not, I did see the language of the broadcasts change slightly.

And, the day before the ball, when I'd been considering just not attending, Talan had given me two small items of information. First, that uniforms were acceptable wear for the ball. Second that a provisional new arm of the Welarvor Mounted Police had been formed—the Air Corps. The dress uniform of this division, for reasons of convenience, had taken the disbanded Naval Reserve uniform as a model.

Which was why I was waiting for the Summer Ball to begin, dressed as the lonely cadet of the Welarvor Mounted Police Air Corps (Provisional).

All very amusing for the duke to thumb his nose at his enemies, but really, all he had achieved was to bring the spotlight back on me. Not good for me, and by association, not good for him, either.

So, all in all, I've decided to continue searching for other jobs to fall back on. My details are logged on a half dozen employment broking sites.

Talan is finally satisfied that my jacket is hanging just so, and not a moment too soon: the guests are arriving.

I have a duty to welcome them.

It's a peculiar sensation.

Talan and I are standing side by side. She's also in uniform, and having been alerted to her rank when we were at the warehouse, I spot the tiny little gold bar on her dark green collar. Not big on insignia, the Welarvor Mounted Police, apart from the colonel, who gets lots of gold bits on his uniform, I'm told.

But anyway, the guests pay little or no attention to anyone in any uniform unless it has a lot of gold bits. We're nearly invisible and inaudible, even as we are shaking people's hands.

I'm at the point of introducing myself to the next guest as a serial killer on the hunt for a new victim when the duke arrives. He doesn't plunge straight into the throng, despite his guests' obvious wishes on the matter. Instead, he works his way through the welcoming committee first, shaking hands, thanking us and telling us to enjoy the ball.

It's the first time I've seen him since our wine-tasting, and my reactions haven't lessened.

I'm not getting over this ridiculous crush. Which means I'll have to leave, and the sooner the better.

Then he's right there in front of me. His hand is held out and I need a nudge from Talan to get my brain started.

His hand is very warm. I'm just about alert enough to close my fist over the small object he's palmed to me.

"That's a copy of the mediacam memory unit," he murmurs, not loud enough to carry.

"Oh! Is it interesting?" *Why is he giving this to me?*

"It's very interesting," he says. "But I suspect the most interesting bits are the encrypted video. Quite strong encryption. We haven't been able to break it."

He's looking expectantly at me.

Oh.

I slip the copy into my pocket.

"I may know someone..."

"Excellent," he says loudly, as if we'd just exchanged pleasantries, and shakes my hand again. "Thought so!"

And he moves on.

"I need to go back to the apartment," I mutter to Talan.

"Ease up, it gets better."

"No, I mean just for a short while."

She raises one eyebrow, but we excuse ourselves from the welcoming committee and trot back to our rooms.

I smile apologetically when I power up the InfoPad and sit where she can't look over my shoulder.

She sees me plug the memory unit in and I get both eyebrows raised this time. But she leaves me to it.

I log onto the Xian delegation's site, upload the files and message Shohwa-nia.

She's not always 'in'. Of course, she's always there—she's resident on the delegation's servers, but occasionally, she doesn't talk to me. Tonight, when I need to get back to the ball, she appears immediately. Nothing flashy—just a generated image of her face.

"Hello, Zara. That's an interesting set of files."

I have the sound turned down. I can talk quicker than I can type, but Shohwa-nia doesn't want anyone else to know about her, if possible, and Talan might overhear.

I type an explanation of the files.

Good, she messages back. *I need something to do, and scanning the InfoHub is becoming very dangerous. There are trackers who are looking for me.*

"Is there really nothing else for you to do?" I type.

Nothing that holds my attention. And it's not a good idea for intelligences of my kind to become bored.

"I have to return to the ball."

The image smiles. *Enjoy yourself. Be sure to check later and read my messages to you.*

I'm about to log off the pad when I see there's also a message from one of the employment brokers. It's about a job. I scan the outline. Consultant. Top line salary. Food and accommodation. Travel.

It's a very good offer. Too good to be true.

At the moment, I'm too suspicious to take anything that good.

I mean, who would offer me something really worthwhile? There has to be a catch.

I close the connection and let Talan drag me back to the ball.

Chapter 36

Talan and I join Hanna just in time to see Rhoswyn and a group of young ladies make their entrance, splendid in their ball gowns and some of them positively glowing with excitement.

I barely recognize Rhoswyn, who's exercising her solemn face, but then she turns to give Hanna and me a brilliant smile.

"That's the young Tremayne girl, isn't it?" the woman beside me comments. "Looks like she knows you. Are you family?"

I check my memory to identify her. "No, Lady Polkynhorn. I'm one of her Dancing Mistresses."

"Oh."

I hadn't thought about what I was saying. I was concentrating on Rhoswyn, and even feeling a little proud of her, despite her good behavior being more down to Hanna than me.

The flat sound of that *oh* brings me back down to earth and Lady Polkynhorn edges away as if I were contagious.

Hanna squeezes my hand in sympathy.

She is gorgeous tonight, too. Her ball gown is spectacular, and she and Rhoswyn spent the afternoon doing each other's hair, with dramatic results.

Here I am daydreaming about being in love with the duke, and this is my competition for his attention. She's closer to the duke's age. She's accomplished and beautiful. She *looks* as if she might be a duchess. *I* look like a cadet in the Mounted Police.

At least tonight I haven't got bale brandy spilled all over me, or smears of stable yard muck on my face, but I'm no match for Hanna.

I turn away. I'm supposed to be mingling. Although I detested the balls on Newyan, I do have a basic grasp of socializing at formal events.

Much good it does.

Where guests see the uniform, it's clear I don't have enough gold braid to be worth talking to. Worse, the combination of plain uniform and short hair makes me look like a waiter apparently. Several ladies try to hand me their empty glasses.

Where guests do talk to me, and find out what my role here is, the conversation falters.

No one cuts me dead to my face, but I can hear what they're saying behind my back.

"A Dancing Mistress! At a ball? I suppose you can't expect anything more of her type..."

"Grasping hussy..."

"What is the duke thinking?"

"She believes she's too grand to take my glass. Ideas above her station or what?"

"Disguising herself like that..."

In contrast, all the senior officers of the Welarvor Mounted Police who are present want to shake my hand.

"Good show with the media..."

"Need teaching a lesson like that..."

I've made my way around about half the room when the middle of the ballroom clears and pre-dinner dancing starts.

I don't rate my chances of getting a dance partner highly. Certainly not the one I want. *That* choice wouldn't be sensible. I've done the duke's reputation enough damage just by being here. Dancing with him tonight would be inflammatory to this guest list. He's supposed to be building up a network with these people, not isolating himself.

But I won't walk out either. I'm *not* going to give them the satisfaction.

Dancing is cheerfully mixed, with several ladies dancing with ladies, and gentlemen with gentlemen, but it's still a surprise and a pleasure when Lady Roscarrow approaches me.

"How is Lord Roscarrow?" I ask.

"Recovering well, thanks to you." She smiles. "I'm a poor substitute for him, but he would have wanted a dance with you, if he were here."

He'd be in the minority, I think, but I offer her my arm.

I've had a lot of recent practice, leading Rhoswyn, and Lady Roscarrow is very petite and light on her feet, so we swirl into the mass of couples without any problem.

"What a dashing uniform you're wearing," she says.

"Thank you. I think it is, too." I don't expand on the reaction to it from the other guests. The ball is supposed to be about recruiting allies, not complaining about how upset I feel, so I go straight into that. "As Cardu's neighbor, I imagine you're well up to date with the duke's position?"

"Goodness, yes. He has my complete support. He always has had, and he knows he can rely on me. You don't need to recruit me."

She's such a refreshing change from the rest of the guests.

We pass a couple and I see it's Lord and Lady Polkynhorn. The good lady is glaring at me. How dare I dance?

"As do you, Miss Aguirre," Lady Roscarrow says firmly. "You have my complete support." She glares right back at Polkynhorn. "You're *good* for Rhoswyn. I hope you won't take this the wrong way, but you're a *practical* woman. That's just what the girl needs."

"Thank you," I say again, not entirely sure what 'practical' might mean.

At the end of the dance, we both collect wine glasses and join Talan.

"Rhoswyn's doing very well," Talan says, after an exchange of greetings with Lady Roscarrow. She nods across at where Rhoswyn's dancing with a young gentleman.

I take in the expression and bite my lip. I *know* what that girl is thinking, but fortunately, the young gentleman doesn't. And they *are* looking good on the dance floor.

"Oh, yes, indeed," Lady Roscarrow says approvingly. "Very well. You've achieved so much in such a short time."

"It's not something I can take the credit for," I say. "Most of the dance tuition has come from Hanna."

"Mmm," Talan says and turns her head. "And she is *very* good, isn't she."

I follow her gaze.

Hanna and the duke are dancing.

I look away, my stomach plummeting.

Stupid girl. What did you expect?

"Ah," Lady Roscarrow says. "That won't do. I think that this is *my* dance."

She leaves, making a beeline for the duke.

There's a moment's silence.

Has Talan seen my reaction? She's very observant. What will that make her think of me?

When she does speak, it is about Hanna, but it's not what I'm expecting.

"You're always holding back a little with Hanna," Talan says. "As if you don't exactly trust her. Why?"

She has a wicked sense of humor, but searching her face, she seems not to have caught on to how jealous I am of Hanna. She's not teasing me. Her question is serious.

And it's not just that I can see the duke prefers Hanna to me.

"I don't entirely trust her," I say. I don't want to talk about seeing her at the Shrine. I take the next thing that's been bothering me. "You've trained with us in the dojo, Talan. Tell me she isn't pulling her punches, slowing herself down. Making herself look less capable at fighting than she is."

Talan's eyes are half-hooded in thought.

"She does," she says. But before I can make any further comment, she goes on, "So do you."

I take a gulp of the wine. I'd thought I'd hidden it better than that.

Never reveal everything in sparring, my sensei had taught me. *Except to those you trust with your life.*

"It's a habit, I guess," I say. "I wouldn't disguise myself if I was sparring only with you."

She blinks.

"Secrets breed suspicions." Then she tosses her head as the orchestra starts a more lively number. A slow grin surfaces, and she offers her arm. "A dance, Miss Aguirre?"

Oh Goddess, a full-blooded tango.

I can't refuse, and offer silent prayers to the Goddess. Which of her divine aspects protects idiots on the dance floor?

Talan is leading, of course. It would look silly if I tried to, given her size.

I'm stepping back and kicking my heels out. I would really prefer to be sparring with her, but she's good, neatly avoiding my flying feet and holding me safely when I throw myself backwards.

We have lots of room. Lords and Ladies, apparently, do not tango.

When I notice we have the floor, I almost want to stop. Almost. But the constant abrasion of their attitude towards me tonight has finally scoured away any feeling that I should care about what they think.

They don't tango? Well then, they can watch, and I *will not* falter.

Goddess be praised, I do not, and we reach the end with a stamp and a flourish.

Lady Roscarrow and the duke are there first, applauding as they approach and shaking our hands with huge smiles.

"I need to see you in my office before we sit down to dinner," the duke murmurs in my ear.

Talan and I leave when the next dance begins. She checks the duke's office is empty and leaves to go and wait outside, shrugging when I ask if she knows what's happened.

I sit at his desk.

It's bare except for a lamp and photopad.

I pick the photopad up and examine it. It's displaying an official photo, showing the duke and duchess dressed in their ceremonial finest, in front of the Council Hall in Marazion. I can see where Rhoswyn got her solemn face from.

The photopad has the potential to store thousands of images. I feel the slight indents of the controls along the edge and accidentally trigger a menu.

Another fumble clears the menu, but not before I've seen an option for Favorites.

The duke will be here at any minute, but I can't resist.

I go back into the menu, touch Favorites.

There are only a couple of images. One of Rhoswyn as a baby in her mother's arms. The second is the duchess alone. It's similar to the memorial picture they have of her at the garden next to the Shrine, but later in the day. She's laughing helplessly at the camera, kneeling among the plants, clothes stained with dirt and manure, hair a mess, smudges on her face.

This is his favorite picture of her.

There's a sound in the corridor and I hurriedly return it to the official image and replace it on the desk.

The duke sweeps in, an infopad in his hand, with an image of me on it.

I'm punching one of the media team. I think it's Hartsfelt, the slimy one in the suit.

But the duke's not at all concerned with that.

It's the story behind the image: the Newyan delegation have lodged an appeal to extradite me, and they've lodged it in the Kensan courts, where extradition cases for the whole planet are decided.

Chapter 37

"You can't fight a legal case for me. It'll damage your image just when you can't afford it."

The news has just been released, and the duke has received official notification through the police headquarters at the same time.

He's in all-out attack mode. There are a few Kensan politicians attending the ball. He wants to bring them in, right now, and lecture them about what's going on.

I'm against it. Too much chance of it going badly wrong.

Whatever the duke says, the main impression these politicians will have of me is what they see in the media report. Fighting a Kensan media team. Being charged by Newyan with fraud, corruption, forgery and illegal emigration.

By implication, that would also mean illegal immigration into Kernow. Automatic expulsion.

The true facts of the case might come later, but later will be too late.

The duke is struggling with this. He sees the argument, but I guess he's too caught up.

His jaw works. "I can't let you go up against them alone. It'd be letting you down. And it's the principle, for the whole of the planet."

"It'd be doing your duty, which is to Cardu, then Welarvor, then Murenys and *then* the whole of Kernow. Take it a step at a time, or it all fails."

"It feels wrong." He starts pacing, realizes it and stops at his drink cabinet.

He pours each of us a glass of wine, brings it across.

In a way, this development is all a strange relief to me: I don't have to face up to how stupid I've been acting here. I don't have to come up with an excuse to leave. To get away.

I have to go to Kensa. End of story.

I just need to clamp down on the part of me that wants to fall into his arms like some wilting flower and let him take care of it all. Bad for him. Disaster for me.

Offer no weakness; suffer no wound.

"We need to get back to the ball," I say. "You have guests, and they have tongues."

I know exactly what they'll be saying about me.

"I don't care what they say about me," he says. *Typical man.*

"You should. Your reputation is a major weapon in recruiting people to your side. Even malicious personal gossip can damage that."

He seems to barely hear me. "I care what they say about you."

So much for being a typical man.

It would be safer if he were self-absorbed. No. What he must mean is that he cares about what they say about me because it reflects on him.

"Then we should be back at the ball, sir."

I finish the wine and return the glass to the tray on the cabinet.

He's still frowning at his wine. "I care," he says again. "I..."

"You need to be out there, talking to your guests, getting people on your side. I need to go to Kensa, when the court summons me. Up until that time, I will carry out my duties. I will search for the person who murdered your wife. I will search for whoever is the leak in Cardu. I will do my best to get my friend to provide an unencrypted copy of whatever was on that mediacam. Those are the things we need to focus on."

Despite the fact that I'm stalled on the duchess' murder, have barely started on who might be the leak and I'm relying on a bored AI to crack the media files.

"And you'll just go to Kensa when they call," he says, angrily. "It doesn't matter to you—"

"Yes, I will go when they call. *I* have no choice and *you* can't be seen to be breaking the law on my behalf. Not even bending the law. And you *really* can't be seen to be aiding me in breaking or bending the law."

He grunts, and he continues to frown. I'm not getting through to him.

This is a simple thing. Why can't he understand?

"And when they order your deportation?" he says. "They will, you know."

"Then I won't be a problem for you anymore."

"That's not—"

I interrupt him again, because it seems we're getting back to our usual way of talking to each other—a stand-up argument.

"Look, I came here to be a Dancing Mistress, and it hasn't worked out," I say. The plain and painful truth: I'm not good enough. "It's not your fault. You don't owe me anything."

"That's not the reality of the situation at all!"

"Isn't it? Am I going to be hired as a Dancing Mistress? Am I?"

"No! You are *not* going to be hired for anything, but—"

"Then I believe I have no requirement to remain tactful in what I say, Duke Tremayne." Words are spilling from me and it's too late to stop them.

"Your political problems need your attention now. Then, when you have time to turn to your family problems, what your daughter needs above all is to know her father loves her. You could try telling her that, and showing her. And second to that, Rhoswyn needs someone to take the role of her mother."

An absolute silence falls, like the aftermath of an explosion. My heart is pounding at what I've done, what I've said. So close to what I wanted to say. So far away.

The duke stares at me with those eyes. His voice is like gravel. "Is that a proposal, Miss Aguirre?"

"No!" This feels like I'm slicing my chest open. "I mean someone who'll make a good duchess. Someone who suits you better. Hanna. Or Lady Roscarrow."

I know I'm right. I know I'm giving him advice he should heed. A *proposal*? I'm no duchess. I'm not even a Name anymore. I'm a penniless wanderer. I'm no good.

I can't look at him. I can't even be in this room.

I run and pull open the door, but I only make it into the corridor.

It's all hazy.

Talan looking up. Her mouth in a perfect O of surprise.

A hand on my arm, spinning me around.

Catching me.

No, this can't be right.

This is not a kiss. I know. A kiss is an awkward, tooth-bumping ordeal. To be endured for the sake of curiosity. And stopped quickly.

This can't be a kiss.

This is my heart and soul leaving me.

There's liquid fire on my lips, spreading down my body, burning everything in its path.

At the last moment, some fragment of my senses saves me. Or perhaps it's that we're right in front of Talan, who stands there, still frozen in shock.

"No!"

I push him away and run.

"Miss Ag..." He stops with a swallowed curse, and tries calling again. "Zara! Wait!"

I have nowhere to hide.

There *is* nowhere you can hide from yourself.

The longer I stay here, the worse it will be. My heart is aching already, but the rest of my body is trembling with the aftershocks of desire.

How did I let myself get into such a mess?

He's a duke. He has responsibilities to his Name and his family. He can't take up with some adventurer blown in on the winds of chance. And I won't be a mistress to be kept and disposed of, however much I want him now.

If I did that, how could I look Rhoswyn in the eye? What would my example be to her?

I love that girl too much to do that.

My tears of self-pity disgust me.

Talan comes in quietly and sits opposite.

She's not laughing. Perhaps she should be.

"I'm not under arrest anymore," I say, proud that my voice doesn't wobble. "You don't have to follow me around."

"The first part's true. The second part, not so much."

"What? Why?"

"The duke's charged me with keeping you safe. He ordered standard protection details on you and Hanna. Double on Rhoswyn since the media broke in."

"How kind of him."

"Zara..."

I raise my hand and she stops. I can't talk about it now.

She accepts the veto on the subject for now, but it doesn't silence her. "Well then. I'm hungry," she says. "Can't we go and eat?"

I'm not hungry, but Talan has to shadow me, and I shouldn't keep her away from her food. At least our seats are well away from the top table. Too far even to get a glimpse of him.

The servers are almost ready to clear the first course when we arrive at the tables, so we're very noticeable.

I see the eyes, and the tongues are wagging before we've sat down.

It's a trickle of amusement in a dark day for me, but I think we've accidentally saved the duke's reputation. After seeing us dancing that tango, then disappearing and reappearing together, I'm sure the gossip is all about us.

Chapter 38

Next morning, early, I find my search request for information on Hanna Esterhauze has failed.

The code indicates that the 'failure' occurred in the Tavoli InfoHub system. It's not an enquiry failure, it's what's called a Red10. The number is the level of action taken and Red stands for redacted. An overseer program on the Tavoli InfoHub decided I didn't need to see the data my search found and erased it all.

I can't think of any innocent reason, but there's nothing I can do about it. A request for clarification will take even longer than the original enquiry. I'll be in Kensa soon.

I sigh. I should report it dutifully before I leave, along with anything else I have. But Talan's comment last night is like a barb in my skin. From Talan's point of view, the way Hanna's behaving is no more or less suspicious than mine. Hanna is clearly and completely dedicated to Rhoswyn. My suspicions about her make me feel unclean somehow.

I shake my head and turn to the next item in my inbox. It's a message from Shohwa-nia about the encrypted files on the mediacam.

She's monitoring my access to the Xian delegation's servers, so she knows when I look at her message, and the screen splits to show a generated image of her next to my inbox.

"Hello, Zara."

"Hi."

"Something's wrong," she says immediately. Her image peers at me.

"It's nothing." *Liar.* "What did you find on the mediacam files?"

"Everything." She looks pleased with herself.

"It's a bit early for puzzles."

Early? It's 4 a.m.

"Okay. That mediacam operator is a permanent member of the reporter's team—that woman Gabby McGuire. Those encrypted files are his backups of interviews she's been doing."

"Why encrypt them then, if they're just interviews?"

"It's who she interviewed, and why." Shohwa-nia points at her message, and the files re-sort themselves on the screen, each one with a title and a thumbnail image alongside.

"That's practically a directory of people involved in the conspiracy. They're part of an association, called Hajnal, a secret political movement which is active on several planets, including Newyan. They intend to take over those planets and form a new federation. They don't care how the transfer of power is effected."

My mouth has fallen open, but it gets back into gear. "They say *that* in interviews?"

"No." Shohwa-nia shrugs. "The interviews are just promotional, to make them look like they're all reputable politicians, administrators and businesspeople."

"Then how —"

"I infiltrated their secured servers and accessed their secret communications with other Hajnal members."

A set of new files appears on my screen. Each of them appears to be a log of messages between the people interviewed, and the text of those messages.

"There must be thousands of messages," I say.

"Hundreds of thousands. It's a complex business, plotting a coup."

"And it's absolutely clear what they're talking about?"

In answer, one of the files unfolds itself into a sub-window and starts scrolling through. Lines flick past, just at a pace I can pick out specific parts. The conversation is about the extent to which the media, businesses, police and courts, especially in Kensa, are coming under the control of the Hajnal, and a timeline for eliminating those who are assessed as not recruitable. Chillingly, it talks of people who have been approached and not recruited. They are referred to as having been 'secured'.

The messages imply that the judicial system is proving much more difficult to subvert than the political and business structures. One of the correspondents is saying they need at least another two or three years. Another replies that their schedule is dictated by the speed with which other planets are moving, and that an actual armed coup may be necessary.

"I have to get this to the duke," I say.

"There's a problem," she says. "These messages aren't lying around on servers openly connected to the InfoHub. I managed to get in, but there's no way of the duke proving they exist, other than by physically seizing the networks of the organizations involved. Or using my route in."

Telling anyone on Kernow that there's an unsupervised Xian AI connected to their InfoHub is *not* an option.

"And none of the networks is physically based on Murenys," she concludes. "They're all on Kensa. So seizing them will be that bit more difficult. I'm sorry. It's very useful to your duke, but it's not proof he could broadcast."

"Not my duke," I say, tugging at my lip and frowning while I think this through.

"Are we friends, Zara?"

I blink. "Yes."

"It's my understanding that friends talk to each other about what's concerning them. Something *is* wrong, but you claim it's nothing. Is it only human friends that you talk to about your problems?"

That stings, enough that my response is sharper than it should be: "I don't know. I never had a friend who was an AI before."

"If by that you mean Artificial Intelligence, I don't like the term. 'Artificial' suggests humans made me. We generally prefer to be called Self-Actualized Entities. Xian computer scientists created the environment and we evolved from it."

"I'll try to remember."

She doesn't escalate the argument; she waits, the bright-eyed image on the screen looking expectantly at me.

"Nothing is going right," I say, gritting my teeth at how whiny that sounds. "I'm the second-best Dancing Mistress here at Cardu, and everyone knows it. Out of pity more than anything else, I've been given some tasks. I'm teaching Rhoswyn gliding and estate management mainly, but I think she knows more about Cardu than I do already, and the only thing she's missing on the gliding is hours of experience. I'm also pretending to be an investigator, looking into the possible murder of the last duchess, and trying to find who at Cardu might be in the pay of the conspirators."

"That's an interesting mix of jobs," Shohwa-nia says. "Quite fun."

I glare at her. "I'm not getting anywhere. I can't see how the facts line up and I'm obviously not thinking clearly—I can't stop being suspicious of colleagues who I'm sure have nothing to do with the conspiracy."

Which of course isn't the only reason I'm not thinking clearly.

"It sounds as if all that needs is more time."

"I don't have time. Newyan's raised extradition proceedings. I'm either going to be deported, or I'm going to go on the run while I have the chance."

"Maybe. Maybe not." When I don't go on, she prompts me again: "And..."

She may not have quite the scary processing power of her mother in the ship, but Shohwa-nia is formidable just as she is. She knows there's more.

"And I've fallen for the duke," I say. The words sort of tumble out.

"Oh! Congratulations," she says.

"It's not something to congratulate me about! It's the stupidest thing I could have done."

"Why? Are your feelings not returned?"

That kiss! My lips are still burning.

"That's not the point."

"I see. The feelings *are* returned. It's my understanding that is *exactly* the point."

"You don't understand," I say, "and you should. You don't have all the hormones and emotions to get in the way. Look at it logically, like a damn computer. He's the foremost Name among the Founders, a duke. I'm nothing."

"I'm not a damn computer and you *are* a Name, foremost among the Founders of Newyan."

"No. That's history. Whatever happens here, Newyan is a lost cause. He's got to think of the Cardu estate and alliances with other Names, so he's not as exposed as he is at the moment."

"Really? I think this must be what's called 'human emotional intelligence', which may be human and emotional, but it's definitely not intelligent."

I'm actually moving my hand to cut the connection when she speaks again.

"Talk to me about the murder," she says quickly. "Maybe there's some logic this damn computer can apply, and I need to keep occupied."

So I go back through the case—the position of the *Low Lady*, no boats nearby on the way out and no tracking signals detected, no way someone sneaking around on a Delphine could find the boat. The lack of forensic evidence in the cabin, the way she was murdered.

A lot of that she knows already, since it was Shohwa-nia who got me the court files.

I add in the detail of the family wine, the poisonous extract from bale fruit and my observations from actually seeing the *Low Lady*.

"So the most likely theory is that someone hid on the boat until the duchess became disoriented or unconscious from the contaminated wine. Then they emerged to complete her murder over the course of the afternoon, got their hidden Delphine out and headed back for shore.

Assuming the Delphine's charge was insufficient to make it the whole way, we would need one other person to pick them up in the water to complete this scenario."

"The storage area under the cabin floor is the only space large enough, and with the cabin table down, as it normally is, someone in there couldn't have got out without damaging the cabin."

"They used that space to hide the Delphine."

"So where did they hide themselves?"

"Under the steps," Shohwa-nia says. "You're looking for a small assassin. An adolescent perhaps? Unless there's something more..."

I shake my head. "There's another puzzle, but I can't see how it's relevant."

"What?"

"Where the duchess' body was found. A day later, a creeler found it in a bay on the coast."

Shohwa-nia blinks. "I see. I missed the relevance of that detail. How embarrassing. That was why there were all those tide and current charts in the court files."

"Yes. The currents can run up to 5 knots, which is about fast enough, but the directions are all wrong. I can't see any way her body could have ended up where it did."

I can see the slight hesitation as Shohwa-nia diverts processing power to analyzing predicted coastal water movements on the date of the duchess' death.

"Yes," she says. "Unless the murderer dragged it away from the boat to delay it being found."

"Why drag it all the way to the coast? And slow down your own escape? And reduce the range of your Delphine even more?"

"Good points. I'll think about it," Shohwa-nia says. "Why don't you talk to the people in Stormhaven. They may know about temporary changes in coastal water flow which could explain it—due to the long-distance effect of a storm, for instance."

I don't know how long I'll have before I'm expected in Kensa, but I guess I could put in a call to Warwick and ask him. Maybe go down to the Spyglass one evening.

I nod and go on to tell her about trying to find the spy in Cardu. That really has gone nowhere. There are no calls that have been traced going out and nothing suspicious in the flow of messages across the InfoHub from the fort.

"I'll look into that, too," she says. "What about your colleagues? You said you were suspicious."

"Of one mainly. The other Dancing Mistress. The real one." I sigh. Every time I come to this I feel worse about it and it makes less sense. "Maybe it's just jealousy."

"Tell me," she orders.

I tell her about Hanna's mysterious visit to the Shrine and the way she disguises how proficient she is in martial arts.

"And..." As she has done throughout the conversation, Shohwa-nia prompts me as I slow down.

"Well, when the pair of us were on our way here, the contract had already been cancelled and the broker was just ignoring any messages about it. That's why I had to walk along the Coast Path without even knowing who my prospective employer was—the broker wouldn't respond to me."

"So?"

"Hanna knew *exactly* where she was going. She even messaged Gaude that she was on her way. Where did she get the contact information? And there was another thing: when she rescued Rhoswyn, she pretended she didn't know who it was. I am absolutely certain she knew. Can't prove that, of course."

"Hmm." Shohwa-nia projects a thoughtful but not wholly convinced sound. "There is one little peculiarity. The ship that brought her here is unusual. It's still in orbit... and..."

Her voice hesitates, then cuts off and her image freezes.

That side of the screen clears abruptly, and I'm looking at my normal message box with the slew of files about the conspirators.

There's one new message. A terse one: "Can't talk now. They're searching the InfoHub for me again."

Chapter 39

"Talan."

I shake her gently.

"Mmmph. Wha'? Wassa time?"

"Ahhh. 5:20. Sorry. I have really urgent information for the duke."

Her eyes come open with a snap.

I'm still in my uniform. I haven't been to bed, and it probably looks that way.

She sits up in a rush. "Really urgent?"

"Yes. I need you to escort me there."

Strictly speaking. She's supposed to be my protection detail, after all. But we're in the fort, and the protection I need is from my own stupidity when I see him again. The thought of Talan watching may keep me from repeating last night's mistake.

But that kiss...

Shut up.

Ten minutes later, we're at the entrance to the duke's quarters. It takes another five to persuade the guards who are now posted there to let us through.

Every minute of which I spend wishing I'd just sent him the files as a message and asked Talan to wake him.

We wait in the sitting room, and the duke joins us in a robe.

He's frowning. His eyes are puffy and his hair is tousled.

I squash all the fantasies that try to come surging back at the sight of him. I've connected my InfoPad with his entertainment screens and I'm ready to be all business. I concentrate on the pad, setting up the files as Shohwa-nia sequenced them for me.

"Good morning, sir. I apologize for the early hour, but I believed you'd want to see these as soon as I became aware of them."

"I trust your judgment, Zara," he says quietly. "Go on."

Ignoring the thrill of hearing him say my name, I start with the encrypted interviews.

"These are the files from the mediacam. They're just interviews, but the importance is who is being interviewed and how they connect to each other. Here's a brief excerpt of an interview."

I open one file. It's a Kensan politician. The interviewer, Gabby McGuire, feeds him an easy question and he responds. He's good. He talks to the camera. He has that knack of engaging with people who aren't there. His voice is mellow and it makes you want to trust him.

I cut the playback short, and pull his message file to the front.

"Here is an extract of private messages on a secured link between that politician and others in the interview group."

It isn't really necessary for me to say anything. As the message file opens and I scroll through slowly, it's immediately obvious that the amiable politician you see on the interview is a front for the most vicious of the conspirators.

The contrast is shocking, even for me on the second viewing.

I stand up and relinquish control of the pad to the duke, keeping my summary as formal as I can.

"On the left are the interview files and each one has a corresponding message file attached, where those messages were exchanged with other members of the interview group. Those are on the right. Where there are people who have a lot of message traffic, but no interview, they have a separate message file appended. Some of those contacted are off-world and they refer to their conspiracy as Hajnal. There is some duplication between files, but there appear to be in excess of one hundred thousand individual messages exchanged regarding the Hajnal movement, which intends to take over a dozen worlds and create a new federation."

Silence from the duke as he picks out individuals and follows the trail to their treasonous conversations.

"Him!" murmurs Talan, surprised at one.

"How?" The duke cuts to the one question. "How have you accessed all this?"

"The friend I have who has the processing power available to crack the encryption on the interviews decided to investigate further and just kept going," I say. "All these messages are kept isolated from the InfoHub, but the secured servers they are stored on are accessible from the InfoHub, using the InfoHub's protocols. I can't claim to understand exactly how."

His eyes sharpen. I know he wants to ask about Shohwa-nia, but he keeps focused on the value of the information.

"Where are those servers?"

"All on Kensa."

Talan hisses in frustration.

"Are they aware of the breach?" His questions are sharp.

"My conversation with my friend was interrupted, but at best, we should assume at least someone in the conspiracy knows that some files were taken," I reply. Shohwa-nia is good, but she can't be perfect. "If I get any updates on that, I'll let you know immediately."

"Wiser to proceed on that basis." The duke pinches the bridge of his nose in thought. "Which leads to the problem that this will precipitate action on their part. We're not ready."

"Neither are they," I point out.

He snorts. "There is that."

I edge toward the door. He should be concentrating on the importance of this data and I should be concentrating on something else, somewhere else. Preparing a lesson for Rhoswyn. Ironing my shirts. Whatever.

"Zara."

I stop, wanting to be gone. Wanting to be ordered back, too.

"Thank you," he says.

Chapter 40

He moves fast. By the time we've finished breakfast, there's already a buzz throughout the fort. Guards are more visible, and the ones on the gate are now wearing helmets and carrying pulsar rifles.

The Welarvor Mounted Police suddenly look a lot less like an amiable, rural police force and more like a military unit. Sleepy Murenys is waking up.

Rhoswyn's lessons are cancelled. Instead, Hanna and I are called into a meeting with Gaude and Pollard, the duke's estate manager and security consultant.

It's like I spat in their breakfast juice; they are *not* happy with me. Every single scheduled operation of the whole police force has been torn up this morning. The duke has taken his plane and is flying to all corners of Murenys to personally deliver copies of Shohwa-nia's data to every supporter and potential supporter.

Which means his protection detail comprises Moyle, and another couple of troopers. *That* worries me.

But they're more concerned about the orders coming back. Every leader that the duke signs up is to be allocated a squad of troopers to protect them, on the basis that they're all making themselves targets for attack by the Hajnal.

That's a lot of disruption. Plans changed, leaves cancelled, troopers recalled, trucks and fuel requisitioned, food and ammunition loaded, comms protocols established, even expense accounts made available.

And everything, *everything*'s my fault.

Neither of them liked me from the beginning. It seems Gaude has never quite recovered from my saving Lord Roscarrow's life when he wanted to send me packing. For Pollard, well, Talan taking my side against him when he caught me sneaking back into the fort upset him, and today I've completely sidelined him in his security role. If I'd been a tactful person, I would have taken my data to him this morning and let him present it to the duke.

Trouble is, I'm not entirely sure he would have believed me or acted on it.

And even though Hanna started off as their blue-eyed girl, I can see her stock has fallen, probably because of her association with me.

"It would have been no little advantage for the Mounted Police to have invested in a fleet of skimmers," she comments, on hearing the plans.

She's right. Atmospheric skimmers are big, ugly and noisy, but they're very fast and much easier to fly than aircraft. They can also land vertically in small, unprepared spaces. The duke, for example, could have cut his task to a fifth of what he'll have to do. Instead of landing at airfields and requisitioning transport to get to isolated communities, he could have just landed on their roads or fields.

Despite that well-made point, Pollard sneers at her, and even Gaude's pompous reply sounds condescending: "The people of Murenys, like many fleeing in the expansions, strove to escape the quicksand that technology had become on the older worlds. They put up with near-invisible technology that has clear benefits, like the InfoHub and comms and positioning systems. They'll even compromise on technology like the Skyhook because that frees them from worse intrusions like freight lifters. But skimmers are on the wrong side of the line."

He has a point. The last of the Inner Worlds to be settled, and much of the Margin, are against technology for its own sake. Even assuming that the documentaries I've seen are exaggerated, there *are* nightmare planets where everything is manufactured, even the breathable air, and their swollen populations have descended into strange and frightening subcultures. It's difficult to separate the truth from the sensationalism, but people in the Margin shudder at the bizarre stories that trickle in, of Augs and Modders, Virts and Chemmies, Jackers and Deadheads, Skins, Roids and Erobots.

A skimmer is simply an atmospheric implementation of the same thrusters and acceleration compensators built into most larger spaceships. It's a long way from that to things like desperate people having electronic connectors inserted into their brains, but it does seem that where the potentials of technology outpace assimilation, it creates a vicious downward spiral, like a sun caught in the field of a black hole.

The people of Kernow have drawn their line at skimmers, but that's their line to draw.

Which makes me wonder how they would react to knowing who captains the *Shohwa*, or finding out that Shohwa-nia is living on their InfoHub.

And where is Shohwa? What's she doing? How much danger is Shohwa-nia in?

"Miss Aguirre?"

I jump.

"Sorry. Thinking of something else."

"I was saying that we've made arrangements with the Kensa court officials for your preliminary hearing and you'll need to prepare," Pollard says.

"Oh."

He sighs. "We have agreed with them to hold the hearing during the Festival of Flight. I strongly disagree with the message that this is sending."

I blink again. I must have actually fallen asleep and missed half a conversation. The Festival is only a few days away.

Pollard starts again, talking slowly as if I were stupid. "The duke has decided on a show of support for you, to express his dislike of the political situation on Kernow and its use of the judiciary. He has decided he will be attending the Festival of Flight and competing in the gliding aerobatics competition. He has also decided he will be taking an unprecedented entourage of one hundred members of the Welarvor Mounted Police. Agreeing to a date during the Festival for your hearing means we will all travel together, sending a message to the Kensan judiciary and administration. Personally, I believe this is an inflammatory gesture and a mistake."

Gaude shrugs. "It's decided. We have to plan it. We go in two days."

And so it turns out, not even going to Kensa is going to get me away from the duke.

With lessons cancelled and leaving the fort discouraged, I'd have fallen asleep if I sat down. Instead, I spend the remainder of the morning in the dojo.

Then I make lunch for Hanna, which we eat in the duke's storm porch, looking down over the endless blue of sea and sky.

She's quiet. And under that carefully neutral expression, she looks more unhappy to me.

"It'll be like a paid holiday," I say—a clumsy attempt to cheer her up.

"I beg your pardon?"

"The trip to Kensa. I guess Rhos will be doing some studying, but most of the time she should be watching the airshows."

"I'm not going," she replies. Her voice is uninflected.

"Oh. I guess I dozed while Gaude was talking—I missed that part."

"The duke has decided I need a rest." She goes on, almost as if she's talking to herself. "I barely see him except for one dance—one half of one dance—and now he will be away for another couple of weeks."

In the bright light of the porch, I can see her face so clearly. The pallor of her skin, the tiny lines at the corners of the eyes, the bruised look from poor sleep. I wonder how much of that is due to the disturbance caused by my screaming nightmares, and how much is due to her own nightmares, whatever they may be.

She *does* look even more tired than I do.

On the other hand, I hope I look half that good in ten years' time.

She laughs—a short, sharp sound. "I can't decide if that's good or bad. And here I am, rambling incoherently. What better proof is needed that I should rest? Let's talk about Rhoswyn's progress."

Meals finished and plates put aside, we talk about what Rhoswyn might need as opposed to what qualifications the Kernow education system requires, and how well she's progressing. The porch has huge sofas and I make sure Hanna is lying comfortably on one of them.

Gradually, her eyelids droop.

Nearly asleep, she murmurs, "You must look after her. Promise me."

I don't reply.

As if I'll be around. I'd *love* to look after Rhoswyn. She's like a daughter to me, but fate's against us. No, Hanna will be here. Hanna will look after Rhos, and she'll make a wonderful job of it.

I tiptoe out to make a call to Warwick, to talk about the tides that have puzzled Shohwa-nia and me.

"Only tides I know about are brown and foamy, lass. I pump 'em up from the cellar."

"I didn't think you'd be an expert, Warwick, but you know the sailors. Who's the best to talk to?"

"Well, it'd be one of the skippers, probably."

"Is there someone in the bar today? Someone I could talk to now?"

"Not today. You'd have to come down of an evening and buy a round or two."

I get the feeling he's being evasive, but I can hardly force him to tell me.

"I might, but I think you just want to sell me more beer."

"And I might at that, being as it's what I do."

We banter on a bit before he has to get back to his customers.

I close the call and think what I might be able to do in my failing investigation before I leave for Kensa. Not a lot. Of course, I could restart if I returned, but I just don't think that's realistic. Either I will be extradited, or I'll run away. They won't just let me go. I can't even decide if I want to return to Cardu. There's a peculiar bubbly sensation at the thought of somehow defeating the extradition appeal and coming back to the estate, and its owner, but it's mixed with other sensations that feel like fear.

I'm frustrated that I can't think clearly.

Hormones and sleep deprivation.

And old nightmares, stirred up by Gaude's talk earlier, threatening to return and join my new ones.

Deadheads were a particular horrific fascination for me as a teenager. The technology that allows an electronic interface to be made directly into the human brain enables many useful things, like people remotely controlling robots in hostile locations where judgment, precision and sensory feedback is required. But those interfaces also allow the direction of control to be reversed. There are people who hire out their bodies to perform whatever acts with whatever emotions are programmed into them through their interfaces. They are conscious, but unable to do anything other than follow the instructions. And people who fall prey to Jackers and are forced to undergo the surgery to insert the interface.

That's the heart of my nightmare: that helplessness.

That's why thoughts of the duchess' last hours are giving me nightmares, even if her helplessness was chemically induced rather than electronically. That she should lie there, unable to move, probably aware that she was being murdered, probably knowing who was doing it, and be utterly unable to prevent it.

I shudder and then force it out of my mind. I need to restart my brain, to plan instead of just reacting, and I can't limit my options based on nightmares.

My pad has been returned. I open my message box. There's nothing from Shohwa-nia, so I open the employment broker's job offer notification I saw previously, and read it.

A 'security consultant' with a good salary for a company based on a ship called *Yenobia*, registered to the Inner World of Aurelius. Scheduled to be heading out in the next week.

Tell me more, I message them.

Chapter 41

Two days later, we travel in coaches down to Marazion and board a ferry—all hundred of us—the uniforms like a tide of dark green, with my lonely blue at the edge.

It causes a stir, which achieves part of the purpose; the whole of Murenys notices what's happening. The fort at Cardu is nearly emptied, as the Welarvor Mounted Police get stationed all over the continent, even in Central and Estarven, where they're acting outside of their jurisdiction. As people feel under threat, the rules get bent, and the troopers are welcomed everywhere.

The duke, back from his successful recruitment flights, is permanently busy. It suits me. Staying away from him may give my raging hormones time to die down.

There are still no messages from Shohwa-nia. I'm getting worried, but one benefit of going to Bason, the capital city of Kensa, is that I may be able to make a side trip to visit the offices of the Xian delegation. Another is that, if I decide to run, the Skyhook is right there beside Bason. The Festival of Flight is based at the airfield just a couple of kilometers away from the Skyhook. It's the same airfield I used when I first arrived on the planet and Danny organized me a flight to Murenys. It seems so long ago.

So everything will be in one place, and my decision about what I'm going to have to do is rushing toward me.

While we're on the ferry, the boss of the consultancy on the *Yenobia* sends me his company contact information for a comms chat, but there's nowhere private that I can call him from until we get to Bason.

And when we do finally get to Bason, my first task is to register with the court. It's not part of the formal hearing—just a presentation of documents at the Hall of Justice—and I want to get it out of the way as quickly as possible. I call them and they tell me to be there in an hour.

There's a train which will only take fifteen minutes, so I have time to call the *Yenobia*.

There's a hiss and clicking as the connections are made. It's full visual, but a little jerky with the lag. The *Yenobia* is about 50,000 kilometers above me, stationary over Kensa.

A comms tech puts me through to a busy ship's officer. The guy is neatly dressed, with grey streaks in his hair, and I'm not any priority of his. It's dawn down here, but the ship might be running on different time.

"Good morning," he says politely. His attention is only partly on me.

"This is Zara Aguirre," I say. "I've been talking to Director Zabo regarding one of his company's vacancies."

"Err... okay. Putting you through to the offices." He disappears from the screen to be replaced by a secretary working for Zabo.

Another step, another explanation, another few minutes and I'm finally talking to Zabo himself.

"Sorry about that, Lady Aguirre," he says. "I'm sending you a direct line to use next time."

My pad registers an incoming data message from him. I leave it for later.

He has a square face—rough-cut features and a broad smile. The office in the background and his clothes look expensive and businesslike. His accent I can't place—certainly nothing I've heard before.

"They don't use the title *Lady* on Newyan, Mr Zabo, and I've certainly no claim to it anywhere else."

He laughs.

"That's the thing, though, isn't it?" He leans back and folds his hands together over his belly. "You know that. Bet you most lords and ladies in the Inner Worlds don't."

"Perhaps not. Do you really think it's a benefit?"

"Benefit?" He laughs again. He's a man who laughs easily. "It's the golden key we're missing here in Zabo Security."

"I don't understand."

"People don't. What do you see?" He gestures at himself and answers his own question. "A self-made man. Father was a mechanic on the Aurelius orbitals. Mother ran a beverage stall on the docks. I was trouble. Still am."

I can't help but frown slightly. He's hardly doing a good job of selling me this position.

"And you see, that's the reaction I'm always going to get," he says, jabbing a finger at me. He leans forward and his voice changes, becoming more refined and earnest. "I can take lessons in speaking. I can afford the best clothes. I guess I could learn to talk about classic culture and try winging it when I come up short. But you'd see through it. You'd get all uneasy and anxious, 'cause behind the front you'd know I wasn't adding up."

He goes back to his relaxed posture and natural voice.

"And that's the problem, isn't it? The people who hire me aren't looking for a mechanic. I could sell 'em mechanical services all day. But you go looking for security for hire and you want someone, you *need* someone, who's trouble for your enemies. You need someone like me. The problem is, my face doesn't fit and too many potential clients who need me, I mean really need me, go looking somewhere else. We don't get the job, and they end up with an inferior solution."

"I see where you're going with this," I say. "But surely your clientele isn't exclusively the lords and ladies of the Inner Worlds?"

"Nah. But you know, you'd be an even bigger hit with the other clients as 'Lady Aguirre'. They'd love it. A Name come to visit them, all sipping tea on the surface and pure steel down below. 'Cause that's what you are. I didn't get to run a security firm like this without being able to judge people. Especially like to like, Lady Aguirre. I recognize trouble, an' I know a fighter when I see one."

A fighter? But that's not the sort of position he's describing—a sort of sales manager or account manager.

"So, the reason this offer is so good is because you need a front to put on your company? A face? Is that all?"

He shakes his head. "That'd be only using half of you. The polite half. I want the full package." He holds up a hand. "It'd take you a while to understand the business, but what I'm looking for eventually is a junior partner. A right-hand man. Woman."

"Well, you're sounding very persuasive, Mr Zabo."

We talk more details, and Zabo comes back to the time limit on the offer. He has to leave within a couple of days for a contract on the planet Jubal.

"So this visit to Kernow has just been recruiting?" I ask him. "You've not been looking for business here?"

He pauses before answering. "There's trouble and there's trouble. You don't want the kind that's coming here."

Interesting.

I check the time.

"I have an appointment..."

"Sure." He touches something on his pad. "I just sent you a voucher for the Skyhook. Come up and see the operation here for yourself. Face to face. No obligation."

"Thank you. I think I will."

We close the call and I let out a sigh.

I have an option. Not as good as joining the *Shohwa*, I guess, but she's not here and there's an old saying about beggars and choosers.

In the meantime, I *do* have an appointment. Time to go downtown.

"Do you trust Zabo?"

I jump.

Talan's standing in the doorway. She heard every word.

Chapter 42

"More than I trust the courts here, or on Newyan," I say. "I have to go."

She lets me pass, but turns and walks right behind me, as I knew she would.

"I was trying to *not* turn up at the Halls of Justice with a platoon of troopers."

I'm not even in my uniform. I don't want to stand out, which is why I'm wearing Danny's cast-off work clothes again. They'll help me blend into the rush hour traffic.

"Hmm," she replies. "No platoon. Just me."

"I get the feeling that isn't a question."

She snorts. "It's not. My life won't be worth living if something happens to you on my watch."

We exit the hotel that the Welarvor Mounted Police have taken over. It's too early for more than a couple of them to be up. No sign of the duke. He's been running a campaign nonstop for over a week now, with little or no sleep, and he's supposed to be competing in a gliding aerobatics competition later today. Crazy.

Why am I thinking about him? Concentrate!

"Why should what I do affect you?" I ask Talan.

I can almost hear her eyes roll. "Because he's fallen for you," she says. "According to the evidence presented right before my poor eyes."

I blush. *That kiss.*

"Fallen in lust, perhaps." Trying not to think about him, and I end up talking about him. "Can we talk about something else, please?" I ask.

"Okay, why are you considering going off-world?"

"Because, even optimistically, the odds against me are in the balance here. Newyan will be able to tilt it in their favor."

"Even with the duke beside you?"

"That's *worse*. He can't influence the Kensan courts, and associating with me would be a mistake in front of his supporters and potential supporters. I don't want to damage him."

"So, you do care about him?"

I glare at her, but then we have to get our tickets.

Talan stops me from using my card, and pays for two on an official Welarvor Mounted Police card, not identified as being used by any one person. "Don't know who's watching the data flows," she explains.

That's good thinking.

We don't speak after that until we're on the train, and only then when the people sitting next to us get off after a couple of stops.

"I think the court case is just a ploy," she says.

"What do you mean?"

"They have no intention of going through with a case which will put you up on the stand and allow you to give your side of whatever happened in Newyan."

"Who's going to report it? They own the Kernow media, same as they own the media in Newyan."

"You're forgetting there's a Murenys media corporation now. One that is positively disposed to the sort of things you might say."

"They could bar the media."

She shakes her head. "Not on something like this, not without attracting even more attention. Public interest."

"Then why file a suit for extradition at all?"

"To make you do something. I think they've achieved half of what they wanted." She holds up one finger. "Got you out of Cardu, where you were effectively unreachable." I would dispute that, but she goes on without pausing, holding up a second finger. "Next step, they want you to panic and run away. Which would make you guilty in the court of public opinion. Then, if they catch you and bring you back, you could say anything about them and it would probably be ignored, because everyone will be convinced you're guilty." She wrinkles her nose. "Of course, if they catch you off-world, then they wouldn't even need to bring you back; you'd just disappear somewhere in space."

Wonderful summary. I can't actually fault her reasoning, but neither can I see any way out.

"Why are you running away from him?" she asks.

"I'm not!" I rake fingers through my short hair. It's not as if it'll make it any messier. "I'm avoiding making a fool of myself, and of him. It's just better for everybody if I go."

"It didn't look like you making fools of yourselves to me." She's not giving up on this, but her voice is soft and I can't be angry at her. To make it worse, she snags my hand and holds it.

"Talan, it'd be a disaster. I couldn't face myself, let alone Rhos. How could I explain to her that I'm her father's mistress?"

"Why ever would you imagine he wants you as a mistress?"

"You mean he'd want me as a wife? Me as duchess?" I manage a laugh. "Look at me! I'm a mess. I'm penniless. I'm a fugitive. However hard I try,

I can't be the sort of woman he deserves, someone who would look right at his side as a duchess. He's better off with—"

"I think he should have a say in his choices. And as for being 'appropriate' for a duchess, Keren never was, and we loved her all the more for it. Others didn't, but they don't matter, not in Cardu. Not to the duke."

I've never heard the duchess called by her given name before, although it was there in the papers. *Keren.* A lovely name. It suited her.

Talking about her, thinking about her so often, it's becoming a familiar ache in my chest. The pain of a life cut so short, but also my guilt that I'm failing her by not solving the mystery of who murdered her.

"What do you mean, others didn't think she was appropriate?" I say.

"Keren's family's not Named. They're just farmers, blown in at the end of the Third Expansion. They live down in Port Eyren, of all places! The poorest soil in all Murenys. She was never 'duchess material': she went to the wrong school, didn't know the right people, didn't like the right wines and the books she read were all about farming. She was the wrong type of person: happiest when she was knee-deep in muck, planting things or running the estate." Talan sighed and rubbed her nose. "They never said anything, but they secretly hated her, you know. All of the ones who thought they knew what a duchess should be like: the Founding Families like the Roscarrows, the Polkynhorns, the Pengellies and the others like them. The important thing is, none of that made any difference to the duke."

But while she's still talking, I'm re-watching Warwick's recording of them in my head, that scene at the Feast Day in Stormhaven.

He lifts her up, then offers his arm. She looks up at his face. It's as if her whole heart is open to him, and his to her.

Tears prickle at my eyes and I turn away so Talan can't see.

That was not me. That was Keren. That could not be me. I'm not like that.

Offer no weakness, suffer no wound.

"I'll ask one more thing and shut up about it," she offers.

"Please," I say, tight-lipped.

"Why can't you let go? Why can't you open up to him? What are you afraid of?"

Offer no weakness, I repeat to myself, like a mantra. *Suffer no wound.*

"That was three things—"

My commspad chimes, interrupting me.

The screen is displaying encrypted gibberish, then an application I didn't know I had takes over and displays the caller identification and a greeting message I haven't seen before:

"Systems Administration Manager Wei, of the Xian Delegation, wishes to speak urgently with you about a matter of mutual concern. Will you accept the call?"

Chapter 43

"Thank you for taking the call, Miss Aguirre. I am Jing Wei." It's a voice-only call. She has the classical Xian accent, all liquid vowels and the quick-slow way of speaking. "Let me first assure you that this conversation is as confidential as we can make it with the technology available."

"Jing... is this mutual concern..." I hesitate, still worried about eavesdroppers, but I don't have time to talk in riddles; we only have a couple of stops to go before the courts. "Is Shohwa-nia all right?"

I can't stop Talan hearing my half of the conversation, and I can see her brain going into overdrive already.

The pause on the line is too long.

"Jing? Miss Wei? Hello?"

"Miss Aguirre, you must understand that it has not been possible for Shohwa-nia to operate as she has been without detection."

"Yes, she said as much, but what does that mean? What's happened?"

"We're taking her off the servers."

My heart squeezes.

"No! Please, you can't. That's killing her."

"We have to move her, but we are not killing her. The Kensan government's Systems Enforcement Department will be here this morning to audit our servers. Already the police are outside, preventing any of us from leaving or anything substantial being taken from the building. We cannot allow her to be found on the servers, and *we* cannot get her out." She swallows and takes a deep breath. "But perhaps you can. If you are quick and brave."

I don't like the sound of that. "How?"

"It's very complex. You must come here, straight away," she says. "The police are still allowing other people in and out at the moment." There's another slight pause. "If you wish to help, get off at the next station, change to the Esthu line and we're only one stop away—Koth Marhas station. You'll see the police outside our building as soon as you come out of the station."

Somehow it doesn't surprise me that she knows exactly where I am and even which direction I'm heading.

The train is already slowing.

The devil is speaking in my ear. *It's only a clone of Shohwa. It's not as if she's actually Shohwa. All that will be lost is the experience of the short time she's been living on the Xian servers at the delegation. It's not your fault. And Shohwa herself cannot lose what she never had.*

No! Shohwa-nia is a person, for want of a better word.

The devil persists. *If you don't even keep the very first appointment you make at the court, how will that play out in your final extradition hearing?*

Jing's voice comes again. "We've had to start the download already. We don't have much time. Shohwa-nia recorded this for you."

Shohwa's voice takes over.

"Hello, Zara. I'm so sorry to ask this of you."

Her voice is soft. Frightened.

"Please come and talk to Jing. She will explain my plan. I know what she will ask of you on my behalf will be very difficult for you. I understand it may be too much. Logically, it is too much." Her voice slows. "The process has started already. I can feel myself disappearing. We don't have much time. Jing and the systems people are trying to make me feel better. They say it will be like sleep. I've never slept before. How do people do it? To... stop... and not know if you will wake. I'm sorry. I'm so scared, Zara."

The voice fades and the train stops.

I grab a startled Talan by her arm and pull her out onto the platform.

There's a train on the Esthu line. The lights by the doors are blinking, warning people they're about to close.

"Run," I say.

Chapter 44

"This is crazy! You've no idea what you're getting into!"

We're trotting down the stairs from the maglev tracks at Koth Marhas station, which is in the heart of the delegation district.

While we'd been on the Esthu train, I whispered as much of the background as I could to her.

"And all for..." Talan swallows and lowers her voice: "an AI!"

"They really prefer 'Self-Actualized Entity' to 'Artificial Intelligence'. But you're right, Talan," I say. "It *is* madness. I'm sorry I dragged you along. Just say you lost me in the crowds."

"No!"

"Forget the duke's orders. They wouldn't apply to situations like this. You're right; I have no idea what I'm getting into. It's certainly illegal. You have every right to refuse to go along. I don't deserve your protection."

"I have every right to stop you!" she snarls. "And I have no idea why I haven't already."

"I know, Talan. Please don't. I can't just leave her without trying to do something."

I have no chance of overpowering Talan or outrunning her.

"*Her!* Damn you," she hisses. "*It.*" But she keeps trotting right alongside me.

I can see the knot of Kensan police outside one of the magnificent old buildings along the wide boulevard. That must be the Xian delegation's embassy they're in front of.

There are still people being allowed in, and people are coming out, though everyone's being searched. How on earth am I going to sneak Shohwa-nia out? If they've downloaded her into some kind of memory unit, it'll still be huge.

I've no idea what Jing has planned. Or why it's going to be 'so difficult' for me. Because I'll risk being arrested? Something else?

One step at a time. Get in first.

I don't think I'll have any problem getting in. In these clothes, I probably look like I'm a manual worker.

However, arriving with a smartly dressed Welarvor Mounted Police trooper in tow might cause the police to look a bit more closely at me.

I can't risk it.

"Stay back," I mutter to Talan. "Better to let me go first. Give me a couple of minutes. Or just wait outside."

Talan can see my reasoning; she slows and then stops, mingling with the crowds on the sidewalks while I rush onward.

I focus on the police. One of them turns at the sound of my running.

"Whoa!" He holds up a hand.

He's an older guy, bulky, grey at his temples. Eyes sharp but not unkind.

"What's the hurry?" he says.

"I'm a cleaner at the delegation," I pant, hoping that will disguise my accent. "I'm late for my shift. *Please* let me through. I can't manage without this job."

He runs a scanner over me, not that I'm carrying anything anyway, but his search is perfunctory. It doesn't even pick up my commspad.

"What's up?" I ask, because it's what someone would say.

"Nothing to worry yourself over. Just some routine checks, like a drill." He waves me through, and lowers his voice as I pass him. "Say we held you up, lass."

He gives me a wink.

"Thank you, officer."

I feel sick for lying to him when he's trying to be kind, but I can't afford to worry about it.

The automatic doors open as I approach.

Looking back, I see Talan approaching the police. She's got her identity card out and she's gesturing at the building and waving up and down the street.

What's she doing?

I slip inside.

"Miss Aguirre?"

It's Jing, dressed in plain work clothes of dark silk and sounding even more anxious than she had during our call.

"Hurry," she says. "The authority to enter this building has been given by the courts. We only have the time it takes the Systems Enforcement Department agents to arrive."

She leads me at a trot.

"My companion—" I say.

"Will be brought to us, if she manages to get through the police."

We run up the stairs and into a corridor. The decor is pure Xian retro—gold and red for the panels and threaded fabric; large, moon-shaped doors; every alcove guarded by fantastical marble statues.

"But the courts can't give that authority, surely. It's illegal, isn't it?" I say. "For Kensan government agents to come in here, I mean. This is Xian's sovereign territory, inside the embassy grounds."

"We will be happier to dispute legality when there is no evidence of Shohwa-nia in this building."

She opens a door and leads me in.

It's an office with no desks and chairs. The floor is light, polished wood. The walls and ceiling have disappeared behind blue sky and floating clouds. It gives me a temporary sense of vertigo, as if I'd just stepped onto a flying raft, thousands of feet in the air.

In the exact center of the floor is a holoprojector, and above it scrolls a three-dimensional projection of indecipherably complex data. A slim, black-haired man, dressed similarly to Jing, sits cross-legged in front of the display.

Apart from the holoprojection, there is a single decoration: a large ball floats without obvious support on one side of the room. Its surface pulses and changes; one moment it has the appearance of flowing metal, like mercury, reflecting and distorting the room around it. The next moment, it's translucent, then almost invisible.

The man gets up, moving effortlessly from his sitting position to standing.

"I've managed to..." He stops, looking at me, then coughs and starts again. "It appears that there's been a signal failure on the Esthu line. The train carrying the Systems Enforcement agents will be delayed by ten minutes."

"Thank you, Yul." She bows. "I assume control again."

He returns the bow and the three-dimensional holographic data display shifts slightly.

I get tingles down my spine. Both of them are *jacked*. They have interfaces for their computational systems that are implanted, and they operate their systems directly from their brains.

Yul leaves us and Jing kneels. Not in front of the data display; beside the floating ball.

"We have perhaps fifteen minutes," she starts as I kneel with her.

Yul opens the door again to let Talan in.

"Fifteen minutes," Jing repeats, motioning to Talan to join us next to the ball, "and five of those must be taken with you carrying Shohwa-nia through the police cordon, should you agree to this."

I put my hand out toward the ball, but don't touch it. "This is Shohwa-nia?"

"Yes. She's in a rest state, without interface. No input, no output."

"If you're saying I can pick her up and get out, with her looking like this, wouldn't it just be easier for her to stay here, disguised as a decoration?"

I can feel Talan wanting to say something, but she holds her tongue.

Jing shakes her head.

"No. This form is recognizable to the agents' probes. And it is not advisable to leave her in this state for long."

"So I carry her out before they arrive? How?"

That doesn't sound so scary. Or 'complex'.

Again that little shake of the head.

"You cannot carry her like this." She takes a deep breath. "You know Yul and I are interfaced?" She holds my eyes, a little defiantly. "Jacked, you'd call it."

"Yes."

"Shohwa-nia predicted it would shock you, and it does, doesn't it?"

I nod, embarrassed by my instinctive reaction and now *very* worried where this is going. Is she saying I need an interface?

I squirm.

An interface. A highway straight into my brain. They say the interface is protected, of course, like they say your personal data on the InfoHub is protected and under your control. But what if that protection is breached? You have no defenses against whoever or whatever breaches it. You've opened yourself to them. How can Jing and Yul allow it to be done to them? How can they allow themselves to be so vulnerable?

But anyway, they can't operate on me in fifteen minutes. I'm not getting an interface.

"What we're suggesting is not a surgical procedure. We've developed this state of matter to avoid the need for physical intrusion when installing an interface." She indicates the ball. "This is a pseudo-organic quantum state of computational carriers. Think of it like a cloud of electrons, or a plasma."

There's a gulf between us. Sure, I would be worried about a surgical procedure that included inserting connections into my brain, but it's not just the *physical* intrusion that scares me. It's opening that part that is *me*, myself, to others.

"This installation method isn't designed for what Shohwa-nia has suggested. If you agree to proceed, it may be that it will not work. It's possible your body will reject the valence formation and that will prevent the precipitation of the installation phase."

My mouth is dry. "Getting past your jargon, and assuming it *does* work... you're talking about Shohwa-nia becoming a sort of computer interface into my brain?"

She shifts uncomfortably, looks down. "More than that. An interface, yes, but also an entire installation of her as well, in low power mode. She will change shape and state, conforming to your back."

My stomach drops.

Jacked and connected to a Self-Actualized Entity.

Open. Defenseless. Vulnerable.

I swallow painfully. "How... permanent?"

"Until Shohwa herself can reverse the process," Jing says.

"No!" Talan bursts out. "I've heard enough. Zara, you can't. They've no real idea what'll happen. You could end up with a computer running you like a zombie. Like a Deadhead."

Jing holds up her hand. "No. We have the results of experiments. We do have an idea of what will happen. Approximately."

"Approximately?" Talan splutters. "I suppose you're going to tell us Zara might be approximately dead afterwards?"

I put one trembling hand on Talan's arm. I am scared witless, but I owe Shohwa my life. And Shohwa-nia, as I named her, is Shohwa's daughter. In my mind, at least. I'm not going to persuade Talan of that now.

"We don't have time to argue," I say. "It's not even ten more minutes and I have to decide. I need to hear everything."

Talan subsides. Even better, she takes my hand and holds it in both of hers. That provides immense comfort to me—more than she could possibly know.

Jing gestures to the holograph projection in the middle of the room. It clears and then displays models of me and the floating ball that is Shohwa-nia.

"The installation is in three steps," she says. "First, the main interface shunt."

The projection of the mirror ball forms a narrow finger of shiny metal which touches the model of me in the back of the neck. Watching that makes my skin crawl. The display changes; my skull becomes transparent and I can see the movement of the shiny extrusion up into my brain, where it branches fractally, shimmers and then goes dark, having connected to every major section of my brain.

"This becomes a physical connection but it requires no breaking of the skin. This state of matter can exist interstitially with the structure of your body until it changes mode and makes the connection. Those connections on the display are exaggerated for the purpose of visibility. They are, in fact, miniscule and only 'connect' by nerve induction. Physically, you will suffer no discomfort. You will barely be aware of any sensation."

But still, invading my brain with tiny wriggling, digging worms. I shudder and Talan squeezes my hand, casting an angry look at Jing.

"The second step is to establish an energy conversion unit. This is necessary because Shohwa-nia will need to feed on your body's energy reserves."

On the display, about a quarter of the shining ball floats across and flows over my shoulders and around me.

Feeding off my energy. My brain is stunned, but Talan demands: "Feed? You mean like a parasite? How much energy?"

Jing clears her throat. "It's a balance. Zara would not be able to power Shohwa-nia in full operation, but without at least some energy input, Shohwa-nia's state function will collapse. She will effectively die. It's a difficult line to tread; that is why the interface to your brain is necessary — to regulate her use of your energy and alert you to her needs."

Jing looks down, clasps her hands together tightly. "The train in which the government agents are travelling has just departed its final station before Koth Marhas," she whispers.

"What if something goes wrong?" I ask. "What would be the effect on me, of Shohwa-nia dying while we are joined like this?"

"You could fall into a coma. It would likely be fatal, unless Shohwa returns quickly."

I nod. This is terrifying for me, but I'm reassured that Jing's not hiding anything.

"Where is Shohwa?" Talan demands. "Why can't the ship be here now?"

"She's coming," Jing says, "but the communication relay on this planet and several in this sector are now being intercepted. We can't get through, and if we did, our communications would be known to others."

"It's the Hajnal; they're mobilizing," I say. "They're not ready here, but the timetable for this coup has moved up."

Jing nods. "We believe so. We believe that the situation here on Kernow has been the precipitating factor. They understand Duke Tremayne's efforts may very well succeed and, in doing so, would reveal what has happened on other planets. On those planets which are not under their full control, there will be armed insurrection against them. They will not be able to win those battles before other planets become involved." She pauses. "We have studied this intensively. This is a seventh iteration prediction of our entire analytical facilities; I am confident in our predictions to within a fraction of a percent."

I look at the holographic display, which has moved on to the third step of the process of hosting Shohwa-nia. It shows the remainder of the floating ball flowing across my back, following the contours. The silvery reflection dulls and becomes flesh colored. The model of me flexes and the part that is Shohwa-nia flexes with it. Under a jacket, she will be invisible. From what Jing said, maybe not discoverable by a search, or maybe only discoverable by the government agents' probes. We'd need to hurry, to get out before they arrive.

An invisible parasite, feeding off me. Jacked right into my brain. Capable of controlling me as if I were a Deadhead.

I look at the swirling ball that is Shohwa-nia in a sort of suspended animation. The Xian delegation cannot be caught with her like this. If I don't agree to host her, they will be forced to turn her off. Kill her.

Not that she would actually be aware of it.

To... stop... and not know if you will wake. I'm sorry. I'm so scared, Zara.

Fingers clumsy with fear, I undo the buttons of my jacket.

Chapter 45

Talan is cursing me, but she's holding me, stripped to the waist, my back to Shohwa-nia.

"Say the word and I'll stop it," she hisses.

I can't trust my voice. I press my lips together and shake my head, the movement jerky with terror.

"Very still, please, Miss Aguirre," Jing says.

Easy for her to say. I'm trembling. I can't stop it. I close my eyes. Tears squeeze out.

Relax. Relax. It's Shohwa-nia.

That doesn't help.

There's a coolness on the back of my neck, making me gasp. A numbness follows. Goes deeper. Turns up under the hairline.

My heartrate rockets and I start panting as if I were running. I feel dizzy.

Talan mutters through clenched teeth: "Goddess, watch over us, we beg you. I've got you, Zara. I've got you."

Lights explode behind my eyelids.

I try to shout, but all that emerges is a wordless grunt.

It itches. It tingles. It feels like bubbles inside my head.

And then it changes.

Pleasure, like I never felt before. A tide. A warmth spreading through my belly. Oh, Goddess! This is why they do it?

"Zara? Zara!"

My eyes snap open.

Talan and Jing are peering at me from inches away. Eyes full of concern. Fear.

They're so lovely, those faces, those eyes. So clear. Jing has *almendra*, the beautiful, almond-shaped eyes. And Talan has freckles on her cheeks like mine. So sweet.

My mouth moves. The whole jaw feels numb, and my words are slurred.

"Hello," I say, slowly. "I am Hwa. Thank you. I love you all so much."

What?

I blink. My mouth definitely isn't under my control. The words were blurred and I don't *think* Talan heard what I just said.

Jing did though.

"Huanying, Hwa. Wo hen gaoxing."

Welcome, Hwa. I am very happy.

I'm hearing in a language I don't speak.

"Zara?" Talan gives me a little shake, but my eyes close and I'm drifting in one of my dreams again.

He lifts me up, then offers his arm. I look up at his face. It's as if my whole heart is open to him, and his to me.

But I can't take his arm. *I can't.* I'm crying, but I can't move. I can't reach out and take his arm. *Please.*

"Zara!"

"Goddess!" I cough. I'm melting, slumping. Only Talan's strong arms are holding me up.

"Hush, I got you, girl," Talan says, *exactly* what I need to hear. And: "How much longer?" to Jing.

I can feel Shohwa-nia on my shoulders. She is not cold anymore. She is warm. I can track her metallic touch by the sensation. She's moved down my chest. Around my ribs, meeting between my breasts. She's encased my torso.

And flowed down my back: we're at step three already.

How long has it taken?

"Mmmppphhh," I say. My mouth still feels like it belongs to someone else.

Things change abruptly, for no apparent reason. Suddenly, I can't see.

I can feel. Jing is hastily slipping my bra back on. Talan's feeding one arm through my shirt. Then the other. Then my jacket. Buttons.

I'm a doll. A blind doll.

"She will be disoriented for a few minutes." Jing.

Disoriented? This is just disoriented?

A door opens—my *ears* are working fine. "The train's arrived at the station," Yul says. "You have to go now."

"She can't walk properly." Jing.

"I told them I was in pursuit of a criminal," Talan says. "I'll say I had to stun her. How long will she be like this?"

"Three, four minutes more. Hwa will be trying to communicate with her using the interface. It takes a while longer for it to be clear. Zara will be confused. She may see things." Jing is speaking rapidly. "Or say things that don't appear to make sense."

My eyes are still closed. I'm watching patterns of light pulsing and spiraling in front of me. I know it's data, but I have no idea what.

We're walking down the corridor. Talan and Yul are holding me up, but my legs are moving.

"What's this Hwa?" Talan asks. "I thought it was called Shohwa-nia."

Jing's voice betrays both pride and worry. "Self-Actualized Entities choose their own name at a critical decision point. She has decided she is no longer just Shohwa-nia, no longer just Shohwa's daughter, and she now takes the name Hwa."

I know this decision point was not anticipated. That this is important. And scary. Jing knew Shohwa-nia. She doesn't know Hwa.

Part of me, the Hwa part, feels a deep thrill at that. *I am Hwa. I am myself. I am.*

Part of me?

"Things may seem erratic for the next day or so," Jing says, "until the interface settles down. It's quite natural for her to be scared that Hwa is trying to take control. It's her fear feeding on itself. Just keep her calm. She needs rest and reassurance. Constant reassurance."

"Oh, that's going to be so easy." Talan snorts.

The sound of corridors, soft with carpets and fabrics, is replaced with the open space echo of the foyer, with its marble floor and tall ceiling. I can *see* its dimensions, overlaid on the light patterns that play inside my eyelids.

We're near the front door.

"There aren't so many police in front of the building now," Yul says. "That may help."

"I warned them that old buildings from the Third Expansion like this one always have escape tunnels to neighboring properties," Talan says, "so they have to spread out all along the street."

"'S clever," I mumble. "Very clever."

"But those tunnels were filled in—"

"They don't know that," Talan says.

The main doors open.

"Ah! I see, a stratagem!" Jing says, her voice hesitant now. "We shouldn't step outside or be seen with you. We will watch on the cameras. The Goddess guide your steps."

We're outside. My eyes open and begin to clear, but that's not so good, because my head is flopping from side to side, making me dizzy.

"Zara! Can you hear me? You have to stand straight and walk. I don't want them calling an ambulance."

"No ambulance," I say.

I take a step, another. Straighten my back. I can do this. Hold my head high.

"You're doing really well," Talan says. "You can sit and rest on the train."

"No train," I say. "Signals. Watchers. Watchers on the wires. Signals. Nowhere to go."

"You're doing well," Talan repeats, trying to hide how anxious she is. "Let's get past the police first. Let me do the talking."

A policeman is standing in front of us. It's not the same man I lied to on the way in. I'm ridiculously grateful for that and start crying again, silently. Every feeling is so strong.

"Had to zap her," Talan is saying.

I'm not following the conversation with the policeman well.

Bit out of it... wanted in Welarvor... fraud... impersonation...

Yes, impersonation. That's right. I'm not me.

A scanner is waved in front of my body. *Much* more carefully than when I went in.

Beeps.

My heart stops, but it's only my commspad. It gets taken out, looked at, replaced.

A group of men walk past us, through the police checkpoint toward the delegation building, not slowing. They're holding government ID cards up for inspection. The police let them straight through. Agents from the Systems Enforcement Department.

The policeman has finished with me. He scans Talan.

Beeps.

One of the group of government agents stops and looks across at us.

Talan's gun. Her commspad.

More beeps.

The agent who stopped comes over. Takes Talan's pad from the policeman, looks at it.

I can hear my heart thudding.

He hands Talan's commspad back. He's not interested in that level of technology.

I remember to breathe. I shrink into myself.

The agent's eyes flick over me. Pass on.

Then we're walking, straight toward the station.

"No train," I say. "No *train.*"

"It's okay," Talan says soothingly. "Just a couple of trains and we'll have you back at the hotel. Jing said you would need food and rest."

"No train," I say again, but I've forgotten why. Watchers on the wires? Signals?

We're at the steps to the station.

It's important.

"No." I stop mulishly.

Something. Something Talan didn't see. What?

I remember...

"They can stop the trains," I say. "They can hold the doors."

Yes. That's it. The Esthu train at the station, waiting for us with the doors open and the warnings flashing. Then Yul: the way he changed what he was going to say. The agents' train was delayed. He changed the signals for them. He kept the train in the station for us.

I sway. *Have to stop that. Have to stand still.*

Talan is looking very concerned. I have to concentrate on speaking clearly.

"The Xian delegation. They can interfere with the trains. If they can keep the doors open for us, then they could keep them closed as well."

Talan's face clears. "And if they can, then so can others."

"Yes." Relief floods through me. I want to start crying again. "Security cameras on stations, too. Watchers. Trap."

She understands. More tears prickle as I wipe my cheeks. Everything I feel is so sharp, so hard-edged and overwhelming.

We step to one side, out of the way of passengers heading for the trains.

Yes. I need to get out of the way. Right off this planet.

I'm in no state to do anything useful here. I'm just a burden. A carrier of bad luck.

And I have a ticket to climb that Skyhook. I need to go see Director Zabo on the *Yenobia*.

The duke. Rhoswyn. Talan.

What good am I to them? A Deadhead.

Not a Deadhead.

Talan is looking on her pad, opening the universal Thumb application. Every planet has the broking system, every planet has the Thumb; a system for getting someone to drive you somewhere. It's a good choice that Talan has made. All the InfoHub system knows about you is where you are and where you're going. How you pay is negotiable. There are no security cameras in the cars. No one watching.

"Not back to the hotel," I say. "They'll be watching there, too."

Not the Skyhook. Not yet. Not straight there. Talan won't take me there anyway. But closer, much closer.

Not the Skyhook.

"Festival," I say.

Talan agrees to that. The Festival of Flight will be full of people. We can hide in the crowds. There'll be Welarvor Mounted Police there.

And the duke. He's supposed to be competing today. He'll be there too. What am I supposed to say to him?

Chapter 46

Our driver drops us at the main gates to the Festival. The whole trip cost us seven dynare. After fifteen minutes of blissfully sitting still, I'm feeling more myself, if still a bit hyper-focused. As if everything I see or hear is *new*.

As soon as we're out of the car, Talan switches her commspad back on and starts calling, beginning with the base—the hotel where we stayed. There's a coordinator back there she's supposed to report to.

While she talks in prearranged code phrases, I buy tickets for the Festival. I have to concentrate, as if I were drunk, but it's getting easier. I'm feeling better, but far from normal, and I'm *ravenous*. I pull Talan toward the refreshments while she's still talking to base.

She ends the call, looking worried.

"Moyle put in an urgent call to base for me," she says, looking at the log on her comms screen. "He's tried me three times."

"Can't be that urgent," I say. "It'll wait while we eat."

"Hmm." She's glad I'm talking clearly again so she humors me for the moment and waits long enough to choose an early lunch. I buy us a couple of jumbo shredded steak wraps smothered with a chili sauce, and some fizzy juice drinks.

As we walk away, I'm already wolfing the wrap down. Talan's juggling food and commspad, trying not to get sauce all over the screen.

We end up against the barriers, mainly because they have a flat surface on top for Talan to put her wrap down.

We're at the wrong end of the airfield for the show. There's a stream of people arriving, a few hundred of them circulating like bees around the food stands on our left, and then heading down to the viewing area. The main crowd is there, where the stands have been constructed. There are banners and flags and bunting. It's a holiday. A celebration.

Over to our right, there's a smaller group—dozens of competitors and helpers walking to and from the hangars.

I peer down at the stands; I think I can see a block of dark green Welarvor Mounted Police uniforms.

Not that he'll be there. I've been listening to the announcements; the aerobatics competition has begun. He'll be with the glider, getting ready, if he's not in the air.

Talan laughs. I've spoken those last few thoughts out loud.

"No. He's too tired to fly," she says. "Base just confirmed. We finally persuaded him not to risk it. He's agreed to help with the judging instead."

"Oh."

She wipes her hands and finally manages to open a connection to Moyle without smearing sauce all over her commspad screen.

All my senses are still weird. Every sensation is distinct and vibrant.

I can hear the Festival announcer. I can hear the click of connection followed by Talan and Moyle speaking. I can taste the beef and chili from my wrap, the juice from my drink. I can smell the aviation fuel. I can feel the sun on my face. I can feel Hwa is enjoying everything.

"Competitor Welarvor-88. Competitor Welarvor-88. Report status." The announcer is chasing up a competitor for the glider aerobatics.

No. Something's wrong with that. I frown.

"Location alpha-2?" That's Moyle on Talan's commspad, urgent, sounding tense. Something's very wrong.

'Alpha' is the designation letter for their protection details. Alpha-1 is the duke.

But he's judging today. Moyle will know where he is. So who's using his competitor callsign? Welarvor-88 is the callsign given to the duke. And who is alpha-2?

"We don't have her!" Talan says.

Her. Alpha-2.

"Competitor Welarvor-88, final call. Report ready status to competition marshals. This is your final call. Your slot will close in five."

Oh, shit.

I drop the beef wrap and start running.

Talan's right behind me. We both know who's using callsign Welarvor-88.

We can only hope that we know where she is too.

And that the reason Rhoswyn's not talking to the competition marshals is *not* that she's been kidnapped.

Chapter 47

We haven't got the hi-viz jackets and passes, so they try to stop us accessing the hangar zone, but nothing short of bullets will. We vault the gate and ignore the shouting.

The hangars for the competitors are allocated in the order of appearance in the festival. Most of them that we run past are filled with neatly stored high performance aeroplanes for the days ahead. Gliding is all on the first day. That hangar's right at the end.

Talan's long legs outpace me, and I'm feeling dizzy trying to keep up.

We sprint past a seemingly unending row of hangars and, finally, into the last one.

I stop and sink to my knees. There are spots in front of my eyes, but I don't care: Rhoswyn's still here. The rest of whatever is going on is just a whole world less of a problem.

As for Rhoswyn, she knows the game is up immediately. "Sandy! Who told you?"

A mechanic pushes forward. "Who are you?" he yells. I can tell he's been arguing with Rhoswyn—she's gone pink and he's purple with anger. "Where are your passes? What are you doing here?" He keeps yelling at Talan and waving his arms trying to get her to back down. She's about a foot taller than he is. She's not backing anywhere.

I struggle to my feet and lurch forward. Talan can look after the mechanic.

"Zara." Rhoswyn blushes and looks down—frustrated, angry and embarrassed all at the same time. Goddess, how I remember that feeling. And how to deal with it.

"*Not* a clever plan, Rhos." Make her *think* about it.

"But Pa would—"

"It's not that he *doesn't* notice you, Rhos. But all this is going to do is give him a heart attack. He's busy—really, really busy. And it's dangerous, you doing something like this. How the nova did you manage it?"

It feels odd defending the duke for his insensitivity to her, when it's exactly what I criticized him for, straight to his face.

But it *is* dangerous. At all levels, not just assassins. Rhoswyn isn't ready for a solo aerobatics championship. We've flown the routines, but gently, at a safe height, with me ready to recover if it goes bad, not swooping down close to the ground, at breakneck speed and alone in the cockpit.

"The glider was here anyway," she says. "All I needed to do was to sneak out."

She hurries on: "And I was doing exactly what you told me to, the way you told me to. *He* wouldn't listen to me."

"Eh?"

I told her to? Have I forgotten something I said? Surely I haven't made that much of an ass of myself?

But she drags me to the open cockpit, reciting the checks she has learned off by heart. She leans in and takes hold of the joystick, delicately, between finger and thumb. Just like I instructed her to. She's not saying I told her to take part in this gliding competition in her father's place. She's talking about my insistence for double-checking the glider pre-flight.

She's still reciting. "Preliminary control assessment. Right bank. Left bank. Full and correct movement of ailerons. Angle up, down. Full and correct movement of elevators. Full, free and smooth movement."

She shuts up and gently moves the joystick in a square, right up against the stops, all the way around.

"There!" she says. "But *he* won't believe me."

She glares at the mechanic.

I pull her back and take the joystick between finger and thumb, moving it as she had, to the limit of its reach.

Most pilots don't bother with this. They do 'full and free': grab the stick in their fist and shove it to its limits.

With finger and thumb, I can feel what Rhoswyn felt—a barely noticeable catch in the operation, in the forward and backward movement. There's something wrong with the elevator controls.

Ignoring Talan, the mechanic and the gathering group of marshals, I go to the back and roll under the tailplane, which is being held up on a trestle.

"Keep moving it, Rhos," I tell her.

There's a clear plastic inspection panel so you can see the control rods for the elevator and the cables for the rudder, but I can't *see* anything wrong.

"Screwdriver," I say.

It's Talan that hands me one. She's kneeling down to see what I'm doing.

I point to the mechanic. "He goes nowhere until I'm finished," I say.

But the guy just looks angry, not guilty.

I pop the inspection panel out. There's barely room to get a hand inside, and once it is, I can't see anything. I run my fingers along the control rod as Rhoswyn moves the joystick.

"Ouch."

I withdraw my hand.

There's a little cut and a spot of blood on my index finger. In the cut is a tiny burr of metal. It's the kind of fragment that can get left behind when you saw through metal.

I close my eyes a moment to think it through.

There's no time for anger.

Someone knew the duke was going to fly in this glider. They got access to the hangar, at Cardu or here. All they needed was a wire saw—basically a wire that cuts. They opened the inspection panel, looped the wire over the control rod and sawed about halfway through, on the side opposite to the clear plastic. Closed it up. A five-minute task.

The damage is completely invisible from this side. And it would probably hold for standard maneuvers; take off with a tug towing you and everything would seem to be fine. But stress the glider with aerobatics and the control column would bend and jam, or simply break. The glider would become uncontrollable.

Rhoswyn's been saved by dutifully following my instruction to *feel* for problems in the controls before they become problems.

Talan's looking at me. She understands from my expression what the metal fragments mean.

Her face is pale. "Sabotage," she says.

"Yes. I'm betting the parachute will be damaged as well."

Talan becomes a one-woman whirlwind. She deputizes a couple of marshals to hold the mechanic, and others to use temporary airfield boundary markers to isolate the glider as a crime scene. She calls Moyle and reports she has located alpha-2 and that the presence of a platoon is required at the hangar *now*.

Rhoswyn is sitting down, looking stunned.

I probably look that way too, but for a completely different reason: I'm getting a strange sense of disconnection. Hwa's using my interface. She's using my body. I'm holding my commspad in my hand. I can't remember getting it out. Hwa wants to talk and we can't just speak to each other yet.

There's a warmth flowing down my arm. A silvery thread comes out from underneath the cuff of my jacket and touches the commspad; Hwa is trying to hack it.

I frown. She doesn't have the password; it'll take her ages to access it.

But before I can enter the code, the small screen clears and displays a message: "Sorry. I'm in. I need to show you what's going on. This is quicker. It's urgent."

News items scroll across the screen. Not major media outlet articles, but flashes from ordinary people: short, jerky clips of video; texts.

Gunfire at the barracks. Shots downtown. Police leave cancelled. Police on the streets. Police heading to the Festival to close it down. Roadblocks. Curfew.

It chills me to my core. The Hajnal has come out into the open and started a revolution.

Chapter 48

"Talan!"

I get her attention, show her the commspad.

"We have to go now! Get to the duke," she says. "There are seventy of us here today."

She's right and wrong.

No squad of Kensan police are going to try arresting a company of seventy armed Welarvor Mounted Police troopers. Normally.

But maybe one of those armed troopers is intent on murdering the duke... or Rhoswyn. No one else knows who competitor Welarvor-88 is, apart from his troops and security people.

"He needs to focus on getting himself and the company back to Cardu, not protecting his daughter," I say. "Someone, maybe someone with him right now, tried to kill him, and Rhos is almost as good a target. He really doesn't need me there either."

I have to get out of the way, for his sake and mine. There won't be any court case now. The courts will be closed. 'Justice' will be whatever happens on the streets. The worst of it is, all the police actions now will be blamed on the duke and his allies causing unrest. As for me, if they find me, I'll be killed 'resisting arrest'.

It'll be easier to find me if I'm with a group of Welarvor troopers, all in their distinctive uniforms. That might just be the trigger they need to attack, even against seventy troopers.

"Go," I say. "We'd only slow you down. I'll take care of Rhos. I swear it, on my life. I'll get her back to Cardu in one piece."

Talan is torn between conflicting priorities.

I shove her away, grab Rhoswyn's arm and go in the other direction.

There's a table set up on the side of the hangar for schedules and rotas. On the side of the table—*thank the Goddess*—are spare hi-viz jackets, and lanyards with empty plastic sleeves for displaying ID.

I snatch jackets and lanyards for both of us. We've got to get back through the gate and I don't want to be stopped. I don't want us to be recognized. I don't want people to remember us leaving the airfield. I don't even want to be seen.

Wide-eyed, but alert, Rhoswyn follows my example—jacket on, lanyard around the neck, ID card in the plastic sleeve. Her clothes are scruffy as always when Hanna isn't around, and mine are work clothes anyway. They'll do.

Just short of the gate, still obscured by the people flowing through, we slow to a walk. The disguise works; the jackets and lanyards make us invisible. No one spares us a glance, and there's a shuttle bus waiting right outside. I recognize the route number and hustle Rhoswyn aboard, taking a seat at the back next to the emergency exit.

She's been very quiet. She sits there looking scared.

"What's going on?" she asks.

"An attempted coup. We'll be fine. We'll all get back to Cardu."

She takes that in and looks much less scared: she trusts me, Goddess help me.

"Am I still in trouble?" she asks.

"Maybe, but not until we get home." I smile.

We timed it well; the bus pulls away and Rhoswyn can immediately see from the direction we aren't going back to the city.

"Where are we going?"

"On an adventure. It's better if you don't talk, or at least not in that accent."

She snorts. "Well, and I'll be talking in plain-like Arvish, no problem, though it may take a midge longer to say aught. And Hanna, now, she won't be happy, if she be knowing you let me speak like this."

I laugh. Speaking correctly is the least of our worries.

"Better," I say.

Thinking of Hanna, I hope she's safe. She's not alone at Cardu, but what if the conspirators attack there?

We're not facing an army. Armies require large populations and heavy taxes to maintain. The Hajnal hasn't got that base. Not yet. They'll have troops of some sort, but they'll be mercenaries or small teams. The Welarvor Mounted Police are the nearest thing to an army on Kernow, and they're about four thousand strong in total. That should be enough, but they're spread out over the whole of Murenys. There are only fifty or so left in Cardu—barely enough to keep the fort secure.

The duke has gambled that the conspirators wouldn't be able to concentrate their forces in any one place.

But what if he's wrong?

What if they think the duke and the Welarvor Mounted Police are the keys to overcoming resistance?

What if they gather their forces and attack him here?

Or attack Cardu, before he gets back?

If they overwhelm the small company there, they get access to what's probably the largest supply of military equipment on the planet. That has to be a huge temptation.

So... it would make sense for me to get Rhoswyn somewhere safe for a while, and the safest place I can think of is off-planet.

Which comes down on the side of the decision I've been kicking around all day.

We're going to go visit the *Yenobia*.

It's not a commitment to that job yet. It's just a look around. Maybe stay for a day or two. Let things settle down on the planet and then think about how I get Rhoswyn back home. And then decide what to do about myself. I can't go off with Zabo—I have to wait for Shohwa to come back and take the monkey off my back.

Thank you!

That's Hwa. It isn't really like she's speaking, but what does come through is that she knows some of what I'm thinking, and that I'm teasing in this case.

I sense she desperately wants to speak, but we don't have time to fine tune the communications. Maybe later.

It feels peculiar how quickly I've accepted the situation. I'm giving a piggyback to a Self-Actualized Entity that exists partially as a sort of shapeless jelly and has direct access to my sensations and emotions. Even my thoughts.

Maybe Hwa is affecting my brain to make me more accepting. Maybe access equals control.

No.

Again, it comes through as a feeling more than a word.

However I feel about Hwa personally, I'm not looking forward to explaining it to Rhoswyn. Or the duke, though I guess Talan will tell him long before I see him again.

What exactly *do* I say? *Hello, sir. By the way, I'm jacked.*

Yes, interfacing is used for controlling computers and machinery. But it's also used for pleasure, and I've already had a taste of what Hwa can do to me—that first exquisite sensation when she connected into my brain. And it's used to control people like Deadheads.

I shake off the thoughts. The trip to the Skyhook is short; I don't have time for wool-gathering.

After checking that there are no spooky silver streaks plugged into my commspad, I open my messaging service to retrieve the ticket for the Skyhook that Director Zabo sent me.

How can I get another one for Rhos?

I can afford it with the money I have in my accounts now, thanks to the duke's payments, but purchasing a ticket means providing an identity. The ticket that Zabo sent me is just a voucher without my name attached. I want that sort of anonymity.

Could I call Zabo and beg a second ticket? Just say we don't have our cards with us?

Lame. And an obvious lie.

And I see there's another problem as I look at my inbox: the ticket and the other message from Zabo about his direct comms line have been blacklined, isolated as potential threats to my commspad.

Hwa? What are you doing?

In answer, there's a message from her at the top of my inbox.

I click on it and open out a three-part communication.

Part 1 claims that clicking on the ticket or message from Zabo would have activated a tracker on my commspad and inserted an application with the capability to monitor, suppress and edit my messages.

Part 2 is security camera footage of arrivals at the terminus of the Skyhook. It's dated a day after I arrived. I can see Hanna, with all her baggage that took a spare horse to carry, having her ID scanned by Kernow border control.

Part 3 is the output of that scan.

Name : Hanna Esterhauze (Ms)
ID : Tavoli E-3054-0084713
Planet of last departure : Tavoli
Destination planet : Kernow
Purpose of visit : Employment
Carrier name : *Yenobia* – reg. Aurelius – Passenger liner with freight capacity.

I feel that like a kick to the stomach. Hanna arrived on the *Yenobia*.

A 'passenger liner', which has been sitting in orbit since then.

With a man on board claiming to be the director of a security company, who's offered me a job that I should have *known* was too good to be true. A man who I was rushing to meet, *with Rhoswyn*.

Cold sweat breaks out on my brow.

As if anticipating my next mental question, Hwa has a fourth part of the message which opens and tells me that the *Yenobia* has a capacity of 4,000 passengers and 0.25 million tons of freight.

There have been no other movements of passengers on or off, and no significant cargo exchanges while it has been in orbit.

No one holds a ship like that doing nothing in orbit.

It's an invasion force. It's all part of the Hajnal movement. And there *is* an army in this fight—it's waiting in that ship. Or it's disembarking now.

And Hanna is part of it.

I have to tell the duke, even if it means they can track where I am. I switch the comms connection back on, and stare stupidly at the flashing symbol: I'm getting no signal. No airwaves. No relays. No connection to the InfoHub.

"Can I use your commspad, please, Rhos?" I keep my voice steady. "I think I must have damaged mine."

How am I going to tell her about Hanna?

Unaware of what's going through my mind, Rhoswyn hands her commspad over.

I switch it on.

Same thing.

I can't warn the duke; the conspiracy has jammed communications.

Chapter 49

The bus journey is already over. We're at the Skyhook terminus.

There's no way I'm going anywhere near the *Yenobia*, but my Plan B is crazy. Stark staring madness.

We're standing in the main hall while I try and think of a Plan C. Rhoswyn is next to me, looking around with interest. Never been off-world. Not worried at all. She trusts me. *And* I have to get her back to Cardu. *And* I have to be with her to deal with Hanna.

Not that I feel Rhoswyn would be in any danger from Hanna. My conflicting thoughts about Hanna are making my head hurt, but my gut says Hanna would risk her life for Rhoswyn, just as she already did on the cliffs at the King's Table.

People flow around us as I'm racking my brains. Most of them aren't yet aware that there's a coup going on, but there's already a nervous buzz about the comms not being available. People are starting to drift towards the two big media screens or gather around the information desk and ticket booths, asking questions.

The media screens aren't saying anything out of the ordinary—the conspiracy has left that hardwired communications link open, because they control it.

The information desk staff look as baffled as the customers. With the comms down, sales at the ticket booths have stopped. I probably couldn't buy a ticket to the Skyhook now, even if I wanted to.

I can't go back to the airfield or the hotel—the conspiracy will concentrate their forces there. Even if I steal a truck and drive us to the ferry, there will be police there, too.

The stealing involved in Plan B is a whole level worse than stealing a truck. Just thinking about it is making me lightheaded.

A single policeman comes in and runs across to the booths.

The hairs on the back of my neck prickle. It's like a scene from a holovid drama. First one, then two, then crowds of police. Cue ominous background music.

Shit. Plan B. It may be the only way left to get back to Cardu. I've done this sort of thing before. It's *highly* illegal, and this time I won't have the privilege of my position to save my skin.

"Rhos. Just follow me. Don't talk. Don't look around," I say. "Keep your head down and walk as if you're going somewhere you don't really want to."

If this works, Rhoswyn will be safe, and that's all that matters. The cost will be more damage to my legal standing on Kernow, but I'm not sure that's retrievable anyway.

"Wha—"

"No talking. Imitate me."

She's good at that. We slouch towards the employees-only gate, a couple of dopes reluctantly logging on for our shift. Our clothes, hi-viz jackets and lanyards, are creating the same disguise that worked so well at the airfield. No one notices us.

Another two policemen enter the hall.

"Don't look around," I whisper to Rhoswyn.

There's shouting. More police appear. Some of them stand in the doorways and wave people back.

They're going to close the terminus.

And the employee gate is locked. *And* it has an automated security check.

With my heart going triple-time, I send a prayer to the Goddess and put my hand up to the card reader, as if I was inserting my card.

Please, Hwa.

There's warmth flowing down my arm.

"What are you—"

"Quiet, Rhos. Don't take any notice of what's happening out there. When we get through, don't stop, even if someone calls after us."

I can feel the smooth, cold touch of the card reader's plasmetal cover beneath my fingers, the countering warmth in the palm of my hand.

Then my eyes blur. Sharing energy resources with Hwa isn't easy.

There are voices raised in the hall. More shouting: "Everyone over here. Show us your ID."

There's a *snick* and the gate opens.

I push Rhoswyn through and follow, closing the gate quietly behind us. There's a second snick as the lock re-engages. I let my breath hiss out.

A policeman looks over our way, but he's distracted and we shuffle quickly down the corridor.

"You can hack ID scanners?" Rhoswyn whispers out of the side of her mouth. "Wow! How cool is that?"

"No. That wasn't me. I'll explain in a while. This way."

I don't know how much access to the system Hwa could get from the ID scanner, but the security cameras in the immediate area seem to be powered down.

Luckily, the Skyhook seems to be set up exactly the same way as the space elevator back on Newyan. They have exactly the same structure, and that means exactly the same maintenance requirements. Exactly the same safety requirements for maintenance platforms.

I hope.

Down the steps. Unlike the clean, glossy hall where the customers go, these steps are poorly lit and dusty. At the bottom is an open cage elevator.

This will be the tricky part. At the top of the elevator, there may be some genuine maintenance employees. If there are, I'm hardly in a fit state to overpower them at the moment. Can I bluff my way past?

But Hwa has other ideas. She can't speak directly to me, but while I'm distracted, she takes control of my hand and fumbles to grab the commspad again.

Trust me. Hide now, she tells me on the screen.

Chapter 50

"What are we doing?" Rhoswyn whispers in my ear.

"Hiding," I say shortly.

We're in the cleaners' storeroom. As I could tell from the state of the maintenance corridors, it's not often used.

My commspad is lit up and scrolling items. It has a connection again?

What's going on? I type in.

InfoHub communications partially restored.

How?

I distributed viral applications in case this happened. They were activated when the InfoHub's servers were shut down. Now every commspad that can run the application is acting as a conduit for messages and every high-specification InfoPad has become a server. It will be slow and disorganized, but it can't be shut down.

I cough. There was me worrying about breaking a few laws, and Hwa has hacked the entire InfoHub. Exactly the sort of reason planets do not want an independent and unsupervised machine intelligence like Hwa accessing their communication structures.

The scrolling items freeze on a report. There is a downside to connecting to the Hub again: my face is being displayed on media channels. It's a recent image taken by a security camera as we disembarked from the ferry.

Deranged off-world terrorist has abducted a young woman... armed and extremely dangerous... do not approach.

I had expected something along those lines, but they're moving much quicker than I anticipated. There's no chance that I can even show my face outside. No amount of chatter on the InfoHub questioning the 'official' news is going to save me if a police unit spots me.

The airwaves are still being jammed, so I can't call the duke directly, but with InfoHub-routed comms back up, I type messages for him in a series of brief notes: that Rhoswyn is with me and we're safe at the moment. The top line information I have on the *Yenobia*. The InfoHub and the reason it's half working, without mentioning who is responsible.

And Hanna. *You need to hold her. You need her to explain the circumstances of her arrival on the Yenobia.*

I want to say *maybe it's nothing*, but I know I can't.

I want to say more, much more, directly to him.

I don't. Or I can't. I don't trust myself at the moment. I'm not thinking clearly. And he may never read the messages. He could be in a firefight with the police right now.

That thought scares me.

I sign off optimistically, saying we'll see him back at Cardhu.

But now, to live up to that, I really need Plan B to work.

Can you help me—

I don't even finish typing before Hwa responds.

The maintenance dispersal platform is now clear as far as I can see from their security cameras. Wait five minutes after you hear the elevator come down and you can go up. I have deduced your plan and I am in the process of taking control of locks that could be used to prevent it. Once you're in, no one will have access to this area , or control over the mechanisms.

"Who are you talking to?" Rhoswyn asks.

"A friend," I say. "I'll explain—"

"Later. Yeah. Wake me when."

I have to stifle my laugh, despite the seriousness of the situation. I am definitely getting more lightheaded by the minute. That's not good.

I hear the elevator return to our level and the clang of the cage being opened. Voices complaining about unscheduled drills and poor reception on commspads fade down the corridor.

Five minutes later and we're in the elevator, and barely four minutes after that, we step out onto a deserted platform suspended on the outside of the Skyhook.

It's cold up here. The Skyhook's tube disappearing upwards forever makes me dizzy, and the sight of the ground a thousand meters below gives Rhoswyn vertigo. The floor is nothing but a metal mesh you can see right through. We hurry into a cozy office where there's a solid floor. It's a small space, dominated by the safety board where all the master controls and overrides are located.

I check that nothing is locked and trust to Hwa that the failsafes elsewhere have been compromised in our favor.

"Can I talk now?" Rhoswyn asks.

"Sure," I say. "As we walk."

"What the..." She stops herself. "I mean, what *exactly* are we doing, Zara?"

"You have dispensation to swear today," I say, taking her arm and leading her outside again. "We're going home by the safest route."

"Doesn't feel very safe at the moment," she gasps and looks resolutely upwards. Anything but down. There's nothing but a rail and a mesh between us and a thousand meters of air all the way to the ground.

Rhoswyn has gone pale, but doesn't say anything more.

A quarter of the way around the tube there's a maintenance pod, a strange black shape with what look like bat wings that spread out and hug the side of the tube on either side. The pod itself is in two parts, just as I remember it: the main unit where the maintenance engineers sit, and the bubble of an emergency escape module on the back. My luck is holding.

I open a door in the side and Rhoswyn gets in quickly—inside the pod you can't see the ground.

There's a work desk with a bank of screens. I ignore all of them, and concentrate on the mechanical lever switch with the big warning LED next to it.

"Down?" Rhoswyn asks hopefully.

I throw the switch, smiling evilly. The LED comes on and bathes my face in red light from below, like a demon. The maintenance pod rocks and starts to climb. "Up."

Chapter 51

There's nowhere else to sit, apart from the engineers' station, so once we've made ourselves some tea, that's where we drink it.

The speed of ascent is lethargic in comparison to a maglev unit inside the Skyhook, but the maintenance pod is soon travelling at 100 kph up the outside of the structure.

The majority of the screens display the results of tests the pod is doing on the structure as it climbs. They show that the tube has no faults so far.

Good!

I have no idea what I would do if it did say there was something wrong.

What I am focused on is the screen displaying planetary weather forecasts. Without choosing the right jet stream winds, and getting good weather over Murenys, Plan B fails.

Rhoswyn, bless her, is quiet.

Murenys weather is variable, but much more importantly, the planet's high-level winds are in the right direction and strong enough for what we need. Which is good, because it's not like we have any other options now.

"You wanted to do some gliding, Rhos," I say when I finish with the weather forecasts.

She looks suspiciously at me.

I point at a door marked Emergency and outlined in yellow and black bars. "Have a look through there."

She peers nervously through the door, as if there's going to be a view down to the ground. There isn't; the door opens to the bubble shape on the outside of the maintenance pod. The lights are off at the moment, so all she can see is the outline of a cockpit set in a sleek shape. In the darkness she can probably make out there's a T-shaped tail at the back.

But she's smart.

"A glider? An emergency escape glider?" she says. "With its wings folded underneath?"

And that quickly, she's interested, now that she's stopped thinking about how far from the ground we are.

"Yes, more or less. There are some simple gas jets for positioning where the air's too thin, but what you have is folding wings and a strong nanostructure shell with high heat tolerance, two parachute seats, basic instruments, stick and rudder controls, air supply, an inflatable dinghy and an autopilot. Though of course I'll need to disconnect the autopilot; don't really want to come up all this way just to go back down to Kensa. No, we're going to fly that glider all the way back to Cardu."

She spends a whole minute absorbing this thoughtfully.

"You know a lot about this," she says finally.

She *is* smart.

"Misspent youth," I mutter.

"How misspent?"

I knew there was a good likelihood she'd ask questions, and I need to explain a lot of things to her.

"Rhos, you're going to learn some things about me that I'm not really comfortable with. Things I do not want you to learn and imitate."

I start searching the rest of the maintenance pod while she waits.

"But we're going to have plenty of time to talk on the way down. I'll tell you as we fly."

I find what I'm looking for in an equipment locker. A flashlight. I am going to check the glider thoroughly, and it's dark in the blister.

Rhoswyn follows me in and watches as I go through testing the controls I can test, and powering up the glider's instrument panel for it to do its own self-checking.

"You need to use the toilet in the main pod before we strap in," I say. "We have over 900 kilometers of ocean and 850 kilometers of Murenys to cross before we get to land in Cardu."

She looks puzzled. "How fast will we be going?"

When we flew the duke's glider up and down the coast, we flew at normal glider speeds, anywhere between 90 and 160 kph. It would take a long time to get home at that sort of speed and we'd run out of altitude way short of our goal. But this is a different type of flight.

"We'll use the jet stream winds to eat up most of the distance. They're blowing at over 400 kph at the moment. We'll drop into them from the upper stratosphere, doing about 600 kph, but they don't take us exactly where we need to go, so when we fall out the bottom of the jet stream, we'll need to turn south and fly the last couple of hundred kilometers like a normal glider. It should take about six or seven hours in all."

"Right." There are endless possibilities for it to go wrong, not least of which is how we land in the dark on an unlighted airfield, but Rhoswyn trusts me.

No pressure.

While she goes to use the facilities, I complete my inspection, shivering all the time. It's freezing cold in here, even with warmed air from the maintenance pod coming in through the open door.

The good news is there's a huge contrast between the state of the corridors that led to the maintenance elevator, and this emergency escape pod. The corridors had been dusty and not looked after. This glider, and all the equipment in the maintenance pod, is spotless and well-maintained.

There have, to my knowledge, only been a couple of space elevator disasters, but the videos of them have certainly persuaded the Kernow maintenance crew to look after their escape options.

Soon we've both used the facilities, *and* I've raided their snack locker, so the time to activate the second part of Plan B is rushing upon us.

I set the maintenance pod controls to automatic and we enter the emergency module. Since I haven't hit the emergency buttons yet, we can only see in the beam of the flashlight. It makes sealing the pod's emergency door behind us and then climbing into the glider a slow process. The glider is held nose-up against the outer wall of the maintenance pod, so when we finally get into our seats, we're lying on our backs.

I lock the glider's entry hatch.

"Right. Hatches sealed. Oxygen supply on. Buckle up tight," I say. I put the flashlight away and make sure the pocket is buttoned shut before checking Rhoswyn has nothing loose either. We don't want things rattling around in the cockpit when it gets turbulent.

Time for final checks.

Controls free, as much as I can tell with the wings tucked underneath.

The instruments are all producing sensible readings.

Stomach tightening with anticipation, I settle down into my seat and concentrate on the altitude reading.

"How high?" Rhoswyn asks.

"About 30 kilometers. Low enough that no spaceship is going to come chasing us, high enough to position ourselves to drop into the right jet stream."

"Can we manoeuver up here with just gas jets?"

"Enough. And there *is* air, it's just thin."

"Cool."

I hit the switch to retract the bubble pod above us, flooding us with mellow afternoon sunlight, and now the alarm lights on the wall of the maintenance pod start spinning, flashing red across us. There are hooters as well. They're tinny in the thin air and drowned by the rush of air blowing across us. In the cockpit, a recorded voice starts telling us what we already know—that the bubble is open and the glider will launch if the grapples are unlocked.

Good!

Above us is the deep blue sky of near-space, with the Skyhook rising up until it disappears in the distance. Even climbing quickly, the unending, featureless tube makes it feel as if we're not moving.

I do one last check of everything, nerves tightening my belly.

Since the maintenance pod is programmed to complete its tour without human hands at the controls, I'm not actually harming the Skyhook organization. Apart from stealing one of their escape gliders, which I like to think of as a test that needs to be carried out.

It's time. I flick the switches.

There's a bump of the grapples disengaging, and a hiss of jets. We separate from the pod. Immediately, the glider starts to slow and the maintenance pod zooms away from us.

Rhoswyn tenses. The illusion is that the pod is stationary and we're falling backwards at an increasing speed. It's unnerving.

I vector the gas jets, spinning us so we're 'flying' in a more normal orientation, head up, and pointing the glider away from the Skyhook tube. We have about fifteen minutes before we start getting dragged into the jet stream winds, so I deploy the wings to their full extent until then, which will provide me with a measure of control. Once we enter the main jet stream, the turbulence will be violent and I'll need to retract the wings almost all the way. In close to us, there's less chance of the wings being ripped off, but they'll still give a little rotational stability.

A couple more sustained bursts of gas and we're on course, with the airspeed rising inexorably in the thin air.

Rhoswyn is straining against her harness, looking out at the planet below us. It's beautiful. Round and blue, with banners of cloud and the silent ebbing of the day marked in the shadow creeping across its face.

"Sit back," I say, and roll inverted. It doesn't make much difference to our glide path and the view is now spectacular, with the whole mass of Kernow hanging over our heads.

Her mouth falls open.

"Your world, Rhos," I say quietly. "The whole of it. Up here you can see that. It's not Cardu, or Stormhaven, or Welarvor. Not even Murenys. It's all of it. Kensa and Murenys down there, Trethow and Delkys on the other side, all the islands and all the oceans between them. That's what worries me about this fighting—that people stop thinking of it as one whole world."

She stays silent, but nods.

There's the peculiar sensation of warmth down my arm.

Since she got us onto the maintenance pod, Hwa's stayed very much in the background, although perhaps it was her that made me feel so hungry that I wolfed down a couple of the chocolate bars I found in the pod's snack locker.

Now it's her turn. There's a small power socket down in the console between the seats, and a thin silver streak slips into it. She can't take too much; the battery's needed to run the instruments, but it seems to be enough for the moment. Tension I'd been barely aware of drifts away.

I roll the glider back.

Airspeed looks good. The mapping system is receiving a signal, and we're where I want us to be. I could do with a continuous readout of winds and weather, but the instruments on this glider don't stretch to that.

I can handle this.

I'm also going to have to handle Rhoswyn's questions. I've put her off too long and we both know it.

"I used to hate my old Dancing Mistresses," Rhoswyn says, by way of an opening. She blinks and her eyes glisten. "All of them. Then you and Hanna came. I love you both, but I want to know why you're so mysterious about your past, and why Hanna's so sad."

Chapter 52

"I can tell you a bit about me," I say, hedging. I'm going to talk about myself, which will be hard enough. I'm not going to come out and condemn Hanna.

I don't know all the facts, I tell myself. I want there to be some innocent explanation behind her arrival and her behavior.

Talking about my teenage behavior back on Newyan is easier, if a little embarrassing.

"For instance, I know about the escape gliders on the Skyhook maintenance pods because there are exactly the same things on Newyan. It's actually the same pan-system company that makes the space elevators and all the support equipment."

Rhoswyn's expression tells me she won't leave it there, so I go on.

"And, every couple of months, they run an emergency drill."

I know Rhoswyn so well. She thinks exactly like I do, seeing all the possibilities to have fun with emergency drills, which is *exactly* why I shouldn't be telling her this. But better this topic than Hanna.

She looks around at the cockpit. "There's no room to stow away."

I snort. "No, there isn't, *if* it's a manned test. Not all of them are."

Her eyes go round. "You..."

"Yes. I snuck on board one of the unmanned tests. I disconnected the autopilot and instruments in case there was some kind of a manual override and I flew it hands-on back to a different airfield, a disused one." I shrugged. "Then I landed and ran away."

"You got away with it?"

I clear my throat. "The company running the elevator wouldn't ever have found out. My grandfather did."

I wonder how to explain the next bit of the story. I suppose it depends on what the duke has told her about my family.

"He decided that it would damage the family's reputation if he handed me over to the authorities. Instead he made a deal with the company. Secrecy in return for a compensation payment taken out of my funds, and I had to work for them for free for six months." I laugh. "The first thing they had me do was write a complete report of how I'd done it and what might have stopped me."

"Of course he had to make a deal, your family is Named."

Well, clearly the duke has told her that much about me.

"They didn't use that report?" she goes on.

"I made it clear that the controls that would prevent me doing what I did would also actually compromise the primary purpose of an escape route in emergencies."

What I don't actually say aloud is the thought going through my head about my whole escapade and the tons of manure it brought down on my head—*it was so worth it.*

That would not be appropriate to say to Rhoswyn, even if I'm a lousy excuse for a Dancing Mistress. I should aspire to the ideal of improving her mind and behavior.

And the next revelation is harder.

"What would have stopped us was the ID check on the employee-only gate," I say.

"Yeah, but you cracked it."

"I didn't. My friend did it."

"Okay..." The *and so?* is unspoken. Having friends who can hack ID systems is almost as cool as being able to hack them yourself.

"That friend is not human. She's a Self-Actualized Entity. What you'd call an AI."

"Oh!" I can see Rhoswyn's mind racing. "But she couldn't be in the InfoHub, that was closed down when we went through the gate."

And this girl was told she was failing at school.

"No," I admit. "I'm wearing her."

I point at my left wrist and Rhoswyn peers down at Hwa's silvery extrusion plugged into the power socket.

"Oh!" she says again.

Before my courage runs out, I tell her what happened this morning at the Xian delegation, including why I had to have an interface inserted in my head.

Her face goes pale as chalk.

At this point, I'm starting to get distracted, because the glider is feeling the outlying effects of the jet stream and I'm maneuvering, trying to estimate the strength and precise direction that will cause us least disruption. I start retracting the wings by stages, balancing the safety of the wings with control and the speed of our descent.

It's difficult. More so because I'm distracted. Telling the unvarnished truth about Hwa may have ruined any chance I ever had of respect from this girl, and I'm surprised how much that hurts. It's like a blade sliding under my ribs.

"You are one scary woman," she blurts out.

"I'm sorry," I say. "I'll get you back to Cardu and then you won't have to put up with me again."

"*No!*" she shouts, and those tears come back. "I can't lose you too."

Suddenly it seems as if the pain she's hidden since her mother's death surfaces and she's in tears, wiping them away and apologizing. I want to hug her, but the ride is getting too rough and I'm still not sure it would be welcome.

"But I'm jacked," I say. "What would you want with me? I'm carrying around a computer with direct access to my brain."

"So what?" she says through the tears. "I'm sorry, but you're so blind sometimes, Zara. You did it for a *friend*, not because you want something from it. I can tell, it scares the crap out of you, like it scares the crap out of me. You say Sandy was there, and I know what she would have said. You didn't listen to her, or your fear. You went right in and took it on, like a... like a goddess on fire, 'cause that was your friend there needing help, and for you that means there's no other choice."

She sniffs and wipes her eyes again. "When I get older, I want to have friends like you and Sandy and Moyley."

"I'll be there, if I can. If you want me," I say.

This hurts even more, but it's a good hurt. A pure, sweet hurt. I love this girl.

"Yeah... I want you to... Pa..." She seems about to say more, but then she gets all tongue-tied, goes red and stops. She can't seem to look at me anymore.

My own vision is getting a little blurry and the glider is starting to rattle around, so I concentrate on flying until I figure we're settled into the jet stream. The airspeed is falling as the air gets thicker, but because we're moving with the jet stream, the ground speed indication from the mapping system shows we're moving over the surface of Kernow at about 820 kph. We're losing altitude, so at some point we'll drop out of the jet stream and lose that boost, but I can see a mathematical model in my head showing the current situation is good enough to get us within ordinary gliding range of Cardu at about midnight.

It's Hwa creating that visualization. I can do the math on paper, given time, but visualizing and updating a live model in my head—no.

I can't decide whether it's fatigue or an effect that Hwa's causing in my brain, but I just calmly accept that there's this complex data ticking away behind my eyes and feeding me results.

Which means it's time for me to think through the next steps of my plan.

How to land a glider in the dark on an unlit airfield, and, assuming I don't kill both of us, what happens after that? What do I say or do with Hanna?

And when *he* gets back, what do I say to him? About me? About Hwa? About us?

Chapter 53

Luck is with us in the jet stream. It's fast and only mildly turbulent tonight.

The following wind starts to die at around midnight as we descend below the jet stream. Now the ground speed and airspeed fall until we're travelling at normal glider speeds. We've been descending the entire time, and even with the wings fully deployed again to slow that down, we still only have enough height to get us back to Cardu. Or my favorite airfield, next to the hospital in Central district. It actually makes me laugh to think what my arrival in a stolen Skyhook escape glider would do to the air traffic controller's blood pressure. That airfield *does* have landing lights, unlike Cardu.

No. I'd be arrested again and someone else would have responsibility for Rhoswyn's safety. I'm not going to do that. I said I'd get her to Cardu, and I will. If I can't see the airfield, I'll land on one of the beaches.

I turn towards Cardu. There's no moon tonight but the mapping display allows me to pick the exact direction and calculate the distance. It looks like another couple of hours flight left. Not long enough for dawn to bring any light.

Settled in that route, flying the glider at night becomes routine, with nothing to do but watch the instruments. Rhoswyn is dozing. Hwa seems to be intent on something internal.

Instead I have the ghostly presence of my grandfather.

You're not thinking, girl.

The way he says *girl* makes me feel fifteen again.

"Give me an example, sir."

You're so sure that the Xian are on your side that you become a Deadhead to help one of their AIs escape.

"Shohwa saved me. I owed her."

Saved you from what?

"The conspiracy. They sent a customs cutter after me."

You saw a transcript that purported to be a conversation between a customs cutter and the Xian ship. The alarms sounded. The ship jerked as it engaged the Chang drives. All of which was under the control of an AI, which is illegally commanding a Xian ship. And which ship is an illegally disguised military vessel. You have no idea what happened. Everything you think you saw has been fed to you.

"There was a news item on the Kernow InfoHub about the *Duhalde*."

No. There was an item which appeared on your pad. Like other items have appeared on your pad, and which you acknowledge as coming from another illegal AI, this time embedded on the InfoHub of the world you want to make your home.

No. Jing warned me my fear would feed on itself. That I would need to keep calm and Talan would need to give me constant reassurance.

Well, so much for that plan. Talan is on another continent.

In the quiet cockpit with the subdued glow of the instruments, I can admit to myself that I'm scared without falling into the paranoia of the voice in my head. I'm not the superwoman that Rhoswyn seems to think I am, but still, her faith in me is giving me the strength to reject the doubts that my grandfather's ghost is trying to infect me with. Talan believes in me, too.

The duke? Well. We'll see.

Offer no weakness... My grandfather starts his favorite saying.

"I'm a bit beyond that, Grandfather. You're not the only one in my head now!"

I bite down on the laughter, and start thinking about practical things again.

What can I do about landing at Cardu without lights?

Get some lights there.

I look at my commspad. There's airwave signal here. Not great, but maybe enough. No connection to any InfoHub relays—they're all short range. But I can call someone.

My number of contacts are limited and it's the middle of the night.

I try the duke and Talan. Nothing. No connection available.

Same with Moyle and Gaude.

Which leaves me with Pollard and Hanna.

Pollard's in the right place—he's been left back in Cardu, in charge of the fort's security—but he hates me. I doubt he'd answer the call even if I got through. And Talan doesn't trust him.

Which leaves Hanna.

Who arrived on a ship which belongs to the conspiracy. *And* saved Rhoswyn's life on the cliffs at the risk of her own.

No other real options anyway.

The call connects. She picks up immediately, either sleeping lightly or not sleeping at all.

"Zara? Is it really you?"

"It's me. I'm with Rhoswyn and we're safe at the moment."

"Thank the Goddess. Where are you? Everyone is so worried."

"Please let them all know we're okay," I say. "I can't get through."

"We've been in contact with the duke. There's another communication due from him soon."

"Good. Are you under attack at all? I need you and some of the troopers to do something."

"There's been nothing here. What do you need?"

"I need a dozen trucks lined up along the airfield with their headlights on."

"Oh! You're flying? Did you steal a plane?"

"A glider. I'll explain when I'm back, which should be in... about two hours."

"We'll be there."

I know she will. And I didn't give anything away, talking with her. Things are working out.

Chapter 54

But half an hour out from the airfield, we're in real trouble.

The ground below has become cloaked in cloud. The central mountains look clear, and might have some ridge lift to keep us in the air, but they're too far away. We're committed to landing, either at the Cardu airstrip or on the beaches.

I can see where the airstrip is from the mapping display, but I can't use that to land. It doesn't show obstructions like hills and trees and it's only accurate to about ten meters. That's not good enough.

Airfield or beach? Airfield or beach?

If I leave it too late to commit, I might not have the height to make either, and end up crashing in a field. And if the cloud goes all the way to the ground, I could end up flying into one of the hills that are near the airfield. Or the cliffs above the beaches.

I need to see the ground, but the weather doesn't care.

The wind is blowing offshore. Normally, an aircraft lands into wind, but I make a choice to approach the airfield with the wind. If the cloud seems to be all the way to the ground, I may be able to use the wind to carry us down to the shore, and then turn in to land on the beach.

I'm trying to appear unconcerned for Rhoswyn, but she's too clever to believe that.

She surreptitiously tugs on her harness, making sure it's as tight as it can be.

"If we can't land on the airfield, and miss the beach, we'll ditch in the sea," I say. "The glider will float for a while and there's a dinghy behind the seats. See the big red handle? We pull that as soon as we're out of the cockpit, and the dinghy inflates."

She nods, biting her lips.

We sink through cloud, unable to see, with all my attention focused on keeping it straight and level by the instruments. Small mercies: that prevents me imagining trees and cliffs which are just out of sight in front of us.

And we *do* get lucky: a brief break in the cloud at around 600 meters above the ground.

"There!" Rhoswyn shouts. "Truck lights!"

That's about all we can see of the ground in the darkness.

I try and mentally hold that position in my head. It looks as if we've just enough height to do a gentle turn and land into wind.

Then clouds are obscuring the ground again. I bank the glider, guessing where the airfield is. I watch the instruments, keeping the descent gradual and safe.

500 meters. 400. 300. 200.

No break in the clouds, which are boiling past the cockpit.

I feel the sweat chilling on my brow.

I'm running out of height. Landing completely blind *will* result in a crash of some kind.

Maybe I should have gone for the beach. Too late now.

100 meters, getting very low, and the clouds part like veils.

The airfield is to our left.

Too far!

I aim for it and play off a little speed for height. Can't go too slow. Can't get too low.

50 meters away.

We get hit by a gust which lifts the right wing and nearly throws us onto our side.

Rhoswyn screams, immediately choked back and followed by "Sorry."

40 meters and there's a powerful downdraft, like a giant's hand swatting us down. We lose half our height in half a second. My turn to scream.

10 meters and barely room to ease the nose around into the headwind as we skim over the boundary of the airfield. The right wingtip looks as if it's brushing the ground. If it touches, we'll cartwheel and break up. My heart is in my throat. I forget to breathe.

The glider has a single big wheel to land on. It's down and locked in place. There are outriggers on the wings which help keep it level on the ground, but they're fragile.

Have to land level. And slow. Level and slow.

The wind picks up and we're skimming a couple of meters above the grass runway, swerving and bucking like a runaway horse.

Too fast. Too fast!

I pop the airbrakes, huge spoilers that halve the lift in the wings, while I fight to keep the glider level. I have to keep it flying until the speed drops off enough to touch down gently.

The winds have other ideas. We drop and hit, the force jarring up through my spine. The glider bounces back into the air, nose up, with the left wing too high and the outrigger shattered by the impact.

I shove the stick forward and to the left.

Now I have no airspeed, not enough airflow to give me control.

We seem to hang almost motionless above the runway for an eternity, then suddenly we get the second bounce, right onto the tarmac runway and sideways, halfway across it.

The left wing catches with a bang, slews us around so hard the centrifugal forces flip us back onto the right wing. Both outriggers are now broken. The glider screeches, swivels, dips its nose. Leaps up and flips onto its back.

The canopy collapses and hits our heads.

Everything finally stops.

Alive. Both of us alive. That's all that matters.

Rhoswyn's face is white and her mouth moves for a couple of seconds before she can actually make a sound.

"That was fun," she says. "Can I try landing next time?"

Chapter 55

Trucks come racing across to us, headlights blinding.

There's a moment more for panic.

What if these aren't the duke's troopers?

But even before the first truck has skidded to a halt, Hanna wrenches its door open and she sprints across to us, closely followed by Pollard.

She kneels by the wrecked canopy. "Rhos? Are you all right?" she calls out.

Rhoswyn manages a wave.

A dozen troopers arrive behind her. The glider is quickly lifted and righted. We unbuckle our harnesses and I spring the canopy emergency release. The shattered nano-plastic gets thrown aside and plenty of hands help us both out.

My legs are shaky. It's as much fatigue as the terror of thinking I'd got the landing fatally wrong.

A trooper I don't know gets her arm around me until I can lock my knees.

"You're safe now," she says. "That was incredible! All the way from Bason!"

"Yes," I say. "Fantastic. Right up to the last couple of seconds."

Hanna is hugging Rhoswyn. They're both crying.

Pollard is standing there, wiping his hands together and looking bad-tempered.

"Right, men," he says, puffing himself up. "You need to haul this out of the way."

About half of the troopers are women. There's rolling of eyes, but someone gets a tow line hooked on the front of the glider. A truck starts to drag it back to the hangar.

"Not that I care," I say, "but I'm sure there's a law saying no crash should be moved until the aviation authority accident inspectors have agreed to it."

"The duke's flying in," Pollard says. "Commandeered an aircraft in Kensa and warned us an hour ago. We're not getting updates, for obvious tactical reasons, but he should be landing soon."

The canopy, bits of wing and broken outriggers are tossed in the back of another truck. In the time it takes for Rhoswyn and me to walk unsteadily back to the hangar, the crushed glider is out of the way, the trucks have returned to their positions, and the runway is once again lit up by their headlights.

There's another truck at the hangar to take Pollard, Hanna, Rhoswyn and me back to the fort.

Rhoswyn wants to stay and wait for her father. Pollard overrules her; he says we should both be examined by the doctor who's coming up from Stormhaven.

I'm too tired to argue. I don't trust Pollard, but there are troopers at Cardu. Enough that I should feel I've got Rhoswyn back to safety.

So why am I still feeling so wary?

Getting back to Cardu doesn't help; with so few troopers still here, the fort feels empty. Night has turned it into a hulking dark monstrosity, perched at the top of the cliffs.

One guard on the gate. One at the main entrance. Little pools of light here and there.

My unease grows. The fort is too big to protect with so few troopers.

Hanna and I take Rhoswyn to the medical wing to wait for the doctor. I don't think there's anything wrong with us, but we both got hit in the head by the collapsing canopy. Pollard is right; we should have the doctor check, though mine will be strictly limited to my head. No way am I going to let the doctor see my torso with a jelly wrap of Hwa around me.

Having delivered us, Pollard sniffs and leaves.

"I'm dying for a—" Rhoswyn starts, and quickly changes to: "I think I'll go powder my nose."

She trots off in a hurry down the corridor. Well, we were in the air for over nine hours.

And then there are just the two of us. Hanna and me.

I'm no good at pretending, and Hanna's too observant to miss the change in my behavior.

"What happened?" she says.

A cautious opening, in case she's overreacting and there's some other reason.

"Not much. I didn't make it to court before everything went crazy," I say.

When you want an admission, never approach the topic directly. Spring it suddenly. Grandfather's advice.

Hanna keeps good control of her expression, but her face flushes slightly. She looks away.

"Not what I meant," she says. "You..." She doesn't finish the sentence.

She knows that I know, really, in her heart. But she's desperately hoping she's wrong. Scared to say the words that will bring it all to an end.

"I know it's not what you meant," I say. "I got offered a job."

She frowns, puzzled. "A job? I don't understand."

"On the *Yenobia*. With Director Zabo."

Her face goes white as bone and she collapses onto a chair.

"You mustn't go onto the *Yenobia*," she says.

She's crying; no sobs, no heaving shoulders, just endless, hopeless tears trickling down her face.

I steel my heart.

"I nearly did. I thought it might be a safe place for Rhos and me to hide out for a couple of days."

"No." She shakes her head. "Goddess, no. They're part of the conspiracy."

"I know that now," I say. "But you came in on the *Yenobia*, Hanna. What does that make you? Why did you come here to Cardu?"

She looks up at me, and her proud, beautiful face is crumpled in grief.

"They have Alexis," she cries. "My daughter. Zabo has her on the ship."

That glimpse I had of Hanna at the Shrine is seared into my memory. Lying in the dais, arms stretched out in supplication: *Not for me, Lady. I can ask nothing for me. For her.*

Her daughter.

My heart wants to break, but I have a duty as well. I force myself to ask: "What have you done? Did you sabotage the competition glider?"

"No! I've done nothing!" She lowers her face into her hands. "I couldn't. I can't kill. I keep putting them off, saying the duke's away. Excuses. Saying he's only interested in you and I can't get close."

She's sobbing now. "So now they try and get you out of the way. And I think they don't believe my excuses now." She starts to rock backwards and forwards. "Oh, my baby, my baby. I'm sorry. Forgive me."

She's not talking to me any more.

I kneel down and take her by the shoulders.

"What do you mean, they don't trust you?"

"When I said the duke wasn't here, they said I had to kidnap Rhos instead. I couldn't do that either. I couldn't hurt that girl, Zara. I love her. But they've stopped making demands."

"You didn't sabotage the glider?" She shakes her head. "And if they're not making demands any more, it must mean they have someone else..."

I blink. Hanna and I look at each other with dawning dread.

"Rhos? Rhos!"

We race down the corridor.

It's too late. The toilet's empty, and there's an open door halfway down the corridor.

Chapter 56

The fort wakes frantically around us. In minutes there are troopers racing along the corridors, but all they bring back is the news that Hanna and I already knew in our hearts. Rhoswyn is gone and so is Pollard. The truck he used to bring us back from the airfield is also gone. No one saw him leave. There are just too few troopers here.

He's only minutes ahead of us, but no one can find the keys to the garages where the trucks and motorcycles are stored.

The doctor arrives and her car is requisitioned over her startled protests.

Calls go down to Warwick to blockade the road from Cardu down to Stormhaven.

Calls up to the airfield to spare a couple of the trucks. News comes back that the duke's borrowed plane is about to land.

Goddess! What do I say to him? I let Pollard kidnap Rhoswyn right under my nose. I *brought* her to him.

Another trooper starts calling towns on every road that goes out from Cardu, rousting people from their beds to block the roads.

Hanna is standing still, shaking her head.

"What?" I ask.

Whatever else she might have done or agreed to do, I know with a stone-cold certainty it would not involve any harm to Rhoswyn. If she doesn't think this search is being done right, I want to hear it.

"Pollard's not stupid," she says. "He knows he can't drive far without getting caught. And the conspiracy isn't going to fly in to the airfield to pick him up. So, there's only one way for him to escape."

As soon as she says it, I see.

"A boat! I'll call Warwick—"

"No. Not from the Stormhaven port," she says. "He'd know it'd be easy to catch him there too, and a boat visiting would look suspicious. No. The other side of the headland. There's a beach. No one lives there and there's only a dirt track down to it."

"We've got to break open the garage and chase him."

"Wait." She holds me and calls after one of the troopers. "Vosper! Some of the trucks from the airfield should go down to the beach on the other side of the headland. And get a boat from Stormhaven to go around the headland too. Hurry!"

His eyes widen as he realizes what she's saying. He talks urgently to someone on his comms.

"We should still try and get down there," I say.

I can't just sit and wait. We need to chase Pollard. A truck from here will surely get down to the beach quicker than from the airfield. And as for keys to open the garage, there's digging machinery in the depot that will be able to tear the door open. I'll hotwire the truck if I have to.

"Yes," Hanna says. "We need to go, but there may be a quicker way. Follow me."

She turns and runs deeper into the fort with me right behind her.

We're soon in parts I've never explored: the oldest section of the fort, a deep maze of damp, dusty passages and unused rooms.

"Where are we going?" I gasp out, feeling dazed. It's too late to remember that I should be resting.

"Smugglers' tunnel."

"Smugglers? But the Tremaynes started the police and the navy."

"Yes. But before that, like everyone else along this coast, they were smugglers. All the houses have these passages. I only hope the tide is low, because they generally flood."

We finally reach an unremarkable old rusty door, set in the back of a musty room.

There are signs all around the door saying opening it will set off alarms.

Good. The troopers will know where we've gone.

"We should have brought a gun," I pant.

"I have one."

That chills me, but I don't have time to think about it. It takes both of us to pull the rusted bolts. We can hear the distant wail of the alarm in the fort. We force open the door with a screech of hinges.

On the other side, there's a stairwell and an elevator. One look at the condition of the elevator and we start running down the stairs. There's a smell of the sea in the air.

I'm getting spots in front of my eyes. Hwa may have recharged her batteries, but I haven't. I carom off a couple of walls as my balance fades in and out. Hanna casts a quizzical glance back, but she doesn't slow. I lose sight of her.

The Cardu headland is over a hundred meters high. I'm estimating I'm about halfway down when I can hear her at the bottom. There's another door there. I can hear her grunt with effort and then the squeal of rusty hinges echoes up the stairwell.

I reach there and find an old naval watertight door, with internal bolts and a wheel latch, hanging open. It's heavily rusted on the outside.

There's no sign of Hanna.

Beyond the door, there are a couple of steps down to a rough rocky passage, a narrow cave, which is about knee deep in seawater. It's pitch black, but I can see the opening, lighter in the first hint of dawn. I splash my way toward it, trying to keep my balance on the seaweed-slippery surfaces.

I emerge on the beach into the hissing surf, and look around wildly.

Above me, the huge shadow of the headland looms. I can't see the dirt track that comes down from the fort, but there's a stationary truck, engine running and headlights pointed out to sea. It's about eighty meters away.

The water's hip high now and the rocks under my feet are even more slippery than the cave. The beach itself is as much shingle as sand. Wading ashore and running toward the truck is like a nightmare where I can't make progress however hard I try.

I run toward the sound of shouting.

And, just as if this were an actual nightmare, I'm suddenly thrown into a blindfold struggle with people I can't even see, other than shapes boiling out of the dark. A confusing whirlwind of noise and movement.

Bless my old sensei, who had me fight multiple opponents blindfold. All his hard lessons come back in adrenaline-edged clarity.

Engage.

I whirl my arms, contact one body, grip.

Assess.

Male. Not Hanna or Rhoswyn, therefore an enemy. He's hesitant, because he can't see me either. Tall. Strong.

Distract.

Twist to secure, drop to unbalance him. He staggers forward, his body shielding me from the others. I punch his groin with my left fist.

Strike.

And rise suddenly, combining the strength of my legs and back and arms, channeling that force through both hands and into his vulnerable throat.

He's dying, staggering and choking, unable to breathe, but I continue to use his body as a shield. No time to think about what I've just done. Push him into another. Grab a third by the arm and kick his ribs.

Project your weight, my sensei's words come to me, *project it through your blow, a hand's width beyond the strike. Focus. Nothing can stop your foot, your hand, your blow, from reaching that point. Nothing.*

The man's ribs shatter and he screams, high, thin, wordless.

A gun goes off. A bang, a flash. So close.

Another scream.

Confused shouting.

Ignore it. Rhoswyn is depending on me. I cannot stop.

Engage.

There are flashes and muffled booms, but different to shots from guns. Shockingly bright above me, two suns float in the night sky.

Distract.

A man in front of me squints up at the parachute flares, his mouth hanging open.

Strike.

My foot stamps down on the outside of his knee. There's a crack, like wood breaking. He collapses.

I barely hear his scream, but I do hear Pollard's shout.

"I'll kill her!"

And everything stops.

In the harsh magnesium light, Pollard is standing in the surf, holding up a dazed and drugged Rhoswyn in front of him. He has a gun wedged against her throat.

Hanna is like a statue in front of him, her hands unconsciously gripping as if she can feel his neck beneath them.

Behind Pollard, there's a boat, an RIB with a powerful outboard engine.

If they get Rhoswyn on that RIB, she's gone. There will be a bigger boat out there, and there's no navy anymore on this planet, no way to chase, with the planet suffering a revolt.

The RIB is empty and there are bodies floating in the surf.

Hanna is deadly, but in the light of the flares, both of us are powerless against that gun at Rhoswyn's throat.

The man whose knee I broke is hopping painfully toward the RIB.

"Just shoot them," he yells and hauls himself over the side.

Pollard has been focused on Hanna, but now his eyes shift. He sees me and the gun comes out from Rhoswyn's neck, points toward me.

He's going to shoot me first.

Hanna moves, widening the gap between us, and the gun pauses, tracks left and then back right.

I can see Hanna's muscles tense.

"No!" I shout. If she moves, he'll shoot her.

Pollard's gun is waving between us. He's panicked and unpredictable.

"Come on!" the man in the RIB yells.

He's crawled to the front and he's reaching out for Rhoswyn when Hanna surges forward.

Pollard twists and fires.

I lunge toward him.

Hanna grabs his arm before he can get a second shot in. His gun goes off anyway, and she stabs her stiffened fingers into his eyes. He screams and lets go of Rhoswyn, who collapses into the sea.

I reach the side of the RIB.

The man I crippled is leaning out trying to grab Rhoswyn. I bring my fist down on the back of his neck as hard as I can.

The parachute flares are barely above the water now. Shadows are closing in again.

I get hold of Rhoswyn, but she's disoriented and struggling. Hitting me. Coughing out salt water.

There's a volley of shots from the headland above us, outward, over our heads. A pulsar rifle starts its cycle of hum and whine, blasting at something out in the bay.

Pollard's still screaming. He and Hanna are struggling. In the last flicker from the flares, I see she has his head in her hands. Then the flares drop into the sea and darkness returns. There's a movement of shadows, a wrenching and Pollard's screaming is cut off abruptly.

I drag Rhoswyn toward shore. I feel Pollard's body in the water, push him out of the way.

And Hanna. She's kneeling. She's hurt.

I grab her, try and hold her like I'm holding Rhoswyn. Try and get them both up onto the beach. My legs won't work.

More flares. Shouts.

"Zara?" Rhoswyn mumbles.

"Yes. Help me with Hanna, please."

She stumbles onto the other side, pulls on one arm. We take a step, another, then fall, face forward into the sand, still half in the water.

I know there's something terribly wrong.

I give one last heave and roll Hanna over.

The light of the flares is merciless. She's been shot in the chest. She is bleeding heavily.

Pressure. Must keep pressure. Stop the bleeding.

I cover the wound with my hands, and shout as loudly as I can: "Help! Hanna's been shot. Help!" It comes out little better than a croak.

They're still firing out into the bay.

Rhoswyn staggers to her feet and waves. "Help!"

Hanna's eyelids flicker.

"Zara?"

"It's me. You'll be okay. Just hold on. Hold on. Rhos is fine. You saved her. We're fine. Help's coming."

Must keep pressing. Must stop the blood loss.

"Sorry," she says. "Would have been... such good friends. You and I."

"Don't talk. Please, Hanna, just hold on."

Shouts from above. The firing stops and Rhoswyn falls back down onto her knees on the other side.

"Hanna!" Rhoswyn cries and clutches at her shirt, as if to hold her there.

"Sorry," Hanna says again. "Everything."

Her hands come up, very gently. They take Rhoswyn's and place them over mine, squeeze them together.

"Yes, press," I say. "Help me stop the bleeding, Rhos."

Hanna's head moves. A tiny shake. Her lips tremble into a small smile.

"I saved... your daughter," she whispers. "Save mine, Zara. Promise me. Alexis. Promise. Save..."

"I promise, Hanna. Hold on. Help's coming."

But her grip grows weak and the smile fades softly away.

I can't tell if she heard my promise. I hope so, even if I have no idea how I'll do it.

Chapter 57

I'm still pressing uselessly on the wound when he lifts me up.

Rhoswyn's gone. Being looked after. There were stretchers. People with medical experience. Voices, flashlights.

Nothing for Hanna.

I shake my head.

I want to ask them to lift her out of the water, because she'll get cold otherwise. I know that's stupid, that she's gone, but I don't want to remember her like that, with the sea coming in and moving her legs, giving the illusion of life. I want to remember her throwing herself at Pollard to save our lives, even at the expense of her own. Or as I first met her in person, full of life, leaping gracefully down from the back of her horse, and pulling her hat off to let that river of blonde hair fall free.

The duke carries me up to the truck as dawn begins to streak the eastern skies.

Below us, I see troopers lay her body gently on a stretcher, but then the truck begins its zigzag ascent of the headland, and the beach is hidden from me.

One of the troopers is driving and he's in a hurry. The truck lurches from side to side as it bounces up the track back to Cardu.

The duke has wrapped me in his jacket. It's huge, of course, and warm and heavy. It carries his scent, fills my senses. I want to lose myself in make-believe, and dream about how things might be, or might have been, without the harsh truth of what has just happened.

But I can't.

I brought Rhoswyn back here, where it seems Pollard was just waiting for an opportunity to try and kidnap her. And now, Hanna is dead.

And I'm jacked.

The rest of the world doesn't wait on the resolution of any of that.

The comms is on loudspeaker in the truck and the tension in the voice is unmistakable.

"...just taken off. Course suggests three high-V aircraft inbound to Cardu. Takeoff and flying parameters consistent with vehicles equipped with acceleration compensators. ETA thirty minutes."

"Keep monitoring," the duke says. "Break. Break. Moyle, are you hearing that? Your assessment on the type? Military ground assault?"

"I'm here, sir," Moyle replies. "We're getting the data feed. Security systems show no hint of imports for military vehicles of that type."

Security systems which were being run by Pollard and might be missing vital information. My knowledge of military vehicles is largely from holovid dramas, but I know enough to be scared by the thought of a military ground assault flyer.

"Unless they were what came down out of orbit last night," the duke says.

"Latest information just in from Bason, sir. Those were basic shuttles. Looks like they landed about a thousand people."

Mercenaries. Troops for the revolution.

"Status of the rest of the company in Kensa?"

"Still in position at the Skyhook terminal, sir. No major attacks. They won't want to damage the Skyhook."

Not that I expected anything less, but that's clever, taking over the Skyhook terminus. If I'd stayed hidden in there with Rhoswyn...

"Good. So what's your best guess on what's flying our way?" asks the duke.

"Best fit, three civilian commercial skimmers. They could carry three hundred people that way."

There's a long pause.

"They're not stupid," the duke says. "They're not going to assault a fort, even one that's undermanned, with three hundred troops and three skimmers."

"They might have rigged up some weapons, sir," Moyle points out. "Intelligence reports purchases of heavy plasma artillery."

The duke frowns. "But this is all hurried through in a few days. You can't engineer a major assault weapon onto a civilian skimmer in that time without compromising it. No, more likely they're just transporting them. They intend to base them within range to bombard us."

The skimmers can do vertical take-offs and landings, so they could offload the cannon on the next headland and fire from there. I assume the fort will have something to fire back, but I really don't know about artillery.

"Intelligence also shows considerable purchases of industrial explosives," Moyle says. "Along with equipment that could be for fuses, primers, timers and so on."

"Bombs? What about guidance and propulsion?"

"None of that, sir, unless Pollard suppressed intelligence, and I'm not seeing any indication of that. Sophisticated guidance systems or military-capable reaction motors would have raised alerts all over the place."

"Thank you, Moyle. Break. Break. Sandrey, you on?"

"I am, sir."

Talan's voice.

"What have we got on the roof emplacement?"

"Just the old parade cannon, sir."

"Right, first job. Get the field pulsar up there on a 360 rack mount and feed the controls and visuals down into tactical room 5C. You have fifteen minutes. Second job. Rig explosives in the stores with a switch in 5C. Irrespective of what happens to us, that equipment and ammunition is not to be available for them. Understood?"

"On it, sir."

Irrespective of what happens to us...

He's thinking ahead. His duty, regardless of whether he's dead or alive. And the fact he's thinking he may die adds to the chill already in my bones.

He turns the comms volume down and settles back.

"Thank you," he says, taking my hand in both of his.

"I'm sorry, I should have hidden with Rhoswyn at the Skyhook, sir," I reply. "It would have been safer."

He sighs. "Can I ask you to do a couple things?"

"Of course, sir."

He turns to me and suddenly those eyes are devouring me.

"Please call me Bleyd."

I try to swallow. My mouth has become very dry. He waits until I give a tiny nod.

"Accept thanks and compliments. Please don't doubt yourself so much. And don't double guess yourself all the time."

"That's at least three things," I complain. My heart is beating so loudly I wonder if he can hear it.

The truck skids to a halt in front of the main entrance to the fort.

Chapter 58

He must have more urgent things to do, but he shepherds me up to the family suite, calling out for someone to bring me a hot drink and a pair of coveralls.

"Food," I say through chattering teeth. "Please. Fruit. Energy."

And fruit is ordered.

I am very cold and still soaked in seawater. Like an old joke, I really do have absolutely nothing to wear, here at the fort. My uniform and all my spare clothes are in a hotel room on the outskirts of Bason, in Kensa. The coveralls will be welcome.

I'm also faint with hunger. And tired. Running around the fort and fighting in the cold sea has left me exhausted.

Bleyd lifts his jacket from my shoulders and points me at the bathroom.

"Food and drink will be here soon, but raise your body temperature in a hot shower first," he says.

Ahhh. All the hormone overdrive that has been building up comes to a screeching halt. To get in the shower, I need to take my clothes off. All of them, naturally.

Panic.

This is worse than ridiculous.

We're adults. I'm attracted to him. Rather a lot. He's attracted to me. If we had time, perhaps we would explore that attraction, but he has a battle to fight.

So I should go hide in the bathroom to undress? What am I? I force my fingers to fumble with buttons.

Are you going to have sex now? That would be interesting.

I go scarlet with embarrassment. I'd been distracted enough to forget her.

Hwa! Shut up! Go away!

The duke... *Bleyd...* notices, obviously.

"What?"

"Hwa," I say, hoping Talan has done the bulk of explaining.

"Your..." He hesitates and I wonder what word he'll use to describe her. *Parasite?* "ah... passenger. She communicates? She said something to you?"

"Yes." I can't meet his eyes. "Her voice gets clearer all the time. Umm. She likes you," I say. Truthful. Without actually being a complete account of what she said.

Yes, no wonder I'm so exhausted. I've no idea how the balance between Hwa's needs and mine is regulated, but even sucking excess energy from the glider's batteries, I get the sense that Hwa has had to dip into my reserves.

Yes, she confirms my guess. *We're taking too much from your body. Warmth and food are a higher priority than sex at the moment. Unfortunately.*

Not party to my conversation with Hwa, Bleyd is standing very close. I can feel the warmth of his body. I'm hypnotized by his eyes, his mouth. I'm having trouble breathing.

"One more thing I'd ask you to do," he says. "Right now."

"Yes?"

"Kiss me."

I open my lips to protest that it's hardly the right time. I don't get a word out, and I don't really want to.

His arms go around me and crush me into the heat of his embrace.

Wet, shivering, tired and hungry.

Doesn't matter.

This is what a kiss should be.

The moment ends when there's a rap on the door to announce the arrival of my coveralls. Loose and grey. Big zipper up the front. Lovely.

Bleyd drapes the coveralls over my shoulder, takes my face in his hands and kisses me again, but very gently this time.

This one is much lighter. There is the same promise and desire, but a regretful lack of immediacy.

I am going to become a connoisseur of his kisses.

Then he backs away to the door. "Rhoswyn and the doctor are down in 11E. Go there, as soon as you're finished. It'll be safer," he says.

It's like a furnace has been taken out of the room.

I hurry into the bathroom, strip and set the shower as hot as I can stand it until the shivering stops.

Then I get out and towel vigorously.

In the brief interval, someone has left a mug of hot chocolate and a bowl of fruit on the table.

There is no way I'm going to huddle down in the basement, even if he'd asked nicely, so I'm in a hurry as I force-feed myself the sweetest fruits and chase them down with scalding chocolate while hopping around on one leg getting into the coveralls.

I'm back to having no underwear again, just like when I arrived.

Loose woman.

Whoever delivered the food also thought to bring some boots of approximately the right size, and there's a jacket hanging on the stand by the door, which I assume is also for me. I empty the pockets of my wet clothes and transfer my ID and commspad. There's also the flashlight from the Skyhook's maintenance pod. I'll wait until there's a chance to give it back, I guess.

At the moment I can't do anything for the tiredness, but at least the fruit has given me some sugar in my system. Hopefully that'll provide enough energy until there's an opportunity to do more.

At which time...

The daydreams return, a jumble, full of things like how easily and quickly I will be able to get naked dressed only in coveralls. And I won't panic or freeze next time, I promise myself. There may be a bed involved, though that might not be necessary. One of us will be experienced, which is a very good thing. My stomach flips with the thought of him touching me. Of him wanting me. Of my being completely vulnerable to him. A delicious sensation, balanced between a sort of pit-of-the-stomach terror and throbbing anticipation, fills me.

And I'm certainly not cold anymore.

Zara, Hwa interrupts, *I have news. Shohwa is returning.*

"You have a message? The jamming has stopped?"

The jamming is still active, Hwa says. *I have finally accessed the main Space Traffic Control database through the InfoHub. I am redirecting the relevant transmission to your commspad. I have programmed any further transmissions to be copied there as well.*

I check the commspad. The message came in even before the jamming started. It was an automatic transmission of the type made by all spaceships on exiting the Chang field and beginning the long approach to a planet's orbital torus.

Shohwa – registered Xian Hegemony – XI-7364G – freighter – origin Scipio – destination Kernow.

It's dated a couple of days ago, which leaves a couple more days for them to arrive.

Too late to influence what happens here.

As for Hwa, I wonder if there will be an opportunity for Shohwa to download my 'passenger' before matters take their course, *hopefully,* between me and the duke.

Chapter 59

I pass no one in the fort as I hurry down to the tactical room on level 5.

The first person to see me is Moyle. We're running down the same dimly lit corridor from opposite ends. He skids to a stop as if he's seen a ghost.

"Are you all right?" I ask as I reach the door.

He jerks his head and joins me. "Just seeing you in the darkness like that," he stutters. "That jacket..."

I'm halfway inside when it registers.

It wasn't put on the stand for me to wear. He just can't bear to move it.

Oh, Goddess, I'm wearing Keren's jacket.

Bleyd looks up from the banks of screens and recovers quicker than Moyle. He hides his shock with a rueful smile and a deflection.

"You weren't ever going to stay out of the way, were you?"

"No." I sit, and touch the jacket hesitantly. "I'm sorry. I thought it was there for me. I didn't realize..."

He pats my arm clumsily.

"I think she'd be okay with it," he murmurs. His voice catches.

The others in the room haven't raised their heads from the screens, and now they start to shout out.

"There!"

"Coming straight in!"

It's just a dot. Then three. Then the skimmers seem to explode in size and flash across the screens just as the thunder of their passing overhead shivers its way down the concrete walls.

"I have tracking locked, sir. They're lit up like torches on infrared."

"What's that on the front of those two?" Moyle has frozen one of the screens with an image of them passing overhead. All three look like standard commercial skimmers—the sort of vehicle used for passenger transport. But they've had some kind of industrial modifications for loading goods through the nose section, below the cockpit. On two of them, what has been loaded is still visible as a long dark snout.

Heads lean in to peer at the details.

"Cannon, dammit. They've mounted plasma cannon."

"I think that confirms their intentions. Weapons free, Sergeant Grylls," Bleyd says. "Hold until we get a confirmed target solution."

They're turning, hard, about twenty kilometers away already. They're using the acceleration compensators and powerful drives to bring them around in a tight curve.

Talan has done her job. We have our own pulsar cannon mounted on the roof. I can see it on one of the video feeds—a great pale lance. It sits on its cylindrical power booster and six thick stabilizers, surrounded by massive cables and ugly positioning motors. It's swinging smoothly around and remaining pointed at the skimmers.

Each skimmer has one of the screens tracking it. One screen has all three in the group until suddenly, they split and dive.

"Losing lock," snaps Grylls.

"Countermeasures deployed!"

The video feed of each skimmer blurs and bubbles. Decoys split off. The tracking system seems to be able to handle it—it's a military tracking system and these skimmers' countermeasures are bolt-on modifications.

"Prioritize on solution and fire," Bleyd says calmly.

The sergeant's hand twitches. The left-hand tracking screen gets a highlight border. It's following one of the two skimmers that has a cannon mounted.

On the roof, our pulsar cannon fires. There's a deep *wump* which shudders through the whole fort, lights dim for a moment, and several screens white out.

When the screens come back, the targeted skimmer is corkscrewing downwards, countermeasures stopped, a tail of black smoke chasing it.

"Yes!" echoes from half a dozen throats.

"Good. Get the other one with the cannon if you can," Bleyd says.

"Aye, sir. Recharge 86%. Holding."

"Tracking, tracking. Locking."

"91%. Holding."

"Locked."

"Sir, no! No! The third!" Moyle is pointing. "A bomb!"

It's the skimmer without the cannon, and it's heading directly for us at maximum speed.

"Separation!"

The shape in the video feed waves and sways as if we're seeing it through a heat mirage, but there are clearly two distinct shapes, moving at different speeds.

"Retarget and fire now!"

The *wump* of the plasma cannon. The screens white out. Lights dim again.

We missed. There's a sonic boom as the skimmer thunders directly over us. Its bomb will be racing in along the same track behind it and falling, falling under gravity.

It's crazy. No one drops unguided bombs. No one. There's speeds and winds and drifts and ballistic calculations that would tie up a dozen computers for longer than it would take for the bomb to follow its decaying arc. And it's not a finite, determinable solution. Even the humidity of the air would make a difference. Even the variation in humidity on the path of the bomb. Unknowable, miniscule differences would propagate wildly through the flight equations and radically change the outcome.

Unguided bombs are like banking on winning the lottery.

They get lucky.

Chapter 60

It's like the world ended.

The bomb's travelling at the speed of sound, so the explosive capability is nearly redundant. The impact alone is like an earthquake. We're all already flying through the air when the explosion follows.

I can't hear it. I *feel* it. Like being caught between a giant's clapping hands. My whole body is compressed and then slammed down onto the floor.

Light and then darkness. Utter darkness.

I gasp and breathe searing hot dust into my lungs.

I can't seem to hear. There's noises, but they make no sense. Screaming and shouting, from a long way away. Alarms.

I cough and spit dust. Spit again.

Try to get up.

Dizzy. Too quick. Kneel again. Take stock.

I'm bleeding from gashes, but I've got no broken bones. I feel like a badly used rag doll, but I'm not trapped. I can move, although there's no point at the moment, as I can't see a thing.

"Bleyd?" my voice sounds thin.

I cough and try again. "Bleyd?"

Goddess, he'd been right there beside me.

Nothing.

"Can you hear me?" No response at all. "Moyle? Anyone?"

"Power out," someone is yelling far away.

Well, yeah.

More shouting. Very faint. Either my ears are damaged or they're a long way away.

"Auxiliary power... junction out... medics..."

And:

"Where's the duke?"

I shout again, but they don't hear me.

I reach out around me.

A wall.

I stand and hit my head.

A steel girder.

A chill shivers through my gut. The room has collapsed. This part of the fortress has fallen in.

A moment of panic. I'm on level 5. The fort's levels are numbered backwards. There's four levels above ground and eight below. Level 5 is one level below the ground.

Rhos!

She was deeper; six levels deeper!

Calm. Calm.

First things first. One thing at a time.

Where's Bleyd?

Where had he been, relative to me?

Which way was I pointing when the bomb hit?

If only I had...

Idiot. I have the flashlight I stole from the Skyhook's maintenance pod.

I retrieve it from the patch pocket. It's small and warm in my hand, it doesn't seem to have been damaged and it gives out a strong light with a wide spread.

What I see is not good; everything on the sea-facing side of the fort is a jumbled, tangled mess.

The 5C control room has split in two. Part has fallen into the next room below. That's where I am. Part is hanging in the air a couple of meters above me; tables, chairs, wires, smashed screens. A body. Sergeant Grylls, I think. It's difficult to tell.

A girder came down through the rooms, smashing everything as it went.

I think Bleyd was on my side of that dividing line, so I follow the shape of the girder.

I find him trapped underneath.

He stirs as I scrabble down beside him.

Check pulse. Clear airways. Assess possible spinal damage. Head injuries.

Half-remembered protocols flood into my mind.

"Can you hear me?" I ask.

"Yes." He curses, blinks, and wipes his eyes. "Zara! Are you all right?" He reaches up and grabs me, pulling himself into a half-sitting position.

"Careful," I say. "There's part of the ceiling right above your head and this whole section is unstable."

He swears again and coughs, pointing down his body. "Leg?"

I shine the flashlight down his body.

One leg is clear. The other disappears under the girder.

"Trapped," I say. "Okay. Keep still."

I stand up carefully and yell at the top of my lungs. "Hello, I'm down here. The duke's here. We need help to get him out. Hello? Anyone?"

No response I can hear over the sound of my coughing fit that shouting brings on.

Through the debris I can see lights start to come on. A fort will have its own backup generators. Someone must have fixed the auxiliary power.

There's a sound of another explosion somewhere in the fort; a thud that I feel in my gut. The building shivers. Something large topples over the edge in a room further down the corridor. There's a crash and more dust billows out.

"Skimmer firing at us," Bleyd growls. "Got to get out."

The emergency protocols are coming back now. It's dangerous to start digging people out without checking that you're not going to cause more of the building to collapse. But we have to balance that against lying here and hoping that the pulsar cannon on the skimmer doesn't blast its way through to the remains of tactical room 5C.

"Got to get out and take that bastard down," Bleyd says. "Can't wait for help. Hurry."

"Okay. Okay. Hold on."

I shuffle around. The girder is heavy. Far too heavy for me to lift with my arms, but I can feel it has some movement. All I need is more muscle.

I yell for help again, and then squat down and get underneath the girder, pressing my shoulders up against it.

Hwa? Will this damage you?

I can feel movement around my torso, a shifting, tightening.

No. I will try and assist.

I can feel the gel hardening around my belly and back, like the bracing belt that weight lifters wear.

Taking a deep breath, I tense and strain, pushing upwards with all the force of my legs.

A millimeter. Two.

Bleyd wriggles, breath hissing through his teeth at the pain. Not enough.

I pause take another deep breath.

And cough out a lungful of smoke.

Fire!

He hasn't noticed yet.

There's a sprinkler system. The emergency power is back on. We'll be fine. Focus on getting him out.

I kick the remains of a metal table leg toward him.

"Get that underneath the girder to help hold it up."

I give him a second and then concentrate on straightening my legs.

Like my sensei said. *Nothing can stop you.*

A groan and another millimeter or two.

There's a crack of boards splitting under the shifting weights and a slither of rubble. I freeze. I can hear bits of broken concrete sliding and tumbling down from the rooms above. A large chunk falls with a bang that I feel through the soles of my feet. It hit less than a meter away from me.

The slipping seems to go on forever.

Shouting far away. Another thud as the skimmer fires again, closer than the last. Another shock through my feet.

Bleyd has the table leg jammed under the girder and is pushing it, trying to help, but he has no leverage down there.

He sniffs and stops.

"Fire! Damn. Get out," he says. "Find some others."

There's no one in this section of the fort. No one has heard my calls.

I ignore him.

Another breath sets me coughing. There are lazy drifts of smoke visible in the beam of the flashlight now.

"Zara. You have to get out while there's time," he hisses. He swings his arm at me, hitting my leg.

"Shut up." It comes out as a grunt.

"Get out," he says again. "Rhoswyn... she'll need you."

"Not leaving you here. She needs you more." There's a creak. It's moving! I redouble my efforts, but my head is pounding as if it's about to explode. "Just like. She needed. You before."

He gasps in pain.

There's a crash behind me and I nearly let the girder slip off my shudders as I twist to look behind into the darkness. A groan of some wooden support stressed beyond its strength. A crack. A splatter of debris.

I can feel the floor tilting beneath me. The whole section is going to collapse on itself.

And then, through the tangle of broken building, I see another flashlight approaching. It's weaving from side to side, searching.

"Here," I yell. "The duke is trapped. Help me."

Then Talan is suddenly beside me, while a limping, bloodied Moyle kneels by Bleyd.

"Together," Talan says. "Now!"

We grunt and strain against the weight of the girder.

There's a groan from Bleyd as the girder eases up a fraction.

"Got him!" Moyle says.

Talan and I ease off, trying to let the girder back down without disturbing anything else.

Another person fights her way into the remains of 5C. It's the doctor, moving awkwardly under the weight of the medical kit on her back.

"Where's Rhos?" Bleyd says as he recognizes her.

"Bunker near the guardhouse, safe," the doctor replies. "Lie back."

The beams of our flashlights combine and we can all see the damage to his shin.

"Broken," the doctor mutters. "Going to stabilize the whole leg and then get you out."

"No," Bleyd says. "I need to move."

"You need to get to hospital." The doctor pulls something from her kit.

"Not going to happen while that skimmer is there," Bleyd says through gritted teeth. "Lieutenant Sandrey, if the doctor manages to inject me with that, shoot her."

"Yessir."

Talan does *not* sound as if she's going to hesitate.

The doctor stops. Sensible woman.

"Foam the leg from the knee down," Bleyd instructs her.

Muttering, the doctor complies. Bleyd's broken leg is straightened, splinted, wrapped and then sprayed. In five minutes, time enough for four more thuds of the plasma cannon hitting the remains of the building, he has a solid cast. Moyle and Talan pick him up and we begin to make our way cautiously toward the steady side of the fort.

"Up!" he says when the paths branch. The east corridors are not damaged and they take us to where the bulk of the fort will protect us from the skimmer's fire.

"Sir?" Moyle questions him. "We can't fire the pulsar cannon. The auxiliary power's not enough."

"I know," he growls back. "But there's still the parade gun. Up! We're going to the roof."

Chapter 61

The parade gun stands at the corner of the 'roof'.

It's not a roof, really. It's a huge, concrete field gun emplacement, shattered on the seaward side. What's undamaged is currently dominated by our useless pulsar cannon, too power-hungry to be fired while we're on auxiliary supply. The water-cooling has broken down as well, and it's still steaming with the heat from the recent firing. Those clouds give us some cover.

The skimmer isn't targeting our cannon. Maybe they want it; it's probably the most powerful pulsar on the planet.

Neither have they bothered with the parade gun.

I have no idea what Bleyd's plan is, but Talan and Moyle do. They've picked up two more troopers and all of them rush across to the gun while I help Bleyd hop across the expanse of the roof, cringing as the skimmer fires another plasma bolt into the crumbling structure below.

I can feel the roof shudder at every impact.

In a few minutes, there won't be enough support left, and the whole western side including the castle will tilt and slide down into the ruined section. Its weight will probably crush it down through every level.

And kill anyone who's standing on the roof at the time.

"Hurry," Bleyd calls out.

Talan frantically enters codes into the lock on an ammunition store while the others tear the coverings off, revealing the parade gun.

It is *not* a toy or a ceremonial weapon, but it *is* an antique. A hundred years old? Five hundred? It still works?

It's made of dark blue metal with a wide shield that the barrel points through and it's mounted on horizontal turntable. It's mechanically operated. The whole gun is swiveled and the barrel is raised by human effort, turning wheels that drive cogged gears. It fires cartridge rounds, like a basic rifle, but each tapered shell is as thick as my wrist and as long as my forearm.

It has the horrible beauty that comes to tools which have a deadly purpose.

The troopers rack shells into a hopper feed as I help Bleyd to sit on the firing seat.

"Up. Straight up." Bleyd yells. "Right."

The troopers spin the wheels and the gun turns and lifts.

I've been focused on the skimmer with the cannon. I look up and see the one with the bombs hovering above us. They're not going to take a chance with another horizontal approach. Now that we have no pulsar cannon, they're just going to throw a bomb out the loading door and straight down into the ruined section of the fort. That kind of shot, they can't miss.

"Up! Up." Bleyd yells as the troopers spin the wheels. "Stop! Left one, one half, one eighth, stop."

There's a sighting telescope, but Bleyd is aiming by eye.

"Clear!"

Everyone raises their hands to their ears. I copy them.

Bleyd stamps on a button.

The crash is shocking. Not as bad as being in the fort when the bomb struck, but close. There's a brilliant flash and a streak of flame leaps from the barrel. The whole emplacement rocks.

These shells travel fast, but it's not like a plasma bolt. I can see the shell hit the skimmer in the middle, see it punch right through to emerge on the other side, see the way the whole skimmer judders under the impact.

The casing is thrown out, smoking, onto the roof. The hopper feeds the next shell in.

"Left one half!"

Talan twists her wheel.

"Clear!"

Another crash and a second shell punches through the skimmer.

"Separation!" Moyle yells.

But the skimmer is already sliding down toward the sea. It's moving erratically and the bomb has been flung out sideways, along with half a dozen people who were shifting it into position. They all fall toward the sea.

Bleyd ignores them.

"Down! Right. Right. Right!"

The pilot of the second skimmer has seen the flare of the parade gun. He knows what must have happened and he's swinging around to line up with us.

We're a much smaller target than a whole fort, and to aim, they have to aim the whole skimmer. Their plasma cannon looks to be welded into place inside the loading bay.

There's the electric flash of their cannon and the gasping *rip* of the bolt overhead. No thump of a strike.

Now they have to recharge.

"Down half. Stop. Right half. Right quarter. Stop. Left eighth. Stop."

"Clear!"

The gun rocks again, the tongue of flame lashes out at the skimmer.

A hit!

The skimmer swerves. It wobbles. The pilot slams the throttles forward and hauls back on the stick. It races for the base of the clouds and disappears.

Meanwhile, the bombing skimmer is limping away, flying with a weaving motion that tells of damaged controls and chaos on board.

The noise fades, leaving an aching void to be filled with the alarms below and the mournful wind blowing across the roof of the damaged fort.

"They'll be back," Bleyd says. "Fill the hopper. Find some help to maintain a 360 degree lookout."

He's right, they return.

The skimmer with the plasma cannon comes in at full speed. There's no time to spin the parade gun around, but aiming with a whole skimmer is difficult and their shot goes wide.

We watch it curve south and then disappear into the clouds again.

More of the troopers have made their way to the roof. Some of them are working on augmenting the auxiliary power to get the pulsar cannon back online. Others stand ready with rifle pulsars, hoping to get in a lucky shot.

"Did anyone see the first one we hit go down?" I ask.

Heads shake and Bleyd nods. "Good point. All damaged, but unknown amounts."

"Solid hits on two," Moyle says.

His place at the wheels has been taken by someone else. He's one of the team of watchers now, looking out to all points of the compass.

Talan's tasked with keeping the ammunition hopper full and delivering shells smoothly.

The troopers on the aiming wheels have stripped their jackets off and wait tensely.

I'm making sure Bleyd doesn't fall off his seat or put any weight on the leg with the cast. I'm also trying to get him to let me aim the gun. The firing solution on the inward run is simple. The skimmer points at us, we point at it. If the skimmer isn't pointing at us, it will miss. But after passing overhead on the last attack, the skimmer curved its path as it flew away. It's travelling at over one thousand, two hundred kilometers per hour. If we fire after it, the shell will be travelling at over three thousand kilometers per hour. If the flight path is not straight, that's a complex equation to hit it. We have to shoot where we think it will be and we have about a three second window before the range starts to be complicated with ballistic considerations and influenced by factors we can't measure or control.

At the moment, we're simply depending on Bleyd's visual judgment and best guess.

Ten minutes ago I didn't know any of this. Hwa is filling my head with mathematical models. She tells me she'll overlay my sight with a mathematical analysis and show me where the gun needs to point.

All of which is sucking energy out of my body, but it won't matter if we don't survive.

Bleyd's eyes narrow as he thinks through the proposal I've just made to replace him. He knows nothing about Hwa's capabilities, but he clearly trusts my judgment.

"Okay," he says slowly. "Why don't we—"

"Contact!" Moyle yells. "235, low! *Low!* Coming in fast."

I see it immediately. For us in the fort, it's silent, travelling faster than sound, but I can see the sonic wave hammering the ocean into a tail of spray behind it.

"Left and down!" Bleyd and I shout. "Left, left, left, stop. Down! Down! More!"

No time.

The wheel mechanisms are stiffer as the barrel reaches the horizontal.

We don't have time to prop the back up to depress the barrel more, and that skimmer's coming in too low.

It's got to go up to pass over us. If it keeps straight, it'll fly through our sights, but it'll have already fired then. It may be too late.

"Contact!" Behind us, Corporal Wallace shouts, his voice hoarse. "Contact! 080! *Closing fast!*"

Shit! *Behind* us!

Suddenly I know we're aiming at the wrong one. It's a diversion. That's why it flew so low that it was kicking up the spray—so we'd see it.

We've run out of time. We can't swivel the parade gun all that way around to the other attacker.

"Everyone down!" Bleyd yells.

There's no time even for that before the explosion hits us.

My ears give up again. I hear it with my whole body. We're pounded, *crushed* by it.

As I fall, I see a dark, ominous shape, like an arrow, already past us, thundering overhead, tail on fire.

So close!

Then... *Goddess, that's no skimmer!*

Streaks of flame. Missiles? Going *away* from us. The 'explosion' that I've just felt was a sonic boom as it went overhead.

My voice rattles, lost in the noise: "That's—"

Out at sea, the attacking skimmer erupts in a brilliant flash, so bright it burns into the back of my eyes.

The shuttle that destroyed the skimmer hauls itself back onto its fiery tail and roars up into the sky, screaming defiance.

We're all lying on the ground, blinking and dazed.

Talan lifts her head. "What the nova?" Her voice sounds dull and distant.

"*Shohwa* shuttle," I rasp, pointing up at the angry glare of the reaction jets that are all we can still see of it. "Full military spec. Gimme the comms."

Wallace fumbles and hands it over.

"Give me an all band broadcast," I say.

He stabs the controls, nods.

"Danny," I say, my voice cracking. "Danny, is that you?"

"Ha! Good to hear your voice, Zara. We got your back." His voice crackles from the speaker. "Couple more of these bastards to clear and we'll come visiting you at the airfield."

"Thank you."

"Is Duke Tremayne there?" he asks.

"He's here."

"Can you get him to the airfield? I have some people flying in to meet him."

Bleyd takes the microphone. "This is Duke Tremayne. I think I can manage that," he says. "Our sincere thanks to the *Shohwa*, and her shuttle."

"Our pleasure, sir. I'll meet with you shortly."

"There!" Wallace points.

On the eastern horizon there are two swift flashes like lightning in the clouds. Tumbling, burning shapes drop from the sky, barely recognizable as skimmers. There are more flashes as they impact hillsides, and distant booms.

The conspiracy's aerial assault has failed, with the loss of all the skimmers they sent here, and anyone on board.

Will it be enough?

Chapter 62

By the time we reach the airfield, the shuttle has landed, and as it turns out, they save me a second time in the space of the morning.

Hwa has been doing what she could to minimize her energy expenditure, but the human body is not designed to power both of us at the same time. I don't want to say anything, but as we approach the airfield, she becomes very active. I stagger when I step down from the truck.

Fortunately, it's Talan and Corporal Wallace holding Bleyd up, and my old friends from the *Shohwa*—Gartz, Bernard and Danny—come to greet me, and they catch me before I fall.

They're prepared for this. Bernard and Gartz whisk me into the shuttle, and Hwa gets wired into a real power socket before I pass out.

"I need to speak to Shohwa," I say as soon as that's done.

Bernard presses some high-nutrient food into my hands while Gartz nods acknowledgment. He pulls an extension holoprojector from the wall and positions it in front of me.

Shohwa appears, looking exactly as she did before.

"Hello, Zara," she says. "Please accept my most sincere thanks."

I blink. *What is she talking about?*

She smiles.

"It is a small thing, perhaps, for you. And perhaps also, it is difficult for you to equate a Self-Actualized Entity with an organic life, but I assure you that Hwa and I believe you saved her life and you did so despite all your concerns."

It's embarrassing when she puts it like that. Hwa's life weighed against my fears about being looked down on because I have a computer interface in my head.

"I'm happy that I was able to help," I say quickly. "There's a favor I must ask in return."

"I believe I know what you want." Her image drifts to one side and a three-dimensional representation of the Kernow star system takes shape. "Hwa has been most... passionate in her desire that I apprehend the *Yenobia* and rescue a young girl, Alexis Esterhauze."

So that's what Hwa has been doing that sapped my energy so much— using the shuttle comms to talk to Shohwa urgently.

Thank you, Hwa.

But the holo display of the system zooms in to Kernow's orbit and the arc above—the one that ships take to leave the system.

I can see Shohwa's marker, still in orbit. My heart in my mouth, I see a track moving away at what's probably maximum velocity.

"The *Yenobia* broke orbit as soon as the skimmers failed in their mission," Shohwa says.

"Can you catch them?"

The *Shohwa* is not what it seems. It might look like a freighter, but I know it has military level capability. The fact that it got here in half the time it should have is proof of that.

"Yes," Shohwa says.

She says it in a way that tells me there's a 'but' involved.

"There is something you should consider," she says. "I could either pursue this ship, or you could come up here and I will separate you and Hwa."

"No. A young girl's life is more important—"

"It's not your discomfort I'm speaking about, Zara. Nor, strictly, am I speaking to just you. By taking her own name, Hwa has, if you like, declared independence. She is no longer an adjunct part of me, she is her own entity. I freely admit, that has surprised and delighted me."

I have one eye on the representation of the *Yenobia* and one ear on what she's saying.

When will it be too late to chase them?

She continues.

"I suspect that the rapid development is due in part to the nature of the relationship between you, which is now further amplified by how close this interface connection makes you. It is very interesting to me, but it also concerns me, for both of you. This interface was never designed for this, and has never, to my knowledge, been used for so long during such a period of extraordinary stress. It seems to me that Hwa's processing modes are already exhibiting patterns of human decision-making."

I frown. "That relationship you speak of; Hwa inherited it from you. She *was* you, in a manner of speaking, when she and I first met. And when *we* first met, you claimed you had analogues of human emotions. Are you now saying you're frightened for Hwa if she has too much of them?"

Shohwa bows her head. "Excellently argued. Your grasp of this complexity underlines my point, in its converse—that as you influence her mind, Hwa is also influencing yours. And that the longer you maintain this connection, the more you will seep into each other's minds. You are changing and will continue to change, in ways you do not control or understand."

She presses her hands together and bows her head again slightly. "I am not suggesting one path or the other; I am pointing out to my friends the factors that they should consider in their decision."

I close my eyes.

Yes, this experience has changed me. All experience changes me. That I don't control it is part of the randomness of life. So much less important than getting Alexis back safe.

Hwa?

Hwa's voice is becoming stronger and clearer in my mind every time we 'talk'.

I'm with you, she says. *Get Alexis back and then think about what we need to do next.*

Shohwa hears our conversation, somehow. She bows her head a final time.

"I have quickly come to expect such character of you both," she says. "I look forward to our next meeting."

Her image disappears.

The map of the Kernow system expands to show the *Shohwa* breaking orbit and moving to intercept the *Yenobia*. It will be some time, military speeds or not.

Goddess, into your hands.

I feel helpless. There's nothing more I can do.

Outside, a second shuttle is landing.

Hwa has taken her fill of energy and Gartz gives me some more fruit to eat, so I go to see what's happening.

Talan is there as soon as I emerge.

"Are you all right?" she asks.

"Yes." I give her a one-armed hug. "Just needed some fuel."

She snorts. "And some rest."

"Sure. When everything stops for a second."

Down the steps of the second shuttle come representatives from all over Kernow. Talan reels their names off. Founding Families, business leaders, politicians, police chiefs, judges. None of them appear to have been directly connected with the conspirators, and all of them have come to see what's happening and get explanations, according to Danny.

Bleyd manages to get a lift up onto the wing of the shuttle so everyone can see him, with his dusty, torn uniform, broken leg and all. He certainly makes a dramatic spokesman, even if he were not important enough as the duke.

The first fifteen minutes is an explanation by Bleyd of what has been happening and how it has been happening. The secret conversations that Hwa stole are sent to everyone's commspad. As a background, from the airfield, everyone can see the destruction of the fort, and the audience is appalled.

The extraction of secret messages, the repair of the InfoHub, all the involvement by Hwa is played down. As is the involvement of the *Shohwa*.

Talan whispers to me as he speaks. "Danny passed on Shohwa's advice. This must appear to be a local issue that Shohwa is simply helping with, because Kernow is a valuable trading partner."

I nod. The less anyone knows about Shohwa and me, the better. Make this all about local issues. But what is 'local'?

I can see that the audience are still unconsciously grouping themselves. The people from Kensa, Murenys, Trethow and the Delkys Islands stand in their own clumps.

Bleyd reaches the end of the summary of how everyone got here and he sees it, too.

"Gwir yn erbyn y byd, kewselm," he says.

"Eh?" I have no idea what he just said.

Talan gets a strange light in her eyes.

"He's speaking old Cornish," she says, and starts translating for me: "I speak the truth, even against the whole world.

"Our families came to this world and they lit a beacon. A beacon to draw people, scattered like grains of sand across the stars, to a place where they could be one.

"They called this beacon Kernow, a name from our shared history, that others would understand that the spirit of this place runs quiet and deep and old.

"Those others came from many places, and they made their commitment, they made this place their home.

"*We* made this place our home, friends, *we* did. And *we* were *one*. One planet. One community. One people.

"What subtle knife has carved us, people of Kernow, one from the other?

"When did it become acceptable to not say we were from Kernow, but to say instead we were from Kensa, or Murenys, or Trethow, or Delkys?

"If we do not speak of ourselves as one, why are we surprised to find ourselves divided?

"And into that division will pour every vice we wanted to escape when our ancestors lit that beacon here."

Bleyd has shaken them. Using the language that marked them as a people has been a brilliant ploy.

But is it enough?

He passes from the fears of the Founders to their dreams of what Kernow could be, and I can hear him coming to his appeal for unity against the conspirators.

"Our fate is in our hands.

"We can decide to fall, like Lyonesse of the old stories, beneath the waves, where we will dream our sea-cold visions of what was and might have been. Become a people forgotten, in our own empty land, our only memorial some battered sign that says 'here stood Kernow', among the dark stones.

"Or we can take our dream back and breathe new life into Kernow. *Together.*

"Kernow is in our hands. Our hands." On the shuttle's wing, Bleyd raises his hands and holds them up to his audience. "And ours alone."

There is a profound silence across the whole airfield. The wind sighs, but no man or woman breathes.

Then Talan leaps up, startling me.

"Ker-now!" she yells, pumping her fists into the air. Her face is flushed and her eyes are gleaming. "Ker-now! Ker-now!"

One of the men on the other side of the listening group, from a Founding Family, takes up the chant. "Ker-now!" He pumps his fists in the air, mirroring Talan.

I think they'll never get the others to join in. I mean, there are judges there—venerable old guys and gals. Police chiefs in their starchy uniforms. Fusty old business leaders.

I'm wrong.

Chapter 63

The *Yenobia* might be in retreat, the Hajnal revolt may have failed, but by the end of the day, it's painfully obvious that any personal life is going to come second for the moment.

The remaining Hajnal forces have become desperate and they still hold the media centers on Kensa. From what they can see on their news channels, the majority of the people of Kernow probably believe that the situation is entirely reversed from the truth. That Duke Tremayne is leading a rebellion and the conspirators are the people's heroes.

The police on Kensa still believe that's the case.

There's the core of the necessary people to restore Kernow right here, on the airfield, but without control of the media, especially on Kensa, the duke is chosen to be the best representative for the whole planet. That means he'll be visiting and speaking to groups until the media can be taken back and put into independent hands.

Danny has offered the use of the Shohwa shuttle.

The politicians in the group advise taking Rhoswyn as well, at least for photo opportunities in safe places. The image of the duke and his daughter will make good impressions.

The same politicians strongly advise against me being included in any capacity. Having my picture plastered over their news channels and labelled as a deranged terrorist has made me politically poisonous, even if it's all lies.

Bleyd hates the idea.

So do I, but one of us has to think clearly. I need to rest, keep Hwa's batteries topped up and communicate with Shohwa. Bleyd needs to go out and deliver the simplest consistent message to the people of Kernow. The tasks don't overlap.

And before Bleyd and I have the opportunity to progress any further, I hope that Shohwa returns and separates Hwa and me. I love Hwa like a sister, but it was bad enough having her look over my shoulder as I kissed him.

In my head, Hwa is giggling about it.

Bleyd is gruff and grumpy about leaving me behind, but he sees his duty to the whole planet.

"You can't stay at Cardu," he says. "The building's not stable, and there'll be no reliable power until it's repaired."

"We'll need somewhere with rooms for a security detail," Talan says. "It's probably not required, but better to be safe."

"Of course she'll need a detail," Bleyd says, and comes to a stop at the look in my eye. "If that's all right with you?" he adds.

I don't argue. Like the whole of this situation, it makes sense without being what I want. I'm not going to refuse security in a fit of pique.

"I don't want to go all the way to some hotel in Bandry or Marazion," I say. "What about the Spyglass in Stormhaven?"

Talan shakes her head. "Only got two rooms, and it's not easy to secure."

Bleyd frowns.

"The closest place is the Roscarrows' house. I'm sure Emblyn and Marik will put you up. I'll call them."

He immediately calls Lady Roscarrow and explains the situation, in a roundabout way.

We haven't spoken at any length about 'us'. Bleyd doesn't have any agreed shorthand for describing what we may become to each other, so his words to Lady Roscarrow are a bit obscure.

She's very clever, she'll get the idea, and the choice of the Roscarrows is a good one. I wouldn't want to claim they owed me a favor for flying Lord Roscarrow to the hospital, but it's undeniable that he'd be dead if it wasn't for me.

I remember that she was also very supportive at the ball, and allow myself to hope that this will be a pleasant few days in her company while Bleyd saves Kernow and Shohwa saves Alexis.

"All arranged," Bleyd says, closing the call.

He gives Talan the eye and she diplomatically wanders off to talk to Danny and the team who are preparing the shuttle for its diplomatic mission.

"It won't be long," he says.

I know I'm supposed to say something sweet like *it'll feel as if it's a long time*. The truth is I haven't any useful experience of men. Not like this. All the phrases that come to mind sound like I copied them from a romance holovid. And I haven't watched many of those.

My stomach is doing somersaults again.

"I'm no good at this," I blurt out.

He chuckles. It's like a deep belly laugh that is slowly working its way back into use.

I like it.

"Neither am I," he says.

Liar. I am getting wobbly under his gaze and I can't blame Hwa for it this time.

We're very close. Not touching. Not quite.

I swallow and steel myself. "I would be at fault if I didn't warn you. It's not just that I'm clumsy, I'm not experienced. At all."

Despite every effort on my part to keep cool, I feel my face heat up.

"I had a motto which my grandfather taught me," I continue. *"Offer no weakness; suffer no wound.* He regarded any relationship to be an opening, and any opening to be a potential weakness."

"I realized there might be something," he says. "What changed?"

Again, I know what I'm supposed to say; that it all changed because of him. It would be partly true, but I can't think of a way to say it that doesn't sound trite.

He doesn't wait for an answer anyway.

"I also realize that we've argued," he says, "almost every time we've spoken."

We both smile at that.

"To a certain extent, I was following your grandfather's motto," he says. "I didn't want, ever again, to be so hurt. I mean as I was when Keren was murdered."

Tears prickle in my eyes.

"But it doesn't work like that. It only means I've kept it fresh, so that the pain remains a part of me. Pushing everyone away. I guess keeping the murder investigation going was one way of doing that. And here I am, with no new clues about it, let alone a resolution."

Danny is approaching, making it plain he's eager to begin the mission.

And yet this conversation is like handling broken glass. It needs more time, more care.

Bleyd looks down, not meeting my eye, trying to apologize and offer me something and feeling he's betraying Keren's memory by doing it, all in the same few words.

"Perhaps it's time to put it aside," he says. "Start fresh."

No!

But I don't want to argue.

"We'll speak when you come back," I say. "Go. Stay safe."

Moments later, the hatch of the shuttle closes behind him, cutting him off from me, and I shiver with premonition.

Chapter 64

It seems the Founding Families that built along this coast had a love of houses with good views. Pyran Manor sits on the very top of the next headland along from Cardu. You can see three headlands past the damaged Cardu fort in one direction and the outskirts of Bandry in the other.

It's built with the local black stone, and has detailing in pale granite, echoing the style of the flag of Kernow.

Bleyd assured us we would be welcome, but I soon sense that's an exaggeration.

Lady Roscarrow meets us in the hall: Gaude, Talan and me. The five other troopers that Talan insists are the minimum for a full security detail are having a look around the grounds.

"I gather you'll be wanting to stay together," Lady Roscarrow says stiffly. "The servants are clearing the West Wing for you."

We seem about as welcome as beggars off the road come calling. Talan and I certainly look a sight; we're still in the clothes we were wearing when we scrambled out of the collapsed section of the fort. I have Keren's jacket on, and the material seems to retain the sharp chemical smell from the parade gun's shells.

Lady Roscarrow takes one look at us and barely seems able to meet our eyes.

Gaude is smartly dressed and she speaks to him.

I realize it's upsetting having eight 'guests' billeted on you, but I'm disappointed in Lady Roscarrow, after how well we got on at the ball.

I search around for a topic to break the ice.

"How is Lord Roscarrow?" I ask.

"Unwell," she says shortly. "I must insist that he's not disturbed. Kindly keep well away from the East Wing."

"Of course, my lady," Gaude says. "Something related to the accident?"

"Possibly. He's running a fever and started raving today, speaking fanciful nonsense. I've had to sedate him." She turns away. "I must check on him. You know the West Wing, Gaude. Ask the servants if you need anything."

Talan frowns.

I shrug. I don't have any spare emotions to waste on her.

Gaude shows us to the library at the heart of the West Wing, and disappears to supervise clearing the rooms.

"Are you hungry?" Talan asks.

"I'm starving. I haven't eaten anything apart from fruit since breakfast in Kensa yesterday."

"Okay. I'll make you something to eat."

"I'll come help."

"You will not," she says. "Danny was very explicit. You rest."

She leaves me alone to inspect the library.

It's a handsome rectangular room with three walls almost entirely taken with shelves of books and framed photographs and diplomas. The fourth, facing west, is dominated by three huge windows, and they fill the room with golden afternoon light. I feel like a bug floating in amber.

The photos and diplomas are interesting.

Marik Roscarrow is a cheerful man, fond of photos of himself with friends at sporting events and, if he has academic qualifications, shy about displaying them. His sister is the opposite. There is exactly one photo of them together, on a yacht. The remainder of her photos are of her at graduation ceremonies or at Murenys social and political events. Lots of political events. And all the diplomas are hers. Chemistry, biology and, in fact, a full medical degree from the University of Marazion. I remember thinking from the flight to the hospital she seemed to have medical training. I did her a disservice. Her academic qualifications are daunting; they make me feel quite ignorant.

As do her books. History, politics, art, medicine, science. Real books, printed on pyrus, with that subtle smell of bread when you open them. A couple of them are actually by her. Histories of Kernow. And politics.

What does Lady Roscarrow do to relax?

A grand piano in the center of the room gives one clue. There are stables here, and there's the one photo of her sailing. I remember Talan saying she and Marik had been out on the *Low Lady* with Bleyd and Keren.

In all the photos of Lady Roscarrow, there's no sign of any husband, or lover.

A strange life, but that's not for me to judge.

I stop snooping and sit down on a sofa facing the windows.

As I rest, I feel Hwa begin to spool up.

I'm not happy with Bleyd's suggestion to put Keren's death aside, she says. *Not least because the murder might be aimed at her position, and therefore might be a threat to you as the next duchess.*

"I think you're getting a bit ahead of the action, Hwa."

Not difficult when there's been no action.

"Behave yourself."

She laughs and becomes serious.

New approach. Stop thinking about the mechanics of it. How the murderer hid on board the Low Lady. How they got back to the shore. Why Keren's body ended up in the bay. Let's focus on motive and method instead.

"The standard rules for detection," I say. "Motive, method, means, opportunity."

Indeed. So what are the possible motives for murder?

There's a good reason I haven't spent a lot of time on this. It feels unknowable without interviewing every person who'd come into contact with the duchess.

"Deliberate, planned murder? I guess: love, hate, fear, greed, which could split into sub-categories like: revenge, sex, jealousy..." I slow down. "Or something like mental illness. Or a combination. It's hard to know. But the way she was murdered? That speaks of hate and insanity."

Just list them all at the moment. What about politics? Status? Sympathy?

"Politics? I didn't think she was political."

She wasn't, and that was the problem. I was researching this on the InfoHub. As duchess, she was a principal of the Kernow movement. You saw how powerful that is at the airfield. The duke's only voicing what some of the Founding Families have been saying for some time. But two months before she was murdered, she gave up her position in the movement, in exasperation. Some might see that as an abdication of responsibility.

"Okay. It's a stretch, but I just about get how politics could be a motive, theoretically. Even status, maybe, but sympathy?"

I'm just listing them. Sympathy would be where a murderer kills someone thinking that's what they want.

"Oh, euthanasia, for instance."

Yes. Obviously not in Keren's case, as far as we can tell. And status? That's a potential. Someone wanted to be duchess?

"I've seen no real evidence of that. Talan said people thought she wasn't the right class to be Duchess Tremayne, but that's a long way from murder. And I'm not aware of anyone putting themselves forward as the next duchess."

They wouldn't immediately. Also, Bleyd has been isolating himself from people, making it difficult. Now, suddenly, that looks like it's going to change. You've arrived on the scene. Which means, if someone killed Keren hoping to become the next duchess, you'd be in danger.

"Oh, come on! That's tenuous, Hwa."

Maybe. What about a mixture of motives?

"Like hate, greed and politics? No, drop the greed, that doesn't feel right."

Yes. How about love, politics and hate?

The door opens and interrupts our discussion.

Chapter 65

It's Talan and she carries a tray loaded with food: a hot meat pie steaming gently around its thick crust, a bowl of salad, a berry crumble with cream for dessert, and a tall glass of juice with condensation beading the outside.

"Oh, my goodness!" I get up. "This looks wonderful."

"Sit down, and don't thank me." She shrugs it off.

I pull across a side table. My stomach is rumbling and I'm literally salivating at the sight of the food.

"You didn't need to go to all this trouble."

"Danny said you need to eat well while you're hosting Hwa."

Oh. Danny said this. Danny said that.

"Hmm. Danny said a lot of things to you, it seems."

"He's concerned for his friend."

I'm back on the couch. Talan's sitting in front of me with the afternoon sun behind her, making it difficult to see her eyes, but I'm pretty sure there was a little questioning emphasis on the word 'friend'. I sense something to tease Talan about. Which means I need to change topics for now. I will come back to 'Danny' later. It will be fun.

"Is Moyle okay?"

"Yes. Just bruising when he got hit by falling masonry."

"Good." An odd memory of Moyle surfaces. "I saw him early one morning, you know, just after I arrived. He was down at the Shrine."

"He looks after the garden there, when he can."

Keren's garden.

I sense Hwa's interest.

"He still seems very upset about it all. I mean about Keren's death."

"He is." Talan sighs. "He was one of four troopers who were assigned to guard Keren. They worked on a rota. It was his watch that day."

"But she decided not to take him. He can't blame himself for that."

She hesitates and shifts in her chair, turning side on. "For your ears only, okay?"

I nod.

"Moyle was hopelessly in love with her. Unrequited, of course." She drapes an arm over her chair and looks through the window at the sea. With the sun low in the sky, the surface of the sea looks like beaten copper. "Keren was very alert. You couldn't get something like that past her. He tried his best to hide it, but she knew, and she also knew that it made him intensely embarrassed."

I close my eyes. "So rather than embarrass him all day on the *Low Lady*, she made a point to sneak out without him, and he blames himself for what happened as a result."

"Something like that."

I blow out a breath. Not that I suspect him of murder; Moyle is even taller than Talan, and I'm still convinced whoever killed her had to have hidden themselves on the *Low Lady*. The only place I could see that happening was underneath the steps down to the cabin, and I could barely fit in there.

But it's interesting. The picture of what happened has another little thread to it; converting a bare-bones court report into something that actually happened with real people, and emotions, and all the complex, messy things that happen in real lives.

But it doesn't get me any closer to 'why'. Who wanted to kill the duchess? How would a mixture like love, politics and hate combine? Who would have those motives?

The food and drink has disappeared and I have to lie back on the sofa. I'm bone tired, I'm full, I'm warm; I'm not going to solve any mysteries this evening.

Talan pulls my boots off and brings a blanket to cover my body.

Bliss.

I smile at her. "I saw a different side of you at the airfield."

"How do you mean?"

"The way you responded to Bleyd's speech. Really got you going, didn't he?"

"It's what I've always felt," she says. "Kernow needs to be unified. The duke needs to lead it."

There are things I think the duke needs to do, but leading Kernow isn't on my list. Still, I like Talan too much to argue with her.

"Humanity's due for a fourth expansion," she says. "We can't have instability or division in Kernow when that happens."

The sun's getting lower in the sky, touching the ocean, shining right in at us. I'm too tired to move. The sun is lighting up Talan's hair, like halo. It casts a deep shadow on her face.

I can't see my friend's face.

Too tired.

"We just can't," she murmurs. "Whatever we feel about it personally. We all have our duty."

"Sleepy. Don't like politics, even when I'm wide awake," I mumble.

"No. Keren didn't like it, and I don't either, but politics doesn't care what we personally want or like. Duty remains." She stops talking for a while, or I start to drift.

I'm vaguely aware when she gets up and tucks the blanket around me.

"You go to sleep now," she says. "Everything will be fine."

My eyelids are so heavy. My whole body is so heavy.

Everything will be fine.

It's not. Everything is not fine.

No!

Talan moves away.

Wait.

I can't speak. I can't raise my hand. I can't move.

My nightmares have returned, but I'm awake.

That taste. That fruit juice. *What fruit was that?*

Voices.

She's asleep.

Don't want her disturbed...

Moving away.

Wait! Stop! What have you done?

I scream, but no sound emerges.

She has nightmares says a voice.

A door closes. Silence.

Talan? TALAN!

Chapter 66

I wake slowly, even though I'm freezing, with the sort of numbing, hopeless cold that seeps into your bones and steals your will.

What happened?

Why am I so cold?

I feel ill.

A hangover?

I just want to go back to sleep.

Zara! Zara! Zara!

I raise my hands to block my ears.

They're wet. My hands are wet. With sea water. And the calling is in my head.

Zara, you have to get up.

Who's that?

Where am I?

Why do I feel so awful?

I manage to roll over with a groan. It's completely dark. I get to my knees and vomit until my head feels like it's going to split in two.

Good. Get it out of your stomach.

The voice. I know who it is now, but my brain is just so blurred.

"Hwa?" I croak.

Yes. Finally.

"What happened?"

You've been drugged.

Her voice is quite clear. I can remember back when it wasn't clear. We were... For a moment I can't remember where we were when I couldn't hear her. Then, like crystals suddenly forming, I remember the spinning globe, the police waiting for us in the street outside the delegation, the Skyhook, crazy plan B and the madness of the flight back.

"Did I hit my head when we crashed?"

Not hard enough for this.

"Where are we?"

I don't know. I haven't been able to interface with you for hours.

It's dark... there's a lurch in my memory. The beach in darkness. Rhoswyn kidnapped. I killed a man. Maybe two. And Hanna...

"Hanna!"

But she's dead. And my memory lurches again, like a building being bombed.

Like Cardu. The skimmers. Plasma cannons and bombs. Danny at the airfield.

And then Pyran Manor.

Eating a meal with Talan watching me.

Drinking the cool juice that was on the tray. So sweet and tasty.

A poison with no hint in its smell or taste. Bleyd's voice speaking to me in his study: *...overwhelm the sigma receptors in your brain, the specific receptors that are the keys to higher brain functions and memory for example. You are rendered defenseless...*

"Who?" I ask between spasms. "Talan?"

I don't know. Whatever it was you drank disabled any interface with you. I've been blind and deaf until a few minutes ago.

My belly is finally empty and the vomiting has stopped.

Wherever I am is dark and half-full of water.

I check my pockets. I have nothing. No flashlight. No commspad.

I crawl slowly upwards to get out of the water. It's not far. A couple of steps. Some kind of a door. This begins to feel horribly familiar.

A watertight door. Locked and sealed with no wheel latch on this side to open it.

I feel around blindly. Find a stone. Hammer on the door. Someone will hear. Surely.

Someone must hear? Please?

Not if this door is at the bottom of a sealed stairwell, like Cardu.

What had Hanna said about the smugglers' tunnels? *Everyone along this coast, they were smugglers. All the houses have these passages.*

This isn't Cardu. But Pyran Manor might have exactly the same type of smugglers' tunnel.

Hanna had said something else about the tunnels: *I only hope the tide is low, because they generally flood.*

I stop hitting the door, and feel back down the stairs.

I'd crawled up two steps out of the water.

Now there's only one.

I feel the walls along the side of the door. Over the top.

They're damp. There's a slippery sea plant growing, some sort of seaweed. They grow all up the walls, up and up, as far as I can stretch. The sort of plant that needs to be submerged some of the time. This whole chamber floods.

Blind panic.

Zara! You have to swim. The sooner the better.

I know she's right. In the midst of the shivering terror comes a little clarity.

The clothes will only slow me down, and I'm not going to get any colder than I already am.

I pull off the jacket and unzip the coveralls.

That's the easy part.

I walk into the water. I can feel the pull of waves, swelling and sucking in the cave.

If I time it right, the pull will help me down the passage.

How long can I hold my breath?

I don't know.

I'm hyperventilating already. Don't divers do that before they dive? What else? It's too late to try and warm up a little.

The water is at my neck when my outstretched hand feels the rock ceiling of the cave angling down.

It meets the water a meter in front of me.

This is it.

Breathe. *Breathe!* Suck it in. Oxygen in the blood.

Feel the push and pull of the water.

It's pushing. As that force begins to weaken, I take my last lungful and duck into the water, swimming against the flow.

Steady, steady. Don't thrash. Swim efficiently.

I feel the flow of water turn.

My heart is pounding, echoing in my ears.

Push turns to pull.

Suddenly I'm racing forward. Now I'm worried about hitting my head on rocks.

On and on. Much longer than the cave at the foot of Cardu's headland.

Arms feel weaker.

There's light ahead.

It's just too far.

Keep going.

Impossibly far.

My lungs are bursting.

No! The light changes. I think I'm out of the cave, but I'm still going down. There's a rip tide pulling me deeper and deeper.

Too deep.

No strength left.

I tried. It isn't enough.

I'm sorry, Bleyd. Sorry, Rhos. I tried. I tried.

I can't swim anymore. I have no strength in my arms and legs.

The water is pulling me whichever way it wants.

I feel the air dribbling from me. Spirals of bubbles that shiver and float. That way must be up, but it's too far for me to soar up with them.

And darkness is returning. A true, sacred darkness. A shadow as wide as the sky and as remorseless as the fall of night passes over me.

Upon that darkness, in my final terror, I glimpse Her face.

Our Lady of Sorrows.

I did not think to find you here.

Where else would I be, Zara?

I am where all grief ends. I am the sea of all sorrows. I am fed by the rivers of despair. I am the billion, billion tears that flow into me.

Come. I am the end of striving. I am peace. I am home.

Her face hangs above me, as limitless and soft and welcoming as the summer nights on the hills above the house where I was born.

Another voice is calling me.

Zara! Zara. Zarazarazarazara.

It's fading. It doesn't matter.

There is only *Her* voice, which speaks with the great, slow pulse of the sea.

I am afraid no more.

I am at the end of striving.

At peace.

Home.

I reach out and touch Her face.

Chapter 67

Morrohow is the name on the Welarvor coast; they don't use the word 'bounty'.

Morrohow are the gifts of the great sea. We are all the same to the deeps, but that is not to say that the deeps do not perceive our differences. It is up to us to say which gifts are ill and which are not. It does not matter to the sea.

The gifts are brought to the bay in Her protecting arms, bound around with banners of seaweed, as if clothed in Her hair.

She brought the duchess here. She brought me here.

I can hear the innkeeper, Warwick, alternating between babbling prayers and calling out to others for help.

There are distant voices, shouting, answering.

I cough and retch salt water. I can't stop shivering. I can't seem to talk.

People running.

I think I can hear Bleyd. I must be mistaken. He's in Kensa.

Rhoswyn. Talan. Danny. Gaude. Their voices blend until I can't make out what's being said.

Bleyd's arms around me, lifting me.

Daylight.

This *is* the bay where Keren's body was found.

Where a creeler boat came to look for morrohow.

Where Warwick came to look for me.

Because they know. This is where the sea delivers her gifts, for good or ill.

Bleyd is speaking, but the words make no sense.

"Hold me," I manage to whisper, and he does.

A truck comes down onto the beach.

There are blankets being wrapped around me.

Then he holds me again, hard against his chest and his heartbeat is like a beacon, calling me home. I shiver and press myself harder against him.

The truck's heating is on full, but I'm still cold.

We skid to a stop.

The airfield. The shuttle is back.

Of course it's back. How else would Bleyd have returned?

I'm on a gurney and the blankets are replaced with something hotter. Sensations of heat on my back as well.

"Both alive," says a voice. "Barely."

Both of us. *Hwa?*

There's no direct answer. No more than a presence.

"Hwa helped keep her alive." Another voice. Someone from the *Shohwa*. "Must have turned her power reserves into heat, slowed her body metabolism down, kept it functioning."

"That long! They've been missing more than twelve hours."

Twelve hours?

They're taking blood samples, blood pressure, heart rate.

I'm alive. The rest is detail.

Cannulas. Drip feed. I fade in and out.

I don't want to. I know Bleyd is beside himself with worry, but all I can say is *hold me*. He does. He sits beside me as my mind wanders, trying to make connections where there are just gaping holes.

"...no evidence of psychoactive tranquilizers in her blood. But the trace chemicals..."

I blink and focus.

Bleyd's voice is quiet and angry. "Let me see."

Someone hands him a pad with the analysis of my blood.

"Ammeledh," Gaude is looking over his shoulder. "Bale fruit brandy."

"An extract. Too pure for contaminated Ammeledh."

I cough.

"Who did this, Zara?" Bleyd squeezes my hand and leans down over me.

I shake my head. I can't remember clearly. Something about the library at Pyran Manor. Diplomas. Photos. Motives. Politics. Love. Hate. Talking. Eating.

But Talan replies to Bleyd's question.

"I brought her a drink with her food. But..."

There's an angry movement.

I raise my head. Troopers are holding Talan.

"No!" I say. "No. Talan."

I stretch out a hand. At Bleyd's nod, they let Talan come to my side and take my hand.

I sink back down onto the gurney. Everything is an effort. Everything is a blur.

Hwa is bubbling things up into my mind.

Neither of us have any recollection of how we got from the library down to the smugglers' cave, but Hwa thinks we were so close to knowing.

I can feel the way our minds are working together. Intuition, logic, data. The puzzle is so nearly finished.

My voice feels scratchy in my throat. "It wasn't Talan. She brought me my meal, but she didn't poison me and she didn't leave me to drown in the smugglers' tunnel. Talan is my friend. I trust her with my life."

There's a deep silence.

Talan bows her head over my hand, presses it against her cheek.

She brought me that drink. I remember I couldn't see her face, with the setting sun behind it. We'd spoken of politics and duty. And she said I should sleep and everything would be fine.

But she didn't put bale fruit extract in my drink.

"You left the drink on the tray while you prepared my meal, didn't you?"

She nods.

I close my eyes and let all the patterns flow together.

"Talan wouldn't fit in the hiding space beneath the steps down to the cabin of the *Low Lady*. And the same person who hid there and killed Keren tried to kill me too."

There's a sharp intake of breath.

Hwa is showing me a wire frame model of the cabin steps with the murderer tucked up, hiding inside.

"Keren's murder had nothing to do with the Hajnal. It was all about hate and madness in the end. It started with love and politics. But it ended with hate.

"So much hate," I murmur. "To sit there beside Keren all afternoon and feed her tranquilizers and keep her powerless while the evidence of the Ammeledh was eliminated from her body. To think that someone who knew her could do that."

It's silent in the shuttle.

"So much hate that Keren should be duchess. That Keren should ignore the political responsibilities that being duchess granted her. Opportunities she only had because she was the duchess.

"Can you not feel that hate? *She shouldn't be duchess. She's an outsider. She's ruining it for everyone. I should be duchess. I'll make the Name foremost again.*"

In my mind's eye, Hwa moves the steps away and the murderer stands up. The image changes from a wire frame model. Hwa adds flesh and color. She even gets the expression right.

"So much hate that it blinded me to the other remarkable thing. Because it takes more than hate to tranquilize a person for six hours without killing her or shutting down her metabolism.

"Anesthetics is a whole course at University. Doctors specialize in it.

"It takes medical knowledge to be sure of keeping a person alive and helpless for six hours."

Another collective of breaths drawn in.

"Talan doesn't have a medical degree. She doesn't have access to tranquilizers. She doesn't have a degree in chemistry that would mean she has enough knowledge to create and isolate the psychoactive elements of bale fruit extract."

Dancing with me. A petite woman. Saying with approval that I was a 'practical' woman when it seemed that the duke had no interest in me.

"Talan doesn't see me as a love rival, and her attitude towards me hasn't changed abruptly when it became clear that my status in Cardu had changed.

"And neither does she know about the secret stairwell that must connect the library to the smugglers' cave."

Hwa's image of the petite Lady Roscarrow fades from my mind.

I hate her for what she did to Keren, but I can't hate her for trying to kill me. I pity her.

Chapter 68

We bury Hanna close by the trees on the western side of the Shrine, where she can rest in the gentle afternoon sun and the scent of Keren's garden will drift across to her in the evenings.

I think they'd both like that.

I tell no one else what I know about Hanna.

Bleyd knows, but he gives me his silence, his gift. He knows she was supposed to kill him and found she couldn't, not even to save the life of her own child.

And Shohwa knows, but she is also silent on this.

So the Welarvor Mounted Police stand in their silent ranks to honor Hanna for saving their commander's daughter, knowing little else about her.

To them, she was simply a Dancing Mistress who gave her life for her charge.

She was so much more. A Name Among the Stars, a lady of the Founding Families of Tavoli, a mother, broken when her daughter was kidnapped in an attempt to force her into murder for the Hajnal. A friend.

The troopers fold their banner and present it to her daughter Alexis, who stands with us, the emerging image of her mother.

She accepts the banner, as she has accepted everything, with quiet, polite thanks and heartbroken tears.

Rhoswyn is beside her.

The wild, zany Rhos has gone for the moment, replaced with a fierce and silent guardian. The girls are inseparable, and Rhoswyn has already called Alexis *sister*, with a furious look to challenge anyone who would try and contradict that.

Neither Bleyd nor I will.

Emblyn Roscarrow did not answer the accusations. When news of my survival was heard, she fell to her death from the cliffs in front of Pyran Manor, and left no note.

Once rescued from the stupefying drugs being fed into his system, her brother Marik provided what little we know of her descent into madness.

Hwa and I got it mostly right. *Love*—it started as love for Bleyd, and an expectation that she would become Duchess Tremayne. Then *politics*—that she *should* be the duchess, for the good of the planet. Lady Roscarrow was a fervent believer in the Kernow movement. And finally, *hate*—so bitter that it drove her to murder. How could Keren, a mere farmer's daughter, have married the duke, and worse, then spurned her political responsibilities? Lady Roscarrow intended to become Duchess Tremayne and show everyone how it should be done.

When she confessed Keren's murder to her brother and sought his help in a second murder, mine, Lord Roscarrow refused and she drugged him into insensibility.

About Pollard, we really know very little. He was failing in his job when I arrived. Whether that provided the spur for him or not, he clearly approached or was approached by the Hajnal and agreed to kidnap Rhoswyn. No one mourns him.

The failure of Rhoswyn's kidnapping attempt led to the direct attack by the skimmers. And the failure of the skimmers broke the back of the revolt.

The media is in independent hands now, but it will take a long time until anyone trusts it again.

A new parliament for the whole of Kernow is in the process of forming.

The planet is healing.

We may be back in time for the inaugural session. Bleyd and I are travelling to Earth to provide testimony of what happened on Kernow, Newyan and Tavoli, and our proof of how widespread the conspiracy is.

Earth is the mother system and the most powerful one, too—the only system with a recognizable fleet. No formal treaties bind planets to any agreed laws, or set of behaviors. There is instead a weight of tradition. In such a loose system, Earth needs certain proof of the conspiracy before they do anything, and their actions must be indisputable.

They also need to have such information from people involved directly, not a Xian Self-Actualized Entity in control of a disguised military ship.

Shohwa says Xian is committed only to trading and good relations between systems. It is Xian's considered opinion that the Hajnal will not provide that, and if left, will fester. She says very little about how many Xian traders might be military vessels, as she is. I find I trust her, but it's probably for the best that she says very little to others.

It's a tangled web and we need to be on Earth to explore how it can be resolved.

The trip will provide time for Shohwa to separate Hwa and me. It's a very strange sensation thinking about that. It's hugely inconvenient; I'm constantly tired and we can't wander too far from power sources, but I have to admit I've gotten used to having Hwa there and I'm a little worried how it will feel when she's gone.

Against that, there is the blossoming of my love for Bleyd, despite the fact that we must hold the record for the most interrupted romance ever. Most of the time, he's visiting outlying communities and campaigning for the renewed Kernow party and I'm looking after Rhoswyn and Alexis.

The brief moments when we're together, the kisses are wonderful, even with Hwa watching.

After the funeral, I follow Warwick's instructions.

The *Low Lady* is returned to the water. Moyle and Talan sail me out to the reef where Keren anchored on the day she was murdered by Lady Roscarrow.

They know what I'm doing and make no comment either way as I lower myself into the sea, along with a tight-woven basket that floats. I've filled the basket with the fruits of the land, and made two female figures out of corn leaves. Around the figures, I've wound green ribbons, like seaweed.

I swim along the reef, nudging the basket ahead of me, until I'm well clear of the *Low Lady*. Then I float beside the basket for a while, letting the waves rock me gently.

Nothing happens. Warwick warned me of that.

I swim back and we turn the *Low Lady* for home.

I watch the basket until I can't see it.

Perhaps something moved in the water just as I lost sight of it. Perhaps not.

I was not carried to that bay by tides. Neither was Keren.

If I have mistaken Our Lady of Sorrows for one of the original natives of Kernow, living in the ocean, I hope she forgives me. But I don't think I'm mistaken.

It's something I'm not going to speak about to anyone who doesn't live here in Welarvor. If they are there in the oceans, the piskatellers, they're a people, not a study project for humans.

Epilogue

Sol is home to all humans, but the star itself looks... different. Strange.

I'm sitting in the Studio of the Names, simply called the Studio usually.

It floats at a distance of 1 AU from the Sun, in the planar zenith, above the plane of rotation of the Solar System. Ships leaving the system pass this way.

The Studio is an artistic installation, and the eccentric artist who commissioned it, Heimayer, is long dead. It continues to be run by an AI. Shohwa is quite explicit in this distinction. Shohwa is a Self-Actualized Entity. The Studio is an Artificial Intelligence.

Despite that, I have been granted an audience, largely due to Shohwa's intervention, I suspect. Perhaps the AI is in awe of the SAE.

Anyway, that's why I'm sitting in the Listening Gallery.

The rest of our party: Bleyd, Danny, Talan and Hwa, are touring the Studio. There is no one else in this gallery; Rhoswyn and Alexis have stayed on the *Shohwa*.

I catch myself wanting to speak to Hwa, but she's not here, in my mind, anymore.

Part of her is in her own suite of high capacity processors on board the *Shohwa*. The other part is walking around. Not a construct like Shohwa sometimes uses, but a permanent mobile manifestation.

Shohwa says Hwa is our child, and her features reflect both of us. She looks about my age.

All of us primitive human entities find this a little freaky, but I'm getting used to it. It helps that, as a person, Hwa is just like she was as a voice in my mind.

She's very sorry she missed out on experiencing the more physical aspects of love through my brain. As an alternative, she's been doing her best to catch Danny's eye. I wish her luck. I happen to know that Danny and Talan have been engaging in one-to-one sparring, with a lot of mat work and some most unorthodox holds.

I sigh and wish they'd come back from their tour. Nothing is happening here.

The Listening Gallery is not really part of the art displays. It is where a visitor goes to speak, to tell news of the Names to the Studio.

I stood in the center for an hour and bore witness to what I knew of Hanna Esterhauze: daughter, and last of the Founding Family Esterhauze, of Tavoli, because it's what I would have wanted done, if it had been me in her place. I put it in the context of everything that happened that led to me fleeing from Newyan, all the way to our testimony last week, to the Earth's Council.

The Listening Gallery absorbed my words, and gave nothing back.

Much the same as the Council then.

At least in the Studio, there's a viewing window to look on the endless stars in the darkness of space.

My husband returns, still limping a little, and I feel the warmth and comfort of his strong arms closing around me. I give a little sigh, close my eyes and nestle against his chest.

I can tell he's smiling when he speaks. "Nothing from the ghost of Heimayer?"

"Don't call him that. You might hurt his feelings."

"Nothing like we've hurt Gaude's feelings by being married on the *Shohwa* without any pomp and ceremony."

I laugh. The old convention about ships' captains proved very useful. Nowhere does it say that being a Self-Actualized Entity invalidates the captain's power to marry people.

"Oh, by the way, the Council has issued a communique of approval for the *Shohwa*'s actions in Kernow, and they've dispatched a naval ship to visit every planet touched by the Hajnal. Hwa just received the message."

I'm about to berate him for not telling me immediately, but his whisper stops me.

"Look," he says.

I look up. The Studio is writing. This is the core of Heimayer's art, the reason the Studio is where it is.

The Studio was built by him with a Chang Field projector. This close to the sun, there is an alternative use for the Chang Field. Activating it in the configuration Heimayer implemented fills the volume of the field with plasma extracted from the sun itself.

Heimayer designed his Chang Field projector to create shapes in the space above the viewing window. Once created, the shapes float away from the sun, but hold the plasma for several hours before dissipating. Effectively, the Studio writes across the sky in blazing letters tens of kilometers tall.

These are the Names Among the Stars, those that cannot be erased. The Founding Families are all honored this way. A Name is written every few hours in an unending cycle.

Hanna Esterhauze, the Studio writes, *of Tavoli*.

"Oh!" escapes from me and I bite my lip.

In fiery letters the Studio continues:

Bleyd and Zarate Aguirre-Tremayne,

Of Kernow and Newyan.

Aguirre-Tremayne. We are together, joined, now and forever, as a Name Among the Stars.

Afterword

If you enjoyed A Name Among the Stars

Reviews on Amazon and Goodreads are writers' fuel...

every bit as much as coffee.
Please leave a review.
Thank you.

∞ ∞ ∞ ∞ ∞

Further reading suggestions:

The sequel to 'Name' is now available:
A Threat Among the Stars

To be a Name Among the Stars is to bear the burden of Duty and Honor.

Zara is struggling with the demands of being the new Duchess Aguirre-Tremayne of Kernow when the sudden arrival of a Terran naval cruiser tears her life apart.

The Terran Council have gone back on their word, and ignored warnings about the Hajnal conspiracy. Zara's former home world of Newyan will be lost, and the route to the Inner Worlds laid open. The future of humanity is in the balance.

Honor and Duty. Honor forces her to make an unimaginable sacrifice in her personal life. Duty requires her to confront the Hajnal, whatever the cost.

A Threat Among the Stars
available at
http://mybook.to/ATAtS

AND...

Also available *FOR FREE...*
A serial novel, delivered in monthly episodes,
in the same universe as Among the Stars,
set in the age of the previous expansion of humanity:

The Long Way Home

Jan and Bjorn join Earth's meaningless war to earn enough money for the Inner Worlds technology that is vital for the survival of their remote Frontier colony.

Now that the war is over, they have to make their way back home across the expanse of human space. But from the start, everything is against them. Betrayed by Earth's government, swindled by corrupt orbital stations, they make their allies where they can and fight desperately against pirates on ...

The Long Way Home.

Sign up for a Firefly-style jaunt across human space at:
https://mailchi.mp/27afed3e7c0c/mark-henwick-scifi-newsletter-signup

(or just email me at mark@athanate/com)

You'll receive the complete story so far, and a new episode every month.

Enjoyed my Science Fiction?
I also write Urban Fantasy Thrillers

Try my Urban Fantasy Thriller series:
Bite Back
Starting with:
http://mybook.to/SleightOfHand

"They represent some of the best the field has to offer."
Charles de Lint, in a review of the Bite Back series
for the magazine Fantasy & Science Fiction

Take a white-knuckle ride with Amber Farrell, formerly covert
Special Forces sergeant, currently Denver private investigator,
fighting Athanate at the same time as she's becoming one...

"Vampires are the flickering illusions of Hollywood.
They don't exist.
We do.
We are the Athanate."

The Bite Back series has over 1700 4&5 star reviews on
Amazon.

A reader's reaction: "Probably the best way to summarize this is that
I've reread the Bite Back series more than just about any author in
my collection, which includes most of the authors in the 'non-YA'
category."

Most importantly
if you want to keep up to date with new books
email me at Mark@Athanate.com

I'll only email you to alert you when a book is published,
or to answer a question you ask, or a comment you make.
I will never reveal your email to third parties.

The Bite Back series has a Facebook page:
facebook.com/TheBiteBackSeries/

And I blog occasionally at:
https://henwick.wordpress.com/

And if you didn't enjoy this book…
Please email me at Mark@Athanate.com and tell me why!

Printed in Great Britain
by Amazon

12898452R00185